The Blackpool Highflyer

ANDREW MARTIN

faber and faber

First published in 2004
by Faber and Faber Limited
3 Queen Square London WC1N 3AU

Typeset by Faber and Faber Limited
Printed and bound in Great Britain by
William Clowes Limited, Beccles, Suffolk

A CIP record for this book
is available from the British Library

ISBN 0–571–21901–2

2 4 6 8 10 9 7 5 3 1

Acknowledgements

I would like to thank, in no special order, Geoff Felix, ventriloquial figure maker; Professor Colin Divall of the National Railway Museum; The Blackpool Civic Trust; Peter Charlton, for advice on music hall; Jennifer Pell of the Fred Wade Bookshop, Halifax; Ron Johnson and Clive Groom, ex-train drivers; Dr J.A. Hargreaves; Michael Farr of the Transport Ticket Society; The Lancashire and Yorkshire Railway Society, especially Chris Leach, Mike Fitton and Noel Coates; Conrad Varley and the staff of the Queen Street Mill Museum, Burnley; Bob Vaughton of the South Devon Railway; David White, Rouge Croix Pursuivant at the College of Arms.

These people all supplied me with the hard facts which I then, very frequently, bent.

Author's Note

This story is a product of the author's imagination, and has no connection with anyone who might actually have worked on the Lancashire and Yorkshire Railway, or lived in Halifax or Blackpool in 1905, or given music hall performances in those towns.

PART ONE

Whit

Chapter One

The vacuum was created, and we were ready for the road. As we waited at Halifax Joint station for the starter signal, I sat down on the sandbox and carried on reading yesterday's *Evening Courier*, which a cleaner had left on the footplate of our engine. 'There are cheering reports of the weather from the numerous seaside resorts, and indications that the Whitsuntide holidays will be spent under the most pleasant conditions. Yesterday was fine everywhere and in every way . . .'

That would have been it, or something like, for the glass had been rising steadily since the start of March. 'Enjoyable sports at Thrum Hall,' I read. 'Everybody was in a happy mood at Halifax Cricket Ground this morning . . .'

I folded the paper and stood up. My driver, Clive Carter, was standing on the platform below. Further below than usual, for the engine that had been waiting for us at the shed that morning was, by some miracle or mistake, one of Mr Aspinall's famous Highflyers, number 1418. These were the very latest of the monsters, and I hadn't reckoned on having one under me for another ten years at least.

'Now don't break it,' John Ellerton, shed super, had said to Clive and me that morning as he'd walked us over to it at six, with the sweat already fairly streaming off us.

Atlantic class, the Highflyers were: 58 ¾ tons, high boiler, high wheel rims on account of 7-foot driving wheels, and high *everything*, including speed. It was said they'd topped a hundred many a time, though never yet on a recorded run. They were painted black, like any Lanky engine, so it was a hard job to make them shine, but you never saw one not gleaming. The Lanky cleaners got half a crown for three tank engines, but it was three bob for an Atlantic, and that

3

morning Clive had given the lad an extra sixpence a hexagon pattern on the buffer plates.

The sun was trying to force its way through the glass roof of the platform, making a greenhouse of the place. Next to Clive was a blackboard on which the stationmaster himself, Mr Knowles, had written. 'SPECIAL TRAIN', it said, then came heaps of fancy underlinings, followed by 'SUNDAY 11TH JUNE, HIND'S MILL WHIT EXCURSION TO BLACKPOOL'.

After writing it, Knowles had turned on his heel and walked off. He might have given me a nod; I couldn't say. I'd nodded back of course, just in case. I'd heard that Knowles had started at the Joint by redrawing all the red lines in all the booking-on ledgers so as to shorten the leeway for lateness, and there he was: marked down for ever as hard-natured. But I thought he was all right. He knew his job. If he wanted a word with the guard of a pick-up goods, he'd be waiting on the platform exactly where the van came to rest. If the brass bell wanted shining he knew it, *and* just where the nearest shammy was kept.

Clive called up, so I leant out the side and looked along the platform. The clock said just gone five after, and we were due off at nineteen past. We had eight flat-roofed rattlers on, one with luggage van and guard's compartment built in. Most of the excursionists were up by now, but a couple of pretty stragglers were coming along carrying between them a tin bathtub piled with blankets and food. 'You never do know when a tin of black treacle isn't going to come in,' said Clive, and there *was* one, rolling about on top of the bathtub goods. Clive always had an eye out for the damsels. In society you might have said he was a rare one for the fair sex. At Sowerby Bridge Shed, though, which was the shed for the Joint, they called him 'cunt struck', and I believe he was the only engine man there not married. He lived by himself in a village I didn't know the name of, and came into the shed every morning on his bike.

'Going on all right, ladies?' he called out, and he began smoothing back his hair. Never wore a cap, Clive; liked to give his locks an airing. I knew that he used Bancroft's Hair Restorer, but whether it was to stop going grey or bald I couldn't have said. Even though he was only thirty-five – which made him fourteen years older than me – both were happening to Clive, but in such a way that a fellow looking at him would almost wish to be a little on the grey and bald side himself.

Today he had on a blue suit that was different from the common run of suiting for some reason I hadn't been able to put a finger on, until he'd explained by saying, 'Poacher's pockets', which was no explanation at all, really. Clive wore a white shirt to drive in, where most settled for grey, and leather gloves, which were very nearly kid gloves, and also out of the common. He was a handsome fellow, I supposed, but it was more a question of dash – that and the natty togs.

'Care for a turn on the engine?' he called to the doxies, and pointed up at the footplate. They laughed but voted not to, climbing up with their bathtub into one of the rattlers instead. They both had very fetching hats, with one flower apiece, but the prettiness of their faces made you think it was more. For some reason they both wore white rosettes pinned to their dresses.

I looked again at the clock: eight-eleven.

I ducked back inside and reached across to the locker for my tea bottle . . . but I was vexed by the tin tub. They would be tied together all day carrying it. And what was it *for*? I took a go on the tea bottle, then threw open the fire doors and looked at the rolling white madness. Nothing wanted doing there. The Highflyers had Belpaire boxes – practically fired themselves.

I fell to wondering about the man who'd built these beasts. The *Railway Magazine* would always tell you that Aspinall had 'studied at Crewe under Ramsbottom', but would never say who Ramsbottom was, and I imagined him as being left behind, sulking like a camel at Crewe while Aspinall rose to his present heights as Professor of Railway Engineering at Liverpool University, and General Manager of the Lancashire and Yorkshire Railway.

I wondered if he ever called it 'the Lanky', as we all did.

I stoppered the tea bottle, put it back in the locker. I wanted to be away: to have the benefit of the Flyer in motion – they were said to have a special sort of roll to them – because otherwise I'd be nodding off, with the early start I'd had and the heat from the sun already strong.

Down below on platform three our guard, Reuben Booth – who was generally given to us on the Blackpool runs – was saying to Clive: 'Five hundred and twelve souls, two hundred and twenty tons'. Old Reuben would always give you the number of passengers if he could, besides the tonnage of your train, and with five hundred and twelve up, we were about chock full.

Beyond him, over on platform one, I saw two men talking, and it was like a little play. One was Martin Lowther, the ticket inspector and a right misery. If anyone didn't have a ticket, he took it personal, like. He was looking at his watch, and the porter who was next to him across the way was looking at *his*. It was a Leeds train that was due in there, I reckoned, and Lowther was ardent to be on it. But as he glanced across to our excursion train, the situation cracked, and he broke off from giving slavver to the porter, and headed towards the footbridge, leather pouch swinging behind him. Next thing, he was coming down the steps onto our platform.

'Eh up,' said Reuben, for he'd spotted Lowther by now, and so had Clive. He was looking along the platform at him as he came along, saying, 'I sometimes think that bastard's going to ask *me* for *my* ticket.' Lowther – who was now peering up through the windows of the carriages – lived at Hebden Bridge, and would from time to time be sent down from Distant Control at Low Moor. He had more gold on his coat and hat than Napoleon. Otherwise, he just looked like a murderer, with his black eyes and his big black beard. It would have been a courtesy for him to come up to us and say he would be riding on our train; instead he was climbing up into one

6

of the middle rattlers, roaring – and he *would* roar it out –
'All tickets must be shown!'

Of course, he had to crack on while the train was at a stand,
for the rattlers had no corridors. We were to go to Blackpool
express – without a booked stop, that is – but Lowther would
be up and down whenever the signals checked us, clambering into compartments and asking for the tickets with his
Scotland Yard air and a face like yesterday.

It was unusual to have an inspector on an excursion train, I
thought, taking another look at the fire. An excursion was
meant to be fun.

It was now eight-fourteen.

Clive climbed up next to me, and began looking in the soft
leather book in which he would copy from the working
timetable the details of any turn. It was all part of his exquisite
ways, like not being able to stand coal dust on the footplate.
Down along the platform Reuben Booth was untangling the
green flag from the shoulder strap of his satchel, and trying
not to bring his hat off while he was about it. Superannuation
seemed to have passed Reuben by. He was very old, and very
slow, which a fellow was allowed to be if he'd had a hand in
the building of the viaducts from Settle to Carlisle, where as
many men had died as in a medium-sized empire war.

Steam pressure was climbing, and number 1418 was near
blowing off, ardent to be away. Little ghosts of steam flew fast
towards Reuben.

The starter signal came off with the bang, but just as Clive
reached with his gloved hand for the shining regulator, there
came a noise from the platform.

Chucking down my shovel, I looked out. Two of the excursionists – two blokes – had run across to the machine that gave
cream biscuits. This was the usual sort of carry-on. I'd seen an
excursionist miss his train back from Blackpool Central
because he was monkeying about with a 'Try Your Weight'
machine. Reuben was frowning at them slowly, while Lowther
took the chance to leap down from one compartment and belt

7

along to another, like a little black bomb. The two blokes at the machine were called back by some of their pals on the train: 'Give over, you silly buggers!'

They climbed up again; Reuben waved his flag, and climbed into his guard's compartment. Clive opened the cylinder cocks and pulled the regulator not more than a quarter of an inch. The exhaust beats began, each one a wrench at first.

'That cream-biscuit machine doesn't work, does it?' I shouted over to Clive as we rolled away.

'Shouldn't do,' he called back, frowning. 'Never has done so far.'

And we stood there grinning as the steam surrounded us.

Chapter Two

We came out from under the platform glass and the gleam on the regulator doubled all in a moment.

In winter in Halifax, the smoke and sky were one, but on a good day in summer the sky was the sky and the smoke was the smoke – and every day was a good day for weather in that summer of 1905.

We crawled down the bank from the Joint. Below, and sometimes to the side of us, and sometimes going over our heads on bridges, was the Halifax Branch Canal. The light was coming and going as we clattered along that groove, under the towering mill walls. Then it went clean out as we rumbled through Milner Royd Tunnel, with all the strange screams of the excursionists.

We came out of that tunnel with the sun full on us, and Clive began notching us up while pushing his hair back. 'Special train!' he yelled, as the first kick of speed came.

Well, *all* our trains were special trains.

When I'd first started as his mate, Clive was on local goods. That was back in March, but come April we'd been made the excursion link, starting with a run to Aintree for the Grand National, and after that trip all sorts came along: Sunday School outings, club beanos, flower viewings, scenic cruises, at least a dozen Blackpool runs. And that with the holiday time barely started.

We would often work an excursion to some pleasant spot, then come back 'on the cushions', meaning we would use our footplate passes to return on any Lanky train in our own time, so then, of course, we'd scrub up in an engine men's mess and go out for a glass.

It wasn't all honey, for there'd still be ordinary passenger turns in between, and we'd often be put to working the branch from the village of Rishworth to Halifax Joint, which had no fixed crew. I said to Clive that this was our bread and butter, and he said 'our bloody penance, more like', for it was dull work. It was not above a couple of miles between the two places, and although all of Rishworth wanted to be in Halifax, Halifax didn't seem to want Rishworth, and we whiled away half our time on those turns waiting at signals outside the Joint.

On the crawl down from the Joint we had been going south, but we were heading west now, and the Sowerby Bridge Engine Shed – our shed – was coming up. Clive gave two screams on the whistle for swank and, Sowerby Bridge being a small place, the whole town would have had the benefit. Clive wasn't known for scorching: instead, he would put up *smooth* running, sparing of coal. But he was sure to have a gallop with 1418.

We were tolerably quick through the little town of Hebden Bridge, and on the climb up towards Todmorden, which was a slog with many an engine, the Highflyer had us fretting about the speed restriction. Here a lot of churches went racing past, and for some reason I had it in mind to lean out and look for the church-tower clock that had the gaslit face at night. Clive banged open the fire door and grinned at me: his way of saying that if I had quite finished daydreaming he wanted a bit more on. Chillier sorts would have done it very differently, but Clive would put a fellow straight in a mannerly way.

'What's up?' he shouted, as I caught up the shovel once again.

'Looking out for a clock!' I called back.

'It's coming up to quarter to!' shouted Clive.

Like all fellows of the right sort he never wore a watch and always knew the time.

'I just wanted to see it!' I said. 'It's lit by gas.'

'Advertising, that is!' said Clive.

10

He was notching up once more, and things were getting pretty lively now. We were running down to Rose Grove, and I had to move about just to keep still, if you take my meaning.

'Sometimes,' I shouted, throwing coal and feeling the sweat start to spring out of me, 'you can see more at night than you can by day!'

What Clive made of this bit of philosophy I don't know because he was too busy finding his own feet and looking at his reflection in the engine-brake handle, trying to make out whether the hair restorer was working. I took off my jacket and laid it on the sandbox.

We were galloping past the black house that always had birds flying over it. That meant we'd crossed over from Yorkshire to Lancashire. Next came the schoolhouse on the hill, the one that always had the big cot in the window, which I didn't like to see because it made the place more like a gaol.

I looked at the sandbox, and saw that my coat had been shaken off by the motion of the Highflyer. This was the engine's famous roll.

Clive suddenly stood back and started moving his hands as if he was turning a wheel, and then bang – Clive had seen it before me – a motorcar was alongside of us on the road to Accrington. Clive was laughing. He opened 1418 up a bit more, but this motor was keeping up all right, though it looked to me like a giant baby-carriage. Just then the road snatched the car right up and away, but it came back hard alongside, and I saw the motorist – he might have been laughing, too, behind his goggles.

But then he started to get smaller.

'Eh up,' said Clive.

The car was jumping; the road went out and in again, and this time the motor was left behind us, still moving but only just, and shrinking by the second.

'What's up?' I yelled.

'He's changing gear!' shouted Clive.

Number 1418 steamed like a witch, but our exertions had made the fire a little thin in the middle, so I began patching, calling out: 'How's he doing now?'

'Picking up the pace again,' yelled Clive, who was still hanging out the side, 'only trouble is . . . the bugger's on fire!'

We went into a cutting – a quick up and down – and when we came out we were beginning to lose the road. I put down my shovel and leant out to see the motorist and his smoking car spinning away backwards. Clive gave a happy shout and two screams on the whistle. He knew about motorcars but did not like them. He thought they wrecked all the fruit gardens of Halifax with their fumes. I told him I'd never seen a fruit garden in Halifax, wrecked or not.

Clive was still peering backwards along the length of the rattlers. 'They're falling out the windows!'

Folk would do that on an excursion – lean right out, and their hats would go flying. But with excitement at fever heat they never minded. Green and gold light was flashing about in our cab as we rattled around the Padiham Loop. It was a great lark, but 1418 was wearing me out – not from the amount of coal wanted, but from the need to keep braced against its rolling.

Clive turned to me and gave a big grin. He was a dapper dog. Nice necktie just crossed over, so you could never work out how it kept in place; coat not new but perfectly built . . . and the poacher's pockets. 'It pays a man to dress smart,' he would say; 'shabbiness is a false economy.' He once told me the best thing you can do with a pair of boots was not wear them.

We came through Blackburn and down the old East Lancs line into Preston station, which was all newly painted green and red and gold, like a Christmas tree in summer. A splash on the brakes, and here we came to a stand while waiting for a local goods to leave.

I heard a door bang from somewhere behind, and Lowther was climbing down to the platform, moving from one rattler to another in search of those without tickets, for he wanted to see those folk *most* particularly.

After checking the water level, I climbed down with the oil feeder in my hands, and put a jot in each of the links and glands, wiping away the tiniest little spillages, this being the Highflyer.

When I climbed up again, Reuben was on the footplate beside Clive. 'You two lads,' he said, in his shaky voice; 'You do know what we have on here . . . Don't you?'

Your mind would race as Reuben spoke. I was thinking: well, what do we have on at the end? A red lamp. That would be the usual thing.

'There's one *First* on,' said Reuben.

'A First?' said Clive, 'on an excursion?'

Excursions were all Thirds as a rule.

'And there's only two in it,' said Reuben.

'Two in the whole carriage?' said Clive.

Reuben nodded.

'But they'd have about, what, thirty seats each?' said Clive.

There was a bit of delay here, while Reuben thought it out: number of seats divided by number of passengers.

'That's what it tots up to,' he said, after a while.

'Who are these gentry?' I said.

'Owner of Hind's Mill,' said Reuben, 'and his old man.'

That was queer. Mill owners didn't go on mill excursions as a rule. I climbed down and ran along the platform for a look. The excursionists were leaning out of the six third-class rattlers, and some gave a cheer when they saw me, but it was nothing to what Clive would have got with his poacher's pockets and high-class necktie. When the Thirds ran out, I naturally slowed, for I had struck the luxury of space – four doors on the First, not eight, and wider windows, and those windows had curtains, not blinds, and every one of those curtains was closed, like four little theatres at which the performances had finished.

As I looked back towards the engine, I saw, beyond it, the starter signal go off. With many shouts of encouragement from the excursionists, I ran back, passing a small old lady on the platform whose black dress was out at the sides. I touched my cap to her as I ran and she smiled and said, 'They'll all see the sea today.'

But the old lady was wrong over that.

Chapter Three

Two hundred and twenty tons we had on, as Reuben Booth had said, and five hundred and twelve souls: Whit Sunday Excursion to Blackpool, booked by a mill – Hind's Mill. It was nothing out of the common as far as excursions went, except that the mill owners were riding with us and our engine was the Highflyer.

The boards went off at Preston, and we began to be in motion again. I watched Clive standing with one hand lightly on the regulator, thoughtful, like.

The mighty crunch of the exhaust beats filled the station like something that, though not over-keen to be started, is going to be the devil of a job to finish. Because of our delay in Preston we had time to make up if our five hundred and twelve souls were not to be late for the beach.

As we came out of Preston station we were running against the County Hall, which was like a red-brick cliff face with twelve flags on top: two crosses of St George and ten red roses of Lancashire, although I knew it had been the other way about when the King had come to open the new docks. Beyond this we were put on the fast road, and Clive really opened up the regulator, and I had to find my sea legs all over again while firing. The engine was a beautiful steamer, but it *would* dance on the rails, and it seemed to me that sixty tons of iron, flying along at sixty miles an hour, should *not* be set dancing.

Clive was suddenly hanging across my bows, and the smell of hair tonic was in my face as he looked out my side. 'The bloody lunatic,' he said.

It was the motorcar again – going along the street that was hard by the line for a short while.

'Well,' I said, 'he's only driving along the *road*.'

'He should be locked up,' said Clive.

'Is it the same bloke as before?'

'It had bloody better not be,' said Clive, notching up for the first increase in speed.

'Reckon he's following us?' I asked Clive, but just then the motorist passed us, and for a while he was fastest man in Preston. Clive said, 'Bloody sauce,' and gave a jerk on the regulator so that we re-passed the man, but no sooner had we done it than the spire of the parish church shot in and wedged itself between the road and line, like an axe splitting wood, and we were rocking away left onto the Blackpool line with an almighty clattering.

There was now a bit of a dip in the fire, which I set about filling, but as we swung down the line to Lea Green, I had to keep interrupting myself to hold on. I could never seem to get right on this high-stepping engine.

Clive looked at me, and grinned. He was at the reverser again, putting us into the highest gear. 'Not up to much, is she?'

'How do you mean?'

'Too shaky,' he said. 'Boiler's set too high.'

So that was Mr Aspinall put in his box.

'It's fun though,' he said, and he opened the regulator a little more before standing back, taking off his gloves, and smartly straightening all the many flaps of his many poacher's pockets.

We were coming up to the signal box at Lea Road, and I put my hand to Harry Walker who was the usual fellow in there, but this wave couldn't come off when attempted at speed. The signal box just seemed to whirl once in a circle as we went by, giving me a sight of blank, shining glass. After Lea Road, we were onto the flat lands of the Fylde – the fields before Blackpool. The first of the windmills was coming into view. When the wind was up and they were really working, they put me in mind of fast bowlers in cricket. I put my head out and tried to hold it still in the hot wind as I thought back to my first trip to Blackpool, nigh on two months before, and how, the moment I'd opened the door of the dining rooms on the Prom, the wind had come in with me, and all the table-cloths had moved towards the tables, putting me in mind of ladies protecting their honour.

———◄◊►———

The waitress had given me a big grin, crashed the door shut behind me, and shouted to another waitress: 'Eve, have you got a "one" for this gentleman?'

The other waitress hadn't heard, so I'd been left sort of dangling.

My waitress might have been Yorkshire, and she might have been Lancashire. Even though I suppose I was quite broad myself I couldn't always tell the difference. I sometimes had the notion that Lancashire folk had lower, darker voices that bent like liquorice. They would say 'Lankeysheyore', or 'Black-pewel', putting as many curves as possible into a word. What the two had in common was loudness about the mouth.

'Eve!' the serving girl had yelled across again, '*have* we got a one for this gent?' Then she'd whispered, 'He's come in by his sen!', and I'd been minded to say that I was a married man, and not just some funny bit of goods that couldn't be fitted into an eating house. And not only that, but a fellow freshly promoted too.

I'd wanted to see Blackpool because, after a short time on goods, I'd been put up to the excursion link at Sowerby Bridge Shed, and Blackpool was the excursion magnet. It was the great demand for holiday trains that had left the Lanky short of firemen, and, seeing my chance to return to my home county I'd snatched at it, after all the complications I'd struck while firing for the London and South Western.

'Eve!' the serving girl had bawled, 'for crying out loud!'

That had done the trick, and I'd been led to the table near the window that I'd had my eye on all along.

I'd ordered six oysters, bread and butter, bottle of Bass.

Then I'd asked for salt and pepper, and the waitress had said, 'Condiments ha'penny extra.'

'Ha'penny extra?' I'd said. 'It never is . . . is it?'

But that was Blackpool all over: the wildness of the waitresses, salt and pepper a ha'penny extra – and Worcester sauce and a slice of lemon another ha'penny on top of *that*.

I hadn't minded, though. I was on velvet: going forward in my work (firing at present but with the job of driver in my sights), and happy at Sowerby Bridge Shed, which was just a mile outside Halifax.

I was newly wed, settled in Back Hill Street, Halifax, with three rooms for me and the wife, and a room upstairs to let, all ready and waiting with bed turned down and a spirit stove for making tea. Marriage suited me very well, in a roundabout sort of way. I liked being with the wife, and I also liked being away from her, for a little while at least.

My oysters had arrived and I set to. A woman at the next table leant across to give me the news that she 'could sit by this window, supping tea all day long'.

'Same here!' I said, turning to look out again at a paddle steamer going between the piers. Of course, I thought, they're not real sailors out there, the ones that meddle with wind and wild sea and darkness, but they were coping with quite a swell, for all the brightness of the day.

I then took from my pocket my *Railway Magazine*, to read of high dividends on the Furness Railway, new wagons on the North Staffs; and, after calling for the bill, I fell to marvelling for the umpteenth time at my Lancashire and Yorkshire Railway footplate pass.

The Lanky was run from Manchester. Fifth by size of the railway companies, its territory stretched from Liverpool in the west to Goole in the east, but the millions in between made it number one in population per mile. Every new engine was painted black for weeks on end, and that was because it was going to go to *work*. The Lanky was 'The Business Line' – cotton, wool and coal – but a lot of northern towns now had their own 'wakes' or holiday week, and the Lanky was all for that, because then people wanted to pack up, and they wanted to be *off*.

It was the johnnies in Central Timing in Manchester who planned most of the excursions. They would sit over graphs that looked like sketches of long grass bending in the wind: these were train movements, and the fellows would be squinting along the lines looking to see where the holiday specials could be slotted in alongside the ordinary trains, and if they could be they would be. Many of the excursions were put up by the Lanky itself but a good many more were dreamed up by clubs and societies, who would ask for a train to be laid on, and usually found the Lanky out to oblige, for it was all money in the bank.

One queer thing about wakes was that it was mainly a Lancashire tradition, but Halifax had its wakes. Halifax was honorary Lancashire really – a mill town like so many in Lancashire, and close to the county boundary. It was one of the things that made it foreign-seeming even to those, like myself, from other parts of Yorkshire.

Stepping out of the dining rooms I didn't bother to look at the top of the Tower, knowing it would crick my neck. I continued along a row of shooting galleries and oyster places, coming to a yard with swinging boats. The swings were on frames with scissor legs. There were four going, each with two ladies in. They all swung at the same rate, and I stood there thinking of them as governors, regulating the mighty engine of Blackpool.

There were plenty about on that Sunday, the last in April, but the Ferris wheel hadn't yet been set turning, and the twenty-three excursion platforms of Blackpool Central – the busiest station in Europe, come summertime – were sleeping in the sun.

Further along, on the seaward side of the Prom, I struck a weird-looking building: like a great brick pudding with fancy white icing into which were carved in curly letters the words

'The Seashell'. It was a music hall of sorts. There were three lots of revolving doors and beside each one a potted palm dancing about in the breeze. How they kept them going in that windy spot was anybody's guess.

As I watched, a little fellow walked up, carrying a carpet bag and a long stepladder, heading for the middle door. I thought: now what's his programme for getting those ladders through those doors? But instead he set the ladder down between two of the doors and climbed it, bag in hand. He was the man who changed the bills, and there was a whole alphabet in his bag. I was quite a one for music hall – I had seen Little Titch at the Tivoli just before quitting London – so I hung about to watch.

The fellow with the ladder had just taken down the letters spelling out the bill-topping turn 'Three Jinks in a Jungle', when I spotted a little bloke watching alongside me: dirty boater and hardly any teeth.

'How do,' he said.

'How do,' I said back. Then: 'What's "Three Jinks in a Jungle"?'

'Concertina band,' he said.

A tram went past just then, making a noise of a piano, kettle drum and a baby screaming.

'Where does the jungle come in?' I asked, and the man shook his head, as if to say: Blowed if I know. But it hardly mattered, since the Jinks were coming off anyway.

Then I watched with the toothless fellow as the new ones went up. First came an M, then O, N, S . . .

'Exciting this,' the fellow said.

Next came I, E, U and R, and the man on the ladder climbed down, being able to reach no further across. As he moved his ladder, Toothless tapped me on the shoulder.

'*French*,' he said, and I nodded. 'Glorious day,' I said, and the fellow nodded back.

I would have gone into the Seashell and watched the show, but I'd promised the wife I would be home before tea.

Clive had the rattlers jumping behind us now. We must have been up to seventy miles an hour, and the engine had more to give yet. I wanted to see how much, so even though I'd put nearly a ton on since Halifax Joint, and my shirt was well nigh soaked through with sweat, it was no trouble to keep going with the shovel.

Clive kept looking through the spectacle glass, along the length of the high boiler, *aiming* the engine. I wondered whether he was looking out for Blackpool Tower, like any tripper.

Presently, in a kind of dream of speed, I moved over to the side and forced my head out for a bit of a blow. We were between the villages of Salwick and Kirkham, flying through a simple world of grass and sky, with all signals dropped.

There were two lines: the 'up' (which was ours), and the 'down' alongside. I yelled across to Clive – some word even I didn't know; something like the sort of cries the holiday-makers would give when stepping into the sea. Holding fast to my cap, I twisted about and looked back. All the excursionists' heads were in, and no bloody wonder.

'Clive . . .' I began. But he didn't seem to hear. 'Clive,' I said again, 'the distant for Kirkham . . .'

No answer.

I knew we'd have this distant signal to look out for soon, but Clive was still looking through the shaking spectacle glass, with his gloves resting on the engine brake. Not his hands, but his gloves, which he had removed. He was studying the speed, frowning over it.

I put my head out once more but had to bring it in directly on account of not being able to breathe. I had seen sunbeams zooming along the line. Taking a gulp of breath, I tried again, looking backwards this time, and I saw, miles across the fields behind us, a train drifting and daydreaming along, or that's how it seemed compared to our speed. I knew it to be

21

the 8.36 from Halifax Joint, the regular daily Blackpool express, which ran even on Sundays and had followed us all the way but only now come into view, the country being flat in the Fylde.

Turning back around, I glimpsed the air over our own chimney. It was a smooth grey, steady in colour. I smiled at the sight, as befitting a true-born galloper, but something slammed right into my eye, a bug or fly that set it burning, so I pulled myself back in.

Then there was a different kind of rushing air, and I was swaying forwards, and then came a duller roar, with the train kind of seizing up. Clive had the brake handle pushed hard over. He was mouthing to me, but with the roar of the brake I could hear nothing. I looked again out of my side and could see nothing up ahead but clear line. But something was wrong.

I came in again, and was bounced forward once more by the braking motion: the engine wanting to go on and wanting to stop, both at the same time. We were still running at sixty or so, and the brakes had been on for a half a minute.

I looked out again and saw an extra article ahead: not a signal, not grass, not track, but something on the track – might have been five hundred yards off, and we were fairly speeding towards it, even with the vacuum brake on at the fullest. Clive was at the whistle now, giving two sharp screams for the guard, Reuben, to screw down his brake from his van. I felt that brake come, but still the seven-foot wheels of the Highflyer wanted to go on. We'd be thrown off if we hit the obstruction, no question, and half the fucking train with us. I looked at the reversing lever and Clive was there. It was the last ditch.

As Clive pulled the reverser, I fell, smashing backwards into the door of the cab locker, and the scream of those mighty wheels filled the blue sky. We skated, screeching for a quarter mile, and I saw through the spectacle glass a wind-mill not turning, a bird not flying but hanging in the sky, the whole world stalemated under this new sound. I looked through the glass at the chimney of the Flyer: the smoke was going up, and then came the sight that's lived in my dreams to this day: not only the smoke and steam, but the chimney rising too, and a horrible complicated bettering going on beneath the engine.

When at last we came to a halt, Clive looked at me, and said: 'Wreckers.'

He turned and jumped straight off the footplate. I followed him down, and along to the front.

Well, it was the wrongest thing I ever saw.

The engine had tried to make a break away from the rails. Sixty tons, and we'd taken flight. The front bogey – the front four wheels, that is – were off the rails. Its supporting frame was bent, and the iron rods that were supposed to guard the wheels had been pushed back. Underneath the buffers, like something spat out, was a grindstone about four feet across.

Clive seemed pretty calm, though he was booting the rail twenty to the dozen and kept smoothing back his hair. 'Bastards,' he said. He knelt down next to one of the front bogey wheels. 'Flange is cracked,' he said.

'John Ellerton told us not to break the engine,' I said. 'And now we have done.'

Not much use, that remark, as I knew even at the time.

Clive was now looking back along the length of the train: 'They're breaking loose,' he said.

The Hind's Mill excursionists were climbing down from the carriages.

'They'd have been shaken to buggery in those old rattlers,' I said.

'Aye,' said Clive, 'we might have burst a few noses when the reverser came on.'

The doors were opening all along the train, and some of the excursionists, seeing the six-foot drop down to the grass, stayed put, but others were pitching themselves out. I could also make out old Reuben Booth climbing down from his guard's van. What you can do with when getting off a train at seventy years old is a platform, and Reuben seemed to hang, shaking for a while before letting himself drop. It was strange to see his body fall because normally he was so slow. As he landed, a book he'd been holding spilled out of his hand.

The excursionists were coming forwards now: Sunday suits, boaters and caps: faces frowning at having stopped somewhere short of Blackpool. They *all* wore the white rosettes and looked like supporters of a football team that had no name. Reuben was following behind, and he was reading a book as he came.

'What's Reuben up to?' I asked Clive, still feeling shaken and not seeing things aright. 'He's never reading a book, is he?'

'Looks like it,' said Clive. 'I'll tell you what, it must be a bloody good one.'

But then it came to me that the book must be his guard's manual.

The excursionists got to us first, hot and dusty from the track ballast. They all looked at the grindstone for a while.

'Who put that there?' said one of them.

Clive looked at me and rolled his eyes, before turning to the excursionist. 'Wreckers,' he said.

'You the driver?' said another excursionist, pointing to Clive.

'Depends,' said Clive. He was reaching into his poacher's pockets, taking out one of his little cigars. 'You're not going to start yammering on about being given a rough ride, I hope. We had all on to stop in time.'

'Daresay,' said the first excursionist, 'but Mr Hind's not going to be best pleased.'

Just then, Reuben came up with his book – it *was* his guard's manual. 'Stoppage or failure of engine?' he said, looking up from the book.

You could tell the excursionists couldn't quite credit this, but they shuffled out of the road in any case, to let Reuben see the millstone.

'Obstruction on the line,' I said.

'Then it's wrong page,' said Reuben, and there was a bit of cursing at this from the excursionists. Blackpool was waiting, and they were watching an old man read a book in the middle of a meadow.

Beyond Reuben, Martin Lowther was walking towards us in his gold coat, and behind him came the only man in the field wearing a topper. That had to be Hind himself, or was it Hind's father, for he was getting on in years.

Reuben licked his finger and turned over a few leaves of the manual. '"Should any part of the train in which the continuous brake is not in operation –" No, that's not it.'

There were two excursionists at my elbow. One of them was shaking his head, muttering 'Premier Line, they call themselves'. I looked him up and down: little fellow, coat over his arm. Still sweating, though.

'No sir,' I said, 'that is the Great Northern. We are "The Business Line".'

Well, they fell about at that for a while, but went quiet as Lowther and Hind came up: first a ticket inspector, then their governor – it could hardly have been a worse look-out for the poor buggers. But Lowther stopped twenty yards shy of us. As soon as he saw the stone on the line, he sat down, just sat right down in the bluebells beside the track, all crumpled inside his gold lace. There would be no more ticket inspecting that day. Beyond him, the bathtub was being passed down from one of the middle carriages.

But the mill-owner continued to approach at a steady pace. He was a big, stale-looking fellow of about sixty: the younger of the two Hinds. The excursionists shuffled down the track bank as he came near. Hind did not wear a white rosette. As he walked, the dust from the track ballast somehow did not land on his boots. His boots kicked it away, and I wondered what he'd hoped to be up to in Blackpool when all his people were at the dancing platforms, the grotto railways and hot-pea saloons.

When he spoke, he sounded like the excursionists, but more used to being listened to.

'I see we've nearly come a very nasty cropper.'

'Nearly, sir,' said Clive. 'It was seen in good time though.'

Hind nodded. You couldn't tell if he was angry or not. 'My father, who is ninety-nine, was pitched from one side of the compartment to another,' he said.

'And is he quite all right?' asked Clive.

'He suffers with his heart, but has a very strong constitution . . . which the Lancashire and Yorkshire Railway has today tested to the full.'

Even that might have been a good thing from the way he said it.

'You'll find it hard to credit,' Hind said, 'but this is Father's first time on a train. He cannot be doing with them, but he'd decided to try the experience once.'

I thought: Christ, we're for it now. But Hind didn't seem *too* put out.

'I'm sure there's been no irregularity,' he went on, 'but I'll have both your names if you don't mind.'

'Clive Carter,' said Clive.

'Jim Stringer,' I said.

'Might we get this stone shifted?' said Hind, 'And then get on? My work-people are to be served with early teas by the Tower Company. And I have most important business to conduct on the seafront at Blackpool in exactly two hours' time.'

As he turned and walked back towards the engine, Clive said, 'Who does he think he is? King bloody Canute?'

Reuben Booth, who was still at his book, began reading again: '"When a train is stopped by accident or obstruction, the guard, if there be only one, or the rear guard, if there be *more* than one . . . "'

Hind looked at Reuben for a while, then turned and

walked back towards 1418. As he did so, I looked at the crocked engine. A derailment: it had happened to me. It would be in the papers. The Board of Trade would send down an inspector. I felt like the tightrope walker who has fallen off the tightrope.

'Reuben,' I said, 'we must get the detonators down.'

'That's it,' he said, but went straight away back to reading his manual: '"Detonators shall be placed as follows: one detonator a quarter of a mile from the train –"'

'Is it a job for guard or fireman, Reuben?' I asked. 'What do you reckon?'

'It says here,' said Reuben Booth: '"The detonators should be placed by the guard or any competent person."'

Clive looked over at me: '*You'd* better do it then Jim,' he said in an under-breath, and it *was* hard not to laugh.

'It's all in hand,' said Reuben, 'leave it up to me.'

We watched as Reuben plodded back to his guard's van, climbed up, stayed up there for quite a while, climbed down with the detonators over his shoulder. They looked like belts with boot-polish tins attached. Reuben dropped one, slowly bent down and picked it up, and set off along the track back in the direction of Salwick.

'What's that bit of kit he's got hold of?' asked a fellow from the crowd of excursionists that was by now standing about us.

'Detonators,' I said.

'Explosives, like?' said the first excursionist.

I nodded.

The excursionist thought about this for a while. 'He wants one of them up his arse,' he said.

Clive was puffing at his cheroots.

'He'll lay the detonators on the track,' I said, 'so that any train coming up behind us will set them off.'

'What? And get blown to bloody Kingdom Come?' said the excursionist. 'Can we not just somehow warn it instead?'

It was hard to believe how Hind's Mill turned out any cloth

at all if this was the class of fellow they had working in it, and Clive was grinning so that his little cigar was at a crazy angle.

'They only give out a bang,' I said. 'But there's no need of them really because the signalman back at Salwick won't let another train in this section until the fellow at Kirkham gives him the bell to say we're clear of it.'

'So your pal's wasting his time?' said another excursionist, and we all watched Reuben in the distance, walking like a clockwork soldier because he *would* stick to the track and the sleepers, instead of going along the field, which would have doubled his rate of progress.

'I do hope he is,' I said, and then I asked Clive: 'Do you reckon we can shift the stone?'

'We'll have a go,' he said.

Some of the excursionists offered to give a hand, but there was only room for two to grip it. We had to graft but we got it off the rails. It wouldn't have been so hard to get it *on*, though, for small embankments rose up from the track just at this point. The stone could have been rolled down onto the line.

We'd no sooner shifted the stone than the bloody motorist from before – I was sure it was the same fellow – came skimming along through the field next to us, trailing a great cloud of dust and sand. It looked as if he was driving clean through the pasture alongside the track, but there *was* a road, although a pretty rough sort going by how much the motorist was chucking up behind him. I looked down at the stone.

'It was brought here along that road,' I said.

Clive said nothing. He was again booting the rail, looking gormless.

A train was coming towards us on the other line, the 'down'; it was shimmering in the heat, so that the train itself looked like steam. When it came close, the driver leant out and gave us a wave, then shouted something that was drowned by his engine and gave us a couple of screams on his whistle. It was one engine pulling seven empty tenders –

a water special, coming back from filling the water columns at Central.

An excursionist called to me: 'What's he carrying?'

'His train's empty,' I said.

The excursionist thought about this for a while. 'What *was* he carrying?' he called back.

I didn't want to talk about this. All of a sudden, I had no appetite for railway subjects. 'Water,' I said.

'Where to?'

'Blackpool.'

'Don't they have enough?' said the excursionist.

'No.'

'You'd think they would,' he said. 'I mean, they've the sea for starters.'

'The engines need fresh,' I said, 'and country round here dries fast in this weather.'

Clive came up to me and we started walking back to the Highflyer, which was leaking steam and looking embarrassed at being half off the rails, and walked about by excursionists.

Clive was saying, 'I like these mill girls in their summer toilettes.'

About half of Hind's Mill were down on the pasture by now, and they'd taken their boxes, blankets and bottles down with them. The sun was high; it was about dinner time, and the excursionists were picnicking; either that or they were stretched out reading their penny papers, drinking ginger beer.

I liked mill girls in their summer toilettes, when you could see a bit more of their hair, spilling out from under their bonnets (in the mills it was kept up all the time). The weavers among them could earn the big penny, even the half-timers, and they always had a lot 'off'. They would dash about Halifax, looking always on the edge of opportunity, while the men would sort of mooch along behind.

We came up to Martin Lowther, who was still sitting by the

29

track, sweltering in his gold coat. He would not take it off, for then he'd be somebody else. 'It goes down as "exceptional causes",' he said, in his morngy voice, looking out at the field and not in our direction. 'A train can only be stopped by engine, by signals, or by exceptional causes.'

'Did you find anyone in want of a ticket?' I asked him.

'Not so far.'

'It probably wouldn't do to carry on looking,' said Clive.

Lowther sighed. He'd struck a loser with us. He'd have been better off on that Leeds train he'd been after boarding.

We were back at 1418 by now, watching all the skylarking excursionists. A game of cricket had been got up in the shadow of the half-wrecked engine; somebody was playing a mouth organ. I asked a gang of them who were just lying about: 'Why do you all have these rosettes?'

'It's the white rose of Yorkshire,' said an excursionist. 'It shows we're from Hind's Mill in Halifax, and that we're to be served a free tea and a parkin at the Tower when we get to Blackpool.'

'If . . .' said one of the excursionists, very slowly.

'Your governor wasn't wearing one,' said Clive.

'Well,' said the same excursionist, 'don't think that means he won't be getting a free tea and a parkin at the Tower.'

'Rum,' said Clive, as we walked on.

'I wouldn't work in a mill for fortunes,' I said, and then I felt quite lost because for the first time in my life, I wasn't sure that I wanted to work on the railways.

In the distance ahead I could see Reuben making his slow way back to the train, this time by the side of the track. He'd learnt his lesson about walking on sleepers. You could always bank on Reuben to get there in the end. My guess was that he'd be carrying the chit from the signalman that would let us move on. As I watched, he picked up one of the detonators he'd laid a few minutes before, so I swung myself back up onto the engine.

The fire was in good order, so I picked up the *Courier*.

30

'Hundreds of detectives guard the King of Spain,' I read, but couldn't be bothered to find out why. I leant out and looked along the track. Clive was in front of the engine talking to a lass, so things were going on as usual with him.

How was it, I wondered, that Clive had seen the stone so early? I'd been looking out, my eyes were A1, and I'd not been able to make it out. There again it had been lying flat on the rails. It might not have tripped us up after all; we might have gone clean over it.

I opened the fire doors and pitched the *Courier* in. It fluttered like a bird for less than a second, and was gone.

You'd read about railway wreckers from time to time: little articles in the corners of newspapers. I had an idea about the death rate on the railways: as a passenger, the chances against being killed were 1 in 30 million. I'd read that somewhere in the *Railway Magazine*.

Wreckers . . . They wanted to make a train jump – for fun. I banged the fire doors shut. They were kids; or drunks. Drunken kids.

We were a fair distance from either Salwick or Kirkham, so anyone putting that stone on the rails would have a chance of not being seen; there again you'd do well to have a motorcar if that was your programme. And while you weren't likely to strike a great crowd hereabouts, you'd be exposed to the view of the odd individual for a long time. The stone had been put on one of the fastest stretches of line to be found, so it would have been known that any train coming to meet it would be doing so at a lick. Well, they would have known it if they'd any knowledge of railways.

I stood up to reach for my tea bottle, and saw through the glass that Reuben was playing the gooseberry, interrupting Clive and the woman on the track ahead. Clive was nodding, so I reckoned we'd been given permission to take our train on.

And then there was a woman, her head below the level of my boots, looking up. Her hat was off. She did not look like a person on an excursion.

'Will you come along here?' she said. She was crying. She had a face that should have been happy. Should have been pretty too – would have been when she was younger. It was a sharp, small face. She looked like a sort of older fairy.

'Someone hurt?' I asked, and she nodded.

I put down my tea bottle on the sandbox. Then, with a guilty feeling, I remembered the first-aid or ambulance box that ought to be in the locker of any engine. I opened the locker door, and there it was: a wooden box with the word 'ACCIDENT' hand-painted on the lid. I caught it up, jumped down from the engine and went after the woman.

As she walked, the words were coming between sobs: 'I didn't want her down . . . didn't want her stifled and jostled in that way . . . it was cooler up . . . so I left her on the seat. Well, she was sleeping . . .'

As she spoke, I opened the box. There was a bottle of carbolic, a roll of bandage (not over-clean), a tub of ointment of some kind, and a little book: *What to Do in an Emergency* by Dr N. Kenrick F.R.S.E. etc. Price one shilling. I flipped it open as I followed the woman along the side of the carriages: 'Treatment for the Apparently Drowned'. 'Drowning is a very frequent accident,' I read. Not on the bloody railways it isn't, I thought. But this wasn't a railway book at all. I read on, feeling vexed: 'Cases of Poisoning . . . A List of Poisons.'

We came up to the fourth rattler from the engine, and someone was saying: 'Oh she's been terribly bashed.'

I pulled myself up to the compartment and there was a woman lying across the seats on one side, with three others standing over her, blocking my view of her head and face. They all had the rosettes on; the rosettes were too big, and there were too many of them for this small space. The women shifted, and I got a proper sight of the one lying down: she was very beautiful, with green eyes and fair hair. I could picture her, not in a mill, but as the good fairy in a pantomime, and she looked a little like the woman who had come for me. But as I looked, she moved her head slightly and vomit rolled

32

from her mouth. The stuff was pink. It spread across the red cloth of the seat.

'Oh!' said one of the women, 'and her so neat in all her ways!' She fell to mopping at the vomit with a shawl.

There was a boy on the opposite seat with a dog alongside him. On his knees was a book: *Pearson's Book of Fun*. I looked at him for a second. He was staring straight ahead and his white rosette was bent, as if he'd tried to fight it off. The woman who'd come for me was in the carriage too, talking in a low voice to the women around me. She turned to me and said: 'She was reaching for her box on the luggage rack when the great jerk came. It was to get a book down for her boy. We think she's taken a concussion, but she's not too poorly.'

'Let me see,' I said, 'I have an ambulance box.'

At which the woman lying down was sick once more.

She gave me a half-smile as the woman with the shawl began mopping again. She said something and the woman with the shawl replied: 'You are *not* holding up the excursion, love.'

'No,' I said, 'there's other things doing that. The engine's come off the tracks,' I added, speaking directly to the woman lying down, but she'd closed her eyes by now.

'Just you wait 'til you see that ocean, love,' said the woman with the shawl. 'Just you wait until you do. Like nothing on earth, it is. Why, it never *ends* you know.'

She turned to me: 'She's never seen the sea, you know. She's a widower, and she's always stayed at home with her boy when we've had excursions in the past. She particularly wanted this compartment because it had views of the sea.'

Above the seats, there were photochrome pictures of the Front at Blackpool.

I said, 'I think the boy should climb down . . . And the dog.'

'Why?' said another of the women. 'Whatever are you going to do?'

They all looked at the ambulance box that was in my hand. The rosette on the bosom of the woman lying down rose and fell in an uncertain way.

33

I turned to the lad and said, 'Want to see the engine, mate? She's a Highflyer, one of Mr Aspinall's . . . quite a beast, you know.'

The kid just stared back. He had a complicated face, the sort that can frown without trying. He also had too much hair, and his coat was too short, and too thick for the weather.

As I looked at the boy, I could hear his mother being sick for a third time.

'Oh, may God help her,' said the woman with the shawl, and I knew this was a bad lookout, with God coming into things.

The woman with the shawl was mopping again. I thought the boy was about to cry, so I said: 'It's a handsome dog. What sort is he?'

'A very *good* sort,' said the boy.

I looked at the dog, and all in a moment the sun coming into the carriage had turned its eyes to glass circles.

'He's an Irish terrier,' I said.

'If you *knew*,' said the boy, 'why did you ask?'

'I wanted to see if *you* knew.'

By turning his face about an inch away from me the boy made it plain that he thought this a low trick, but he said nothing.

'Oh, she looks a little brighter now,' the woman with the shawl was saying.

'My dad had one when I was a young lad,' I said to the boy. 'He was a butcher. All butchers have got dogs.'

'I know two that don't,' said the boy.

'Well . . .' I said.

'I can think of *three* that don't,' said the boy, and he added, with a look of fury, 'Most butchers *don't* have dogs.'

I turned back towards the woman lying down.

'First thing,' I said. 'Let's give her some air.'

At this, one of the women told the boy to get down, and with such meaningful force that he obeyed, taking the dog with him.

34

'Now,' I said, putting down the ambulance box and the book, 'let's help the lady sit up a little.'

And I heard a word from the one who'd come to collect me: 'No,' she said. But she said it quietly and I paid her no mind.

I leant forwards and helped the woman into a half-sitting position. Nobody moved to stop me. Directly I touched her head, my hand was both wet and dry: blood. There was a deeper red stain on the red cushion on which she'd been lying too. There was a sort of bony rumble and the woman with the shawl had fainted. I turned back to my patient. She opened her eyes, and the beautiful, surprising green-ness of them came and went all in a moment. The eyeballs had rolled up and she was white as paper. No human should ever look like that.

One of the women shouted: 'May God rest her soul.'

All was confusion after that, with everyone fighting to get to the woman and to bring her back to life, but it could not be done.

At the end of this scramble, with the compartment filled with the sound of screaming, the elderly fairy, the woman who had come to collect me from the cab and who by rights ought to have had a happy face, looked at me: 'What is your name, Mister?'

'Stringer,' I said. 'Jim Stringer.'

'Well, Mr Stringer,' she said. 'You've just killed the sweet-est-natured, most beautiful lass I've ever known, and you've left her boy an orphan.'

Chapter Four

The Halifax Parish Church clock was striking six when I stepped out of the Joint station and lit a small cigar. Clive smoked small cigars. They fitted the bill for a fellow of the right sort. A cigarette was too dainty and fashionable, and a big cigar was for semi-swells: the smaller the man the bigger the cigar, my dad – who did not smoke at all – had once told me.

My way home was along Horton Street, which climbed up from the Joint, and there were many temptations on that cobbled hill, starting with the Crown Hotel that gave 'MEALS ANY HOUR', for although my wife had many virtues, cooking was not one.

I carried on up. Sugden's ice-cream cart was over the road, with the little white pony that looked as if it was *made* of ice cream. I hadn't seen him for a few days, for he would often get a lad to hold the horse's head when he went into the Crown for a glass of beer. The lad would get a penny lick for his trouble.

Sugden saw me coming and called out: 'Weather suiting you?'

'Champion,' I called back, for that's what I always said to Sugden.

Next came the works where Brearley and Sons made boots; then the moving crane, which had stopped, then the old warehouse where they posted the bills. There was a new one up there: 'A MEETING TO DISCUSS QUESTIONS', I read, just as though I didn't have enough questions on my mind to be going on with. But I read the ones set out: 'Blackpool: A Health Resort?', 'Wakes: Curse or Blessing?', 'The Co-operator . . . Does He Help?' At the bottom, the poster said: 'Mr Alan

Cowan, founder of the Socialist Mission, has the Answers', and I wondered what sort of crackerjack *he* was. The meeting was fixed for 18 July – which would be the Tuesday following Wakes Week – at the Drill Hall in Trinity Street.

I walked on, past a grand pub called the Imperial. This I had never been in, but you sometimes got the most wonderful prospect if the two front doors happened to be open as you went by. The saloon was jungly inside with twisted metal lights and big plants moving under electric fans. All seemed to go on very smoothly and quietly in the Imperial Saloon, where the waiters crept about in their patent-leather shoes. One pull on the beer pump, it was said, would give a pint of bitter in an instant.

But I didn't bother to look inside this time.

Alongside the Imperial was my own haunt, a pub called the Evening Star. There was one room, with barrels on stools behind the bar and sawdust on the floor. Most of this room was taken up with a handsome billiard table with red baize – it was as if one day the shavings on the floor had miraculously flown together to create this marvellous article. I was no great hand at billiards so I never played a game on it, and the queer thing was that nor did anyone else.

I walked into the Evening Star and asked for a pint of Ramsden's. It was three days after the stone on the line, and we'd been on the Rishworth branch ever since, but late that afternoon some bit of business with a broken ejector end had kept me back in the shed. Try breathing kerosene and oil inside an engine shed with fires being lit all around you, and the glass rising towards eighty – it's the only thing for discomfort and sick imagination, and puts you in sore need of a pint.

On the billiard table was a folded *Courier*, left behind. I picked it up, and there at last was the report. It was very short. 'Railway Outrage' in big print, then 'Lady Passenger Killed' in smaller, and 'Who is the wrecker?' smaller still.

> A special Whitsuntide train to Blackpool, which left Halifax Joint station on Whit Sunday, had a narrow escape from utter disaster near Kirkham. With admirable speed the driver applied his brakes on seeing the obstruction, which proved to be a grindstone placed squarely between the rails. Some minutes after the train was brought to a halt, a woman was found to be suffering a concussion after a fall in her compartment. At first she seemed to be merely shaken, with bruises about her forehead, but she fell into unconsciousness and died within a short time of the train coming to a halt. A reward of £5 for information leading to the apprehension of the culprits is being offered by the railway.

To speak of a 'narrow escape' was wrong – that would have been something else altogether. Clive had been going too fast.

Then again, was it right to blame Clive for the way things had come out? I knew that I had not shone myself on that day. I took from my pocket the note I had made from the book, *What to Do in an Emergency*, for I had found the right page half an hour after the woman had passed away, and while waiting for the engineers to come out from Blackpool Central had copied down the important part. It came under the heading: 'About Unconsciousness and Fits', and Dr N. Kenrick had not minced words. 'If the head is not getting its full supply of blood, as you see by the pale face, surely it is only a matter of common sense to keep the head low . . . I will go further, and say that if it is a delicate person you are dealing with, to put him or her suddenly upright may cost your patient his or her life.'

That's what I'd found, having looked in the book for reassurance. The woman who'd come to collect me from the engine had been right, and that was all about it. I'd read the passage time and again as the engineers had jacked up the front of

1418 and got it back on the rails, hoping that somehow the words would change, and the meaning bend the more I read it over.

There was to be a Board of Trade inquiry, and the smash had set the police on the move after a fashion. A constable had come to Sowerby Bridge Shed and questioned Clive and myself. Clive had kept pretty quiet, but I'd spoken up to the copper, talking about how the grindstone might have been got to the line, mentioning the motorcar flying past. I wanted salt put on those who had done it. But I had the notion that the constable wanted as little information as possible, because information meant hard graft for him.

I folded up the paper. The mill girl who'd fallen had not been named but I'd learnt it while waiting for the ambulance to come along the meadow track: Dyson. Margaret Dyson, weaver. And the boy she'd left behind was Arnold Dyson.

The ambulance had taken her, and the boy too, rocking over the meadow. We'd started away ourselves then, rolling at five miles an hour – owing to that cracked front wheel – into Blackpool Central. We'd got in two and a half hours late with the 8.36 coming behind, and down by the same amount. The Hind's lot would have missed their teas under the Tower, and the white rosettes would have gone for nothing. But I guessed they would soon have another taste of Blackpool, for any good-sized mill sent its people there at wakes, and the Halifax wakes was in the second week of July, less than a month off.

I put down my pint pot, and my eye fell on the folded *Courier* once more, bouncing from the words 'Robbed Another Lady' to 'Giant Strawberries Expected' to 'Excursionists Alarmed'.

A North Eastern train carrying excursionists from York and district to Scarborough was required to brake with unwonted suddenness before Malton yesterday, as a large branch lately fallen from a tree lay on the line ahead of it. One man, who appeared to have hurt his back in the sharpness of the jolt, was removed by ambulance staff to the hospital at York. No other passenger sustained injury beyond a serious shaking.

The travellers, who were members of excursion clubs at York, were delayed somewhat but nonetheless enjoyed a full four hours to sample the delights of Scarborough before their return.

This train had been heading to the east coast, we'd been heading west, and it had been on the North Eastern, not the Lanky. But it was an excursion, just like ours: a special train. No connection had been made between the two items. According to the *Courier* they were *not* connected. I'd seen the editor of that paper about town: a big chap with a silk beard and a silk hat; I'd seen him stepping in and out of the Imperial, and he looked nobody's mug. But how much thought had he, or the fellows on his paper, given over to the matter?

A branch lately fallen from a tree . . . It had a kind of hollow ring to me: words too easily put together.

I put the peg in after the second pint, as usual, and walked back out into Horton Street. At the bottom of the road, Sugden was sitting on his cart, dreaming of a pint of plain. The dazzle was gone from the day but the heat had not abated. It checked me as I started to walk, and seemed to be slowing down the smoke from the mill chimneys on Beacon Hill.

Back Hill Street is not far above the Joint as the crow flies. It wasn't the best part of town, and it wasn't the worst. We were more fortunately placed than many working people, as I supposed. I had twenty-five shillings a week. I would have been better dressed on the rates of the Great Northern, but it wasn't bad; and the wife had come into fifty pounds on the death of her father.

Our house in Back Hill Street was No. 21. It was an end-terrace, but we weren't side to side with the others. Instead we looked outward and down, so we fancied we were like the prow of a ship sailing into the next street, Hill Street, which was like a continuation of Back Hill Street but with houses of a better class: bathrooms, gardens and electricity laid on.

The house was probably made with the leftover bricks of the terrace: an odd piece, so to speak. There were the two rooms and a privy downstairs and two more biggish rooms up. An outside iron staircase leading to the bigger of the two upstairs made the house more like a place of work than a home, but it was ideal for letting. This was the main reason the wife had wanted the place, although she hadn't said so to the house agent. I used to fancy she was a little ashamed of landladying, even though it was how she'd got her money down in London too.

The wife called the outside stairs 'the balcony'. I would stand on it with one of my small cigars, which she didn't like in the house, and look out at the backs of Back Hill Street. There would be washing on all the lines. When she'd first come up to Halifax the wife had said every day was like a washday. Now every day was a drying day.

Back Hill Street . . . It was just two rows of net-curtained windows to me. One net curtain – at No. 11 – had a fishing rod propped against it. Everyone who lived there had lived there for ever, except for me and the wife, so, while we were pleasant and gave our 'Good mornings' or 'Good evenings' to whoever we passed by, we didn't really 'neighbour'.

They were a daft lot living there really, as far as I could make out, and seemed dafter still in the light of what had happened to Margaret Dyson. Your typical household in Back Hill Street might be one half clerks, but let down by the other half, who would be weavers. Front steps were likely cleaned at night, in secret, so nobody could say for certain that a skivvy hadn't done it. We were the exceptions over this, for the wife just *didn't* clean the front step. We had our net curtains downstairs of course, but the wife didn't bother with them up, and we were alone in that as well.

41

I let myself in. The wife was in the chair by the stove reading the *Courier*. I had told her all about the grindstone on the line, but not about my efforts in the carriage. I suppose I just didn't want her to think she'd married a chump; or worse still a killer.

'Your accident's been reported here,' she said happily, from behind the pages. 'It seems you did very well to stop in time.'

She turned the pages of the *Courier*. It was only one article out of many to her. I wondered if she'd clapped eyes on the item about the Scarborough trip. It wouldn't do to let on about it.

The parlour was painted green. It was meant to be the finished job but always looked like an undercoat to me. Having pushed the boat out for the boiler, we were light on furniture: we had the cane-backed chair the wife sat in, and the red sofa. There was a continental stove instead of a fire, and we meant to have that taken out and the old fireplace brought back into use. The old mantelshelf still stood, and the old *Courier*s were put beneath it, ready for the far-off day when the fireplace would go back in, and the other far-off day when the weather would be cold enough for it to be used. That was the house in which we were to make our future, and to the wife it was too important a matter to be rushed. We had a tea caddy in the bedroom in which, on the wife's orders, we were saving for all manner of household goods of a superior kind.

'They ought to give a bigger reward,' she said.

I walked through to the scullery, and the jug, basin, towel and soap had been laid out by the wife as usual. It was always Erasmic Soap, 'The Dainty Soap for Dainty Folk'. The wife wanted me double clean, for she knew I would always scrub down at the shed after booking off, but she hated the smell of the axle grease and the yellow soap I used to take it off at work. In fact, she didn't want me a railwayman at all, and if I was clean she could forget I was in that line, at least for a while. To the wife, trams were the thing. She was all for things of the future.

'Cape gooseberries from the stores,' the wife called out.

The store meant the Co-op.

'Are we to have gooseberry pie?' I called back.

'They're a delicacy just as they are,' she said.

She always bought things for tea that weren't quite the thing, and she always bought them from the Co-operative Stores. She was a great co-operator, but she liked the idea of it more than the actual buying, so we'd quite often end by going out for a knife-and-fork tea.

'Five pounds for information,' the wife was saying. '*Twenty* would be more like it, but that would be too go-ahead for the Yorkshire and Lancashire Railway. Why, it would be twenty pounds less in the pockets of the directors!'

'It's the Lancashire and *Yorkshire* Railway,' I said. She always got that wrong – on purpose, I believed.

I ate a gooseberry and was rather knocked. No pips. But I would rather have had a chop.

I walked back into the parlour, and the gooseberries were at once forgiven. I even forgot about the accident for a second, for the wife was standing and smiling, looking just the size and shape of a person you could put your arms around.

'Oh yes?' I said, half smiling myself, but a little nervous at the same time.

'Two items of news,' she said. 'Number one. Do you remember that I said I might have let the room?'

'Yes.'

'Well, the gentleman called this morning to confirm that he would be taking it.'

We kissed over that. We'd had all on with this let: adverts in the *Courier* week after week at half a crown a go. The wife had seen five or six folk over it, and every one she said would turn out a flitter. Unknown to her, I'd also written up adverts and placed them about the Joint in hopes a railwayman might be interested. We were handy for the station, after all.

'He's coming on Saturday and has sent the ten-shilling deposit. He has even begun getting his mail sent here.'

We looked across to the old mantelshelf. We had up there the wife's gold crucifix on a chain, which hung across our marriage lines, and a picture showing two kittens playing with a flower, and words along the bottom reading: 'Never a rose without a thorn' – this bought on one of the few occasions that the Halifax Co-op had run to art.

In front of the picture was the little fat envelope that I knew contained my *Railway Magazine*, which would have arrived that day, and a letter addressed to 'Mr George Ogden' care of 'Top Floor Apartments, 21 Back Hill Street.' I picked it up.

'It came by the five o'clock,' said the wife, meaning the 5 p.m. delivery that brought most of our letters and packets.

'He's giving out that he's taken apartments,' I said. 'It's an apart*ment* at best, and I would have thought it was more accurate to say that it was a *room*, and a pretty small one at that.'

'Well it's a very good job *you* weren't put in charge of letting it out,' said the wife.

She stood up and smoothed the green sash around her waist, letting me see her trimness. I liked the way I was not supposed to notice what she was about in this.

'Would you care for a stroll?' she said. 'And I'll tell you my other news.'

I never knew what was going forward with the wife, but on occasions like this I expected her to say that she had fallen pregnant. One day she had given me a most mysterious look, and said that we must clear out the foreign stove immediately because it was dangerous, and I had been ready for it then.

I looked on the back of the envelope for the lodger, and saw that it had been sent by the 'Institute for the Diffusion of Knowledge'. 'He's quite a cultural sort, is he?' I asked.

She gave some thought to this, and as she did so a hundred possible images of this Ogden formed in my mind.

'No,' she said at last. Then: 'Are you ready for off?' She had her bonnet in her hand.

'What line is he in?'

44

'He works for your show,' she said.

'The Lanky?' I said, wondering whether he'd seen one of my notices down at the Joint.

She nodded, saying, 'Come on now, bustle up.'

'Engine man?'

She shook her head. 'Certainly not,' she said. 'He tells me he has very great prospects.'

'But what is he *now*?'

'Ticket clerk,' she said.

There were battalions of clerks at the Joint. I would nod at the odd one, but they were all in a different world.

We stepped out of the door, and the wife turned to me before we'd gone three paces along the street. She was holding a folded piece of paper, which she passed to me. It was a very short letter: 'We have decided,' I read, 'to give you the situation of office clerk at our mill on the terms named, that is £1 15s. per week starting wage. We would suggest you commence duties on Monday next.'

I would not continue to mope over the accident. I kissed the wife, saying: 'I *knew* you would do it.'

When I'd brought her up to Halifax just after we were married, I'd said she shouldn't work, but had soon thrown up the sponge over that particular battle. In some northern towns, if a man let his wife take a job, folks would turn up their noses at him, but in Halifax the women worked because the mills needed them. And the wife went her own way in any case. To her, typists were the best thing out because they were part of the modern world. She'd been doing a course at the technical school, typing and shorthand, and was up to . . . well, a certain amount of words a minute. A *lot* of words as far as I knew. But when she'd gone to see about any situation there'd always been someone else who could do more, and the letters sent back had always begun: 'We have filled up the situation coming vacant . . .' She'd had dozens of those, and the more she got, the harder she grafted at her shorthand and typing.

Shortly after she'd started I had bought her an India rubber, and she'd said, 'Thank you very much,' while opening the window and shying it all the way to Hill Street. 'I will *never* get on with one of those in the house,' she'd said, to which I'd replied, 'Well how will you remove your mistakes?' 'By not making them,' had come the answer.

I had never seen anything bounce like that India rubber.

For weeks afterwards, I would find half-done letters about the house that she'd brought back from the technical school. 'Dear Sir, My directors wish me to convey to you . . . '; 'My directors wish to inform you that the matter you name . . .' – all with imaginary directors named and supplied with hundreds of initials. Or: 'Replying to your letter of the 5th inst, our reqxxxxmentx . . .' And then might come a long line of bbbbs or !!!!!s, for there was a lot of ginger in the wife.

It had not been easy for her to come to Yorkshire from London, and at first she had seemed in a daze, and, when not in a daze, blue. The rain was like prison bars. She told me she thought that Halifax and places around were like Red Indian villages thrown up all in a moment on the side of a hill. To her, coming from London, they were fly-by-nights, not real.

Slowly, she had begun to make her corner. Through ladies at the parish church – to which we went most Sundays, the wife to pray, me to guess the engines coming into the Joint (which was just over opposite) by their noises alone – the wife had joined the Women's Co-operative Guild, which had suited her philosophy to a tee. Equal fellowship of men and women in the home, the factory and the state: this was their line, and it was all quite all right by me, except it meant I would frequently miss my tea, for the wife would be off to some talk on 'Cheaper Divorce', or 'The Air We Breathe', because they were not afraid of tough subjects. I would then go off to the Evening Star or to the Top Note Dining Rooms, which was where the two of us seemed now to be heading.

We walked on through the little streets between our house and the middle of town. It was very hot, but there was nothing in these streets to catch the gleam of the evening sun. You'd see children in all the back alleys. The poorer sort were bare-foot, and the wife would say, 'Poor mites, I don't know how they manage to live.'

They seemed to me to manage all right, going all out to make a racket as they did so: rattling the marbles in empty glass alley bottles, skipping in the sun and counting end-lessly, or echoing about unseen.

The wife was always pleasant to the kids, and told me not to speak of a child as 'it', which I was in the habit of doing, but I noticed she would always walk fast until we got out of the back streets, which happened when we struck the Palace Theatre at Ward's End. This was all Variety, and I would usually stop to have a look at the bills. I'd been inside twice, but never with the wife. She preferred lonely sounding ladies at the piano, of the sort they sometimes put on at her Co-op evenings. She'd once said to me: 'What's funny about a little man in big boots?' and I said, 'Well you must admit, it's fun-nier than a *big* man in big boots.' But no. There was no funny side to boots at all as far as the wife was concerned.

Looking quickly at the Palace bill for that week, I saw the word 'Ventriloquist', and resolved to go along later. After comedians, ventriloquists were my favourite turns; there'd been one on at the Palace just recently, and I'd meant to go along. A good show would be just the tonic I needed.

Next to the bill, another of the advertisements for the 'MEETING TO DISCUSS QUESTIONS' had been pasted up. I pointed it out to the wife, and she said, 'Why do they ask: "The Co-operator . . . Does He Help?"'

'How do you mean?'

'Why "he"', said the wife, 'and not "she"?'

'Well,' I said, 'it's *man*kind, isn't it?'

The wife snorted, and turned away from the poster, saying: 'They don't like excursions.'

I stopped and looked again at the poster. 'Blackpool: A Health Resort?' I read. You could tell they had a down on the place. I wondered what they thought of Scarborough, for that was the same thing on the other side of the country. 'Wakes: Curse or Blessing?' I read once more. 'Mr Alan Cowan, founder of the Socialist Mission, has the Answers.'

'Mr Robinson,' the wife was saying a moment later, as we waited for a gap in the traps and wagons racing along Fountain Street; 'that's the gentleman at the mill who gave me the start . . . He said that he would prefer me a little faster at the keys, but that I was the only one he'd seen over the position who knew what worsted was.'

The wife looked at me, but I was miles off, thinking of Mr Alan Cowan and the Socialist Mission.

'What?' I said.

'Mr Robinson,' she said, 'who interviewed me for the job, said I was the only applicant who knew what worsted was.'

'Doesn't say much for the others,' I said.

'How do you mean?'

'Well, they must have been a lot of blockheads if they didn't know what worsted was – and them living in a mill town, too.'

'What is it then?'

'What's what?'

A tram was coming along Fountain Street, keeping us pinned to the kerb. The driver standing in his moving pulpit – for that's how it always looked to me – had been burned by the sun.

'Worsted,' she said.

'Worsted?'

'Worsted, yes.'

'Well . . . it's a sort of cloth.'

'Cloth made of what?'

'Wool.'

We were dodging through the traffic now. Happening to glance backwards I noticed that all the little high back windows of the Palace were open on account of the heat – a sight I had never seen before.

'What sort of wool?' the wife was saying.

'Well, you know . . . sheep's wool.'

'Long *staple*,' said the wife. And she looked away, and then she laughed. 'Eh, you daft 'aporth,' she said. She was practising her Yorkshire. 'You wear it every day but don't know what it is,' she said, straightening her white bonnet with her thin, brown hands.

'You could have said something quite clever there you know,' I said.

'I believe I did,' she said, smiling at me. The hat was righted now.

'You could have said you'd *worsted* me over worsted –' I said.

'You're loony,' said the wife.

'– if you really *had* done of course.'

We were now outside the Hemingway's Music Shop in Commercial Street. It was the wife's favourite shop, along with the Maypole Dairy at Northgate, where they had very artistic cheeses, kept cool by fans, like the drinkers in the Imperial Saloon. The Maypole could draw quite a crowd in the evening, although whether it was the cheeses or the fans that did it, I never knew. At Hemingway's, the wife always liked to look at the Hemingway's Special Piano they had in the window that was £14. She wanted to have only the best items in our home, and the Special Piano was on the list and some money towards it was in the tea caddy. Meanwhile we had no items, or very few. Whenever we struck this subject of furnishings I always pictured the shop in Northgate that had the sign in the window saying: 'HOMES COMPLETE FROM £10 TO £100'. It was the ten pound part that interested me, but the wife would have none of it. 'I will not equip the house from a cheap john,' she would always say.

'The marvellous thing,' she said, still looking in the window, 'is that it looks just like any other piano.'

'That's one of the things that worries me,' I said.

'But for *fourteen* pounds,' she said.

'That's nigh on three months' wages,' I said.

'There'll soon be two of us earning,' the wife reminded me, 'and now that the room's let . . .'

'But what about the extras . . . *tuning* it, and the two of us learning to *play* the piano.'

The Top Note Dining Room was two doors up from Hemingway's Music Shop, which might have explained the name. Nothing else did. The tables went the whole width of a wide room, and the people eating at them looked like workers in a mill. But they would give you ice in a glass of lemonade without waiting to be asked. The wife and I took our places. We both had steak and fried onions with chipped potatoes. It was the first good meal I'd had since the smash, which had put me off food in lots of ways.

'You see it's not that I don't like Cape gooseberries,' I said, 'I just don't want to eat them for tea.'

'Well,' she said, 'it's just that I've had so many interruptions.'

'I would be willing to make my tea for myself,' I said, 'I *would* . . . almost.'

'Oh, we can't have you living on Bloody Good Husband Street,' said the wife, 'you the dolly mop!' Then: 'Would you like to see the mill where I'm to go on?'

It was one of those lonely ones up on Beacon Hill. The trams couldn't get up there, so we took one as far as the Joint, sitting on the top for a bit of a blow. The sky was a greenish pink with the sunlight leaving it only slowly, and the smoke still coming out from the mills, snaking into the sky, adding to the heat and weirdness of all as they made their slow S's. The smell in the air was twice burnt.

We passed Thomas Cook's excursion office in Horton Street. It was still open for business. The people of Halifax could not do without their outings. I couldn't imagine for a minute how they'd got on before the railways and the excursions started.

'I could make a stew at the start of the week,' the wife was saying, 'and it would *keep*. Do you like stews?'

'Yes,' I said firmly.

'What kind? What do you like in them?'

'I'm not faddy. Anything at all. You should buy the meat on Saturday night.'

'Oh,' she said suspiciously. 'Why?'

'It's cheaper then.'

She said she'd think it over.

The wife was smiling. She had taken off her hat, and as we came to the tram halt, I thought: she looks still more fetching without it, and will look more fetching again when she puts it back on, and so on for ever. She was wrong over trams, however, which were forever either racing or jerking to a dead halt. They seemed to go on by jumps, and I found myself – for the first time ever – a little anxious riding one.

We got off at the Joint, and as usual the wife paid no attention. She did not like railway lines, partly because her house in London had been underneath one. When I first took up lodgings there (for she was my landlady before she was my wife) I used to say: 'What do you expect, living in Waterloo?'

We took the little stone tunnel that went under the platforms of the Joint, and under the canal basin, and under the Halifax Flour Society mill, and a good deal else beside. We came out and began climbing the Beacon, going by the one zigzag lane – half country, half town, with rocks lit by their own gas lamps, and sometimes black thin houses like knives along the way. There was one mill above us all the time as we walked, and this was our goal.

Just then a bicyclist came crashing along. 'Evening!' he called, which was gentlemanly of him because by the looks of things he had all on staying alive. I thought his lamps were going to shake right off his machine, and he did look worried, but he wanted to keep up the speed.

All my work started and finished down in that groove he was racing towards. There was too much life down there, and too much death too, because that's what the smoke was, and the black smuts floating along: that was your death certificate coming towards you. One in thirty million passengers might be killed on the railways, but your chances of coming a cropper if you *worked* on the railways, or anything that moved, were a good deal higher, and you could not avert what was coming.

The black mill was right above us now, made up of three buildings chasing each other in a circle, like a castle in a child's story book. A fellow in a gig was waiting outside in the darkness. As we looked on, a small door within the main door opened; light came out like something falling forwards and just stayed there for a while.

Presently, an old man emerged from the door, walking with two sticks. Well, he was practically a spider, or a little rickety machine. The man in the gig climbed down, and he didn't help the old man, but walked alongside, looking on very closely. He did give him a hand up into the gig, though. The old man was wearing a heavy black coat in spite of the heat, a high white collar that shone like moonlight, and a black necker. He looked all ready for death. His face was small and crumpled, almost a baby's again; he had one lock of no-colour hair going across the top of his head and, as he took his seat in the gig, this fell forwards like the chinstrap of a helmet or the handle of a bucket.

'What's the name of this show?' I asked the wife.

'Did I not tell you?' she said. 'It's Hind's Mill.'

I looked at the wife, but decided to hold my tongue for the time being.

'That must be Mr Hind Senior,' said the wife. 'He's the chairman and founder.'

As we watched, the manservant leant across to put the old man's hair straight, like somebody training a vine. Then the mill door closed and the light went. A moment later, the trap rattled off into the hot night.

Chapter Five

The rest of the week I spent dreaming back and forth on the Rishworth branch, and trying to read a book by a fellow called Rider Haggard, for I was out with the *Railway Magazine*, having developed a strange fear of coming across an item about obstacles placed on the tracks.

Most of the time, the stone on the line was on my mind, and I had made my little speech to the wife after explaining that she had been taken on by the mill that had suffered the smash: 'You go and work at Hind's Mill if you like, but you are not to go on their summer excursion.' 'Why ever not?' the wife had said, and my words had seemed completely daft in an instant. But I had not taken them back.

The Board of Trade had come to Sowerby Bridge Shed. Rather, Major Terence Harrison had come, late of the Royal Engineers. Clive had said the Board always took its inspectors from that show if possible. The major had worn a very good, very tight suit. He was not a full inspector, but a sub-inspector, yet all the fellows in the shed gave him a very wide berth, fearing he was trained to detect ale on a railman's breath at fifty paces. He had talked to Clive in John Ellerton's office, and Clive had come out laughing. Then it had been my turn. Speaking to Major Harrison, I did not sound like myself. I kept saying things like: 'I jumped down from the cab to see whether I could render any assistance.'

He had not wanted to know about my medical attempts, but was concerned only with the engine, the track, the stone and other things not living. He told me he would write a draft report, and that this would be properly finished off when the police investigation was completed. I told him I thought the culprit would most likely be someone owing a grievance to the mill, and Major Harrison said he was sure they would turn out to be from Blackpool. 'It's a damn strange town, you know,' he said.

Well, I thought he was a blockhead, but he did pass on two handy pieces of information after I'd got up the nerve to question him a little. The train before ours over that two-line stretch had been a Blackpool to Preston. It was an ordinary train, not an excursion, and it had gone between Salwick and Kirkham a full hour before we'd arrived there. Nothing out of the way had been seen on the opposite line. So the stone had been placed an hour or less before the smash.

As for the North Eastern train that had hit the branch on the way to Scarborough, he said that to his knowledge no investigation would be held, because the engine had not left the tracks.

He asked me why I'd asked, and I said: 'Well, perhaps it was put there on purpose.'

'You can't drag a great branch down off a tree, you know,' he said, and it was as if he'd *tried*.

No, you clot, I thought to myself, but you can shift one that's already fallen.

———————◄o►———————

Come the Friday, knowing that the wife was off to a meeting of the Women's Co-operative Guild, I fixed on the idea of going up to the Palace directly after booking off, but I was all in, and it seemed to take an eternity for me to walk up Horton Street in the late hanging heat. Sugden was there, with his ice-cream barrow and his little white pony.

'Weather suiting you, chief?' he called.

'Champion,' I said, and it was then that I saw a long-haired man, halfway up the hill, handing out newspapers. He was not one of the Horton Street regulars. He wore a cap on top of his long black hair, so that his head was somehow very crowded. I walked towards him, and he put one of the papers in my hand.

'Cop hold, guv,' he said.

54

The paper was called the *Socialist Mission*, and there were no more than about four pages to it.

'Take it,' said the long-haired bloke. 'Gratis.'

I looked at the front page. At the top of one column were the words: 'Speech by Alan Cowan at Hull Dock Gates'. The rest of the page repeated all the questions that had been on the poster – for it was the same show – but with words beneath: the answers, I supposed. The answers according to this Alan Cowan.

'Are you Alan Cowan?' I said to the long-haired fellow. He took off his cap and brushed his black hair back with a shaky long white hand. He seemed quite surprised to be addressed.

'Me?' he said; 'no, though I keep in touch with him by telegram and letter. We're in the Mission together, the Socialist Mission.'

I looked again at the paper, and the words: 'Blackpool: A Health Resort?'

'Where is Alan Cowan just at present?' I said.

'Dunfermline,' the long-haired fellow said instantly. He was thin and white, like a plant kept out of the light. All the energy and life that might have gone into giving him a bit of colour had instead been directed into the growing of his hair. 'He's at a speaking engagement.'

I nodded.

This fellow could have taken the bottom ends of his hair, and put them in his mouth. But the hair was something forgotten about, like his suit.

'Do you work for him?'

'Publicity Officer,' said the long-haired fellow. 'Mr Cowan pays me fair wages.'

I knew I'd already missed Early Doors at the Palace Theatre, but I said: 'I've a couple of questions of my own, if that's quite all right?'

The long-haired fellow said, 'Aye', though he looked a little anxious.

'What's he, Alan Cowan, I mean . . . What's he got against folk going to Blackpool?'

'Well,' said the long-haired fellow, 'I'd better start at the beginning of you're asking that.'

'Will you step in here for a pint?' I said, nodding towards the Evening Star.

The long-haired man shook his head. 'Don't drink,' he said.

'Would you not have a lemonade or something?' I said, and his eyes fairly lit up at that, so we stepped into the pub.

'It's been so hot out there today,' said the long-haired fellow, putting his hat and his papers down on the edge of the red billiard table. But it was no cooler in the pub, of course: just a different heat, with beer smell and cigar smoke mixed in.

Looking across at the papers, my eye caught the words beneath 'The Socialist Mission'. They read, 'Formerly "The Anarchist Dispatch"'.

I had a glass of Ramsden's for myself, and the socialist missionary took his lemonade, which he drank off in one. Then he fell to looking at me, sideways, like, half trying to see round his hair, and half hiding behind it.

'You're anarchists as well as socialists, are you?' I asked. I was talking as if there were many, but before me was just the one fellow.

'The two go along a little way together,' he said, and then he was off, talking at me, but not *looking* at me once.

He started, as threatened, from the beginning. It was all about how the liberal-labour men had not improved the condition of the working man as they had promised, and nor had the trade unions, and so a new type of organisation was wanted. What was needed was the socialisation of the means of production. 'We must have a straight-aiming struggle,' he said, and 'Alan Cowan believes that class war is its most efficient locomotive.'

Well, at that word I cut in: 'Where do you stand on the railways?'

The long-haired fellow moved his hair about for a while, steeling himself to say something. He had rather long, fine fingers, and I thought: he's never done a hand's turn. He was not part of the working life himself, but a kind of shadow, or echo of it.

'Railways . . .' he said at last: 'Run by crooks, and should be nationalised.'

'And as to Blackpool and wakes and holidays, and so on?'

'Blackpool?' he said. 'Well, I don't call that a very worthy holiday place. The working people go there and what happens? They loiter on the sands by day, suffocate in some cheap place of amusement by night.'

'Been to Blackpool yourself, have you?'

The socialist missionary gave a kind of shrug, as if he didn't *know* whether he'd been to Blackpool. 'What's that got to do with it?' he said at last, and with a little more of the brass neck to him.

'If not Blackpool, where might they go instead?' I asked him.

'Well, they might get out into the country once in a while, but that's not . . . I do wish Alan was here because he puts it all over so much better than I ever could, but the question is: does Blackpool help the working class fight or does it hinder?'

'I don't know,' I said.

'Take this town, Halifax,' said the long-haired fellow. 'It's like a bottle with the stopper in. Fifty-one weeks of the year, everyone's cooped up in the mills, prisoners of the wage slavery. Then for one week – wakes – the stopper comes off and it's the mad dash to the seaside. Now if that didn't happen there's a fair chance the bottle would explode.'

'Why?' I said. '*Why* would it explode?'

He sighed, looked down sadly at the empty lemonade glass. 'I forgot to say the bottle is a bottle of selzer, or maybe beer. Something volatile, any road. Something *likely* to explode. Alan has it right but I can't remember exactly how he puts it.'

'Selzer will not expand in the bottle in any circumstances,' I said, finishing my Ramsden's.

'Well,' said the socialist, '. . . we'll see about that.'

I put down my pint pot. 'So you're dead set against Blackpool because folk like it?'

'In a way yes,' said the long-haired fellow, who now brushed his hair right back from his face as if he'd suddenly lost all patience with it. 'Everything that increases the dissatisfaction of the working man must push him in a revolutionary direction.'

'And what do you think of Scarborough?'

'That's another . . .' And here he muttered something I couldn't catch.

'Another what?' I said, and he came out with it this time, for he was a fellow who warmed up by degrees.

'Another *latrine*,' he said.

'Well then,' I said, 'would you blokes in the Socialist Mission ever stop a train that was carrying working people to Blackpool or Scarborough? Would you ever wreck it, I mean?'

At this, he walked over to the billiard table and took up his newspapers again. 'Why do you ask that?' he said turning around, the newspapers once more under his arm.

I told him.

'Well,' he said. 'You must come along to our meeting to know more, and you must speak to Mr Cowan himself. But I'll tell you here and now that one difference between us and the standard run of liberal-labour idiots is that we understand there is a fever for action in the mills and factories of all the working towns in the country, and if the workers won't rise of their own accord they must be pushed to it.'

I stared at the fellow, with the happy ringing of the till in the background. Had he just owned up to murder?

'But no,' he went on. 'We didn't wreck your excursion.' He half smiled in a way I didn't much like; I'd seemed in a funk, and that had galvanised him in some way. The smile changed as I watched, though, becoming something a little pleasanter. He was only a kid; good-looking, in a way; and Clive Carter would have killed for that hair of his. He should have been out courting on a Friday night like this.

'What's your name?' he asked me.

I was tired of being asked for my name, for I felt I was being written down in all sorts of bad books, but I gave it him anyway. 'Jim Stringer,' I said.

'Jim Stringer,' he repeated. You felt he wasn't given a name very often, and that when he *was*, he made the most of it.

'What's yours?' I said.

'Paul,' he said. And he nodded to me before walking back out into the street.

I took up the paper he'd passed to me and read it over a little. It was all a lot of big, windy promises: 'There will be a general expropriation of vast proportions'; 'All distinctions between classes and nations will be lost', and so on. Half the articles were headed: 'Alan Cowan writes', others were 'by a comrade'. I knew there was something queer about it from the outset but for a little while I couldn't say what. It was like looking at a night sky and slowly working out that there was no moon. Somewhere or other, there should have been a little complicated dull part where you were told who it was printed by and where, and how you might get in touch with the editor. But there was no such thing to be seen.

Chapter Six

I was too late for Early Doors at the Palace, and too late for the start, come to that, but I was let in after the first turn.

I was put into the one seat left, which was in the stalls and directly in front of the orchestra. As I sat down, I knew I'd made a bloomer in coming, for I could hardly breathe. There were too many hot, red people in the theatre and not enough air to go round.

The sweat began rolling off me as a board was put up announcing a dog circus. The fellow in charge of the dogs wore a tailcoat and high collar. He had long hair flattened to his small head by Brilliantine and sweat. He stood still and sweated, swaying slightly as his dogs jumped about him. He looked like a tadpole, and his dogs would leap and hang quivering in the air like jumping fishes. At the moment that any dog made a jump, the fellow with the big drum, who was about four feet away from me, would hit the biggest of his cymbals, worsening my brain ache by degrees. Why can't those damned mutts keep down, I began muttering to myself. And why would the old fellow next to me not keep still?

After the dog circus came six men who were a German or Hungarian band. Oompah music. As they played, the orchestra played along, doubling the noise and doubling the heat; there was a lot of cymbal stuff from the drummer, and I would have liked to belt him with one of the bloody things. The band played against a painting of a pale-blue mountain; the colour dazzled, and I could not look at the mountain top, which was blinding white.

The bill-topper was the ventriloquist, the one I'd come to see, but he turned out to be the sort I don't like: the kind with a walking figure.

As the floods went up he was leaning on the figure, or the figure was leaning on him. It was an English Johnny, or Champagne Charlie. You could tell by the tailcoat and high collar. The head was weird: round, white and lumpy, like the moon or some great fungus, and the grey eyes seemed to be sliding to the side, as if the figure was sad and ashamed at having a perfectly round head. The ventriloquist was also got up like a toff: frock coat and top hat. He was breathing deeply, trying to get a breath in the heat like all of us, and preparing for the walk. The doll, of course, was not breathing at all. Any sort of weather was nothing in *his* way.

The walk started, and as usual a great cheer went up at the same time as the walking music started up. It was as if a famous cripple had got to his feet and taken his first steps in years. The ventriloquist's left hand was at the figure's back, and he was working the levers that swung the legs. The figure moved by a forward jerk of the left leg, which woke up the right one, and brought it swinging along behind, and the left arm rode up towards the chest every time this happened. The doll's right arm was in the hands of the ventriloquist.

They were heading for two chairs half involved in darkness in the middle of the stage, and you could see that disaster beckoned because the ventriloquist's legs (which were shaking) and the legs of the figure were moving further and further apart, so the two of them were starting to make the shape of an A.

In walking ventriloquism, the figures were always the Johnny or Champagne Charlie sorts, so that their funny walks could be put down to them being cut. It was all so samey, but there was an extra sort of desperation with this pair, and I really wanted them to get to the chairs without a collapse.

Part of the trouble was that the ventriloquist wasn't such a great hand at walking himself. He was a big fellow, but trembly from nerves. At one moment he lost control of the figure's head, which swung from left to right, as if saying:

No, I will not go on with this. But they did reach the chair, and sat down to great applause. The ventriloquist beamed out at the audience. He had a red face, shining with sweat, a wide grey moustache held out by wax, and a sharp, pointed beard, the two of them together making a cross on the lower part of his face. He looked so completely jiggered that really you did not want him to have to do any more work. But he presently produced a cigar and put it in the figure's mouth, saying, very loud, 'Well here we are at the eye doctor's!'

While everyone took *that* in, and puzzled over it maybe, and the worrit next to me continued with his infernal fidgeting, the ventriloquist produced from his waistcoat a Wind Vesta, and saying, 'A light of course, we must have a light,' he lit the figure's cigar.

Two things now happened that brought more applause: the lights came up to show a line of figures on seats, stretching away to the side of the ventriloquist and the figure, which was now shooting out puffs of smoke from its mouth. The other dolls in the row were an old lady, a rustic type, a darkie and a costermonger. One was moving: the old lady. Her head rocked up and down, as if she was saying: Well, here we are but we must just make the best of it.

I wondered whether folk were clapping because they thought it was good or bad, because it *was* bad, *shocking* bad. If you were a ventriloquist you ought to be funny – that was the only way you could get away with it. I had seen no ends of funny ones down in London, but they were mainly the fellows with the knee figures: schoolboy, little Johnny, Jack Tar. But it was always *funny* business, with the figure saucing the man, instead of this slow, exhibition stuff.

The ventriloquist took the cigar from the figure's mouth, and the figure said something that I worked out was: 'Can we speak in confidence?'

The ventriloquist looked along the row, and, looking ahead again, said: 'I doubt it, you know.'

I watched the nodding head of the old woman, which ticked like a clock, and watched the orchestra sweat as my own head clock ticked.

The ventriloquist was saying, 'Well, *my* vision is perfect, how about yours?'

It struck me that at this rate it could be as much as ten minutes before the end, and I couldn't take it any more. I was far too hot, and after the conversation with the socialist I'd been quite unable to put away thoughts of the stone on the line.

I stood up and walked out into the foyer, which was a red and gold circle of bars so that I was surrounded by barmen, who were all lining up glasses, waiting for the rush that would come at the end. I picked out one at random and walked over to him feeling strange, with my boots sinking into the carpet. I asked for a glass of water, and he said: 'You look jiggered, mate.' I told him I'd had quite a few days of it. He said, 'How's that then?' and I said, 'Well, I was in a train smash for one thing.'

I told him about the stone on the line, and the death of Margaret Dyson, but the barman wasn't interested in her: 'You, though,' he said, 'you were on the front of the engine, and you weren't hurt even a bit?'

'Well, no.'

'Cor,' he said, 'You're all luck, you are.'

This struck me as the wrong way of looking at things, and made me feel worse about Margaret Dyson. I heard a noise behind me, and was aware that all the barmen in the circle had got hold of the story now and were leaning forward and listening.

'I bet you were shitting yoursen,' said one of them.

'How did the stone get there, then?' one of them called out.

'Put there,' I said.

'You suspect . . . a spot of mischief, then, do you?' asked the same fellow again.

'I reckon it was socialists,' I said, 'socialists or anarchists who've got a down on excursions, because they're put up by

63

the bosses . . . So the stone might have been put there as a sort of warning to the railway company.'

'Well, that's all fairly choice,' said one of the barmen. Another said, 'Anarchists,' very slowly, as if he was trying out the word for size.

Just then I felt extra heat and the ventriloquist was standing right next to me. It was powerful strange to see that marvellous beard and 'tache at large in the real world.

My barman handed him a glass of something mustardy coloured, and nothing was said. The ventriloquist was red, shining with sweat, and panting as if he'd run a mile: he was a fellow not meant to be seen at close quarters. He began to drink the mustardy stuff, whilst looking at nothing. He was bigger than he'd looked on stage, especially in his upper half: he looked cut out for something more than ventriloquism.

'A warning by anarchists!' said one of the barmen, slow on the uptake, and the ventriloquist continued to drink and to look at nothing, but the nothing had now moved further into the distance.

The ventriloquist finished his drink, turned, and disappeared through a door between two of the bars.

'I thought that bloke was on stage just now,' I said to my barman.

'He generally takes a little summat just about now for his vocal organ.'

'He gets through heaps of lozenges, you know,' said another of the barmen.

'But that was whisky and honey he had just there,' said the first.

'What's he doing out *here*, though?' I said.

'There's a bit where he leaves the dolls to it,' said the first barman. 'They're all waiting there at the hopticians –' (he said the word very carefully, and put an 'h' in front of it) '– and they start up with these coughing goes. First one, then the whole lot.'

'How do they cough if he's not there?'

'The movements are all worked from off by the fellow does the props. Rubber tubes and air valves and all that carry on. And property's mate, junior properties – he does the coughing.'

'While Monsieur Maurice drops in here for his little brain duster,' put in another of the barmen.

'And it won't be the last of the night,' added the first.

'Monsieur who?' I said.

'Maurice,' said the first barman, and it came out like 'more ice'. 'Very Frenchified, he is.'

'But not really, though,' added another of the barmen.

'I've seen his name before,' I said; 'it was being put up outside a little hall in Blackpool.'

'Very likely,' said my barman.

I looked at my glass of water and enquired about the price of a pint. On hearing the answer, I told my barman I'd nip back to the Evening Star for my last of the night, if that was quite all right with him. He grinned, and all the barmen watched me walk through the main doors and out into the hot night.

There might have been thirty people in the Star by now, and every man jack avoiding the billiard table. The Ramsden's was off, so I put away a pint of something else that I didn't much care for, and it didn't knock the stone on the line from my mind, so I took another, and that seemed about the right dose.

I came out of the Evening Star for a second time, and a tram went racing past like a comet with advertisements, or the fast drawing-back of a curtain. Looking far to my left, I saw the Joint and Hind's Mill, a black modern castle at the top of Beacon Hill. To the right, at the top of Horton Street, was another beacon of sorts, the Palace Theatre, but the show was done long since and, as I watched, the lights began to go out. I made towards this disappearing target anyway, and turned off before reaching it to enter the side streets.

The wife would have been home an hour since, or more, so I was late. I didn't like to be late back for the wife, and I didn't like to be *bothered* about being late back.

There was a quarter moon, lying on its back, lazy and not giving out much light; there were flies around all the gas lamps, and too much life in the streets, though none of it to be seen: just far-off shouts and cries, and all doubled by the echo of the houses. The shouts always seemed to be shadows of sound, around the corner, or in the alleyways behind the houses.

I turned down a snicket that cut a terrace in half, then pushed along a particular back alley because I liked the racket my boots made on the cobbles, but the clanging of the segs on my heels was presently doubled, so that the sound was more the clip clop of a horse. I turned, and there seemed to be a fast-travelling shadow, but no sound. I carried on walking, and was back to hearing the sound of my own boots. I turned into another snicket, and then I was in Back Hill Street.

The gas was up in the occasional house. I came to ours, which gave out no light, and saw a man or a shadow of a man beyond, in Hill Street. Something about him made me look behind me, and there came a shout from that direction that seemed to jump, so that it was two shouts, and then the noise of something happening in Hill Street, and then nothing.

I unlocked the door, walked into the house and sat down on the sofa, not breathing. It came as a relief, a few moments later, to hear the steady chimes of midnight coming up from the parish church. I stared at the closed door, and thought about how a good cold snap would put an end to all this nonsense in the streets. When the chimes ended, I stood up to put on a brew, and as I did so the letter box flipped open. I flew at the door and looked up and down Back Hill Street, but that's all I saw: the street and the quarter moon, looking like a painting.

Chapter Seven

Bright sunlight and the clanging of hooves woke me up early the next morning, the Saturday, and, as I climbed out of bed, I thought: did I go and see a ventriloquist last night, or did he come and see me? I ought not to have been standing next to the fellow in the bar like that. It was against all the rules. Then there was Paul of the Socialist Mission. I knew I'd said too much to someone. Or had it all been just kids in the streets and bad beer?

Leaving the wife to sleep, I stepped out, and saw a pan-technicon drawing up. The remover was in the driving seat but there was no sign of our lodger.

The remover leapt down, and said: 'Upstairs, is it?' He opened the doors at the back, took out a chair, and darted into the house with it. I watched as the remover took in various articles and, as he did not see any need to say anything, it was like watching a burglary in reverse. Just then a young fellow in a black suit came wandering into the court, and he *looked* a George Ogden somehow: biggish and rather round. He was wearing a high collar even though it was a Saturday, and he was all *waistcoat*, the garment in question being shiny black with many little secret slits and vents and special pockets for small things. Laced into it through special holes was a watch chain, which hung across this fellow's belly like a golden banner. I knew that I had marvelled at this waistcoat before – and that I must have done so down at the Joint.

He was about of an age with me. He stuck out his hand: 'What's your label?' he said, and he not only shook my hand but clapped me on the back.

'Jim Stringer,' I said.

'Which makes you the master of the house.'

'I am the *man* of the house,' I said, carefully.

George Ogden gave me a look – curious, like, but friendly. He had a round face, and a lot of curly hair which looked like smoke that had tumbled upwards from a chimney and stopped.

The remover was toiling away in the background, now carrying a bundle of George Ogden's books. I caught sight of the title of one: *Letters of Descartes*. They were all from the Everyman Library.

'I've come along to see that this man takes proper care of my things,' said George Ogden loudly, and just then he turned to the remover: 'Good morning to you.'

The remover made no reply, but carried on removing.

'Very independent unit, that chap,' said George Ogden.

'The wife tells me you work at the Joint,' I said. I didn't like to say: You're a clerk, because to my ears that sounded unkind. 'I wondered if that's where you saw the advertisement?'

He nodded. 'Presently in the booking office,' he said, 'but I like to think I have the steam in me to go a good deal further. What line are you in?'

'Engine man,' I said, and for the first time since beginning on the footplate I said it without boastfulness.

'What . . . driver?'

'Hope to be in time,' I said automatically. 'But just at the moment firing.'

'I like to think I'm a ticket clerk only on the outside,' said our lodger, at which I took a good look at him, thinking: well, there's a lot *of* your outside.

'Are you on goods or passengers?' he asked. 'Don't say you're on the express runs?'

I fancied he half wanted me to be on the expresses, and half not.

'I'm on the excursions,' I said.

'Oh yes . . . Do you think one of us should hold that horse?' he said, nodding towards the removal man's nag.

'It's standing perfectly still,' I said.

'I know,' said George Ogden, and then he seemed quite lost again for a second. 'But there are some valuable items in that van, I don't mind telling you.'

Wondering about what sort of goods we were getting here, with this funny fellow, I inched my way around to the back of the van so I could get a clue to his character from his possessions, saying as I did so: 'I suppose you spend half your time selling tickets for our show – the excursion runs, I mean, especially the Blackpool trips. There was a stone put on the line to Blackpool last week. Did you hear of that? My mate and me were the ones who found it in our way.'

'Yes,' said George, 'I did hear of that.'

'A lass was killed when we clapped on the brakes,' I said.

'Thoroughly bad show,' said George. 'Not quite *cricket*, if you see what I mean.'

'We'll find out who put it there,' I said. 'You can bet your boots.'

'You've a lot of plants,' I said, for I had now inched my way around the back of the van, where there was a whole forest of ferns and rubber plants.

'They're all new,' said George Ogden proudly. 'I'm a lover of nature, Mr Stringer.'

'Well I'd say they needed a drink.'

'Reckon so?'

'The leaves of that fern – they're sort of crinkly, and look . . .'

A book had been pitched in among the leaves of the fern: a book of plays by George Bernard Shaw. I picked it out.

'They're going brown at all the edges,' I said.

'What? The books?' said George. 'Better get 'em read, in that case.'

'The plants,' I said.

George was looking up at such quantity of sky as could be seen between the two rows of houses in Back Hill Street, which was a small amount, but at that moment very blue.

'Every Sunday,' he was saying, 'I mean to be on my bike, getting to know the beginnings of Derbyshire.'

'What bike?' I said, for there was none in the van.

'It's to be sent by the Nimrod Cycling Company,' said George.

'Oh yes?' I said, scrambling down from the van.

'When they've built it. You see, the kind I've put in for is in advance of any of the machines they have presently available.' He took a little bag of sweet stuff from one of his many pockets and held it out for me. 'So far,' he continued, 'their models are all just so much ironmongery. Comfit?' he said.

'Thanks,' I said, and I put my hand into the bag, but all the comfits were stuck together in the heat so I gave it up after a second, but George Ogden continued to hold out the bag.

'Carry on, old man,' he said, 'you haven't quite gained your object.'

I shook my head and smiled, at which he took the bag in two hands, and began straining to break a lump of comfit off for me, going rather red in the process.

The remover was back in the van again as the comfits cracked. George handed a lump of them to me, and we both stood there crunching away as the removal man worked.

'Interesting what you say about those plants, old man,' said George, very thoughtfully, through a mouthful of comfits. 'I thought the leaves were *supposed* to go brown at a certain time?'

I tried to give him a few points about plants, as the remover came and went, grumbling in an under-breath, sometimes dropping things and not always picking them up.

The subject came back to railway tickets. George said that the ticketing at the Joint was all pills, and that with a brand new way of going on, which he had thought up the night before, the Lanky would be able to double its profits, but I was prevented from hearing about this plan by the removal man, who came up to George when the van was empty: 'That's you in,' he said, at which George Ogden reached into his waistcoat (I wondered if there were as many pockets inside as on the outside), and produced a pocket book. In this he found a ten-bob note, which he handed over to the remover. He was given some change in the form of one coin, which he looked at for quite a while, before giving it a home in his waistcoat and saying to the remover, 'I'm very much obliged to you, sir, you can be certain that I will be recommending you to all at the office.'

As the remover drove off, George bent over and picked up a boot that the man had dropped, saying: 'Did you smell the ale on his breath? And to think I could have hired the van and done the job myself for half the price.'

'Where did you get him from?' I said.

'From the small ads of the *Courier*,' said George, 'the *very* small ads. Should have known not to take a chance on a fellow who can't run to a line of bold type.'

'He did seem a bit surly,' I said.

'*Devilish* surly,' said George Ogden, 'and a butterfingers to boot.'

He then lowered himself down to pick up a book that had also been dropped.

This, I saw, was *Letters of Descartes* again – in Everyman like the last.

'You've two copies of that, you know,' I said. 'I saw one earlier.'

'Well,' said George, 'I take six a month from the catalogue, and sometimes I pick one I've had before.'

'Why?'

'Oh, you know, I do it by accident . . . I'm nuts on literature,' he went on. 'I've got twenty-four Everyman's now, and when I get up to thirty, I'm going to start reading them.'

We had stepped inside the house by now, and the kettle was screaming. I walked into the scullery and called to George: 'Cup of tea?'

'Don't mind if I do.'

I made a pot, and as it was mashing took George upstairs to show him to his room; I pointed out the door at the back that gave on to the iron staircase leading down into the yard. 'You'll probably want to use these mostly, so you can come and go under your own steam,' I said. 'The outside privy is yours; there's use of the scullery, and if you want a sit down in the parlour from time to time, that'll be quite all right I'm sure.'

The stuff had just been put into the room in any old way, with most of the plants off their tables and sitting at crazy angles on the truckle bed. And there were heaps of packets of biscuits on the floor. George Ogden trooped through all this rubble towards the door leading to the outside stair, and the thin window alongside looking out to Hill Street and beyond. Well, the window may have been thin but as much as possible was trying to come through it. You could see across the mill tops to Beacon Hill, with its own few mills, including Hind's, from which this bright morning smoke was dreaming away to the right; and then, more directly below us on the hillside, were all the things the factories had *made*: the Drill Hall, the courts, the hotels, the Palace Theatre, and all the little houses in between, cluttering the place up like the pawns on a chess board. I threw open the window for George and the room was filled with the blaring of a barge on the canal wharf, and the faint cry, rising up from the Joint, of 'Halifax!', which a certain old porter set up whenever a train came in.

The wife was at the door of the room; George was looking at her, and it was strange to think that another man was seeing her morning self, with a sleepy delay in her eyes, and her hair tangled. 'Good morning, Mrs Stringer,' said George, and he bowed. There was no other word for it.

'Halifax!' came the cry from the station once again, and it was as though we were all just waking from a dream, and needed to be reminded where we were.

'I hope you will be quite comfortable here, Mr Ogden,' she said. 'Of course you will always use the stairs at the back.' She had a paper in her hand, which she gave to him.

'They're good quarters,' he said, 'just what I need to be going on with.'

'Please remember,' said the wife, 'there's use of the scullery, but do please knock before entering if the door should be closed. You must keep to the outside privy. You may use the paraffin stove for heating water up here if you like but you are to ask first if that's quite all right. I have taken the liberty of typing out our agreement.'

I liked hearing the pride in her voice as she said that. I knew that she had stayed behind at Hind's on her second day and put in over an hour on this job.

'I will give this my attention very shortly,' said George Ogden, who took the paper, folded it and placed it inside the leaves of *Letters of Descartes*, which was a very bad sign from the point of view of his ever getting around to glancing at it. He then turned to the window again, and we all looked out.

A lot of pride had been put into the building of Halifax, and the builders had a powerful liking for columns and domes, so that to my mind every other building looked like a giant mausoleum, something built in memory of someone or something very grand that had gone before and must never be forgotten. I would always think of Halifax as a town that was down by one person, and that on account of me. But it looked grand this Saturday morning.

George Ogden turned to us and said: 'God's in his heaven, and all's right with the world.'

'It's ten shillings down,' said the wife.

George Ogden took out his pocket book and handed over the money much as the Shah of Persia might if that gent were ever called on to pay ten bob for a lodge. 'Brand new address,' he said, 'and a brand new start.'

And this remark of his bothered me.

Chapter Eight

I saw that we were down for a Scarborough excursion when I read the weekly notices the following Monday. It was booked for the Wednesday – 21 June.

As we were rolling away from the shed mouth on that day, and heading for the coaling stage with a tank engine clanking under us, I saw that John Ellerton, shed superintendent, was walking alongside. It had been misty when I'd booked on at seven but that had cleared, leaving the smoke to battle it out with sunshine. The mills and the houses of Sowerby Bridge climbed the hills in zigzags, and there were golden flashes of sunlight coming off certain windows like messages being sent over the rooftops, across the patches of rocks and grass, over the horses' heads. There was nothing much to Sowerby Bridge – it was mostly Town Hall Street – but it looked fine in the sun, just like its mightier neighbour, Halifax.

It was the tenth day after the stopping of the Highflyer, and this was our first excursion since then. The trip was booked by a show called White's, another Halifax mill.

Of all my particular worries, I'd been thinking of that report in the *Courier* speaking easily of the 'lately fallen tree' that had lain on the line ahead of the North Eastern Railway excursion to Scarborough. We were about to run over those very metals.

After leaving Halifax, we would make first for York, where the Lanky territories gave out. The rest of the trip being over foreign territory – that of the North Eastern Railway – we'd have to pick up somebody who knew the road.

'I have the name here of your pilot,' John Ellerton yelled up; 'fellow called Billington!'

We had the board for the Halifax line now, and Clive was opening up the regulator.

Ellerton stopped trying to keep up, but looked at his watch, then yelled out: 'They've given us him before!' he called. 'And he's a right pill!'

'What's he on about?' said Clive as we began rumbling towards the Joint station.

'He said the bloke we're to take on is a pill.'

As we crawled along, I looked down at a patch of coal, cinders and bright weeds – green and black nothing. But there was a paraffin blow-lamp and grinding wheel there, with a spare grindstone about the size of the famous one from ten days ago. I had never noticed either of these items before, but I somehow knew they had always been there. The question was: had there been a second spare? I would ask John Ellerton, who was standing watching us go, with his bowler right back on his head, pleased at the sight of another engine going off to be at large in the world. Everybody liked John Ellerton: he had very honest blue eyes: Irish eyes, as I thought of them for some reason.

'I believe I know him,' said Clive.

'Who?'

'The pill. They always give you the same bloke at York – he's like a sort of warning not to come back.'

I was more than a little anxious over the run. Paul, the socialist missionary, and his governor, Alan Cowan, were down on excursions. Paul had denied having anything to do with the wrecking of 1418, but would be hardly likely to say so if he had been behind it. But no. If you were wrecking trains to make a point, you *would* own up to it, providing you knew you couldn't be found.

If the wreckers were after mills then here was another: White's. Then again, if they were after Hind's Mill only, we'd be all right.

The wife had settled in there quite nicely, working for her Mr Robinson and not either of the Hinds. She'd told me they were trying to discover for themselves who'd placed the stone. I'd asked her if they knew she was married to me, the fireman of the engine, and she'd said, 'I don't know. I keep mum over that.'

Could it be that the wreckers owed a grudge to Highflyers, or big engines in general?

That was something that had come to me in the Evening Star, and if it was the case, we were in for a trouble-free day, for we had under us one of the standard radial tanks of Mr Aspinall. They were a little longer than your common run of tank, but were to be counted a close cousin of a kettle put up against a Highflyer.

Clive, doing his checks, had found dust on the regulator, on the engine brake – all over the shop, really – but he'd smiled at it. I fancied that after a few long days on the Rishworth branch he was feeling light-hearted at the thought of Scarborough. It was a pretty spot, and something new in that we'd not worked an engine there before. Also, we were not booked to do a double trip, so the two of us would be able to try some of the pubs before 'coming back passenger'.

Our carriages were waiting at platform six at the Joint beside the blackboard on which Knowles, the stationmaster, had written 'SPECIAL TRAIN, WHITE'S MILL', and so on, with all the fancy underlining, even for this little tank engine. He was just finishing off as we came in. He could have farmed out this job, but he had a better hand than anyone in the Joint, and he knew it. As we floated up alongside – Clive had got the cut-off just right, as usual – Knowles looked up fast, then away. I looked at Clive, but he was miles away, holding his leather book and staring at the pressure gauge, even though it was at the right sort of mark. It struck me there and then that I'd never seen Clive pass a single word with Stationmaster Knowles.

Old Reuben Booth was our train guard once again, and he was now waiting below for the coupling up and the vacuum-brake test. Knowles was walking away along the platform. You'd think he'd stay to look over a vacuum test once in a while. It was more important than getting the blackboard right. There again, he would have to talk to us in the process. Maybe he was a shy sort really. Maybe he knew we were up to the job, and could be left to ourselves.

Reuben told us the train weight, then said: 'A hundred and fifty souls,' and as he did so his colour fell and he gave a sigh. He looked all-in.

'What exactly is this trip in aid of, Reuben?' I said.

'Holiday,' he said, and then, breathing hard through just standing still, he looked along the line towards the Beacon Hill Tunnel, which we would be entering presently. After a while of doing that he took out a paper from his coat pocket, saying: 'I have it all set down here . . . Founder's birthday, White's Mill . . . Trip's out to Skegness . . . No, sorry, to Scarborough.'

'Much obliged, Reuben,' said Clive, who turned and rolled his eyes at me. Then he looked back at Reuben, asking: 'Is the founder coming with us, sitting up in first class all on his tod, like that slave-driver Hind?'

'Hind was with his old man,' I reminded Clive.

'From what I've heard,' said Clive, 'that tots up to the same thing as being on his own.'

'No, there's no First on,' said Reuben, 'and, no . . . founder's not coming along today.'

'Why not?' I said.

'On account of . . . fellow's been dead this fifty year.'

So he was one of *those* kind of founders.

The mill hands were coming up to the carriages, trooping along in gangs of half a dozen at a time from the Lamb Inn on platform five, which always opened early for excursions.

'What do they make at this place?' I called down to Reuben.

'Blankets,' he said. 'White's blankets . . . *Red* they are, generally speaking.'

The excursionists all gave a cheer when Reuben waved his green flag, which he did in a way all his own: like a man very carefully drawing a diagram in the air. They were all still leaning out when we got the starter from Halifax, but they dodged back in sharpish when we reached Beacon Hill Tunnel, into which fifty years' worth of engine smoke had rolled, and mostly stayed. It was cool inside, but you got the shaking, shrieking darkness into the bargain. For the first time I felt a little of my new nervousness in the tunnel dark. It was the stone on the line that had done it.

In the tunnel, I took off my coat. Turning about, I felt for the locker. Although stone blind I worked the catch without difficulty, but when I tried to shove my coat in there it wouldn't go. I threw open the fire door, but the red shine came only up to my knees, and did not help me with the locker, so I leant out of the engine, watching the dot of light grow and resolving to be patient.

We came out of the tunnel and the mystery was all up: a carpet bag was crammed into the locker, taking up all the space. Clive was looking across at me from the regulator. 'Not the common run of stores,' he said, 'I know.' He took a pace towards me and heaved at the bag so that it went further inside the locker. He then fished out a book that was in there alongside the bag. He handed it to me, saying: 'Reuben gave me this. It was left behind on the Hind's excursion.'

It was *Pearson's Book of Fun*.

'I've seen it before,' I said; 'it belonged to the kid whose mother died. We'd better get it back to him.'

Clive nodded, in an odd, dreamy kind of way, and I guessed he must be thinking I was nuts: the kid had lost his mother, so he would not be in want of *Pearson's Book of Fun*. I had not told Clive how I had botched things in the compartment after our smash, so he could not see what was driving me on: guilt.

'What's become of the lad?' I asked him, though I had a fair idea.

Clive shrugged and said, 'I reckon Reuben can tell you.'

I could have guessed he would say something of the sort. Clive coasted and glided; he put away all serious stuff.

78

The pill was waiting for us at York all right. Full name: Arthur Billington.

'Now then,' he said, climbing up.

Then, before we could say anything back, the starter signal came off and he bellowed: 'Right then, you've got the road, so *frame!*'

He had a very loud voice.

He was leaning over the side straightway, barging Clive out of the way and eyeing up the big signal gantry we were rolling up to. I happened to give a glance over in the direction of York Minster, which, I always fancied, was sitting on an island, and which seemed to rotate as we went past.

Billington was shouting about signals. 'One, two, three, third from the right – that's the bugger you want. And he's come off! He's come off! You're right as rain for Haxby now.'

Clive gave one of his gentle pulls on the regulator.

'Open her *up*, lad,' said Billington.

'Would you like a turn yourself?' said Clive.

'Aye,' he said. 'Shift over, shift over,' and Clive came across to my side.

Billington gave a great tug on the regulator, and straightway I knew his kind: all hell and no notion. Two weeks before I would have laughed at him. Now, I wanted Clive back at that regulator. He'd been going too fast over the Fylde, but he'd stopped the Highflyer in time, after all. Well, nearly.

'There'll be a nice big hole in your fire now,' Clive told me, in low tones.

I saw that he was right, so I took up my shovel. We ran crashing through the little station at Haxby, and as we did so that tranquil spot was filled with the voice of Billington, roaring: 'What have we got on?'

'Excursion,' I said.

'You two blokes work spare, do you?'

We were rushing through the village of Strensall now, at

79

such a rate that I caught sight of a porter on the platform pushing half a dozen people back from the edge.

'We work excursions,' said Clive, as we shot out once more into countryside. 'We're the Sowerby Bridge excursion gang,' he added.

I thought how much I used to like the sound of that.

'At York,' said Billington, 'you'd be called the *spare* gang. Do you *have* a spare gang at Sowerby Bridge?'

'No,' said Clive.

'That's because you're it,' said Billington.

Clive was giving me the eye, smiling but frowning at the same time.

'What do you do when there's no excursion on?' Billington was shouting.

'Relief,' I shouted.

'Relief, spare . . . Comes to the same thing!' yelled Billington.

Clive showed me by hand signs that he wanted the foot-plate given a spray with the slasher pipe. I was glad of any distraction, and as I set to he hung out of the side with his blue jacket fluttering, looking along the line ahead. Very noble, he looked, with his grey hair lashed back. Was this the thing between him and Knowles the stationmaster? Clive was a handsome sort but just a little bald; Knowles was a well set up fellow, but not so fetching to the fillies (I guessed). They both dressed up to the knocker, so there it was: deadlock.

I hosed down the footplate with the boiling water, calling out to Billington to mind himself, but he was too busy squinting through the spectacle glass and talking thirteen to the dozen about how we had Kirkham Abbey coming up, and how the signals all about there were a mare's nest.

'The only blokes who might be called "spare" at Sowerby Bridge', Clive was saying when he swung himself back onto the footplate, 'would be the pilots.'

Well that hit home, shut Billington up for at least two minutes.

But then he bellowed out: 'Now you've got distant, *outer* home, and *home* signals to look out for!'

'How far short of Malton are we?' I asked him.

No answer.

'It was shortly before Malton that a smash nearly happened,' I went on. 'I read of it in the paper.'

'Kirkham Abbey's five mile short of Malton,' Billington yelled back, presently. 'But don't bother thissen about that, you've the fucking signal to look out for.'

So we were in the danger zone. And I wasn't over-keen on the name Kirkham Abbey either – too like Kirkham in the rival county of Lancashire where Margaret Dyson had come to grief at my hands. I would not give it up yet.

'But where was the tree on the line?' I shouted.

However, Clive was at Billington's shoulder now. 'You can shut her off for a bit now, can't you?' Clive asked him; 'let her cruise through.'

'What do you think this is?' said Billington. 'A bloody yacht?'

Clive shook his head and sat down on the sandbox to read *Pearson's Book of Fun*. I carried on with the shovel, trying to fix the fire. With the sun right overhead it was very hot work.

'Natty dresser, your mate!' roared Billington.

I was trying not to look along the line, for I had no control over what might be placed there.

'Shabbiness', I shouted back at Billington, 'is a false economy.'

'Is it buggery,' said Billington. He had views on everything.

We were now running up to Kirkham Abbey station, and we would have been touching seventy when I spied the distant signal through the scratchy spectacle glass. It was off.

'Did you spot that?' shouted Billington.

'Aye,' I said, and he seemed put out. I wished he would slow down. A distant signal, even when off, meant proceed with caution.

'Now the "home" is the hardest spot on the whole bloody line,' Billington was saying. 'Half hidden in the bloody

81

woods . . . It controls the level crossing that's just around the bend here.'

'All the more reason to slow down, then,' I muttered, shovelling coal. Ninety-nine times out of a hundred, if the distant was off then the home would be off too, and there'd be no trouble, but a cart stuck at that level crossing would put the kibosh on all right.

We were really galloping now, and the damned wood seemed more of a forest, unwinding endlessly around the bend on the 'down' side, with no sign of the home signal. You could see very well how a branch might have fallen. There were so many of the buggers, after all.

I was glad to see Clive put down the book and stand up.

'I'll take her back now if it's quite all right,' he said to Billington.

'What for?'

'Well it's just that we've only got three ton of coal and the way you're going –'

'It wants some knowing, this signal does,' Billington was saying, and the words seemed to be shaken out of him by the motion of the engine. He was refusing to give up the regulator.

On the 'up' side was the ruined abbey. I caught a glimpse of white stone and white dresses against the bright green fields, a parked motorcar and some toffs standing within the broken walls, as if they were downhearted at having got there before it all collapsed.

We were being shaken to buggery, running far too fast for this stretch. Billington should not have been at the regulator. I fancied that he was racing because he wanted me to miss seeing the signal. Then he could point it out and get the glory. We should have told him about the stone on the track the week before because it might have checked him, made him think us jinxed.

I looked across at Clive, who was sitting on the sandbox. He would be going through hell at what Billington was doing to the engine, but he was back at the *Pearson's Book of Fun*.

82

Billington was shouting to me: 'Signal's coming up your side. Got your eye out?'

Clive looked up, and I thought he was going to say, 'She wants a brush on the brakes!' Instead he began to read aloud from the book: '"Why"', he shouted over the rattling of the engine, '"is a football round?"'

'What?' I called out, because I couldn't credit this.

Then three things happened: Billington yelled: 'Any second now!' Then he gave a cry of *'Bang* off!' and there was the home signal for Kirkham Abbey, half hidden as promised. It *was* off so we were fine, but Clive was back at the regulator, Billington was tottering away towards my side, and we were slowing down. Clive hadn't exactly crowned him. There could have been nothing more than a shove, but it might have been the devil of violence, for I had never seen Clive riled before, or even move fast, come to that. Why, he must have risked crimping his trews, and *Pearson's Book of Fun* was left lying before the fire door. I put my shovel down, picked it up and brushed the coal dust off. I was going to return this to the kid, and I meant to return it clean.

The book was mainly riddles and the solutions were at the back. I was so light-headed that I searched out a poser from the first pages. 'Why *is* a football round?' I said, as we went through Kirkham Abbey station at a speed moderate enough to let me see a puzzled look coming onto the face of the porter.

At first Clive didn't answer, and I asked again, this time nodding to Billington – who was sulking like a camel behind me – to let him know that he might have a hazard too, but of course he wasn't game after what had gone on.

'Because if it were square,' Clive shouted back, 'the players would be kicking too many corners!' He turned to me and grinned.

When, not long after, we came up to the great signal gantry at Scarborough, which must have had fifty boards mounted on it, Billington spoke up for the first time since Kirkham Abbey: 'Work it out your bloody self,' he said.

The tracks going under the gantry were a mass of X's, and I wished we could look up the answer at the back of *Pearson's Book of Fun*, but we picked our way by degrees to the right excursion platform, and Billington bolted as soon as we got in.

But the queer thing was that so did my mate. No sooner had Billington scarpered than Clive was jumping down from the footplate, with the carpet bag in his hand, joining the steeplechase of excursionists racing down the platform for the ticket gates.

'Sign off for us, will you?' he called back.

I looked at the platform clock. It was nearly midday.

'Who's to put the engine in the shed?' I shouted at him.

'Thissen,' he said, with a big grin.

'Won't we take a pint?' I called, feeling quite dismayed.

'Sorry, Jim!' he called back. 'Got a bit of business in hand!' And he was off along the platform, but he turned after a few seconds, and with the excursionists flowing away on either side of him he called back once again: 'Scarborough and Whitby Brewery Company – South Shore.'

'Shall I see you there?'

He shook his head. 'The pale ale,' he said. 'It's the best thing out!'

I opened the fire doors, put on a bit of blower, then I stepped down with *Pearson's Book of Fun* in my hand. There were about twenty excursion platforms in all at Scarborough. Three-quarters were taken, and the rakes of silent carriages were like empty streets, but streets standing under glass in a milky light. Reuben Booth was coming towards me along the empty platform, moving dockets from one hand to another, like a conjurer trying a card trick he can't remember. It was all luggage-in-advance business.

As soon as he saw me he stopped and looked at the book. '*Pearson's Book of Fun: Mirth and Mystery*, edited by Mr X,' he said slowly. 'Clive gave it to you then, did he?'

'I mean to return it to the lad,' I said.

'Right you are,' said Reuben, and he nodded to himself for quite a while. 'The boy's been left –'

Here he stopped to wheeze for a time, and I thought for one crazy moment that he was about to say, 'He's been left a thousand pounds.' But no.

'– orphan.'

That word again; the fairy-like woman proved right again. Why couldn't that old bitch take the kid in herself?

'So it's Crossley Porter House for him then?' I said to Reuben.

The Crossley and Porter Orphan Home looked over Savile Park in Halifax. It was a school with orphanage above. The orphans were looked after by matrons or masters who were all immense; the masters all had big beards, and the women would've if they could. Or maybe it was just that the orphans were so small. The orphans slept on the fifth floor; everybody in Halifax knew that. If you were left without parents, or even just fatherless, you would be climbing those stairs.

Reuben looked down at his dockets.

'And what's to happen to his dog?' I asked.

'The dog?' said Reuben. 'That's at my place.'

Reuben was a kindly, untidy fellow – just the sort to have dogs. He lived in a house on the edge of Halifax which you could see on the run down from the Joint to Sowerby Bridge. It was on its own hill: tall and thin in the middle of tall and thin trees, and looking liable to topple forwards into its own garden.

'It won't be the first I've taken on,' he said.

'No,' I said.

'Folk put them in the van, label on the bloody collar: "Give water at Bradford", "Put off at Hebden Bridge", and I'll tell you what . . . half the time there's no bugger *at* Hebden Bridge to collect.'

'Don't they give a name and address when they hand a dog over?'

'I'll tell you summat else for nothing,' said Reuben sound-

85

ing quite galvanised just for a moment, 'I've no notion of this beast's name.'

'I'll ask the boy,' I said. 'I'll take him back the book, and I'll ask him. I could take him a bit of sweet stuff too . . . Comfits,' I said, remembering George Ogden, 'only they don't like the hot.'

'Farthing Everlasting Strip,' said Reuben, 'that's the thing for a lad. Mind you, they en't really everlasting –' He stopped here, and seemed to be thinking of something a million miles away before continuing: '– but they really do cost a farthing.' He was smiling, which I had never really seen Reuben do before, and all over a bit of toffee.

I asked him if he'd have a drink with me, and he said he would, so we fixed up to meet in the station booking office after I'd disposed of the tank engine.

I uncoupled it and ran it round to the Scarborough shed, where I signed my own name and Clive's. It was a sacking matter if discovered and reported, but you'd do it for a pal. Then again, you usually knew *why* you were doing it.

They didn't have an engine men's mess at Scarborough shed. They had an engine men's 'lobby', which sounded fine, but in the washroom there was no soap: plenty of Jeyes smell and acres of white tile, but not a smidgen of yellow soap. I'd known country stations where they'd lay on a pail, but even in those spots there'd always be soap.

When I met Reuben back at the station, he was looking at himself in the window of the booking office, a steady look with a tired sort of question in it.

'Do you have any idea where Clive's off to?' I asked him, and it came out quite short, for I was still vexed over the soap.

Reuben gave me one of his looks which meant he was getting ready to say nothing.

'The fellow's been moving in narrow ways all day,' I said.

Reuben was still looking in the window, but now sly, like. There was gold lacing on his coat and cap, but it meant nothing to him. His beard was like what's left of a thistle after the flower has gone.

'There was no soap over yonder,' I said, 'so all I could do was take a piss.'

'Aye,' said Reuben, looking away from the glass and towards me at last, 'well tha must do what tha can.'

Where was Clive? And why had he not seemed put out by the smash or anything that had happened since? Why had he come out laughing from his interview with Major Harrison of the Board of Trade?

I looked down at my grimy hands. Clive could not have put the grindstone on the line because he'd been with me since first thing that Whit Sunday morning, and the stone had been placed within the hour before we struck it.

And anyway: *why* would he do it?

Chapter Nine

You'd have guessed the weather was set fair even under the glass of the excursion platforms, but when I stepped out of the station with Reuben I was startled at what I'd been missing: rows of glass charabancs waiting under the high, burning sun; the widest of clean blue skies somehow letting you know that the sea was at hand, though not for the present to be seen; and, across the road, the Westfield Hotel, fairly dazzling in its whiteness.

When we were clear away from the shadow of the station, Reuben stood still for a while, nodding and saying over to himself, 'Gradely . . . gradely,' even though it was hardly the weather for old men in gold coats.

We were now on the Valley Road leading down to the South Shore: Italian gardens, lily ponds, rock pools, bamboos and all vegetation out of the common; white ladies with the smaller sort of parasols in the miniature zigzagging roads, laughing at all these corners they were made to turn in order to get nowhere at all. But it didn't matter because whatever way they faced gave postcard views: the Valley Bridge connecting fun with more fun, the mighty Grand Hotel high on its own cliff – a cliff all to itself! – with its stone starfish and dolphins all around the roof. I'd been born just along the coast at Baytown, and the one telegraphic address I knew as a boy was that of the 'Grandotel Scarborough'. Many messages under that head, it was said, were sent out in code for they were starting wars, or finishing wars, and all that kind of carry on.

The harbour, down below the hotel, was like a sort of circular village in the sea, and the beach was a creamy brown – *sand*, I mean – whereas at Baytown it was rocks, and the sight of anybody sitting on it was a sure sign a drink had been taken.

We walked on, and the sound of a brass band floated up to us and expanded to fill the sky. If you could imagine a whole town saying, 'I am first class – I am in the pink,' well, that was Scarborough in the summer.

Reuben was next to me as we took it all in. At large in his guard's uniform, he looked like an old campaigner from some forgotten war, which to my mind he was, having had a hand in the building of the Settle–Carlisle line. I had read that the winds on the high viaducts there could stop a locomotive in its tracks.

As we walked on, I fancied I could feel the heat of the sun and an extra heat on top – the coal dust burning on my skin. I took my coat off, but my shirt and my undershirt were like a further two coats, and these I could not take off. How Reuben was managing under his thick coat I could not imagine. The further we walked, the more my boots and my woollen trousers became my enemies, but we eventually struck the Scarborough and Whitby, the pub Clive had spoken of. As we walked towards the door, I noticed a torn scrap of a poster on its wall: 'SEE MONSIEUR MAURICE', it read, 'THE VENTRILO-QUIAL PARAGON AT THE FLORAL HALL, SCARBOROUGH'. The bloody man cropped up everywhere.

Stepping into the Scarborough and Whitby, you saw the truth of the day: everybody's face was red. The sun had fairly exhausted them, or beaten them in a fight.

'What's yours?' I asked Reuben.

'Shilling of brandy,' he said, in a thoughtful sort of way.

I took a glass of pale ale, as recommended by Clive, while wishing he'd been on hand to take one with me. It was very hard to talk to Reuben, because everything he might have to say was buried so deep.

'Clive's gone off,' I said again. 'Don't know where.'

There was a bit of a question put into that, but Reuben said nothing.

'Odd that he shouldn't let on,' I said.

Reuben didn't seem to have heard this, but something must have progressed in him, for he said, nodding: 'It's a rum go.'

Nothing was said for another short while. Then I had an idea: 'Reuben,' I said, 'why is a football round?'

It was a quarter to one by the clock over the bar as I said this. At getting on for five to, Reuben said: 'Well . . . it would *have* to be.'

'But why?' I said, and I saw the daftness of the whole thing. The riddles in Pearson's didn't work without speed.

Reuben had finished his brandy. 'Thinking on . . .' he said, '. . . I had two of these, last time I came here.'

'Will you take another, Reuben?' I said.

He shook his head. 'Just thinking, like.'

'When were you last over here then?'

'Nineteen hundred,' he said.

I nodded, hoping he might continue, and he did after a little while.

'Generally speaking,' he said, 'I'll only take one drink.'

'But the last time you were in Scarborough, you had two?'

He nodded. 'Aye.'

We were back to square one. I bought another glass of pale ale and Reuben watched me drink it. There were so many questions I could have asked him that in the end I asked none at all.

Reuben made his way back to the station when I'd finished my beer, and I walked out a minute later. It had been a mistake to have a second drink, as I learnt the minute I struck sunlight. I walked past the Spa, which had four domes and was like something out of *Arabian Nights*. It was all French windows at the front and a black and white floor inside that I knew was supposed to be a marvel of the age. They didn't charge you for standing on it, but walk in there and order a cup of tea and you'd get a nasty shock when the bill came. That was all on account of the fancy floor. It had cost fortunes to put in, and they had to be got back. There was a band playing, which put me in mind of the Hemingway's Special Piano that might one day be sitting in my parlour. The wife would enjoy a trip to the Spa. She would hate it but she would enjoy it too. And that went for the Grand Hotel in spades. The Spa was nothing compared to the Grand.

I carried on, going uphill now towards the Esplanade: all the South Shore was the superior end of town, and the Esplanade was the pinnacle – home of the seaside gentry. I looked across the South Bay towards the castle, where a lot of dressing up in olden-day costumes went on, maypole goes, and things of that kind. There were benches along the Esplanade, and not one without its spooning couple. But one bench was longer than the others, meaning that the lovebirds were a decent distance away.

I sat down, feeling like the filthiest thing out, and the lad was saying to the lass: 'Oh *do* let on, Rose.'

It was strange to think, from their closeness on the bench, that they could have any secrets from each other, but there it was. They were not factory folk. He would be a clerk, a George Ogden sort, except without the appeal of that funny fat fellow. The pair of them had fallen to staring at me now, and I wondered what they made of me: a collier let loose from his mine, they were probably thinking; the wrong sort for the South Shore, any road.

Rolling away below the bench was a hillside park with rockeries and tinkling little streams looked after by a gang of men in uniforms. Below the park was the South Bay pool, which was really just a walled-off section of sea. On the landward side of it were smartly painted blue chalets for changing – and every time a swimmer came out it was a different story: sometimes they would be straight in with no shilly-shallying, sometimes one foot would be dangled down followed by a lot of walking about the edge and thinking. There was no skylarking in the pool because this was the South Shore, and everybody swam very daintily, their heads tipped sideways. I looked out for the prettiest doxy, of course, but it was hard to spot the faces under their water bonnets. And then my eye fell on a head I knew. It was Clive's.

I stood up and called down to him, but all that happened was that one of the park keepers half looked up and the clerk alongside me on the bench said to his girl: 'Would you like to see what's going off at the aquarium?' which really meant, Let's get away from this vulgar fellow.

As I watched, Clive pulled himself out of the water and, with not a glance at the lady swimmers (which was not a bit like him), walked into one of the blue chalets. By now, I could feel the skin of my face tightening. I was being burned by the sun, but I would not move from my post. After ten minutes, Clive came out of the chalet, and I lost him in the throng standing about the turnstile of the baths. But I got him in my sights again as he began walking up the paths of the park.

He still carried the carpet bag, and his swimming costume (an article I would not have expected any fellow of the right sort to possess) must have been in there, but the bag looked emptier than before. He kept putting his hands through his hair. He wanted the sun to dry it, but he wanted the sun to get it *right*.

As he climbed towards the Esplanade, I made up my mind: if he saw me I would be friendly, otherwise I would keep back and watch.

He did not spot me, and I began walking back in the direction of the Spa and the Grand. I fretted that I ought not to be spying on a pal, but I knew that my reason for doing so was in some way connected to the stone on the line.

I followed Clive back up the Valley Road towards the station. He stopped for a while under the Valley Bridge. He started walking again, and I thought he might be making for the station, but he turned off before he got there, or dissolved into air before he did, for the next time I looked he was gone.

Clive couldn't have put the stone on the line, but he could've asked somebody else to do it. He could have paid them fair wages, just as he paid the cleaners to put a hexagon shine on the buffer plates of the engines he fancied; just as the socialist missionary, Paul, was paid fair wages by Alan Cowan.

Chapter Ten

We were back on the Rishworth branch the Thursday and Friday after the Scarborough run. I was able to get nothing from Clive over his movements at Scarborough, and had eventually given up.

On the Saturday afternoon, the wife went off to the Co-operative ladies to hear about 'Health in the House' and 'Thoughts on the Minimum Wage', and when she'd gone I took down my *Railway Magazine* and lighted on an item about 'the largest signal gantry in New Zealand'. It wasn't very big, as even the *Railway Magazine* admitted: 'From the photo it is evident that New Zealand is far behind the mother country.' It was meant to be a joke, I supposed.

The words of Dr N. Kenrick came back to me: 'It is only a matter of common sense to keep the head low.'

I would take a stroll. And I would try to find some company. I walked upstairs ready to tap on George Ogden's door, but I saw that it was ajar. I was full of curiosity about this fellow, who I had seen nothing of all week. He had use of the scullery, but he never *did* use it. He would go up by the back stair late at night and very quietly, but it was a kind of quietness – by which I mean not *very* – that told me he'd taken a drink.

I pushed the door and George was inside, sitting on the truckle bed, with the plants – half of them quite dead – on the floor around him.

'George,' I said in an under-breath, and he came to life, like a penny-in-the-slot mannequin.

'What ho!' he said.

'I'm off up to the Albert Cigar Factory. If you knock on the back door they give out cigars that have got a bit bashed.

They've usually only had a little nick and they come very cheap, less than half price.'

'They're quite all right, are they?' said George, standing up. It was heartbreaking to see him so galvanised over such a little thing.

'They have 'A's and 'B's,' I said.

'Good,' said George, 'I'll have an 'A'. This will be our first step to better acquaintance. I'm to book on at two, but I'll have plenty of time, won't I?'

He stood up, collected his hat, picked up a letter that was lying on one of his boxes, and caught up one of the packets of biscuits. 'Care for a cream biscuit?' he said. He sounded like an advert, and his face looked like an advert too as he bit into the biscuit: a big smile decorated with crumbs and bits of white sugar cream.

'Don't they sell those down at the Joint?' I said.

'That's it,' he said, 'from the penny-in-the-slot machine.'

'I didn't think it worked,' I said. 'Well, the excursionists can never make it work.'

'Excursionists?' said George. 'Daft lot! I expect they just put their money in and hope for the best!'

I said I thought that was more or less the recommended procedure.

'It is if you're a juggins. Now listen, there's an address on the side of the machine,' said George. 'You write in to it if the thing is not giving out biscuits, and they send you any number of them back, gratis. Duggan's Sweetmeats, 54 New Clarence Road, Bradford.'

'You have it by heart,' I said.

'That's the best way,' said George. 'You ought to give it a go.'

'But I've never put money in the machine,' I said.

George said nothing to that. 'You get a very gentlemanly letter of apology too,' he went on, 'signed in person by the chairman himself.'

We were crossing Ward's End, dodging the darting wagons and traps and their hot, cross drivers. All the pavements

95

were chock full, as if the heat had turned the whole town inside out.

'You're very lucky in your Mrs Stringer,' George said.

'Yes,' I said, 'I know.'

'She's rather pretty.'

I thought to myself: now that's going a bit strong, but I didn't really mind it coming from George Ogden. It would have been different if a dog like Clive had said it.

'She stops at home as a rule, does she?'

'Used to,' I said. 'She works at a mill now.'

I could not bring myself to say the words 'Hind's Mill'.

'I wouldn't fancy that myself,' said George. 'You'll see a lot of weavers in some pub of a Saturday night, crowding around the "Try Your Fortune" machine, startled at whatever comes up, and it's enough to make a fellow weep. I mean to say, the tickets might just as well read: "You're a weaver in a mill, you will stay a weaver in the mill, and when you are quite worn out you will leave the mill, and then you will die."'

After that little lot, I found that I didn't quite *know* George Ogden. I would have to think on.

I said, 'The wife is in the *offices* at her mill, you know?'

'Of course she is, old man,' he said. 'Don't mind me at all.'

A tram was stopping outside Victoria Hall, and George Ogden suddenly made a run for it. It was an unnatural sight, George running. It was like a man having a fight with himself while on the move, and it seemed that half the street came to a halt in order to marvel at the spectacle. He jumped onto the tram then jumped directly off with the conductor bawling at him. There were post boxes on the trams, and George had just posted his letter. You weren't supposed to do it like that though. The boxes were for fare payers only.

As he strolled back to me, the conductor was giving us the evil eye, but luckily his tram was carrying him further off by the second.

'You want to watch he doesn't open the box and take your letter out,' I said.

'How will he know which is mine?' George said, and then he smiled and then he frowned.

'It's a letter to my best girl,' he said.

'Where does she live?'

'She's out in Oldham,' he said.

'Do you get over there very often?'

'Not so *very* . . . It's a fair way, you know.'

'Matrimony on the cards, is it?'

George, who had wandered onto the road, now had to scuttle out of the way of a delivery bike and was nearly flattened in the process. His legs were too short. He was all brain and belly.

'That's . . . it's never quite settled,' said George. 'Your Mrs Stringer,' he said. '*She's* got her own mind, hasn't she?'

'It's all the woman's role, and so on,' I said. 'She's ardent for freedom.'

'Bit hard on you though, old sort?'

'Well, she wants better conditions for all.'

'What about lodgers?' he said, quite sharply.

'How do you mean?'

'It's just that I'm in rather low water in present, financially speaking, and –'

'If you want a rent cut it won't wash, George,' I said. 'You've only been in a week.'

'But with all her beliefs about fairness –'

'No,' I said. 'As far as all that goes . . . You see, a part of freedom for her is being able to charge you five shillings a week rent.'

'Oh,' said George, and he stopped dead on the pavement, looking quite abashed. 'Anyway, it's quite all right,' he said, starting to walk once again. 'I'm a socialist myself, you know.'

'Yes,' I said, 'so am I, but I will not go to lectures on the minimum wage on Saturday afternoon.'

And I will not put grindstones on railway lines on account of being one either, I thought, and it came to me that I hadn't seen Paul, the socialist missionary, hanging about Horton Street since our conversation of eight days ago.

'There's just nothing to be done about it,' said George, who was still thinking of his rent. 'I shall have to reduce my savings.'

'Well you could stop going out for knife-and-fork teas every night,' I said. 'You do have use of the scullery, you know.'

'I do not have knife-and-fork teas,' said George, 'I have damn good *suppers*.'

'And I suppose you'll have a bottle of wine too?'

'I will take a carafe,' said George, and he said that last word with very great care. 'That would be nothing out of the way.'

'What is a carafe?' I asked him.

'It's a sort of small jug,' he said, and then he stopped and smiled: 'But not *too* small.'

We walked on, skirting past People's Park, where all the benches were full. I was trying to spy the rainbow in the fountain, while thinking violently about George and money. He either had too little or he had too much.

'Where did you lodge before, George?' I said.

But he ignored this question completely.

We were by now at the Albert Cigar Factory, whose two chimneys did look like cigars puffing away, but nothing had been made of this for advertising purposes. I took George round to the back of the factory, where there was a small blue door with a broken metal sign on it. The only words remaining read: 'ALWAYS DELIGHTFUL TO INHALE'.

I knocked, saying to George, 'You sometimes have to wait a while.'

But the door was opened straightway by a young fellow in a dust coat. He was standing in a kind of shop – a take-it-or-leave-it kind of show, not out to please, where the goods were just left in crates and kicked about as needed.

'What ho!' shouted George, and the cigar man sprang back. For a minute I thought he was going to crown George.

"A's or 'B's?' the cigar man asked.

"A's for me', said George. 'Take a dozen.'

"B's for me,' I said. 'Half a dozen.'

Mine were two shillings, George's four, and they came to us in boxes without lids.

'Do you have any tubes?' said George to the cigar man.

'What sort of tubes?' came the reply.

'Cigar tubes,' said George.

The man turned to one of the crates and George turned to me, muttering, 'Extraordinary fellow!'

George got one tin tube, gratis – which he thought a great thing to bring off – and as we walked away he took a little clasp knife out of one of his dozens of pockets, chopped the end off his 'A', and lit it. It was more than twice the size of one of my 'B's.

'Sound smoke,' he said after a while, and he carried it off pretty well. Folk looked at him as he walked by. Then he stopped, and with the smoke racing into his eyes, unlaced his watch from his waistcoat: 'Fancy a stroll down to the Joint?'

I said that I did, and we set off down Horton Street, carrying our cigar boxes.

'You really ought to get 'A's, you know,' said George.

'Why?' I said, even though I'd been thinking the same thing myself.

'They're bigger,' he said, taking a puff, 'and better. You're an A1 fellow, so have an A1 cigar.'

'Thank you,' I said, because there didn't seem much else to say.

After a few paces he turned, with a flaring match in his hand, saying 'Won't you join me, old man?'

So I bit the end off my 'B' – which George frowned at – and started smoking it.

I might have taken two draws on the cigar when we came alongside the Thomas Cook excursion office in Horton Street. They were queuing out the door as usual, but the window was boarded.

'Hey!' I called to George. 'That's been smashed.'

George didn't even stop walking; didn't even remove his cigar from his mouth. 'Friday night, old man!' he called. 'High spirits!' Then he added: 'I've no use for that place myself. I won't go in for your whirligig holidays. Besides, the trains can be dangerous from all I hear.'

'It's not the trains,' I said, staring at the boarded window. 'It's the loonies with the bloody millstones.'

Without a word to George, I stood on my cigar, crossed over Horton Street and began pushing towards the front of the queue of excursionists, apologising as I went. As I did so, I realised that George was behind me, not apologising, but saying, every now and again, 'Step aside there', and the funny thing was that his big cigar allowed him to get away with it.

There were three clerks inside the excursion office, all looking very hot and bothered, and surrounded by posters of people standing at the seaside in golden sun, and grinning fit to bust under straw boaters. There were some Lanky posters up there as well, and two or three of the same one: a poster showing a steam packet, and the words: 'STEP ON AT GOOLE FOR THE CONTINENT'.

'Who smashed your window?' I asked one of the clerks, who was in the middle of serving an elderly party in a dinty bowler.

'Mr Bloody Nobody,' he said, and then, after a quick glance at me, 'It wasn't thissen, by any chance, I don't suppose?'

George was right behind me, smoking into my ear. 'Bloody sauce,' he said. 'Why, it's slander, is that.'

The clerk now turned to George: 'And will *you* get out of here, and leave off poisoning us all with that dratted great cigar.'

'That was slander as well,' said George, when we were back outside in Horton Street.

'Come here,' I said, and I led him back across the road to the wall of the old warehouse. The poster was still there: 'A MEETING TO DISCUSS QUESTIONS'.

'I reckon it was that lot that smashed the window,' I said. 'They want to stop all excursions, and they want to frighten the railways off.' And I told George all about Paul, the socialist missionary-cum-anarchist, and how there might be a connection with the stone on the line.

'Anarchists . . .' said George, when I'd finished. 'There's a lot of those blighters in Germany, from what I read in *The Times*. Bomb-throwing's meat and drink to them, you know. Then there's the bloody Fenians too.'

'Well, that puts my mind at ease, I must say,' I said. 'Why do they do it?'

George puffed on his cigar, using it to think. 'Get in the newspapers,' he said.

We walked on, heading for the Joint, and George said, 'Do you care to know my theory on your little bit of bad business?'

'Go on then,' I said.

Walking down a hill didn't suit George Ogden any more than walking up a hill. With every step the breath was knocked out of him, escaping with a little whistle, which was sometimes accompanied by a jet of smoke from his 'A'.

'It was wreckers,' he said.

'I know that,' I said.

'But this is what you don't know,' he said, quite sharp: 'they were going for the next train.'

Above the station, the flag of the Lanky and the flag of the Great Northern slept side by side in the great heat.

'Why would they be doing that?'

'Beats me.'

'Well, what makes you think they *were*?'

'Simple,' said George. And the next speech he made standing still in Horton Street, with his fingers in his waistcoat pockets and his cigar always in his mouth: 'The next train was *known* of. The Blackpool Express. Runs every day, even Sunday: eight thirty-six. Famous train, and the only timetabled one of the day from Halifax to Blackpool. It was in the *timetable*, do you see, there to be found by anyone picking up the month's *Bradshaw*. Yours –' Here he took one hand out of his waistcoat, to point at me, '– yours was an excursion, and a late-booked one at that. Some excursions get into the *Bradshaw*'s, those known of long in advance. Yours didn't. Some – those known about a little less in advance – get into the *working* timetables. Yours didn't. Some get into the fortnightly notices, but yours missed that as well. The first we all knew of yours was in the weekly notices.'

'Do you fellows in the booking office get the same weekly notices as us engine fellows?' I asked.

'Wouldn't be much point in having different!' said George.

That was true enough.

'Wreckers are sometimes just kids out for fun,' I said. 'They want to make the train jump. They wouldn't be particular as to which train they tripped up.'

'No,' said George. 'But another sort might be. If they *had* planned to send one particular train galley west, odds on it would have been the second.'

'Yes,' I said slowly, 'unless they *had* seen the weekly notices, and they knew of our train.'

'Yes,' said George, even more slowly.

'But that's half the Lanky,' I went on. 'Every stationmaster and signalman from here to Blackpool, and everyone who reads a stationmaster or a signalman's notices, which, since they're pinned up all over the shop, is hundreds.'

'Thousands!' said George.

We now carried on walking towards the station, with me wondering where this conversation had got us, but thinking very hard over it, and over the broken window of the Thomas Cook office.

Chapter Eleven

There were two booking offices at the Joint: one for the Lancashire and Yorkshire, one for the Great Northern. That's why it was called the Joint. They were on a sort of wooden bridge, in a building that was like a pier pavilion and went over the tracks and platforms. You climbed dark dusty steps which smelled exciting in some way, and fanned out to left and right, depending on whether you wanted the Great Northern ticket window – which you would if you wanted a connection to London – or the Lanky side.

Between the ticket windows was a door, which I supposed was as good as invisible to passengers, for it was through this that only the ticket clerks came and went. Once through the door, things split into two again. To the left, small letters on a door said 'GN TICKET OFFICE'; to the right, small letters on another said 'L&Y OFFICE'.

As I prepared to follow George through this second one, I asked him: 'Have you ever been through the other door?'

'Wouldn't care to,' he said, shaking his head.

'Why not?'

'Because it's exactly the same as this show, except with different printing on the tickets.'

As he said the word 'tickets', that's what I saw. The walls of this big wooden room were made of them, and they muffled any noise. I could hear the station below but it might have been a mile away. All around the walls were dark cabinets with wide, thin drawers, and above the cabinets were racks in which the different types of tickets stood in columns. The tickets, thousands upon thousands of them, were imprisoned in their long thin racks. They were dropped in through the top and could only be slid out from the bottom.

In those few wall spaces where there weren't ticket racks, there were pictures. One was the famous Lanky poster that had been in the Thomas Cook excursion office, 'STEP ON AT GOOLE FOR THE CONTINENT'. I thought of holidays, and again of the broken window at the excursion office. Had Paul done it? Or even Alan Cowan himself?

There were two other clerks in the office: one sitting at the ticket window, another leaning against one of the racks. George introduced them as Dick and Bob, and as he did so, all of their voices sounded lost, as if they were outnumbered and beaten down by the tickets on all sides.

I had seen this pair before and secretly thought them a very medium pair of goods. They might have been in any line of business. There was nothing railway-ish about them. They both shot me funny, complicated looks, because they knew me for an engine man, and an engine man does not wear a stiff collar. But he does start at the head end of the train, and that's the important thing. Or so I'd believed until the smash. Being at the front end put you in the way of trouble. I had struck trouble, and been found wanting.

I shook their hands, and then they fell to staring at George and his cigar. 'Better not let Dunglass or Knowles see you with that thing in your mouth,' Dick said.

Dunglass was the chief booking clerk.

'Smoking's only allowed in the general room,' added Bob, rising from the seat at the ticket window. The ticket office had the wooden, empty smell of a cricket pavilion.

'Nonsense,' said George, who now took Bob's place at the ticket window.

In front of George at the ticket window was a great wooden guillotine that could be dropped down at the close of business, or, as I was to learn, at any time that suited. George also had a money drawer, and at his elbow a date stamp which looked like an iron head with a thin mouth for the tickets to go in.

There not being any passengers to be dealt with, George

swivelled around in the chair, which was set on wheels, and, using his cigar as a pointer, indicated the racks, saying very loudly: 'First-class singles . . .'

There were lots of these.

'Second-class singles . . .'

More still of these.

'Third-class singles . . .'

Yet more – a good two dozen racks of these.

'Heaps of Thirds, aren't there?' I said.

'What?' said George, sitting back, taking a pull on his cigar. 'Well, nine out of ten passengers go Third. It's a third-class world, I'm afraid . . . except for some of us.' At this, George swivelled right round in his chair, with his boots lifted up off the ground, and the face of a kid riding a whirligig. Bob and Dick looked at each other and smiled. George was the star turn of the booking office.

'First-class returns,' George continued, putting his feet down to stop the chair and pointing to another part of the booking office, 'Second returns . . . Third returns, policeman-on-duty tickets, clergymen tickets, staff privilege, angling tickets, market-day specials, platform tickets.'

He was going on rapidly now, his cigar jumping about; I couldn't make out where he was pointing.

'Now,' said George, 'your first-class singles are white, your second-class singles are red, your third-class singles green. Your first-class returns are white and yellow, your second-class returns are red and blue, your third-class . . .'

'Tell him the interesting stuff,' said Dick, or Bob, very timidly.

'What do you think I *am* doing?' said George, quite indignantly.

'No, the *really* interesting stuff.'

'Is there any way of recalling who's bought a ticket on any particular train?' I asked the office in general.

George frowned. 'You can say which tickets have gone,' he said, 'but not who's had 'em.'

'Unless you happen to remember the person,' said Dick.

'Or the ticket they get,' said Bob. 'A notable ticket number might do it. I sold a ticket for Todmorden this morning: third-class single, number one, two, three, three. That's a highly interesting ticket.'

'Why?' I said.

George answered for him. 'Because the next one's going to be one, two, three, four, see? Collector's item.'

If George was right, and the wreckers had been aiming at the 8.36, the regular Blackpool express, the train after ours on that day, it might be handy to know who was riding on it. But I would not find out here.

Just then, somebody tapped on the ticket-window glass and George swivelled around to face the customer.

'Good afternoon, Doctor Whittaker,' he said, thrusting his cigar-holding hand down below his counter. 'Second-class return to Bradford?'

At this he gave a sudden kick with both legs and his chair went flying backwards so that he was level with second-class returns to Bradford, or so I supposed. Bob and Dick gave me silly smiles as he did this. George reached across to the rack, and suddenly the ticket was lying in his hand. He had the trick of flicking it from the bottom of the rack. Then, by means of a strange, sitting-down walk, he dragged himself and his chair back to the ticket window, sliding the cigar into its tube as he did so.

'Ninepence, Doctor Whittaker,' he said.

But then he had to lean again towards the window, for the doctor – evidently a regular customer – had further require-ments.

'Cycle ticket in addition?' said George. 'That'll be one six-pence, Doctor Whittaker.'

He gave a greater kick this time, sending himself back a good fifteen feet, the cycle ticket being a more out-of-the-way sort of thing than a second-class return, therefore kept further from the window. George took one from the rack, and went back to Doctor Whittaker, who it seemed was not done yet.

'Cycle *insurance* also?' asked George, quite peeved after listening for a moment at the window.

The doctor then had something else to say – something pretty sharp, too, that I could almost hear through the glass. When the speech had finished, George said: 'It is no trouble at all, sir, only you might have said first time. If you had *said*, you see, I would have *known* . . .'

He shot himself backwards once more, towards bicycle insurance, muttering as he went: 'Not being a great hand at mind-reading.'

When the sale was completed, George wheeled around to us all once more, beaming.

'Quite a card, our George,' said Dick.

Just then there was a knock at the door. It was a kid I'd never seen about the Joint before. 'Any of you blokes come across a photographer?' he said.

Everybody said they hadn't, and the fellow left.

'Rum sort of question,' said George, frowning when the fellow had gone.

On the other side of the room, Bob, who was looking down onto the platforms through one of the windows, gave a cry: 'Hi! She's back!'

George left off fiddling with his cigar and dashed over to the window along with Bob. I walked over more slowly.

'What's going off?' I asked.

'Mrs Emma Knowles,' said Bob, grandly.

'Who's she?' I asked. 'Stationmaster's daughter?'

'Wife!' said George. 'If you can credit it.'

A tank engine was pulling out of platform two and a lady in white was walking along the platform in the opposite direction: little clouds of steam were flying towards her from the engine, like blown kisses. From the ticket-office window I could only see the top of her hat, but some hats promise beauty beneath, and this was one.

'She looks lonely today,' said Bob.

'The finest woman in the town,' said George very sadly, as he walked back to his rotating chair at the ticket window. 'One day, I'm going to go down there and talk to her.'

'You ought to, George,' said Dick, 'she couldn't eat you, after all.'

'Actually,' said George, 'I wouldn't mind a bit if she did, you know?'

'What would you talk to her about?' asked Bob.

'I could put her straight about this show,' George said, indicating the whole of the booking office.

'You'd talk to her about railway tickets?' I asked.

'Only at first,' said George. 'Just to break the ice.'

Emma Knowles walked on, disappearing under the building in which we stood.

'Oh we do like her,' said Bob, turning away from the window and folding his arms.

'Why does she come here?' I asked.

'Take the air?' suggested Bob.

'What air?' I said. 'It's all smoke, like any station.'

'Old Knowles likes to show her off,' said George. 'Just rubbing it in, you know, look at me: villa looking over People's Park, housemaids, company cab at my door each morning, and this vision in my bed every night.'

'She's quite often seen at the station,' said Bob. 'And she doesn't just come here to see Knowles.'

'Why does she come then?' I asked him.

'Catch a train,' said Bob.

'Where to?'

He shrugged.

'Being married to the SM she has a pass all over the line,' said Dick.

'So you see,' Bob put in, 'because we don't sell her the tickets, we don't know.'

Now all was quiet in the booking office. George seemed half asleep in his chair all of a sudden, with the cigar lodged in one of his waistcoat pockets. Dick was leafing through a book of accounts. Bob was looking out of the window with his hands in his pockets.

There was another knock on the door and Dick opened it. A grinning kid stood there with a box in his hand. 'Afternoon, mates,' he said. He uncombed his hair by smearing his hat across his sweaty head, then he passed the box to Dick, handing across a docket at the same time. 'Fleetwood singles,' he said, 'numbers five hundred to six thousand on the nose.'

Bob passed a book to Dick, who'd begun unwrapping the parcel, which contained bundles of tickets tied with white ribbons.

But George was scowling from his seat as Dick began to record receipt of the tickets in the ledger. 'We're counting on a full complement this time, old man,' George said to the kid.

There was something funny about the way Dick wrote in the ledger. At first I couldn't see what it was; he just looked greedy to get the words and numbers down, but it struck me after a second that he was holding two pens, writing with both hands.

George saw me watching. 'Like a blinking octopus, en't he?'

Bob, who seemed proud of Dick over this, said: 'He can do sales and receipts at the same time.'

'Five hundred to six thousand exactly,' said Dick, looking up from the ledger and turning to the ticket bundles. 'Looks like they're all here.'

'Have you lot seen the show they're putting on down there?' said the kid, pointing at the floor, but meaning the platforms beneath.

'What show, old man?' said George to the kid (even though he didn't look more than fifteen).

'Picture-taking,' said the kid. 'Photographic artist. He has all the brass lined up.'

Dick walked over once more to the window.

'You'll not see it from there, old man' said the kid, who then gave a funny look towards George.

'I'm off down to look,' said Dick, and Bob went too.

'Good fellows if they can be turned the right way,' said George, when they'd gone. 'Not a lot of steam in them really, but . . .' He got to his feet and began putting away the tickets from the new parcel, or trying to. He couldn't quite reach the top of what I took to be the rack for Fleetwood singles. I asked if I could help, being six inches taller than George. 'It's quite all right,' he said, and took a stool from the other side of the room. 'They must be put into the racks in a certain special way.'

'Well, yes,' I said, 'in number order, lowest number at the bottom.'

'Bit more to it than that, chief,' said George.

But there wasn't, as he knew very well.

'Where do the tickets come from?' I asked.

'From Headquarters in Manchester, of course,' said George. 'They're sent over here in parcels as needed.'

'All in number order?' I said.

'That's the idea: in number order, and parcelled in batches of two hundred and fifty.'

With none of the Fleetwood singles put away, George walked over to his revolving seat once more and sat down. Just as he did so, there was a passenger at the window, and he had to sell a ticket.

When the sale was complete, George pitched the coin into the wooden drawer and turned again towards me: 'They go in runs of ten thousand, you know,' he said, and then gave me a sideways look to see whether I *did* know. Well, I had a vague notion but didn't let on, so he continued talking like a penny book. 'It's the Edmonson ticket that's used. Has been for donkey's years. For every type – Liverpool singles, let's say – the run is ten thousand, but the system only allows four digits to be printed on the tickets so how can that be since ten thousand is five?'

I gave a shrug, for I really didn't know.

George smiled. 'Rather a pretty little catch, en't it? Well, what's the number of the first ticket in a run, would you say?'

'One,' I said, looking again at 'STEP ON AT GOOLE FOR THE CONTINENT'.

'*Nought, nought, nought,* one, you mean,' said George, 'because remember that even though you can't have more than four digits, you can't have fewer than that either.'

'I see,' I said.

'So that's your answer, is it? First one in a run's nought, nought, nought, one?'

'Yes,' I said.

'Quite sure of it, are you?'

'Well it's obviously not,' I said, 'from the way you're carrying on.'

George was grinning like a street knocker.

'Very well then,' I said, 'what *is* the first number in the run?'

'Fish and find out,' said George, and he spun around in his chair.

I could have brained him there and then. 'I give it up,' I said.

'Oh come on,' he said. 'Take a shy.'

Something I'd read in the *Railway Magazine* came back to me, and I knew the answer, but I had a queer feeling that it would have been quite crushing to George if I'd come out with it, so I said again: 'No. Can't work it out.'

In celebration of his victory, George gave one more spin on his chair, and said: 'The first number's nought, nought, nought, nought. That way, the last one's the ten thousandth even though its number's only nine, nine, nine, nine. I must say, old man, it should be no riddle to anyone of normal intelligence. It's a very good thing you're not in this line of work.'

I was not having this. I had let him have his victory, and now he was making me eat dog over it. 'Well, I knew that all along,' I said.

'Oh leave off,' said George. He sat still in his chair, took his cigar out of his waistcoat and looked at it. 'See that the cigar bears the name of the registered star band,' he muttered quietly to himself, and when he looked up at me again, his cheeks were red. 'The next time the four noughts come up,' he said, 'I'll buy the ticket myself, as long as it's not a really expensive one like a First to Liverpool, and then I'll let you have it, old man. Gratis. Folks will give worlds to get 'em.'

'Well,' I said, 'no need to trouble yourself over that.'

I wanted to put our little set-to behind us, and I thought of a question that would help me do it: 'You said there was some trouble over the tickets coming in?'

'It's just this,' said George. 'Some blockhead in Manchester keeps sending us short batches – causes the devil of confusion, puts all the ledgers out. It would turn your hair pink in streaks if you knew the half of it . . . everybody kept back hours after booking off time . . . as if it's not bad enough, being stuck in this poky hole.'

I looked again at the steam packet on the Goole poster, and, to change the subject, said: 'I have hopes of taking the wife to Goole.'

George nodded. 'As a shipping centre, it's hard to beat,' he said. 'The barges go along the canal like trains – all tied together, and when the ride is right there's some big ships to see.'

'The company keeps its own fleet of steam packets there I believe,' I said. 'It's a bigger show than Fleetwood, and I've not yet been out that way.'

George looked at me very gravely for a while, then took his plunge: 'Would you like a ticket for yourself and Mrs Stringer?'

'Staff privilege, you mean?'

George nodded.

'Well, I have my footplate pass for getting back from turns, but staff priv . . . Three a year you're allowed if you're an engine man, and you've got to put in for them weeks in advance. They're like gold dust, aren't they?'

'They are *rather*,' said George.

I tried to keep a carefree tone, but I had a bad feeling over this. 'And they must be signed by Knowles,' I said.

George nodded solemnly once again. 'I put 'em under his nose, and he generally signs 'em without looking.'

112

'Well –' I said.

'Only sometimes I don't bother.' George picked up a pen, stood up again and walked across to one of the racks – the one holding the staff-privilege tickets. He flicked a ticket out from the bottom and returned to the ticket window with it. He had burnt his boats now, for he would not be able to put it back except at the top of the stack, and then it would be out of order. 'I know Mr Knowles has got a lot on, and so to ease his burden a little I sometimes do the job myself,' said George. He was waving his pen over the blank ticket, working himself up to the moment, and I was looking at a new George. Except that somehow his being a little on the fly was not so *very* great a surprise.

'It's quite all right, old boy,' I said, thinking to soften the blow of my refusal by putting it in his own sort of swell talk.

'Oh that's *quite* all right,' said George in turn, putting his pen back into his coat pocket. He then began walking back over to the rack from which he'd taken the ticket. 'I was only skylarking in any case,' he went on. 'Now of course, it does sometimes happen that we take one out, and it turns out not to be needed . . .' He laid the ticket on the little ledge at the foot of the column from which it had come. 'So it stays there until it *is* required.'

I could've split, and George would have been stood down immediately, with worse to follow. So in a way I should've felt flattered, because he was showing me trust.

'Do you know what I'm going to have in my apartments at Back Hill Street?' George asked, suddenly.

'Your room, do you mean?'

'Damask curtains. I've got a *mind* to have 'em,' he said, standing up, 'so I'm jolly well *going* to have 'em.'

I nodded. 'The wife doesn't really hold with curtains,' I said. I wanted to keep talking to get the ticket business behind us. 'She won't do things in a sixpenny way,' I said. 'She must have the best of everything, and so she will wait until opportunity calls.'

'And do you know what's wanted in this office?' said George.

I shrugged, still a little dazed.

'What's wanted is a revolving ticket cabinet to go next to this revolving chair. That would save me having to sail backwards every time.'

'Wouldn't things become a little confusing, with you and the tickets both revolving? You might end up going one way, the tickets another.'

George stood up and walked over to the window. 'Glad to know your view on the matter,' he said, but of course he wasn't in the least. He looked through the window for a while, before turning to me and saying: 'Shall we go and watch the photographer?'

'But what about anyone coming to buy a ticket?' I said, at which George turned about and slammed down the hatch.

'They can buy 'em on the trains,' he said. He then lobbed a small amount of coin into the money drawer and took out another ticket from the racks. This he handed to me. 'Take it,' he said. 'It's a present. All paid for.'

It was the third-class single to Todmorden mentioned earlier: number 1234.

'Thanks,' I said.

'Come on,' said George, who was holding the booking-office door open for me.

We walked along under the canopy of platform two. It was all shaded, and I wanted to be out of it quickly, into the world of light beyond where the photograph was being taken. That's the thing about sunshine day after day. It spoils you. You get so as you can't do without it.

The camera was set up at the platform end. Knowles was there, his two assistant stationmasters, the head porter and a handful of other high-ups. The photographer was at his camera, looking down into it through a sort of concertina tube. He had his own assistant alongside.

'It looks smart to have an assistant even if you never use

114

him,' said George, as we stepped up to join Dick and Bob.

Knowles was at the front of the group, and Mrs Knowles was looking on. She was beautiful and she was smiling. Knowles was not.

'You small fellows go to the side,' Knowles was saying.

'All he wants is a whip,' George muttered.

Knowles had a brown, square face and a thin black moustache which was there to prove the care he took over shaving and everything else. He spoke fast, with a mouth that was like a machine. 'Where do you want me, sir?' he was asking the photographer. 'In the middle?'

At this George turned and rolled his eyes at me. 'A stationmaster isn't gentry, you know,' he said.

'How do you mean?'

'Just watch him.'

The group was all ready, like a small army in gold, except that too many of them looked like farmers.

'Now stay quite still,' said the photographer. Then he said, 'Stopping down', and began fiddling with the camera, while the assistant looked on, flinching every now and again. The photographer looked up, half towards the sun with a hand shielding his eyes. He looked away, very downhearted. The day was too bright.

Presently the photographer looked into his camera once more, then looked away again and took up glaring at his assistant. He then returned to his camera, but broke off at some small gust of wind that seemed to bring with it a change of light.

'Fellow's making a meal of it, en't he?' George whispered to me. 'I've messed about with a hand camera in my time . . . a touch of portraiture . . . Nothing to it really.'

Knowles coughed, being the only one in the party of photographic subjects who dared.

'The pharmacy up on New Bank has a dark room,' George continued in an under-breath. 'I have use of it at special rates.'

The photographer went back to his camera and peered into the rubber tunnel once more. 'Busy day for you fellows?'

asked the photographer after a while. He was still looking through the camera.

'This is a *railway station*, sir,' said Knowles, and just as he was doing so the photographer pressed a button and the camera clicked.

'Oh, heck!' said the photographer, and, standing up straight, he said to the party: 'Look, if I ask a question don't answer it, all right? I'm just thinking aloud.'

Meanwhile the assistant had gone live, darting towards the back of the camera, from which he removed something, smuggling it into the black bag. Then he smuggled something *out* of the black bag and fitted it into the back of the camera where the earlier article had been. The photographer was standing with his face tipped up towards the sky, eyes closed.

'Fellow's a perfect fool,' George whispered.

The photographer now walked a fair distance away from his camera, and just stood there with his hands on his hips.

'I've an important train expected in on platform six in three minutes,' called the stationmaster, 'and I *will* have to attend to it.'

'Yes,' said photographer, 'well now the sun's in the wrong place.'

'I expect Mr Knowles will be able to sort that out for you,' said one of the assistant stationmasters. It was a jest, so a bit of a risk, but Knowles's wife laughed – a lonely tinkle like breaking glass – and Knowles himself gave a smile. Well, nearly.

'Look at him now,' said George, 'dignity maintained at all costs. But I saw him in the Imperial once with Dunglass, and it was all "thee" and "tha", and when the waiter asked if they wanted beer or wine, he said, "nawther". He's teetotal, you know.'

George looked again at Emma Knowles. 'If I could just once . . .'

Knowles was now giving George the evil eye. Then his stare shifted to Dick and Bob, who both looked nervously back at George, waiting for him to speak up for them.

'Ogden,' said Knowles. 'Who is presently in the booking office?'

'Just at this present time, sir?' said George, and two untidy red marks had appeared on his cheeks, like two maps of India. 'Well, fact is that business is rather light, sir, and we all came down very briefly to see whether we could be of assistance.'

'I am standing here, Ogden,' said Knowles, 'and I am trying to smile for this gentleman –' he pointed to the photographer '– and the cause is not helped by –'

But just as George was about to get what-for, the 'important' train – which didn't look in the least important to me, being a little local with three rattlers on – came bustling into platform six as threatened. Knowles broke away from the picture group to see to it, or to pretend to. As he dashed across the footbridge, I saw a man stepping off the train with a bulky portmanteau in his hand. He wore a cap and had too much hair. It was Paul, of the Socialist Mission. Close behind him walked a tall, thin man in a homburg hat. This one, who'd stepped off the same train, carried no bag, but had a bundle of papers under his arm.

'Hi!' I yelled. But it's a tall order to shout across four platforms with an engine in steam close by, and the two fellows were quickly up onto the footbridge.

I edged up to Bob. 'Where's that one from?' I asked, pointing to the train that had come into platform six, and was now rolling away.

Bob looked at his pocket watch and thought for a second. 'That's in from York, I reckon,' he said.

That was good enough for me. It could have connected there with a train down from Scotland. I was blowed if the second fellow wasn't Alan Cowan, leader of the Socialist Mission. Well, he looked just the sort. I gave a general nod towards the photographic party and began to give chase.

Chapter Twelve

I fell in behind the two as they walked past the cab rank outside the Joint. The thin man wore a suit of decent brown tweed. I could picture him in Scotland; I could see him in Dunfermline.

He kept a dozen paces behind Paul, and I thought: they don't want to be seen together. I couldn't go up to him, for I didn't know the fellow, so I ran past him and stopped Paul at the foot of Horton Street.

'Remember me?' I said. 'I stood you a lemonade at the Evening Star,' and even as I spoke, I thought it was a pretty poor beginning.

He put down his portmanteau. The long hair, coming out from under the bowler, made him look old-fashioned, and then it came to me from childhood books: Richard III.

I pointed back down Horton Street, and said, 'Would that fellow be Cowan, because if so . . .?'

But even as I looked, the man in the brown suit was stepping into the Crown, looking just as though he was after a spot of dinner, and I knew I was wrong.

'*Who*?' said Paul.

'Sorry,' I said, 'made a bloomer.'

And the nasty smile went crawling across his face.

'Where's Alan Cowan just at present?' I said.

'Piccadilly Circus,' Paul said, instantly. 'Well, that's where he was speaking at midnight last night. Meeting of the unemployed.'

If they're unemployed, I thought, why must they wait until midnight to hold a meeting? 'Keep pretty close tabs on him, don't you?'

'I'm not the only one,' said Paul. 'He's a world-class ideologue, is Alan.'

'Would you take another drink with me?' I said.

Nasty smile as before. 'All right,' he said, and he picked up the portmanteau once again.

In the Evening Star, he left the bag with me at the bar and went off to the Gentlemen's. As the barmaid came up, I was torn between looking into the bag and another plan, and it was the second that won out.

I ordered a Ramsden's for myself, a lemonade for Paul, and a tanner's worth of gin, which I dashed quickly into the lemonade. The concoction was surging up as Paul came back and threatening to overflow the glass, but he didn't seem to pay any mind, and just drunk the stuff down at once as he had done before.

'You've been to York, then?' I said.

'No,' said Paul, and he smiled.

I thought: damn, the drink's taken him the wrong way.

'Why Piccadilly Circus?' I said. 'Why was Alan Cowan speaking at Piccadilly Circus?'

'It's one of the usual propaganda patches,' said Paul. Then: 'You laid hands on your train wrecker yet?'

'No,' I said. 'The whole of the company's on the look-out for the culprits,' I continued, 'and there's a retired army officer leading an investigation.'

Paul gave a snort: 'Let me guess. Stumped, is he? We have plans for his sort, I can tell you . . .' He looked at his empty glass, maybe with a bit of curiosity. 'We mean to make very short work of that class of gentry, and the coppers, and *all* the upholders of law without order.'

'But they have the guns,' I said.

The smile once more. 'Oh we have available to us certain chemicals and clever mechanics, certain lead patterns for the manufacture of certain items.'

'Did you pitch the stone through the excursion-office window?'

He turned away from me to look through the door of the pub, which had been propped open on account of the heat.

'We'll make a bonfire of this place,' he said, looking out at Halifax; then he picked up his portmanteau. 'Take my advice,' he said, 'and leave the railway slavery. It'll be worse for you if you don't.'

'What's your game exactly, mate?' I said.

'Propaganda,' he said, already turning away. 'Propaganda by deed.'

A tram came clattering past the door of the Evening Star, and the fellow was out and on it with bag in hand, all in a moment.

Chapter Thirteen

It was the following Monday, but only just, it being three o'clock in the morning. George had been moving about upstairs in the night. I'd already been awake, and the wife had stirred after a while, saying: 'What *about* him. Do you think he's flitting?'

'I wouldn't think so,' I said.

'He was late with his first week's rent.'

'But he did pay it?'

'He did.'

'Well then.'

We talked for a while about a subject first raised the evening before: about how she might compose a letter to the Crossley Porter Orphanage asking whether I could see the boy, Arnold Dyson, to return his book.

'It'll be neat enough,' she said. 'As to the wording, we have a book of letter forms at the mill, but it doesn't include writing to an orphanage about the child of a dead employee.'

'No,' I said.

'It should do,' she went on, 'with the number of folk put into an early grave by the work.'

Then she said, rather slowly and carefully: 'Mr Robinson, who took me on at the mill, has been stood down.'

'The one who asked you about worsted?'

She nodded.

'Why?'

'Over a new line of suiting. At first I thought he was on leave, but he's definitely left. It's all solicitors' letters now.'

'Just out of interest,' I said, 'was he on the excursion?'

'I don't know.'

'So you're now at the mercy of Hind, father and son?'

The wife sighed: 'Looks like it.'

'How are you going along with old Hind?'

'Do you mean old Hind or really old Hind?'

'*Really* old Hind, I mean.'

'Old Hind barely moves, let alone speaks to the likes of me. The other one's all right, though I don't like the way he carries on with some of the lasses.'

'How do you mean?'

'I'm not saying.'

At this, the wife rolled over and gave me a kiss.

'The next excursion,' she said, 'the Wakes one . . . It's all fixed. It goes on the Sunday of Wakes, comes back on the Friday. The mill starts up again on the Monday.'

'You're not aiming to go on it yourself though, are you?'

'The office must keep going, so I'm to work that week,' she said.

'Good,' I said.

'But I do have the Sunday off, so I'll make a day trip of it. I'll go with the lot of them on the train, and come back by myself in the evening.'

'You bloody won't,' I said.

'Why ever shouldn't I?'

'You're itching to see a train wreck at close quarters, are you?'

'There won't be another outrage,' she said. 'That's why they're called outrages, you know, because they don't come along so often.'

The wife then went downstairs for a cup of water.

It was two weeks 'til Wakes. But I had a Blackpool excursion before then – an evening go, coming up in just about fourteen hours' time. Paul had smashed the windows of the excursion office, of that I was sure. He was out to get the excursions. That was his mission, which he called socialism. He was a nutcase, him and Alan Cowan both, but just because they were crackers, it didn't mean they weren't dab hands at killing.

122

When the wife returned she was fretting about the Standard typewriter, which she had at the mill but which they wouldn't give to another office girl, which she thought was unfair. 'The Standard is a very superior typewriter,' she said, climbing back into bed.

'Then they should call it the Superior,' I said. 'What is the advantage of it?'

'The keys go down quicker, so it's much faster.'

'Well then,' I said, 'it's only making you do more work.'

The wife thought about that for a while.

I said: 'Would this other office girl be so worried on your account if you were the one without it?'

'I don't know,' said the wife. 'And what's that got to do with it anyway?'

She then asked me why the Co-operative Society should not be allowed to use the royal crest. I said 'Why would you want to?' and she said 'We jolly well *don't* want to.'

I put a stop to this subject by starting a bit of love-making, after which she went off again: this time to do something I knew to be connected with a little booklet she had called *How to Check Family Increase*. At first this had stayed at the bottom of the wooden box at the foot of our bed, and I'd thought it was being held in reserve, because doesn't there have to be an increase before an increase can be checked? But since she'd started at Hind's I'd seen it half hidden in several places about the house, and guessed it was being read. The wife had passed on no instructions to me concerning checking family increase, and it was an embarrassing matter to speak of, so I had carried on as normal.

When she came back, I wondered whether to tell her about George Ogden being on the fly, but it would only bother her. Instead, I said: 'George told me something I never knew: all railway tickets come in runs of ten thousand, they all carry four digits only, so you can guess the number of the first one in a run.'

'One,' said the wife, sighing.

'No,' I said, 'nought, or rather four noughts in a row.'

Her interest was not picking up.

'Can you imagine why it's nought?'

'I'm sure there's some perfectly good railway reason which is perfectly idiotic,' she said.

'It's because if you started with number one you'd get to number ten thousand.'

'So what?'

'Well, ten thousand is five digits, isn't it?'

Talk of railway tickets sent the wife drifting off to sleep, but I lay awake fretting. Blackpool was a dangerous place. It was just because it was such fun. There was no *reason* for Blackpool except fun.

I don't recall whether I then slept for a little while, but I know that I was awake at four and staring at the bedroom window as the hour chimes floated up from the parish church. It was a second after the fourth one that the stone came bursting through the window and, as if kept in the air by the wife's scream, sailed over the bed and crashed directly into the mirror on the opposite wall.

I moved straight to the window, but checked myself, for there was glass all over the tab rug we kept beneath the sill, and I was bare-footed. Hill Street – where the stone had been pitched from – had the look of a place somebody had just left. The warm air rolled up and in through the broken window.

I moved to the bedroom door and saw across the corridor that George's door was half open. He was peering round the edge of it. 'What the blazes was that, old man?' he said. He had on a nightshirt, and his hair looked wild, which made me think he must wear something on it by day.

'Stone,' I said. 'Came through the window.'

'Christ on a bike,' said George. 'Drunks, was it?'

'Happen,' I said.

'Anything I can do, old man?'

I shook my head, and George closed his door.

I walked downstairs but thought better of going out.

Instead, I caught up the brush and pan and a couple of old *Couriers*. When I got back upstairs, the wife was already picking up glass. She gave me a look, and it was one big question.

What to do in emergencies.

'It was two fellows,' I said. 'They were canned. I just got a glimpse as they scarpered.'

'Did you?' she said.

'Yes,' I said, and I reckoned she didn't believe it any more than I did, but she *wanted* to.

We picked up the glass together, wrapped it up like fried fish.

'What did they look like?' asked the wife presently.

'Two swells,' I said, and I began to see them in my mind's eye: a pair of Champagne Charlies like in the music halls. 'They were a pair of proper chumps,' I said. 'One fell as he ran off, and had to be helped up by the other . . . The trouble is, you see, we had the gas up, and we've no curtains . . .'

The wife was back in bed now. There were little particles of glass in my hands from picking the splinters out of the tab rug. I walked over to the gas and looked at my finger ends: it was like a kind of frost. I climbed up next to the wife. I couldn't touch her because of the glass in my hands.

We sat back on the bed, both wide-eyed and not saying much, but listening to the sounds of Halifax that came in through the burst window.

At five we heard the clattering of the milk cart, then came the rattle of clogs – a sliding, shuffling, slithering – as the weavers of Back Hill Street set off to their mills, which was followed by a noise of metal fighting against stone: the first tram of the day coming down Horton Street.

'It's odd that anybody should be drunk at four in the morning,' said the wife at one particular moment. 'I mean, midnight, yes. But not four.'

'It's quite possible to be drunk all night,' I said.

'Well you'd know,' said the wife, and gave a grin. She didn't seem too downhearted. Perhaps my story had taken, after all.

'We'll pay for the new glass out of the tea caddy,' she said, as I thought: if this is the work of Paul, why does he not go off and smash a boss's window instead. Old Hind's would do – any one of the hundreds he had to his name.

Presently, the sunshine came spreading, and then, when all the cobbles were quiet and the hands were inside the mills and fit to be baked or roasted, came the heat, which sent the wife off to sleep for a little while. She woke at seven to go off to Hind's Mill, very sadly removing a ten-shilling note from the tea caddy and saying, 'This puts Hemingway's Piano further off than ever.'

She said she knew of a glazier up on the Beacon near the mill, and she would call in on her way to work. She said she would be back from work at the usual time in the evening, and I told her that I would be late back because of the evening run I had coming up. I told her it wouldn't hurt to lock the door from the inside when she got back; she asked why, and I couldn't think of a way of putting it. Then I gave her an extra special goodbye kiss, for I knew I was about to come a cropper on the Blackpool line.

Chapter Fourteen

Beginning shortly after dinnertime, I spent a lonely three hours in the shed fettling up 044 tank engine No. 7 (not one of Aspinall's but one of Mr Barton Wright's) for an evening cruise to Blackpool. It would be the first Blackpool Special from Halifax Joint since the occasion of the stone on the line.

As I bundled the paraffin rags into the firehole and afterwards the baulks of timber, the same thoughts revolved endlessly. The stone could only have been thrown by Paul. He'd followed me home on the night after we'd first spoken, so he knew where I lived. He wanted to make news over the stone on the line, whether he'd put it there or not, and the stone through the window was another push to get the whole matter in the papers. Then again, the poster advertising 'A MEETING TO DISCUSS QUESTIONS' was still in place on the wall of the old warehouse. That was pretty brass-necked of them, if they really had turned terrorists. You either fought or you held meetings. You didn't go in for both.

Why didn't I tell the papers? Then the Socialist Mission might leave me alone. And why didn't I tell the coppers, which would come to the same thing? But what was there to tell?

As I lit the fire, my mind moved on to the bigger matter, the question of wrecking.

The odds were that any engine man would meet no more than one attempt at wrecking in his life. But what good were the odds? One out of thirty million had been killed on the railways in the previous year, 1904, but what good was that to you if, like Margaret Dyson, you happened to be the one?

I thought of her again. It was crazy to go through your life without seeing the sea: seeing it only in photographs. Margaret

127

Dyson was not down-to-date. She had not caught up with the railway world. But then *it* had caught up with her.

Question after question came as I lit the fire, and one of the big ones was this: Where had Clive disappeared to beyond the Valley Bridge at Scarborough?

That gentry swung his snap-bag, followed by himself, up onto the footplate at 3 p.m. He just grinned at me, and began checking the oil pots as I fettled the fire.

We came rolling out of the shed in the bitter blackness of our own smoke, which broke and cleared as we came into the light like blackbirds appearing one after another out of nowhere and rising off our chimney top. I looked up into the little valley town of Sowerby Bridge, at the blue shining sign: VAN HOUTEN'S COCOA. It should have been a sign for seltzer or dandelion and burdock; better still, ice. Some fellows were skylarking in the open-air water tank on top of the coal stage as we took on coal. It was strange to be in an engine underneath men swimming. They were getting cleaner by the second, and we were getting filthier as the coal smashed into the bunker. The coal would always come in like an accident; I could never get over the din.

As we rolled on, readying to go off shed and make for the Joint, I knew why Clive had been swimming in Scarborough. He'd done it to get clean.

Just then, I looked back and saw John Ellerton coming towards us from the shed, waving his hands. He wanted to see us in his office, so Clive braked the engine and we climbed down.

John Ellerton's office was full of light and full of paper. It was built onto the front of the middle of the shed, like a sort of toll booth. The engines went in and out on the roads either side, and the office was three-quarters glass, so John could see all the comings and goings. He stood behind his desk and passed papers to Clive and me. It was the draft report into the smash by Major Harrison, sub-inspector of the Board of Trade. It started: 'I have pleasure to report . . .' Then the facts of what had happened were set down. Next came the write-ups of the interviews with Reuben Booth, Clive and me, and finally the conclusion, which I jumped straight to. Skimming it over, I read: 'It is found that no want of caution was shown in the operation of the engine. The fireman is a young man of twenty-two, only recently put up to the job, but the driver is experienced, and appears to me deserving of commendation for preventing a far worse disaster.' And this was the last word of Major Harrison: 'It is not possible to say how the obstruction came to be placed on the line.'

'Well I don't reckon much to that,' I said.

'I think it's first rate,' said Clive, grinning all about his head.

I said nothing, but the report was wrong even as regards the known facts. Clive oughtn't to've had to use the reverser. It was throwing on the reverser that had done for Margaret Dyson. That, and me not knowing what to do in emergencies.

'There's one other matter,' John Ellerton was saying.

I said: 'I know what it is,' but nobody paid any attention.

'I've just had the *Halifax Courier* on the telephone regarding a telegram they've received,' said Ellerton. 'Now I'll read it out.' He picked up a paper and read: '"Hind's Mill Blackpool Excursion checked by Socialist Mission. Similar to follow. End wage slavery."' Ellerton then gave a pleasant, embarrassed sort of smile, adding: 'How it ends wage slavery to stop a train I do not know. And why did they not say they'd done it straight after instead of waiting 'til now?'

'Is the *Courier* going to print that?' I asked.

'Course not,' said Ellerton.

'The coppers should go to the Drill Hall in Trinity Street,' I said. 'This lot have a meeting booked there. They're anti-excursion. There's posters for it all over.'

John Ellerton nodded. 'I know,' he said. 'A constable was sent along. The meeting was booked, and the money taken, but no address was given. And summat else . . . it was up to the hall to sell the tickets, and there've been no takers at all.'

I looked over at Clive, and he was gazing out of the window – at one of the radial tanks being led out of the shed by the two horses that were kept at Sowerby Bridge. When he turned back around, his grin had gone, but not completely. 'Well they either did it,' he said, 'or they read of it in the paper, and thought they'd *like* to've done it.'

'That's what I first thought,' said Ellerton, 'but it was apparently not mentioned in the *Courier* that it was Hind's Mill on the excursion.'

'They knew of it,' I said, 'because I told them.'

So it came out about my chat with Paul, and this character Alan Cowan somewhere in the background. And I was the chump all over again. I would certainly not make matters worse by mentioning the stone that had come through the bedroom window.

'Unless,' I said, 'I was only telling him in that pub about something he knew of because he really *had* been the cause of it.'

At that, Clive drifted over to the window again with a sort of sigh, and John Ellerton had a good laugh. Irish eyes, I thought: they might be a good thing on balance, but they can get you down sometimes.

'At any rate, I think we should have extra gangers walking the routes to the coast,' I said.

'He's like a monkey on a stick, this kid,' said Ellerton to Clive, who was still at the window. 'The cops have been informed, and I'm advising the pair of you now to go steady today over the stretch where you came to grief last time. And that's about all I can do.'

As we walked back to tank engine No. 7, I asked Clive: 'Who is it we're taking to Blackpool?' It hadn't been clear from the notice I'd read.

'Don't know exactly, but I reckon they're toffs,' he said.

Not wage slaves, then.

'How do you make that out?' I asked.

'It's an evening cruise,' he said. 'Think about it.'

'I am doing,' I said.

'Evening,' he said. 'What do *you* do of an evening?'

'Sit at home with the wife, generally.'

'All right, but what would you *like* to do of an evening?'

'Just that,' I said.

He gave me a long, steady look – something new for him. 'Very well,' he continued, 'but most working fellows are in the pub come seven, and they have no great hankering to take a train cruise.'

All was explained when we got to the Joint, for as we backed onto our carriages on platform two we came to rest alongside the stationmaster, Knowles, and one of his artistic blackboards. He muttered something as we stopped – could have been speaking to himself – and moved away, leaving us to read the word 'SPECIAL' done in the usual fancy way. Underneath was written: 'HALIFAX SUNDAY OBSERVANCE SOCIETY – EVENING THEATRE CRUISE TO BLACKPOOL.'

'Rum,' said Clive, when he saw it.

We collected our guard. He was a Bradford lad, so I'd never seen him before. As I gave him my good evening, a new thought came to me: if it were not the socialists who were the wreckers, but some fellows who were after old Reuben Booth, our usual guard, then we would have no trouble on this trip. But who would want to put Reuben's lights out? Anyone wanting him dead had only to wait, and not for very long.

Twenty minutes later we were well on our way to Blackpool, and climbing towards the little school just before Todmorden. The children were in the yard, doing exercises, making letter Ts. They jumped, and the Ts became Ys; another jump, then Xs. It was too late in the day for them to be doing that. Why were they not at home? The giant cot was there in the high window behind them, and I imagined them all put into it every night, imprisoned by the sheets and blankets. I thought of Arnold Dyson, and *Pearson's Book of Fun*, and the wife's letter to the Crossley Porter Orphanage.

It was a beautiful evening, and all the chimneys of Accrington, Blackburn and Preston could not put a stop to that. On every section the signals were favourable, as if to say: hurry on, we want to see what happens to you *next*. But Clive was back to his steam-saving, smooth-running ways, and there was not that wildness to the shaking of this engine that we'd had with the Highflyer, or with the Scarborough engine when that blockhead Billington had been aboard.

When we saw the first windmill of the Fylde I became a little anxious, even so. But this anxiety was checked by a friendly wave from the fellow in the signal box at Lea Road, and my mind was put onto a different channel completely when Clive, who'd just finished putting the reverser back to its full for our launch across the fields, said: 'I'm to have a medal, you know.'

'Like Ramsden's bottled beer,' I heard myself saying. (Advertisements were forever telling you of the prizes won by that class of ale.)

Clive gave a grin on hearing this, which proved the whiteness of the man, because by rights I ought to have been shaking his hand. 'It's for saving the train when the stone was on the line . . . Extraordinary vigilance and presence of mind in the conduct of duty, that sort of thing.'

I'd seen words like that written under the pictures of the engine men who got into the *Railway Magazine*. As a rule they were older than Clive, and wore beards.

'You must be chuffed,' I said.

'I'd rather have a day off *any* day,' said Clive.

'Is there to be a big do when it's presented to you?'

'Give over,' said Clive. 'It comes by post.'

'Well, I'll bet it comes first class at least,' I said, and I finally did step across the footplate to shake his hand, which left us feeling a pair of proper buffleheads.

'Are we to have a bit of a beano in Blackpool on the strength of it?' Clive asked me.

'I should come straight back,' I said, thinking of the wife alone in Back Hill Street.

'You can't,' said Clive, sharpish. And he explained that since there were no direct trains coming back, it'd be a case of going via Preston (which I knew), and that by the time we'd got in to Blackpool, run round our carriages with the engine, and booked off at the central shed, I'd have missed the one Preston train that connected in good time with a Halifax service.

'Your earliest train back's at midnight,' he said. 'This lot –' and he nodded back at the train '– they're all going back first thing tomorrow.'

'That's no bloody good,' I said, thinking again of the stone sailing through our bedroom, graceful, like, but about the size and shape of a fist.

'What's up?' said Clive, with a little grin.

I was blowed if I would tell him the truth, so I just said: 'I've a wife to look after, you know.'

'I'll stand you half a dozen oysters,' said Clive.

'What's that set against a marriage?' I said, and I was grinning myself now.

'All right, a *dozen*,' said Clive. 'A dozen and a couple of bottles of Bass.'

I hadn't bargained for having to make this decision, being so sure we were going to be tripped up by some obstacle on the line.

We were now rumbling past the Blackpool gasometers – bright rust in the evening sun – and Clive was shutting off steam. We coasted past the gaps in the houses, where the glittering sea would come and go. The biggest gap was where the line went over Rigby Road, which had the beach right at its end, and you would gasp as you went over, just as if you had at that moment been caught up and *put* into the sea.

We came swinging into Blackpool Central at dead on seven o'clock with two empty water specials streaming out on either side of us. We were put into excursion platform seven, where an assistant stationmaster told us to leave the engine. The next crew booked for it would take it off to the shed, and we could sign off in the SM's office.

Clive turned to me, saying, 'That's handy for you. If you sprint across directly to platform two, or three, in the main station – I can't just remember – you'll be back in Halifax . . . ten-thirty, sort of touch.'

I thought of the wife in bed alone, and the stone, the indoor comet. 'Well, I'd best go,' I said, knocking off the vacuum ready for uncoupling, as Clive leant out of the footplate watching our passengers walk towards the ticket gates.

'Aye,' said Clive, 'you'd better had. I'll sink a couple of pints on my own.'

Some of the passengers thanked Clive as they went, but they were respectable sorts, not factory, and not the kind to give a cheer for the driver. One of these worthies shook Clive's hand, and handed up to him a letter, saying, 'Apologies for not sending these along earlier.'

At this I tapped Clive on the shoulder, and asked, 'What's that?' because I feared he might stick it straight in his pocket, making another chapter in the Scarborough mystery. But he obliged me straight away, taking out from the envelope two theatre tickets and a handbill, which last he passed directly to me.

'What is it?' he asked.

'A play called *Man to Man*,' I said. 'It's on at the Grand.'

'Not music hall, then?'

'It's a drama,' I said, reading the handbill.

'Oh yes?'

'It's in four acts.'

'Is it now?' said Clive.

'There's two intervals.'

'*That's* good,' said Clive. 'That's the first good thing I've heard about it.'

I began to read from the handbill: '"Mr Frank Liston is as manly and impressive as the Rev. Philip Ormonde. As George Gordon, Mr William Bourne submits an earnest and incisive . . . "'

'Will you give it here for a moment?' said Clive.

I did so, and he put the paper directly into the fire.

'You didn't really fancy it then?' I said.

'Too improving,' said Clive, 'and I will not be improved. I *can*not be as a matter of fact . . .'

From a distant part of the station came the sound of an engine moving in.

'Well, I reckon you've missed your early service,' said Clive.

'Bugger,' I said, and Clive shook his head, grinning at the same time, because he knew I'd done it deliberately. The stone chucker had done his worst. He wouldn't be back. Also, I felt in need of a bit of fun, and that was all about it.

We walked along the platform, shadows of clouds moving fast across the canopy glass. The station was half busy: a few trippers on the platforms waiting to go home, and so looking downhearted. Yet Clive and me had the town, and the evening, all before us.

Chapter Fifteen

In the Gentlemen's at Central, Clive was stooping over a sink. His shirtsleeves were taken up to the very tops of his arms, with perfect folds all the way. He'd lathered his face, ears, back of neck, and was looking in the glass at the results. My own wash and brush-up had been finished minutes since.

'There was no soap at Scarborough,' I said, just to see how he'd answer. But the words were lost under the great belch of water going down the plug in Clive's sink.

'What's that?' he said, but he was refilling the sink with rinsing water.

I now stepped outside, just in case he wanted to apply a touch of the Bancroft's.

When he'd done, we walked through the horse smell, cigar smoke and the greenish light of the station, and came out onto Central Drive, where the gulls were screaming. There were the morning gulls and the evening gulls, and the second sort made a sadder sound. It was an in-between time at Blackpool: cocktail time for the toffy sorts, as I supposed; some men and ladies far out in the sea, the more serious sorts of swimmers – swimming and thinking, working things out as they went along.

'I wonder why folk go bathing?' I said, thinking again of Clive in Scarborough.

'Well,' he replied, looking straight ahead. 'Why are some others continually *fishing*?'

We continued to look out to sea: all the little waves trooping off together in the same direction, which was sideways, not towards the shore but heading up the coast towards Fleetwood.

I thought of Margaret Dyson. This was what she'd never seen. If you saw the sea once and it was a certain way, you'd probably think it was always like that.

The bathing machines had been put in a straight line, sideways to the sea as if to say: that's your lot for today, fun's over. Clive was lighting a little cigar, and a sandwich man was walking towards us – seemed doolally, like most in that line, traipsing along, clearing his throat over and again. You wanted to box his ears and shout: 'Frame yourself, man!'

His board was advertising a music hall: 'MONSIEUR MAURICE,' I read, 'SEE THE VENTRILOQUIAL PARAGON'. It was the fellow I'd seen, and then stood beside, at the Palace Theatre in Halifax. According to the board, he was now giving his turn at a spot called the Seashell; topping the bill too, for underneath his name were the words 'ALSO THE FOLLOWING ARTISTES . . .' I remembered about the Seashell. It was that weird little humpbacked music hall I'd seen on my first trip to Blackpool. Monsieur Maurice had been topping the bill then as well.

As the fellow shuffled up towards us, I pointed to his board and said, 'This place anything like?'

'It's the only thing,' he said, without stopping.

'Let's go there,' I said to Clive.

Clive turned around so that his back was to the sea. He looked at the sandwich man, who was walking away towards the North Pier.

'There's a ventriloquist on who's quite good . . . Well, he's not good,' I went on, 'he's shocking bad, in fact.'

'Righto,' said Clive, and put his cigar under his boot.

We went first over the road to an oyster room with a model ship in the window, where we put down a dozen oysters and a couple of bottles of Bass apiece. Then we pushed along the Prom to the Seashell.

It really was a rum show, built of bricks covered over with plaster and looking like something between a brick kiln and a funny kind of hat. Inside, it was like a sea cave: no sharp

137

edges, with all the roofs low and sloping. The floor rolled up towards the box office, where we queued for our tickets, marvelling at the place, which was all painted browny red with pictures of the Prom and the Tower jutting out from the walls because of the way the walls curved.

When we'd bought our tickets we saw the word 'BAR' written in yellow on a green wooden board clipped to red curtains. We walked through, but all the spots were taken by a lot of red-faced old brandy shunters who were stretched out with their drinks on red couches, looking like they were lying in a Turkish bath. But they did have such an everyday article as a barrel of Plain on the go, and it was only a penny a glass.

When the bell rang, we took our seats under a low, wavy roof, painted green, pink and gold. As soon as I sat down I felt sucked down almost into sleep, what with all the beer and the work and having been awake most of the night before.

The number '1' was carried across the stage by a boy, and there followed a cross-eyed banjo player, who you kept expecting to make jokes. But he somehow never did. Next were two women, 'Grace & Marie', dressed up as pixies and singing. They started in straight away with a song, but a good bit of it was lost in the cheers from the audience. This was on account of their dresses, which were tiny and made from leaves, or so you were meant to think. Afterwards they played a tune with hand bells, and the drums coming in towards the end, which made their bosoms shake in a way that had me feeling rather hot.

I looked across at Clive, and he was just nodding to himself.

There was some wrestling next, with no music but just the growling of the two big fellows. It was brought to an end by a voice saying out of nowhere a name, and then 'Mr Jefferson Byrne . . . Just him . . . and his shadow.' All went extra-dark at this. After what seemed a precious long time, one light came up, then another, and there was a man in white dancing with his shadow. After a while everybody started booing.

138

'I've never seen anything like this before,' I said sleepily to Clive.

'No,' he said, 'and never will again probably.'

As Jefferson Byrne was leaving the stage, Clive said, 'Now if he did one thing and the shadow did something *else*, he'd have something.'

In the quiet times between the turns, when the number was being walked across the stage, I would hear a noise, and I couldn't tell whether it was the sea just outside, or the breathing of everybody in the theatre. Then I started to think of the band as being the noise of the sea. Every time they struck up, it was waves coming in with a great rusty crashing, and then the waves ran back and a new person was left on the stage.

After the shadow dancer came an immobile comedian with a turkey head. Next was a ventriloquist – not Monsieur Maurice but one of the new kinds with a small doll placed on the knee. The turn announced itself. The man was Henry Clarke, the doll was called Young Leonard. Leonard had a boy's head, but wore a man's suit – and could move his eyes or smile.

The ventriloquist asked the boy: 'How old are you?'

'That depends.'

'What do you mean?'

'Well, I'm thirteen at home . . .'

The doll's eyes moved slowly away from the ventriloquist, and that was the thing that set you laughing – the eyes.

' . . . but under twelve when travelling on the railway.'

I liked that, and I wondered how it might go down with Martin Lowther, the narky ticket inspector.

'And speaking of figures,' said Henry Clarke to the doll, 'I believe you are a great hand at mathematics.'

'That is correct,' said the doll, who nodded away for a while, looking very pleased about it.

'Well, can you multiply?' asked Henry Clarke.

'I can multiply very rapidly,' said Leonard.

'Yes, they say that fools are multiplying very rapidly these days,' said Henry Clarke, and it wasn't the line that brought the house down, but the looks that went between the two afterwards: Clarke seeming to be rather embarrassed at his own crack, and the doll quite mortified.

Some clever stuff with numbers came next, then Leonard broke off, saying, 'I'm sweating badly.'

'That's rather vulgar,' said Henry Clarke; 'why don't you say "perspiring"?'

At this Leonard rolled his eyes and looked about the theatre with his amazement growing by the second. It was all pretty good, and the best thing of all was the end, when the doll smiled and moved its eyes *at the same time*.

Next was a man doing a boot dance, like Little Titch's, but not really up to snuff; then came a ballerina.

'They ought not to have dancers on one after the other,' I whispered to Clive.

'Yes,' he said, 'but get those legs.'

The whole audience felt the same; you could tell because it went quiet.

The Elasticated Man was next, followed by the star of the evening, Monsieur Maurice. As before at Halifax, the lights went up to show him standing at the side of the stage gasping for breath with the moon-headed Johnny hanging on his arm. When the two started the walk, the applause began, but there was not so much of it as there had been in Halifax. A Blackpool crowd had more than likely seen walking figures before, or Monsieur Maurice himself come to that, for, as I had noticed myself, he had been in Blackpool at the start of the season.

The two staggered up and down a fair bit this time, with Monsieur Maurice calling out that they were 'taking a stroll' and 'promenading', and the figure was made to wave at the audience from time to time. The only good part came when Monsieur Maurice said, 'I believe we are being hailed from the pier', at which the two looked out at a far corner of the audience and a voice really did seem to be coming from there, so that a fellow sitting in that particular spot in the audience began shaking his head and grinning, as if to say: Look, it's not *me* that's calling out, you know.

The lights went down, and when they went up again the two of them were on a bench, supposedly looking out to sea.

I looked at Clive. He was asleep.

After some seagull noises (worked up in the orchestra), the ventriloquist said, 'Blackpool, famous for cold sea, warm beer, hot pies and scorching sun . . .'

As we all waited – those of us that were awake – the dummy turned its head to the ventriloquist; a crater on the moon opened, and the word 'Sometimes' came out in a deep croak. I knew it was being worked from behind, and thought it a swizz for a ventriloquist to have battalions of fellows helping out.

Afterwards there was some business where the dummy turned its head to watch a make-believe paddle steamer go hooting by. Meanwhile, the ventriloquist lit a cigar with both hands to prove he wasn't the one *moving* the head. You couldn't take your eyes away, partly because it was frightening.

At the last, there was a man whose hair went into funny shapes, and a man whose hair was normal. Funny Shape also went in for sad faces. He started singing a song called 'Home' and that's where everyone was going as he did so. The more they sang the more they walked out.

'I'm off,' said Clive, suddenly waking up, but I always sat through the chasers, owing to feeling sorry for them. It was selfish in a way, for I could never enjoy my after-show beer if I'd cut the chaser.

'I'll see you in the bar,' I said, and he went off, lighting a little cigar.

The trick was to get out of a music hall just between the finish of the chaser and the start of 'God Save the King'. But you had to move fast because they'd try and trap you with the national anthem, and when they'd got you standing to attention, they'd try to deafen you.

I timed my escape to a tee, though, and Clive was waiting for me with a glass of ale.

'I've made enquiries,' he said, 'and Grace and Marie will be next door in five minutes.'

'What's next door?'

'Supper rooms used by the turns.'

'What do you want to see that pair for?' I said.

Clive looked at me and frowned. 'You can spend the evening with the Elasticated Man if you *want*.'

I knew what was going forward, of course. Clive was after a bit of spooning with one of these two, but it was more than that. I was to be put to choosing whether I wanted to try my luck with the other. He was saying: look what can be yours for the taking on a night in Blackpool, but for the vows you have foolishly taken. He would never say so, but he was out to prove I was wrong to be married.

The supper rooms were over the road and along the Prom a little way, and we got a fair old blast as we stepped across to them. It was a warm wind, but strong, and the black sea was starting to get lively. The electric lights along the front were all lit, like a swaying pearl necklace.

The first thing I noticed was the Elasticated Man eating a chop. He wore thick trousers and no coat; white shirt with collar open at the neck. Clive saw him but paid him no attention. He was looking all about for Grace and Marie.

It was a long, low room with no curtains. The Promenade – and the occasional speeding hansom – could be seen through windows on one side, and the sea beyond. There were benches and tables running along beneath the sea window. In the middle of the room was a billiard table, like a peaceful green field. There wasn't much to say it catered to the show business: just one poster showing acrobatic cyclists.

When Grace and Marie walked in, they were no longer pixies, of course, but ladies of the world in quite good dresses, carrying straw hats. My first thought was: They are not as beautiful in life as they are on stage. But still they *are* beautiful.

Clive was ahead of me, talking to them, and then he was walking back with the two of them following. 'We came up here by train, yes,' he was saying. 'As a matter of fact, we were *driving* the train!'

'Get away!' said Grace or Marie. 'Both of you?'

Clive gave me an extra big grin – he was coming over all unnatural for the benefit of these doxies.

'It takes two, yes,' he said, 'but no need to go into the mechanical details. Would you take a drink?'

Two minutes later we were all sitting down on the sea side of the room. Grace and Marie had glasses of punch; they asked what we were drinking, and Clive said, 'This stuff is "Plain", which would never do for bonny lasses like your-selves.'

It made me quite ill to listen to this talk.

On stage Grace and Marie had been all eyes (and legs, of course), but now you got their noses too. Grace's was a long nose but a good one – a whole story with a beginning, a middle and an end. Marie's nose was sharp, and she had a face that was round *and* sharp, like a vole's. With her dark, mischievous eyes, she reminded me of the wife, and I liked her best. I wondered how it would sound for a man to say to his wife: 'I went off with the one that reminded me of you, dear.' I supposed it had been done, *and* said.

We had barely started on our drink when Marie said to Grace: 'There's your bill-topper.'

I looked up. 'Monsieur Maurice,' I said.

'Which one was he?' said Clive.

'He has the walking figure and the drinking figure,' said Grace.

'No,' said Marie, 'the drinking's out now.'

'Is it? He was giving them Champagne Charlie until last year.'

'Oh he's had them all,' said Marie, looking across at me; 'multi-dolls.'

'Wasn't he giving the eye test shena a while ago?' asked Grace.

'Read the writing on that wall!' Marie suddenly commanded.

'What wall?' said Grace, and they both laughed.

I guessed this was part of Monsieur Maurice's turn – the one that I had walked out of in Halifax. But Clive was looking cheesed-off at all this shop talk.

'It's a bit like the two of us,' he whispered to me, 'going on about steam pressure.'

'Why don't we *do* that?' I said, finishing my glass of Plain. Well, I was canned by now.

'The Boer War!' said Marie. 'What a blessing that was to us all.'

'How could a war help two singing pixies?' said Clive, a bit crossly.

'You could play all the service towns, you see,' said Grace, and I could see she was a little gone on Clive.

'Broken hearts being in favour, you see,' Grace continued.

'So the sad songs *went*,' said Marie.

'Went where?' said Clive.

'What kind of turn plays the Seashell?' I asked the two of them.

'You know Marie Lloyd?' she said.

'Yes,' I said.

'Well, she's never played here.'

They both laughed.

'Little Titch?' I said.

'Getaway,' said Marie. 'Little Titch is far too *big* for this place.'

The ventriloquist, Monsieur Maurice, walked across just then. 'I will not mince the fact, ladies –' he began, addressing Marie and Grace. Then he looked at Clive and myself and stopped. His beard rocked as his mouth came to a quite definite close. His beard was very sharp, the moustache was very wide – it was like a music-hall turn in itself.

144

Marie said: 'These gentlemen are from the railways.'

At this, the ventriloquist looked all about him; as if he wanted to start a whole other conversation with a whole other lot of people. But with the drink in me, I was at him straight away.

'I liked the walking business,' I said, 'how's it done?'

He looked away. 'Wouldn't do to say exactly how it's done,' he muttered, looking over towards the bar. 'Champagne,' he said to himself, and he went off. With his over-theatrical face, he looked like one of his figures: a waxwork gone live.

'Will Monsieur Maurice be bringing a bottle over, do you think?' I asked Grace and Marie. I had never tasted Champagne, and meant to do so. It had been wanting at our little wedding down in London, in the supper room of the Waterloo pub, as Dad had more than once pointed out on the day.

'His real name is Morris Connell,' said Marie, 'and, no, he will not be bringing a bottle over here if past history is anything to go by.'

'How long have you known him?' I asked.

'Since the first of the Seaside Surprises,' said Grace. She turned to Marie: 'When was the first of the season?'

'Oh, early,' said Marie. 'April-time wasn't it?'

'We've all been back here every two or three weeks for the one-week runs ever since,' added Grace.

'All the same turns?'

'Yes. That's how it works with the Seaside Surprises.'

'Nothing very surprising about it,' said Marie, 'when you come to think of it.'

So that was how Monsieur Maurice had come to be in Blackpool, then in Halifax, and now back in Blackpool. I looked over to the bar, and he was standing there eyeing me.

'The one-week runs that you have here . . . They always begin on Mondays, do they?' I asked Grace.

'Mondays,' she said, 'that's it.'

'And does that fellow live here in Blackpool?' I said, nodding towards Monsieur Maurice.

'He has digs here,' she said, 'but he has a lodge in Preston as well.'

I remembered that I'd also seen his name in Scarborough, and mentioned this.

'Yes,' said Gracie, 'he's often at the Floral Hall there.'

Monsieur Maurice was walking back towards us carrying one glass of iced Champagne. As he sat down, he looked at me for a while longer, then he turned to Grace and continued his shop talk: 'Two whistles down the speaking tube to say you're on, and that's to the star room, so the question is: what's become of the call boy?' Shaking his head, he continued: 'I don't know . . . Half-pay for matinées, and my expenses going on just as usual.'

'What did you think of the two of us tonight?' Grace asked him, and I could tell that as long as he was at the table, all remarks would have to be addressed to him. You could tell he wasn't keen to think of Grace and Marie at all, but he seemed to put his mind to it for a second, after which he said: 'You two must decide if you are to be stars or specialities.'

'Well nobody wants to be a speciality,' said Grace.

'It's why we've brought in the new closer', said Marie, 'with the drumming.'

'That was the best bit of all,' Clive put in, 'the way you shook those . . . you know . . . bells.'

'I felt it suffered rather from a want of daintiness,' said Monsieur Maurice.

'It got a good hand,' said Grace.

'Especially from me,' said Clive.

Monsieur Maurice turned around just as a new man entered the room. 'People will always clap for decency's sake,' he said. 'Now there's somebody whose performance I *must* commend,' he went on, standing up and walking over to the new fellow.

'There's twenty vents on the sands,' said Grace, as Monsieur Maurice moved off, 'and they're all better than him.'

'Why does he top the bill then?' said Clive.

'There,' said Grace, 'you are into the very crannies of a mystery.'

'Could be money,' said Marie; 'thirteen consecutive fronts paid for in the *Era* don't hurt.'

'Special New Year's card to every manager in the country,' added Grace.

'Sounds a good notion,' said Clive, trying to cut in again.

'No,' said Grace, '*we* send *telegrams*.'

'Wire best offer!' Marie suddenly shouted. 'We're coming!' and she looked at us all with wide eyes. I did like her, but I had a feeling Clive would fare better alone.

I found a wobbly pair of legs and walked over to the bar. Monsieur Maurice was standing by the billiard table, shaking the new man's hand and saying: 'You were quite a favourite tonight.'

The new man – who was the ventriloquist that had been on first, Henry Clarke – was thanking him. Off stage, he looked an amiable sort: brown eyes and silky hair parted down the middle like a church roof.

'Let me stand you supper,' Monsieur Maurice said to Henry Clarke. 'The fish pie's rather good here.'

'That's awfully kind,' said Henry Clarke. 'Only they *will* put cayenne pepper in, and I don't care for it.'

'Nothing easier in the world than getting a helping without,' said Monsieur Maurice.

'Well, I did ask yesterday,' said Clarke, 'but in the end I had to go for the mutton instead.'

'Oh I think we'll be able to manage,' said Monsieur Maurice.

I looked over to where Clive was sitting with Grace and Marie. More drinks had come from somewhere onto their table, but I wasn't keeping track of my own let alone anyone else's. Clive was laughing, looking only at the two women, especially Grace, so odds-on she was his favourite. You could watch Clive for ages in a room, and he would only ever look at the women, no matter what the men were up to.

147

I thought I might go back over to Marie later. It wouldn't hurt to talk a little longer.

Next to me at the bar, Monsieur Maurice was shouting at the serving girl: 'What do you mean by "It can't be taken out once in"? I *insist* on having a fish pie without cayenne pepper!'

The serving girl went away into the kitchen and came back, and something along the right lines was worked out, for Monsieur Maurice ordered Champagne in a friendly voice and not only paid for Henry Clarke's fish pie, but stood him a glass of beer into the bargain. So he wasn't such a tightwad after all.

I stood in the middle of the room for a while, thinking of ventriloquists, Blackpool, trains and the wife – a hundred things and nothing at all.

As I wandered across to the Gentlemen's a moment later, I could hear Monsieur Maurice saying to Henry Clarke: 'Do you know the words that frighten me most *in all the world?* "Wanted: for children's party, a ventriloquist".'

They didn't seem very frightening to me.

Henry Clarke was smiling in a shy way, eating and trying to be polite.

'Second only', Monsieur Maurice was saying, 'to "unexpectedly vacant all season".'

Henry Clarke smiled again.

I looked out through the window. The moon was there above the sea, the last entertainment of the evening laid on for the trippers. The room became like a boat in rough water as I started crossing it. Then I struck the billiard table, which I looked at long and hard: the long green gaslit field, against the storminess of the sea – telling the sea how to behave.

'He's a dear old pal of mine,' the Elasticated Man was saying to somebody while staring at his picked-over chop; 'helped me when I was down.' Looking again at the Elasticated Man, I could see that he was old himself – sixty or so. Yet still elasticated.

When I returned to the table where Clive and the two girls were sitting, I heard Grace saying:' . . . because I don't want to be a step girl, stuck down some warren with two kids, and expecting again.' She looked all about the room before adding with a sigh: 'This is a jungle sort of life though.' She turned back to Clive and sighed again. I had never seen Clive spooning at close quarters, and had little experience of the art myself, having married very young, but I somehow knew that with all this sighing, things were progressing for him.

Marie said to me, 'You look all-in.'

Clive was saying something in my ear that I couldn't catch. Now he was standing up, taking Grace by the hand, but my eyes were on Monsieur Maurice, who was sitting and watching Henry Clarke eat fish pie. Clarke looked pretty uncomfortable, as well he might, and the drunken thought came to me: if for whatever reason it was Monsieur Maurice who'd thrown the stone through my window, then the wife was sitting pretty at the present moment, for she was in Halifax, and he was here.

A little while later Marie was also standing up, saying to me, 'Will you stroll on the beach?'

There was a shivering mini-sea on the beach, left over from the tide going out. The electric lights on the North Pier were reflected in it. Two figures were walking under the North Pier: Clive and Grace. As I watched, they stopped and kissed. For all that Clive was due his medal, this was his true business: not driving engines but kissing. *And* the next lot.

'Well!' I said to Marie, who was very surprisingly nearby.

I turned and saw a tram coming along the Prom, all lit up like a theatre. Its lights took away from the moonlight. I watched it stop at the North Pier, then move on.

'You've missed *that* one,' said Marie, 'but you must get the next.'

'That's right,' I said, 'I certainly must.'

I gave a small wave, which was returned, and as I began walking, thinking of the wife in Back Hill Street reading her

149

Pitman's Shorthand manuals by the bad light of the gas mantel, plotting and planning for the two of us (and, as I sometimes thought, for the whole of the world) I felt glad to have said goodnight to Marie.

I hurried back along the Prom, for I knew it was close to midnight. The trams kept coming by, and they were noisier in the night. Or perhaps it was the Prom that was quieter, with just the odd lonely person looking out to sea. You'd get these lonely sea watchers even in Blackpool, but only ever late at night. The lights went along the Prom, up one side of the Tower, down the other, then continued along.

Central station, right under the Tower, was nearly but not quite dead. You can *feel* it when there's just one engine left in steam, but that locomotive was somewhere out of sight, and the stationmaster must have booked off, for the ticket collector had a bottle of Bass in his hand. How did he get on the railway, and once on, how did he stay on? He was very thin, and his hair was white and shaggy. He looked like a cornstalk but dangerous with it. His coat was too big for him, and there were egg stains down the front of it clear as day. He was talking to a fellow who had his back to me, and wore a tiny jacket, narrow-go-wide trousers, big shiny boots and a cap pushed right back – not a railway man. He had a big head but a little nose, tilted up like the cap. I put him down as one of those reverse swells, an underminer.

This big-headed kid was saying to Cornstalk: 'It's a job though, Don, and tha needs brass.'

'That's fair do's, Max, that is,' said Cornstalk. The voice was high, and it carried. It was Lancashire . . . Lancashire or Yorkshire, but light.

'Every ticket with its little triangle clipped out,' Cornstalk was saying, 'and after a while, you know, I get so I can't look at that triangle or any fucking triangle. It's wrong, like, I know, but I don't like fucking triangles any more, and when I see a bottle of this stuff with the fucking triangle on the label . . .' He stood back, and the bottle of Bass was in the air, and when it came down the pieces of brown glass raced to all parts of the empty station.

'Will you look out?' I said, as I came up to the two of them.

'Sorry about that, mate,' said Big Head, but Cornstalk himself said nothing, never looked at me either as I walked through the gates.

The last Preston train was on platform five. It was a clumsy, late-night sort of tank engine of the kind I didn't know; the kind of beast that wakes you up at midnight as it crashes through your town with its driver cursing at the controls.

I climbed up and took a seat in Third – it was a corridor carriage. The smashing of the Bass bottle had sobered me up, and I wished I had something to read. Two toffs came by fast along the corridor, one saying to the other, 'It's just this way, now, follow me,' very much at home, as though the train was his personal property. They were looking for first class, I supposed.

From the platform I heard the guard blow and give the right away, then there was an extra bit of business. The guard was calling to somebody. 'Hurry up now, sir,' and by the respectful tone of voice, I judged it to be another toff coming along at a clip, also making for First. I heard a carriage door slam and Monsieur Maurice, the ventriloquist, was walking along the corridor, breathing heavily. He turned into a compartment two or three along.

I sat under the flaring gas, looking at the Photochrome pictures over the seats opposite: they all showed Nelson's old flagship washed up on the beach at Blackpool. I waited until the gas works came up, which at night became lots of tiny blue lights spread out along the tracks. I stood up, moving along the corridor until I saw the ventriloquist. He was asleep with his head on his chest, the point of his beard going into his chest like a knife. Across his knees was a newspaper. There was a small cloth bag at his feet. He was more Morris Connell now than Monsieur Maurice.

I went back to my carriage and thought about Clive. Would he still be under the pier with Grace? More likely he'd be pegged out in the barracks – the engine men's lodging over the road from Central. He'd have to be on the milk train at four though, and back over the Pennines before first light, because the two of us had a seven o'clock go-on at Sowerby Bridge shed. How was he able to be so cool about the prospect of another smash? Maybe it was just his nature. Perhaps that was how a fellow of the right sort ought to be. Then again, perhaps he knew for a fact there wouldn't *be* another smash, the first one having been arranged by himself. But why would he do that? So that he could get his medal and come out the hero. But why would he *want* to come out the hero? He was not so determined to get on in his work, as far as I could see. He had never once mentioned that he was aiming for the top link or anything of that nature.

Ten minutes out of Blackpool, we started rattling wildly over the Fylde, like something being blown along. I looked out of the window for a while and saw the signal lamps coming up, shining green, green, green all the way.

I fell into a doze, and heard the bang of the starter signal going off at Halifax. The wife was aboard the train, and we rushed away and had a smash, but the wife was all right because she explained that it hadn't been a real train but only the echo of a train.

At Preston, I was woken by mailbags being thrown onto a barrow and the shouting that always goes along with that job. My connecting train for Halifax, which would be emptier still, was waiting on the opposite platform. I picked up my cap and walked along the corridor. The ventriloquist had left his carriage but his paper was still there. Thinking it could come in for the ride to Halifax, I picked it up. It was a paper for the show business, and running right down one side of the front page was a long thin drawing of a long thin comedy policeman. I picked it up, and saw that one item on the front page had been circled in pencil: 'Henry Clarke and Young Leonard: A Laughing and Applauding Hit in May at the

152

Palace Theatre, Halifax. Re-engaged for the First Week of June. Too Strong for All Rivals.'

Clarke, the good ventriloquist of the evening just gone, must have been the one I'd meant to see at the Palace in Halifax but missed; I'd gone along later and got Monsieur Maurice instead. I looked again at the paper and for a second thought of ventriloquism as a job like any other, with one man put up against another in the fight for wealth and ease of living.

I returned to Halifax at getting on for two o'clock, and, hurrying along Horton Street, I looked on the old warehouse wall for the Socialist Mission poster. It was still there, speaking of the 'A MEETING TO DISCUSS QUESTIONS'. If they do go ahead with it, I thought, it would be them answering the questions, and the coppers doing the asking. Alongside it was a poster for the Halifax Building Society: 'AS SAFE AS HOUSES' read the slogan, and that made me hurry along faster still towards Hill Street, where there was just one light burning – upstairs in our house.

I was through the front door and up the stairs in a trice. But quietly. The wife was asleep, having left the gas turned low for me. There was new glass in the window and I looked through it. When you have a new window, the bit of the world it shows looks clean and new as well, even if, as in this case, it should only be the gas lamps and sleeping houses of Hill Street.

As I looked at this scene, George Ogden walked slowly into it, coming from the direction of Back Hill Street. He had his hands in his pockets. Then he turned and looked up. When he saw me looking back, he grinned, and put up one fat paw to wave. He was signalling me to come down.

It was well past two by now, but I crept back down the stairs, out of the front door, and round to the side, where George was still beaming. 'Evening, old man,' he said. He

153

was pulling his waistcoat down over his belly, so that I could see the assorted shapes of the little items in the pockets.

'Evening?' I said, 'It's getting on for dawn. Where've you been?'

'Supper at the Crown,' he said.' Anchovy cream of turbot, then veal kidneys with gin and juniper berries, turnips, asparagus a la crème and roast potatoes on the side, followed by pears à la cardinal with apricot syrup and brandy, cheese plate and biscuits, pot of coffee and liqueurs. But that's by the way.'

'Hardly,' I said.

'It seems to be the window-breaking season in this town,' he went on. 'Thinking it over, you're blaming the nutty dynamitists, I suppose.'

'You what?'

'The socialist-anarchists?' He was holding out a ten-bob note; he pushed it at me. 'They seem to have fixed on you as the fellow to blame for the hardships of all the working men in Halifax, which seems to go a bit hard, since you're a working man yourself and not taking home above, what, twenty-seven bob a week?' He pushed the note at me. 'I'm feeling rather flush just at the moment, so you'll oblige me by pocketing this forthwith, old bean.'

Well, I was so tired that I just took the money. 'Thanks, George,' I said, 'I'm much obliged to you.'

'But how did they ever get your address?' he called to me as I made for the front door.

'Turn in, George,' I said. 'It's late.'

Chapter Sixteen

I clattered on the small door inside the big door at Hind's Mill, for there was no bell in sight.

We'd booked on at five that morning, taking a special to Fleetwood for the Drogheda steam packet, then coming back light. The engine had been running hot; I'd scorched the back of my hand on the motion in finding out, and had been on the look out for carbolic ever since. Meanwhile my hand was wrapped in a mucky bandage. It was Friday 30 June, four days after the late turn at Blackpool. We'd not been back since and there'd just been one other excursion in the week: church ladies to Southport on the Wednesday – trouble-free, but I'd been fretting about George Ogden, who, by paying for the window, had only made me think he must have been the one who smashed it. But he couldn't have been, because I'd seen him in his room only a second later.

The door of Hind's was opened by a bonny, plump girl in a white dress with a red ribbon round her middle. She looked like a sort of very nice cake, all prettily wrapped up. 'Oh,' she said, 'I thought it was going to be Mr Hind Senior. He generally comes along Friday afternoons with his gentleman's gentleman for a nosey . . . An inspection of the weaving hall, I should say.'

'Good evening,' I said, taking off my cap and trying not to be put off in any way; 'my wife works here in the offices, and –'

'You're Lydia's husband?' she said. 'Oh, come in.'

I shook her hand. 'Jim Stringer,' I said, and she said, 'Ever so happy to meet you. Cicely Braithwaite.'

I stepped through the little door and found myself in a kind of vestibule with wooden walls on either side, with bob-holes cut into them. Cicely lifted the hatch on one of the bob-holes, and I saw the wife talking on the telephone as though to the manner born. She was the only one in a light, wooden office with a high desk and tall, shiny-topped stools.

Cicely Braithwaite dropped the bob-hole door and said, 'As you can see, she's on the telephone presently. She's talking to Manchester, so best not to interrupt.'

'Who's she talking to?' I said, 'if you don't mind me asking.'

'Most likely Michael Hardcastle. He's our, you know, travelling gentleman.'

'I see,' I said, but I did not.

Cicely Braithwaite was going red. 'He doesn't like to be called a salesman,' she said. She was going redder still, crimson now. 'But that's what he is,' she added, firmly. 'That's where I work,' she continued, lifting the opposite bob-hole. There was an office inside, but no people. It came to me that she must be the other office girl, the one spoken of by the wife; the one not allowed the Standard typewriter.

'My boss is Mr Robinson,' she said. 'Well, *was*. He used to be one of the partners.'

'He's left though, hasn't he?'

'Yes,' she said, 'he's been sacked.' The redness came surging up again. She couldn't help talking out of turn, and couldn't help blushing over it afterwards. 'The other office, the one Lydia's in . . . That's Mr Hind's.'

'Old Hind's?'

'No. When we speak of old Mr Hind we always say "Mr Hind Senior".'

'Or "the fossil",' said the wife, who'd opened the bob-hole of her office and put her head through. 'Your hand!' she then cried, and came out into the corridor. 'Hold it up!' she said.

'It's nothing to fret over,' I said, as Cicely asked the wife, 'Shall I go and fetch something for it?'

'Boracic acid,' said the wife, 'that's the best thing.'

Cicely opened the door to the second office and came back holding a bottle of something and a glass of water, saying, 'Drink this. You look parched.'

Cicely handed the bottle to the wife who, looking at the label, said: 'Linseed oil. It'll have to do.' The wife began unwinding my bandage, saying to Cicely, 'Do we have another of these?'

Cicely said, 'They'll have bandages in the weaving room.' She opened a door beyond the two offices, at which moment all conversation with the wife had to stop on account of the racket.

I was looking through the door at the same thing done over and over again: row upon row of crashing looms, each row under a drive shaft, all the looms connected to this shaft by rolling leather belts, so that the machinery on the floor was tangled with the machinery on the roof, as though a giant spider had climbed over everything making a web as it went. The walls were white; the white was light, and everybody inside looked as though they'd just seen a ghost. Margaret Dyson, the woman I'd killed, had worked in there. No wonder she'd been so keen to get away to the sea, if only for a day.

The long blister under the bandage had burst, and there was coal dust inside the wet remains. The wife was shaking her head over this as Cicely Braithwaite came back, shutting the door behind her. The silence was beautiful.

'Was it Michael you were speaking to?' Cicely said to the wife, handing over a length of bandage.

'It was,' said the wife, 'and he's having to take one thirty-second of a penny on the –'

'Not on the twelve-ounce?' Cicely Braithwaite put in.

'Yes,' said the wife, 'on the twelve-ounce.'

'I *knew* it would be the twelve-ounce,' said Cicely, as we all went from the space between the offices into the wife's office proper. She took me over to a desk and made me rest my hand on top of a *Kelly's* Directory. Nearby were many other books lying open, with pages made of different kinds of cloth. I knew what they were: sample books, of the kind seen in draper's shops.

'What's the twelve-ounce?' I asked, as the wife poured on the stinging stuff and set to with the new bandage. Every so often she would flash a glance over at the telephone, as if expecting it to jump.

'Twelve-ounce suiting,' said Cicely. 'What do you think about that?'

I didn't think anything about it, so I just shrugged. It was Clive knew all about suits.

'Have you not told him about the twelve-ounce?' Cicely Braithwaite asked the wife, who did look a bit embarrassed over this. There was a kind of force about Cicely Braithwaite that could make you feel a stranger even to your own wife.

'I'm only just beginning to understand it myself,' said the wife.

'It's the biggest disaster going,' said Cicely, very happily. She turned to me. 'Let me put you straight, Mr Stringer. Now look at your coat. A lovely bit of worsted, that is. It's quite filthy, and it's full of burn holes but it's a lovely bit of worsted underneath. I reckon that would be about a twenty-ounce cloth. Most suiting is from twenty to twenty-eight ounce. Well, Mr Peter Robinson, the gentleman I worked for in that office over there –' she pointed in the direction of the second office '– he had the notion of making something much lighter than your common run of summer cloth: twelve-ounce suiting. Light green suiting.'

'But do you mean light, green suiting, or light-green suiting?'

'Why, both,' said Cicely, 'when all our suiting up to now has been normal weight and blue.'

'Well it sounds a perfectly *good* notion,' I said, as the wife wound the bandage. 'I'd feel a lot brighter in a thinner suit.'

'I daresay,' said Cicely, 'and in some spot like Italy, where it's stifling the year round, it would be just the thing. But they can't *give* it away here, and they're saddled with miles of it.'

'Well,' the wife put in, 'have they not thought of trying it in Italy?'

'Whatever do you mean?' Cicely asked.

'It would go perfectly well in Italy,' said the wife, 'and

would do here too, especially in summers like this, if they just once gave it a starting shove.'

'How do you mean by a shove?' asked Cicely.

'Advertising,' said the wife.

Cicely nodded. 'You would have liked having Mr Robinson here, dear,' she said to the wife, 'if you'd got to know him properly, got to know his ways. He was go-ahead like you. Have you told Mr Stringer of your programme for the filing?'

'I've not,' said the wife, 'because he is not particularly interested in filing.'

I finished off my glass of water and gave Cicely a grin.

'In fact he doesn't even file his own nails,' said the wife.

'Tell me of your programme,' I said.

'Very well,' said the wife, who was finishing off my bandage with a pin. 'When I come to take dictation from Mr Hind, he always ends, "Kindly acknowledge in due course", which means that for every letter sent out we get one back, and half the time the other person puts "kindly acknowledge" on their letter of acknowledgement, so you can see that the smallest little bit of business does rather go on for ever. But when I mentioned it to Mr Hind, and suggested that he stop writing "kindly acknowledge in due course", he said, "It's quite impossible. How can you be sure you've sent a letter if you don't have a reply?"'

'Mr Hind is *not* go-ahead,' said Cicely, turning to me.

'So,' the wife continued, 'I said you must just put a little trust in the Post Office, and that way you could save pounds every year, to which he replied, "How am I to finish my letters? What am I to put instead?"'

'Well, what *is* he to put instead?' I asked the wife, after a little while.

'"Yours truly,"' said the wife, and she stepped back from me, for the bandaging was now done.

'He'll never do it,' said Cicely.

'No,' said the wife. 'But *I* will. He never reads over the correspondence after dictation.'

'You can't,' said Cicely. 'You'll be stood down if he ever finds out, and –' She suddenly gave it up and stopped, saying directly to me: 'I'm expecting that buzzer any minute.'

I nodded at her.

'That's to tell us to stop working,' she added, although she had in fact not done a hand's turn since I'd arrived.

'The weavers *clock* off,' explained Cicely, 'we *book* off, and where Mr Hind Senior has got to I really don't know.'

'Will the weavers be coming through this way?' I asked, for I didn't want to clap eyes on the woman who'd all but accused me of murder.

Cicely shook her head. 'They leave through the main doors. They only come through this way on Thursdays.'

'Pay day,' put in the wife.

Then the telephone did start ringing. The wife answered it very smartly, saying, 'Hind's Mill, Office of Mr Hind', and fell to discussing a sale of looms.

'Mr Stringer,' said Cicely, who seemed to have no inclination to stop doing no work and go home, 'your suit has more scorch marks on it than my uncle Jasper's tab rug, which is always getting burnt on account of him piling too much free coal onto his grate.'

I frowned at her.

'My uncle Jasper works on the railways,' she explained, climbing up onto one of the high stools.

'Well then,' I said, 'so do I.'

'Lydia never told me,' said Cicely.

'She doesn't really care for the job,' I said. 'She thinks it's mucky and dangerous and not, you know . . . Well, it is true that you can't be an engine man and not be bowed down by it.'

It was the first time I had admitted anything of that sort, but nobody was really listening. Cicely had a faraway look, and the wife was still talking into the telephone.

'Mr Stringer –' said Cicely again.

'I was firing the Highflyer,' I cut in. 'I mean the engine that carried this mill's excursion to Blackpool: the one that got stopped.'

'Oh,' she said, except that it was really only half an 'oh', about the smallest sound you can make while still speaking. Climbing down from the high stool, she said: 'Would you care to see the weaving room, just while Lydia's busy?'

We walked along the wooden corridor between the offices, and I tried to collect my thoughts together. Why had the wife not let on that I'd been firing the engine on Whit Sunday? Well, she would not be popular if it was known she was married to one of the men who'd kept the whole firm waiting in a field for half a day. We'd promised them a holiday, and then made a smudge of it. Or maybe Cicely *had* known that I was part of that show, but didn't let on that she knew, so as to save embarrassing me.

Cicely opened the heavy door to the weaving room for the second time, and now I was ready for the noise. There must have been four hundred looms, and every one rocked and buckled as the shuttle inside it was pitched back and forth. The weavers were mainly women. They would dart in and trim at the cloth in the thrashing machines with tiny scissors, then stand back, looking over all parts of the contraption before swooping back in again with the scissors.

There were five rows between the lines of looms and men walked along these, pushing trolleys on which were spare bits of kit for the looms, to be stopped as needed.

Most of the lot in this room would have been on the excursion. Cicely was standing next to me, with a handkerchief in her hand, looking along the middle row of looms. She looked quite grave, which did not suit her. It was getting on for five o'clock on a roasting hot day, but the inside of the mill had a feeling of near-dawn on a cold day. I looked up at the sky-lights, but they weren't sky*lights*, for they'd all been white-washed to keep out the glare.

'Which loom did Dyson, the girl who died, work at?' I shouted to Cicely.

She leant towards me and I shouted my question again. She heard it this time and pointed. My eye flew from her finger end to a loom in the centre of the weaving hall, where stood the superannuated fairy, my accuser. She was looking straight at me once again, as a great scream came in on top of the clattering of the looms. It was the buzzer, and even as it continued, the place wilted, the machines wound down, and all the madness came to an end, for the steam had been turned off.

But the woman was still staring.

I turned to Cicely and said: 'Who is that woman?'

'That's Mary-Ann Roberts,' said Cicely.

As Cicely looked at her, Mary-Ann Roberts finally left off staring at me and turned away to join the crowd moving towards the door at the opposite end.

'She knew Margaret Dyson, the one that died, didn't she?'

Cicely nodded. 'She was her elbow mate: worked at the next loom. She's moved along now to take Margaret's. She didn't want –'

Cicely was looking up, and now she was crying. All the weavers were walking out of the weaving room at the other end, and I was alone with this crying woman.

'. . . The ladies with her in the compartment,' Cicely said, 'they thought at first she was getting on nicely, but –'

And she was off again. I just stood there like a mule. My programme was to get her back to the wife, because the wife would know what to do. An idea struck me – not a very good one. 'Do you want a cup of tea?' I said. 'Come this way.' I didn't know where any kettle was, leave alone tea, and Cicely Braithwaite *knew* that I didn't know, but she followed me back to the wooden corridor between the offices. The wife was still talking on the telephone. Cicely was sniffing mightily as she walked, and starting on a speech.

'I've worked here five year,' she was saying, 'five *years*, I mean. I was taken on as a weaver and a friend said you should go typist because there's better prospects, so I did my typing course. In my first year, the Whit excursions for this mill started: it was to be an extra treat in advance of the Wakes Week trip to Blackpool. It was Mr Robinson's idea – he's the fellow that's gone now. He said it had to be Blackpool of course, and everyone from the mill was to go, and there was to be a tea at the Tower. Well, when we came back it was always given to me to write to the Blackpool Tower Company, and it was always the same letter.'

She took a big breath, and I was afraid of another big crying go, but she carried on, just as if reading this letter she'd spoken of: '"On behalf of the work-people and officials of Hind's Mill, I beg to thank you for the excellent manner in which you catered for our party of five hundred."'

A *very* big sniff here.

I could hear the wife, through the wooden wall, saying: 'You must telephone later when Mr Hind himself is here, or can you not write a letter?'

'"The tea"', Cicely was continuing, '"was admirably served, and the attendants left nothing to be desired . . . and . . . the fact that we have not had a single complaint out of the very large number –"'

Another mighty sniff.

'"– speaks for itself."'

That last part did it. She was off crying again, saying how the tea was never served that day; and how it was to have been such a spread, how it had been the thing Margaret Dyson had been looking forward to most particularly; how the Wakes Week holiday that was coming up really would be a wake. But now the wife, having at last finished with the telephone, was stepping out of the office and putting her arms about Cicely, and things were set to rights while I was sent outside to wait.

I walked around to the side of the mill and stood between the chimney and the mill pond. They made a silent pair as always. The sunshine was sending a golden V shimmering out across the water. My heart was beating fast, just as after the smash. What I wanted was another smash, and there would then be a person lying down in a carriage, having taken a concussion. I would go in and I would not attempt to lift their head.

The last of the weavers were trailing away down Beacon Hill.

Walking further along the mill wall, I came to the boiler room. The door was half open and things were still in full swing inside. I could make out two boilers, with fireholes set below. There was one man to each, and now that the fires were finished, the two were scraping out clinkers with long irons. The sound they made was a desperate kind of clattering, for they wouldn't get home until the job was done.

There was a tug on my coat and the wife was standing next to me. We began walking down the hill to the town. Far below us, trams and horse buses were cutting through Halifax at a great rate, and folk were filing down all the streets that led to the Joint, which was full of engines coming and going. Freedom for the wage slaves: that's what we were looking at, for the Friday buzzers were going off all over.

'Do they talk much in the mill about the lass that died?' I said.

'Some do,' said the wife. 'She was popular – a bonny girl.'

'Do they ever say she might have been saved?'

But the wife didn't seem to hear that.

'Cicely is a good soul,' she was saying, while looking at flowers by the roadside, 'but she has an awful time of it. Hind treats her like a slavey – just like one of the work people, even though she's been in the office for donkey's years.'

'Where is Hind?'

'He has a yacht,' said the wife, 'and he's on it. Has been for a week.'

'Where?' I said.

'Cruising off Llandudno. You can send letters to it by posting to somewhere in Llandudno. He can send them back as well, worst luck. All week, the correspondence has been letters from Mr Robinson's solicitors saying that the price offered for his share in the mill is not acceptable; Hind saying that no more is to be offered because the light suiting of Robinson's has brought the mill almost to bankruptcy; and letters to wine retailers asking for Champagne to be sent out to Hind's yacht. If I put the wrong letter in the wrong envelope there'd be fun.'

'You mean if you sent the Champagne to the solicitors?'

'No, you nut. If the solicitors for Robinson found out how much Hind was spending on himself.'

'What about Hind Senior, the founder. What does he make of all this?'

'That fossil! Who knows if he thinks at *all*. Hind's the only one who talks to him. It was in King William's day when he founded this mill, you know, and it was powered by water.'

'Do you think he's on the yacht right now with Hind?'

'Is he heckers, like,' said the wife. 'The fossil hardly ever leaves Halifax, and he's due at the mill right now.' Then she pointed to a roadside flower: 'Foxglove,' she said quite fiercely.

'But they did lose money over the light suiting, and it *was* this fellow Robinson's fault, wasn't it?'

'It had been his idea, but young Hind had agreed to adventure it. I'd help Mr Robinson if I could . . . He has a little boy, you know, Lance, rather grown-up for his years, and he wrote a letter to Cicely to pass on to Hind. It was asking for his dad to be given his job back. Quite heartbreaking it was, according to Cicely. Well, that boy's mad on engines. Peter Robinson's often over here with all this solicitor business, and I thought you might show the boy about the station.'

'I'd say you were sweet on this Robinson,' I said.

'Well, he had his points, you know.'

'Like what?'

'He gave me my start, for one thing. He was always gentlemanly to the workers, even if he was flogging them to death.'

'Where is he now?'

'At home.'

165

'In Halifax?'

The wife shook her head. 'He lives in Lancashire, at St Anne's.'

'Oh, you'd like it there,' I said. 'It's just before Blackpool; it's like Blackpool with everything taken out. Peaceful, like.'

'What I *would* fancy,' said the wife, very slowly, 'is a trip to Hebden Bridge.'

This was a turn up. The wife was not a great one for taking trips. 'Hebden would be a start,' I said. 'It's the prettiest spot within ten miles of here.'

'In fact I *am* going – tomorrow afternoon, with Cicely. She did want cheering up, you know. Would you come along?'

'I book off at one o'clock tomorrow,' I said, 'so I could do. Shall I ask George?'

The wife shook her head. 'I don't care for that one . . . I've read there are lots of wild flowers in the hills above Hebden.'

'You bet your boots,' I said.

'Jim . . .' she said. She did not often use my name, so I was certain she was going to say she was expecting. Instead, she said: 'I mean to take more of an interest in nature.'

'It's all the rage now,' I said.

'I mean to plant something in the garden.'

It was the first I'd heard it called that. 'You mean in that tub we have in the yard?'

'Tub in the yard! You're no loss to house agency, are you?'

'What are you going to plant?'

'Mint,' she said.

We'd drifted halfway down Beacon Hill Road. Two coal trains were crossing under the North Bridge, both going slow – lazy in the evening heat, and sending an echo all around the town. The wife had stopped again; she was looking down at some heather by the road.

'When did Robinson leave the mill?' I asked her.

'Friday 26 May he got the letter. It was the day after he'd interviewed me for the job.'

'A fortnight before Whit, then?'

'Aye,' said the wife.

I said: 'I do think the coppers might ask that gent a few questions about what happened, you know.'

The wife was still looking down at the tiny flowers. One of the coal trains had come to a halt between the Joint and the North Bridge goods station; the other had disappeared.

'Why would he want to stop the excursion?' said the wife. 'It was his flipping idea in the first place. There's any number of hundreds who *might* have had reason to do it, mind you. I spend half my days writing letters to people saying we can't take them on at the mill. Bobbin-setters, reelers, duffers. They might not want to see the ones that *have* jobs gallivanting off to the seaside. If it comes to that . . .'

'What?'

'No, I shan't mention it. You'll only go flying off.'

'No,' I said. 'You must.'

'If it comes to it,' said the wife, 'when they stopped making the light suiting they laid off two hundred weavers. But half of them were taken on a week later at that show.'

She was pointing at the letters spelling 'Dean Clough' standing up on the roof of the building just beyond the North Bridge. Each letter was taller than three men, and although the North Bridge was high enough to fit the goods station underneath, those letters towered above it. The Dean Clough Mill seemed to have been built by men who'd never seen another mill, and so had no notion of the correct size, but what they did have was an endless supply of bricks. You could fit twenty mills of the common run inside it. It was built by the Crossleys, who'd also – along with a certain Porter – put up the brass for the orphanage where young Arnold Dyson now lived.

As we watched, the buzzer at Dean Clough went off, and it was loud even to the two of us, half a mile across town and halfway up a hill. After a minute, the workers came out, like oil spilling from an engine casing. As they poured forwards, crossing through the shadow of the great chimney, the wife said: 'Eight thousand carpet designs possible . . . Four thousand colours possible . . . Six thousand two hundred folk employed.'

'Wage slavery,' I said, thoughtful, like.

A motorcar was coming up the hill towards us. We stood back on either side of the road to let it pass, and the wife looked after it in a dreamy way. When it had gone she said, 'That's a bobby dazzler!' Then she laughed at me from across the road, because this was one of her new Yorkshire sayings.

We walked on a little way, and there was a trap stopped in the road, with a man standing up in it. There was something else in the trap: it was a small scrumpled-up something, and, as we got closer, we saw that it was a person, and that it was dead, with the little eyes in the little head closed and quite sealed up for ever.

I got in before the wife. 'Hind Senior,' I said.

Hind Senior didn't look as though he'd ever been a great talker, and nor did his gentleman's gentleman, but this fellow had to call out, for otherwise he would have been in league with the dead body at his side.

'Hi!' he yelled. 'Are you two down from Hind's?'

'I work there,' called the wife. 'Drive up there, and ask for Cicely. She'll let you telephone from the office.'

'What happened?' I called out.

'He was ninety-nine, Jim,' the wife whispered.

'Motorcar,' the man in the trap was saying, 'it was the bloody motorcar finished him off.'

Chapter Seventeen

Cicely Braithwaite was waiting for us outside the front of the Joint, with all the cab drivers eyeing her. She kissed the wife, saying: 'It was you sent him up to the mill, wasn't it dear?'

'It was,' said the wife.

'Of course, you know what did for the old man?' she said to us both. 'His heart.'

'Go on,' I said.

'Well,' said Cicely, 'it stopped.'

'And it was on account of a motorcar, wasn't it?' I asked her.

Cicely nodded. 'Frightened the life out of the old man,' she said, and then she coloured up. 'You know, it's the first time I've said that when it's actually been true.'

'Did the motorcar do anything?' I asked.

Cicely shook her head. 'Barley, that's the old man's man . . . He said it just came too close as it passed by . . . and it was going at a fair rate of course, as they all do.'

I could hear Knowles, the stationmaster, shouting at a porter: something about an out-of-date auction poster and how it wanted taking down sharpish. I looked at the clock over the station. 'If I nip up fast for our tickets,' I said, 'we should be in time for the one thirty-two – stopping train for Blackpool. Hebden's first stop.'

'Does he have *Bradshaw* off by heart?' Cicely said to the wife, as I climbed the steps to the ticket office.

As I waited at the ticket window, I thought about motorcars. The one that had run alongside us before the smash had looked like a giant baby-carriage, and so had the one on Beacon Hill. And so did they all, except for a certain other kind that looked like boats. I'd asked the wife, and she'd said that her Mr Robinson owned a motorcar.

The *Courier* was always going on about how they were the terrors of the countryside, I knew that much, and it was said they should be taxed. I didn't believe the Socialist Mission could run to one, even though old Hind might have been in their sights as an operator of wage slavery.

Dick served me at the ticket window. I could see Bob in the office behind him. I tried to remember the difference between them. Dick was the one who could write with two hands; Bob was the one that couldn't.

'George about?' I asked.

He was not; day off.

'I can't understand *Bradshaw's*,' Cicely was saying, as I returned. 'Whenever I find the train I need, I look down the page and there's a note saying "Only on Weekdays", and it never *is* a weekday that I want to take a train.'

'There's worse than that,' said the wife. 'Only go on Thursday afternoons, half of them.'

The train came in on time, pulled by one of Mr Aspinall's 060s, but that was lost on the ladies. We found an empty compartment in Third. I sat next to the wife on one side, Cicely sat on the other. As the whistle was blown, Cicely said, 'I suppose Mr Hind will have to break off his sailing holiday. He'll be awfully cut up to hear the news.'

'Rubbish,' said the wife, and Cicely frowned as the engine started away.

'Well, it's a shame that the poor old –'

'Fossil,' put in the wife.

'The poor old *gentleman*', said Cicely, 'did not get to a hundred, because then you receive a telegram from the . . . Oh, now that reminds me.' And Cicely began telling a story about Hind's Mill. 'Before he went off sailing, Mr Hind asked me to take a letter, which always gets me in a tiz. He's so fast, it's very hard to take him down verbatim, although I'm sure *you* can do it, love.' She touched the wife on her knee.

'He usually writes out the letters he wants me to send,' said the wife. 'I've only taken one from him verbatim.'

'How did you get on?'

'I asked him to talk more slowly.'

Cicely went wide-eyed and forgot all about her story for the moment, looking the spit of Young Leonard, the doll of Henry Clarke. 'Well he must be dead keen on you then,' she said, 'or you'd have been stood down in a moment.'

The wife was smiling, looking out of the window and kicking her foot, smiling at the flashing sunshine and the smokeless Saturday-afternoon mills going by. I pulled down the window strap and lit one of the last of the 'B's that I'd bought with George Ogden. A man went past in the corridor, and I thought: now by rights he'll be envious seeing me sitting here with two beauties. Though I'd lain awake most of the night as usual, trying to make a connection between the death of old Hind and all else, I was now feeling a little better about things: I would just go on searching until I knew the name of the person who'd put the stone on the line. Meanwhile I was dead set on having a pleasant afternoon.

'Do carry on with your story, Cicely,' I said, and I put on a bit of a swell's voice for that, so the wife gave me a funny look.

'Mr Hind had me into his room,' Cicely went on, 'and after a bit of doing his usual –'

The wife was frowning at her; we were rattling past Sowerby Bridge.

'You know,' Cicely said, 'the funny . . .'

'Funny what?' I said, puffing out smoke.

'The funny-osity. He never says anything, but just puts his hands –'

The wife shook her head, as if to say: not in front of a man, which was a shame, because I'd have liked to hear more about the funny-osity.

'Anyway,' Cicely continued, 'Mr Hind said, "I would like you to take a letter." I said, "Who to, Mr Hind?" and he said, "To the King!"'

'He never did!' I said, and the wife gave me another look.

171

'I've not told you this, dear,' said Cicely, grinning all around her head, 'because I was saving it up for today. Anyway it was a very long letter, and it was to go with six suits that we were sending His Majesty.'

The wife rolled her eyes.

'The letter was saying, you know, please find herewith six suits, only in a smarter way, and was all about how they were made from the finest woollens. I never knew this, but Hind's Mill has been sending the Royal Family six suits for the staff at Balmoral every year for forty-seven years, and when we send off the fiftieth lot of six, we're to be in the *Halifax Courier*, Mr Hind says.'

'You'd think he'd want to keep quiet about such a daft scheme,' said the wife.

'Why six?' I said.

'I don't know,' said Cicely. 'Nobody knows.'

'To think what it must cost,' said the wife, 'and Hind laying people off in their dozens over the light suiting.'

'The letter was to go to the King's Secretary,' Cicely continued, 'who's the Right Honourable Lord . . . something, with a lot of letters after his name – more letters after his name than *in* it. I have the letter by heart if you want to hear.'

She looked across the carriage at the two of us; again she was dividing us, because I wanted to hear, and the wife, I knew, didn't care to.

'Go on, Cicely,' I said, blowing smoke.

'My Lord,' said Cicely. 'We would be grateful if His Majesty would be so gracious –'

'Makes you quite *sick*,' said the wife.

'– so gracious,' Cicely continued, frowning at the wife, 'as to receive this gift of six suits for the royal staff at Balmoral.'

But such a frost had been created by the wife that Cicely just said, 'Eee, Lydia,' and gave a very Yorkshire sort of sigh. Then she perked up, saying: 'Oh, talking of letters . . .' And she passed an envelope over to me.

I didn't have time to picture my worst fears before they

were actually there on the page. It started straight in with: 'I saw you yesterday at the mill with Cicely, who says your wife is the new one in the office. This letter is in case you want to know more about Maggie Dyson, the lady you killed.'

Cicely and the wife were talking. I read on, but not every word. I kept my eyes half turned away, as if looking at the sun.

There was something about Dyson's husband, how his heart had given out at a young age; something about the boy, who was so quiet where his mother was lively, but still she doted on him: 'No living child was better fed or clothed.' There was another part about the boy's dog, which was quiet too, and didn't need looking after, 'even on railway stations'. It seemed to be good that the dog was quiet, but a worry that the boy was so silent.

It ended: 'To think that in her hour of need she had YOU. It must be a judgement upon her, but why only God knows.'

There was a looking glass on the opposite side of the carriage: I saw in it a boy smoking a cigar, trying to be something he was not.

'Who on earth is writing to you?' asked the wife.

Cicely answered: 'It's from Mary-Ann Roberts, love, one of the weavers. She saw Jim at the mill yesterday and stayed behind to write a letter. She asked me to give it him. What it's about I don't know, I'm sure.'

'It's just about the smash,' I said.

'What about it?' said Cicely. And I was sure the tears were coming again.

'Oh, nothing to speak of,' I said.

I stood up and pitched the letter through the window, sending my cigar flying after it. The girls looked at me strangely for a moment; then carried on with the chatting. On top of everything, I felt a coward for covering things up.

We climbed out at Hebden Bridge and stood before the notice on the platform: 'FOR HARDCASTLE CRAGS: AN IDEAL SPOT

FOR PICNIC PARTIES'. The sound of our train departing gave way to the clattering of the weir by the station. The town was a little way to the west, with woods coming down to it from the hills on all sides. There were mills at Hebden, but they were small ones: house-sized, family goes, putting out thin trails of smoke instead of black fogs.

As we set off walking, I picked up the wife's basket with the blanket on top. 'This is a rather light picnic,' I said.

'We'll pick up a bite in the town,' she said. 'It's on the way, and there's a Co-operative Stores.'

We crossed the river Calder by a bridge called the Victoria Bridge. We walked in a line, dawdling, Cicely in front twirling her sunshade, calling out that this spot could be just as good as Blackpool, if only there were afternoon dances to be found, and me cursing Mary-Ann Roberts. There was a swan going along underneath us, with signets following behind, like a train.

Then the wife caught sight of a baker's van heading into the town, and said we must follow it because it had the words 'HEBDEN BRIDGE CO-OPERATIVE SOCIETY' on the side. We followed it into Commercial Street, and the wife got excited over the store having a butchery as well as a bakery. It was funny how easily people could enjoy life when they didn't have a death to answer for.

'If they can lay their hands on the coin for that,' she said, 'there must be hundreds of members.'

The wife picked up bottles of cola, Eccles cakes, apples and eggs. But when she came out with our divvy number, the shopkeeper shook his head and said, 'That's a Halifax number.' The wife believed you should be able to use a Halifax divvy number in a Co-op at Hebden Bridge or anywhere else, and told the man so, but he didn't seem bothered either way. Even though he had a butchery *and* a bakery, he was not go-ahead.

He told Cicely that some of the eggs she was looking over were pre-boiled, all ready for picnicking. Cicely laughed, and said, 'Shall we take them and drop them to test it?' and the man said, 'You can do what you bloody want after you've paid for and taken them away.'

'You've a hope of getting new members if that's how you talk to customers,' said the wife.

'I'll not have people cracking eggs on my floor,' he said.

As we were leaving, though, the shopkeeper walked out from behind his counter and, throwing one of the eggs towards Cicely, shouted, 'Catch!'

Cicely did catch it, going very red in the process. 'Well,' she said, as we walked down the road with our full basket, 'he was all right in the end.'

We walked up to a cluster of finger posts on a pole. They showed the way to Granny Wood, Common Bank Wood, Owler Bank, Wood End, Hardcastle Crags.

'What's *at* Hardcastle Crags?' asked Cicely, a little anxiously.

'Rocks,' I said.

'Do they do teas?' said Cicely.

'Do *who* do them?' I asked.

'Lonely spot, is it?'

'Except for the hundreds of trippers,' said the wife.

'It's known as Little Switzerland, or England's Alps,' said the wife. 'I read about it in the library. There's a mill up there that's now a tea room, but was in full cry until only a few years ago, working dozens of little weaving girls half to death.'

'It is very pleasantly situated, though,' I said.

We walked along Lees Road, which was in the valley of Hebden Water, and, after passing Nut Clough Mill, fell in with a line of trippers trooping on one another's heels up to the Crags. Occasionally a gig would come along with some toffs on board, and fairly bulging with up-to-date patent cookers and whatnot.

It was scorching hot, and because of what Cicely had said the day before, I fell to thinking about my good suit, which was probably twenty-eight ounces like my work ones. Well, it was *too much*. I wore it every single Sunday, but for half the year I'd be far better off without it.

We walked on, and after a mile of hard going Cicely's sunshade had stopped twirling, and she'd fallen behind.

'Clog on!' called the wife, turning and grinning at her.

'That's proper Yorkshire, that is!' Cicely called back, but she didn't pick up the pace.

We knew we'd come to Hardcastle Crags when we began to see oak trees on the hillsides. Underneath them, the light and shade was all criss-crossed. There were lots of signs telling you not to use patent cookers, and lots of people using them. Each little group would look up and scowl as you went past, just in case you were thinking of sitting near. It was the valley of a stream that was out of sight below, but noisy with it. We sat down next to a party that was just leaving. They looked well-to-do, and had managed to have a knife-and-fork dinner. They were now cleaning the knives by sticking them straight into the ground and yanking them out again. Cicely was quite hypnotised by this. 'I'll bet it doesn't work with the forks,' she said after a while, as if coming out of a dream. Then, looking all about, she said, 'The forget-me-nots are all on the go.' She sighed, adding, 'Oh, they're so viewsome. They've always been my favourites.'

We stretched out our blankets and ate our dinner, which took about five minutes flat. What I'd have liked was a bottle or two of beer, but instead I said, 'Who'd like to walk a bit further up?'

'What happens up there?' asked Cicely.

'You hit the tree line where all the vegetation gives out.'

'Doesn't sound so exciting,' said Cicely.

A few minutes later, the wife spotted a little sign reading 'FLOWER OFFICE', and pointing up. This was a round hut where flowers were explained. It was very close inside and smelt strongly of plants, although there were only *pictures* of plants on show, with the parts – roots, flowers and stems –

shown separately like the parts of a machine. In the middle was a glass case containing books open at certain pages and showing maps of the Crags. Everybody shuffled around in a circle, boots making a din on the floorboards.

There was an old lady standing in the hut. Everybody had to keep dodging around her, but it turned out she was there to be asked questions. A couple of smart sorts came out with a few, speaking the Latin names of the plants for swank.

Cicely asked the old lady: 'Is it allowed to pick any of the flowers round about?'

'It is not,' said the old lady. 'And there is a ten-shilling fine for those that do.'

Cicely walked directly out, and the wife followed her.

A minute after, I came out myself, and the sun had suddenly swung away. Well, it was not completely gone. There were floating shadows and patches of light in the trees; then would come a surge of cool wind and rattling leaves. I saw the wife walking through some yellow flowers with her skirt lifted almost to the knee.

'Where's Cicely?' I asked her.

'I don't know. I've looked all about. The way she was spoken to, and it's the second time today –' And here she raised her voice so that it might carry to where we'd just been: 'If that woman was not standing there everyone would be able to walk around the hut properly. Has anybody thought of that?' She was now looking down at the ground. 'All the flowers are labelled with little tickets,' she said, 'it's like a shop.'

'I thought you liked shops,' I said.

'I would rather find out about the flowers by myself.'

'How?'

'I would save up for a book which had pictures and explanations, and I would match those up with the ones I see growing.'

'You'd be walking about all day,' I said.

'I might very well be.'

177

She took off her hat, and, keeping it in her teeth, changed her hair at the back. She asked me if I would pass her the shawl that was in the basket. She pulled it around herself and put both her arms around my waist.

'I'm *froz*,' she said, practising her Yorkshire again.

Rain came with the next gust of wind, and you could hear the cries from the trees all around as picnics were brought to an end. I picked up the basket and we walked up, away from the stream towards the dining room in the old mill. When we got there, we saw a big sign on the wall saying 'TEAS AND DANCES', and we knew Cicely would be inside.

She was eating chocolate and drinking tea at one of what seemed like hundreds of tables. Even so, the old mill looked empty. They hadn't put as much back in as they had taken out.

When Cicely saw us, she shouted: 'Oh do come on, or else I shall finish all this chocolate cake!'

'She seems quite herself again,' said the wife.

'The dancing starts shortly,' said Cicely when we reached the table. 'And there's a programme.'

'Do they run to a waltz?' asked the wife.

She passed over a piece of paper. The wife read it and, sitting down, said to Cicely: 'The two of us shall have a waltz, dear.'

The wife was a good dancer.

In short order, the floor was full of people waiting for someone to walk over to the piano. I looked up at the roof. Brackets that had held machinery were still stuck out from the tops of the walls like gibbets, and there were flowers jammed in at odd places. When I looked down again there was a man at the piano.

The waltz began, and, as Cicely and the wife walked hand in hand to the dance floor, I decided to take a turn outside. It was raining more heavily, but the sun was out once again.

Two minutes later, I was walking in the woods in the rain and the sun, when I heard a crashing noise that shouldn't

178

have been made by any picnicker. I stood still, and the noise was followed by a crack and a shout.

Down below, the stream was racing on as before. I heard another cry. Walking smartly towards the sound, I struck a rock that had been broken in two by a tree that had been growing up through the middle but was now dead, and itself broken, and, beyond these, making up the complete set, was a broken man.

I knew him, even without his gold coat: it was Martin Lowther, the ticket inspector. He lived in Hebden Bridge. His head was half beard, half blood. He was in shirtsleeves, with cuffs undone and no gold on his clothes to protect him. Without his coat he looked like a tortoise without its shell. And both his legs were in the wrong positions, as if they'd swapped sides. It was the impossible before my own eyes; the sun and the rain together; engine number 1418 half off the tracks.

As I crashed down through the bracken towards Lowther, I saw a long, thin man down at the beck. He was running hard along its banks, leaping the water as clear flat grass for running came up on either side: long feet, big strides, like Little Titch in flight, with legs as wings, and head going backwards and forwards like a pump. It looked as if he was racing the water itself. He was nobody that I knew.

Letting my coat slide off my shoulders, I tumbled down the little mountain and fell in behind him.

The long fellow scarpered up a bank and struck the valley road, Lees Road. But as I went up the bank to follow, a thorn scraped through my bandage and touched my burn. I stopped for a moment to stare as the red line came alive with blood; then, smearing the bandage back round as best I could, I set off again.

There were not many on the road, just a few half-hearted stragglers: tardy sorts, and now they were all in my way. They'd seen one man running, now they saw another. They didn't connect us – at least no one called out any encouragement.

The trees seemed to be rolling in a light wind. This was blowing the rain away, and the sun was coming out with a violent force. It had got a taste for shining that summer, and was out to cause a sensation. I forced myself on like a human hammer, boot segs clattering on the stony road. I could not see the killer but when the road twisted in the right way, I'd see the oncoming crowds part and come together, as if someone was going through them at a lick. Ahead of me, shaking in my line of sight at the bottom of the valley, was Hebden again. A rainbow was over the top of the town, and beyond that was a second rainbow, fainter but bigger – for Mytholmroyd further along the valley.

I came into Hebden, and the sound of my boots changed to a ringing echo in the streets.

The place was full of happy excursionists: the skylarking, drink-taking sort who didn't fancy the hike up to the Crags. They roved between the pubs, or stood crowding pavements near the jug-and-bottle doors. I skidded into half a dozen streets about the main square, seeing nothing, and came to rest in front of the town chapel. But the sound of one desperate fellow's boots clattering continued. The runner, with his jerking head, was five hundred yards off, the only man on Burnley Road, and he was going hard for the right turn that'd take him over the canal and river, and into the railway station.

He was on the bridge as I came onto Burnley Road. As I hit the bridge, the railway station swallowed him up. I shot past the booking office and onto the down platform. The light changed, got brighter and darker all in a moment. Light rain was coming down all around the station, but I was under the canopy. I could see the rain but it was not real to me. I was far too hot for anything, and the platform did not seem to be quite level.

I turned and turned. There was a porter standing next to me on the down. A clerk was coming out of the General Room. There were four passengers on the down, more in the waiting room. All my thoughts were of the down. A train came in, blurring everything. Very short train, three rattlers on. The porter shouted 'Rochdale train!' The four on the plat-form looked at him and got on, as if they were obeying him. The engine began to blow off steam – bad driving – and as the steam turned to rain there was another noise from beyond and behind. I turned and saw the finger-pointing sign to the footbridge and the 'up'. In my mind the sign was saying, Hurry up to the up! There was another train in – already in and waiting on the up. I was over the bridge, and onto the platform and into the train.

A bloody rattler. No corridor. The last of the doors was slammed and I heard the tail end of the guard's shout of 'Manchester train!' As we moved out of the station and began shaking through fields, I threw off my waistcoat, but the sun soon found my compartment and ran alongside the train, roasting me all the same. I could not cool down in the com-partment, which I had to myself. I sat on the seat, and a lot of dust came slowly up, sucking the breath from my lungs. There was no longer any possibility of any more rain ever. I was on the same train as the running killer, and we were going towards Manchester, the London of the North, the city where the Lancashire and Yorkshire Railway had sprouted from.

I stayed sitting, leaning forwards on my seat, which some-how seemed the best way of coping with the burning, falling feeling. We came to some little station on the Lanky that I'd never been in: I caught the name as we went through slowly: Littlebord. One proud stationmaster in shirtsleeves, viewing miniature trees in tubs.

More hot, lonely fields came up, sheep moving away with short, bumpy runs – couldn't be bothered to do more. We rolled into Smithy Bridge station, going slowly along the length of a poster showing a row of happy faces: it was an advertisement for Blackpool. But our three-carriage train did not stop, and we were into fields again, smaller ones, rising and falling beside us like waves. I could not picture in my mind the route from Hebden Bridge to Manchester that I was

181

now following, and I could not remember the direction, could not move my thoughts.

I got to my feet in the carriage and turned a slow circle to help me get my bearings. I then recalled that I had boarded the train on the up. The direction we were moving in was south. I wanted to put my head out of the window to see whether the killer was looking out from his own compartment, but I could not rise.

I knew that a big town lay between Hebden Bridge and Manchester, but could not remember its name, was too hot to remember its name. Directly we stopped, I would put my hands on the other fellow, then shout for the nearest constable. But why? I clean forgot for a moment. It came back to me in a blue flash, like electricity. He had killed Lowther, the ticket inspector. He had done it for some reason to do with the stone on the line.

What would be the first stop? Looking up, I saw a mighty advertisement for Victory V lozenges go rocking past. I heard the friendly echoing of a station, and I knew this was Rochdale, but I also knew I had brain fever from the heat. I grasped the window strap to pull myself up, but our driver was proving very tardy in shutting off steam. If he doesn't push that regulator to the home position in a minute, I thought, there'll be no station left. But the exhaust beats continued, steady as the ticking of a clock. Our train may have been short, but it was very determined. I sat back down with the notion that if we weren't going to stop at Rochdale, we weren't going to stop anywhere until the end of the line.

I fancy that I may have slept before Manchester. I do not recall approaching the station: Manchester Victoria.

When we arrived, I stumbled out of the compartment, and saw the illuminated display revolving in the hot dirty air: 'VISIT THE ARDENNES'; Visit . . . somewhere else; 'VISIT THE ARDENNES' again. I turned to look at the platform gates, and there was the long thin man going through fast, leaving money in the hand of the ticket collector.

I broke into a run, but it came out wrong, all wobbly, like, and I knew I was being marvelled at by a lot of people coming down off a train that had pulled up on the opposite platform. I had my waistcoat in my hand, but no jacket and no pocket book. I had left them behind in Little Switzerland, England's Alps.

The ticket collector was coming up to me – 'Where's your ticket, mate?' but he didn't say it, I was only imagining him saying it. There seemed to be some difficulty in my head as to what was happening, and what I thought was happening, for although they were mostly the same, they were sometimes not.

I got past the ticket collector because he'd seen somebody he knew. Somebody was walking towards the fellow and putting his hand to his cap, ready to raise it and say 'Now then'. So the collector forgot his business for a moment, and I was through the gates and in the clear. But there was another revolving sign that delayed me: 'ENGLAND' . . . 'CONTINENT' . . . 'ENGLAND' . . . 'CONTINENT'. I dragged my eyes away. I was in the great hall of Manchester Victoria station, which was all white tiles, like a giant washroom. The offices of the Lanky were hard by, I knew, tacked on to the station.

There was no air. Close to the entrance was a refreshment room, where a man was drinking a glass of water. I saw the silver sparkle of it, and that delayed me too, but the drinking of water was something that went on in another world.

I stepped out of the station. The cathedral might have been carved from coal, and there was a river smell floating up around it. In the mystery of Manchester, I was keeping my eye out for anyone moving away fast from the station, but there were dozens doing that, even though it was early evening on Saturday. All along the steaming wet roads they went, for it had lately rained; under the hot orange sky they went, under the mighty gas lamps, the size and shape of diamonds.

On all sides enormous words were being carried across streets by viaducts and bridges: 'GRAMOPHONES BELOW COST', 'UMBRELLAS RE-COVERED'. It seemed to be a city of policemen with slowly turning heads, and everybody a winner or a loser and nothing in between. There were great statues in the streets, controlling the people, and the trams were like moving spiral staircases, everybody walking towards them full of mean thoughts, not really walking but pushing on grimly. It was hard to credit that only one train could bring a fellow from Little Switzerland to here.

The sun was sinking, but still I could not get cool. I thought I might raise a breeze by walking fast so tried that for a while. It didn't work, so I sat down in a coal yard near the cathedral. There was a grindstone there, and a fellow lifting sacks of coal onto a cart. I stared at the grindstone, and the coalman looked at me for a longer time after every heave, until I walked over the road to a pub which turned out to be tiny – just a dark, tiny box of hot air, with dusty pictures of soldiers all around the walls. I bought a glass of beer, handing over what I realised, too late, was my last shilling. Then I bought another because the damage was done. Besides the barman, there was one other fellow in the pub. He was smoking a clay pipe. He was one of those old men with eyes that are frightening because too young and lively: the kind that haven't done enough in life.

'I saw you,' he said, 'sleeping in a coal yard.'

'Was not,' I said. I might have been five years old.

'Hard on, you were. You're barely awake now.'

'It's not a crime is it?' I said.

'So you admit it? You'd better watch him,' he said to the barman; 'turn your back for a minute, he'll be out like a light.'

He turned to me again as I tried to tuck my hand bandage back into place. 'What are you up to?' he said.

'Looking out for a murderer,' I said.

The old boy just muttered something very quietly to himself at that, and went back to his pipe, disgusted that there was somebody even stranger than himself about the place.

I came out of the pub and immediately saw a very promising sign reading 'ICE STATION'. But then a tram moved and it was 'POLICE STATION'. I thought about walking in and saying I believed a man who had done a murder at Hebden Bridge was now at large in Manchester. It would be like saying that I believed him to be 'in the world'.

I decided to do it, though.

As I walked into the copper shop, it was hot, but in a different way again, which turned my head. I realised that my bandage was dangling down from my wrist like a dog lead with no dog on the end.

I started to tell my story at the long desk, and a man who was something between a policeman and a clerk said the smart thing would be for me to sit down on a bench. He talked to somebody else about me, and the only words I heard were 'no effects', which he said with a laugh. But it was all songs and whistling in the copper shop because a man was fitting an electrical fan into the ceiling.

I sat still for a while, working on my breathing. The trouble was that I was unable to take in as much air as I was breathing out. Other people who were waiting to be seen, I noticed, were taken off to special rooms, and I couldn't work out whether it was good or bad that I was kept on the bench. I told at least three policemen that I wanted to make a statement in connection with a crime, and nothing was done, but glasses of water kept coming for me, and I would watch the scenes at the desk. Mostly it was people with complaints that came in, and mostly the complaints were about horses.

Presently, a fourth or fifth copper came up, saying: 'How about a spot of grub?' He gave me a menu chart, divided up according to different times of day. I looked up at the clock, thinking it was about six, when bread and butter and tea came to an end going by the chart, and pea soup started, but somehow it was quarter to eight, when hotpot was nearly finished; and the fan, although not turning, was quite fitted into the ceiling with the stepladder below it, and I knew then that I must have been asleep.

Manchester had been so large, and now it was so small: just this police station and the question of the fan.

The pea soup was brought on a tray, with suet pudding and syrup and half a pint of tea. As I started to eat it my bandage, which I had tried to fix, came unwound again and dropped into the soup, so it became green, but it became sticky too, so that when I wound it back – which everybody in the copper shop saw me do – it stayed put.

The copper who came to collect the pots when I'd finished had a sideways sloping face, and teeth going backwards. I reminded him that I had a statement to make, and he said, with eyes to the floor: 'Yes, you've taken a funny turn, but we mean to get it down.'

But I did not believe him because he wouldn't look at me.

He finally took me into one of the writing rooms, using more pushing and shoving than I cared for. I said, 'I've had a fair wait, you know,' and he said, 'Well, we wanted to take a look at you for a while.'

'Why?'

'You seemed a bit steamed up . . . bit of a beer smell coming off you . . .'

He was looking away all the time, so there was no telling if this was the real reason.

'I have been running for miles,' I said. 'So I have taken a glass of beer.'

The policeman nodded.

More water came from somewhere, so I drank it. 'You boys must have had me down as loony,' I said, 'a loafer.' I knew you ought not to call policemen 'boys'. It was asking for trouble.

The policeman smiled very uncertainly while producing a pen and a ledger from the drawer in the desk. He said: 'All right now, you've come here on the train from Switzerland but you don't even have a coat . . .'

It was a long statement, starting with an explanation of the difference between Switzerland and Little Switzerland, which I became better at as I went along. I told the policeman all, and he wrote it down. Well, mostly. I told him about the stone on the line, and my notions concerning it, including that it could have been the first attempt by the runner of today to get Lowther, but even as I spoke, I remembered that nobody could've known Lowther would be on the train. I myself had seen him *decide* to get on it.

The copper came in with: 'Why would a fellow wreck a whole train on the off-chance of doing for one man on it?'

That was my question too, but I said: 'Well, it has been known.'

'When has it?'

I thought of all the *Railway Magazine*s I'd ever read, all the reports of smashes and inquiries but nothing came of it.

'I couldn't say for certain,' I said, feeling that this was throwing away all the work I'd put in to make him think I was of strong mind.

'What happened today,' said the policeman (and I knew that he was thinking '*If* it happened'), 'might very well have started out as an argument over a fare. Ticket inspecting can be a dangerous line to be in, you know.'

Yes, I wanted to say: if you were canned, or just the violent sort, you might crown a ticket inspector if your blood was up. But you wouldn't follow him on his private Saturday afternoon jaunts, when he was minding his business and not wearing his gold, and do him then.

The policeman ended by saying he'd be sending a letter to Hebden Bridge Police, and writing me out a chit that would see me from Manchester Victoria station back to Halifax.

Well, he had to get out of it all somehow.

When I walked out of the police station, Manchester was all aglow in the hot, soft darkness, and the river air was spreading, yet somehow I was feeling stronger. To stand at shoulder height like the statues in the streets would be nothing. As I approached the booking office with my chit, I wondered whether I needed to explain how I had come by it, or did they see a hundred roughyreds a day in possession of police 'specials'? Another fancy came to me as I approached the booking office: If the murder of Lowther was not to do with one ticket, it might very likely be to do with hundreds. George Ogden had told me tickets had gone missing. And George Ogden was on the fly.

Chapter Eighteen

When I came half stumbling through the door of 21 Back Hill
Street, the wife was in the process of walking across the parlour, and my coat was lying on the sofa looking as though it
was taking a rest in my place. I put it onto the floor and lay
down.

'Are you all right?' she said, but she did not kiss me and
continued on her way to the scullery. 'A man of your descrip-
tion was seen flying through Hebden Bridge,' she called out,
while moving pots within the scullery, 'then leaping on a
train to Manchester . . . Without a ticket, the booking clerk
said.'

'If you knew I was going towards Manchester,' I called
back from the sofa, 'why didn't you tell the police? Then they
could have had men waiting.'

The movement from the kitchen stopped for a second at
this, but soon started up again. The Erasmic Soap and the
good towel were laid out for me next to the tub, and the tub
was near the open window, which was the summer equiva-
lent of in front of the fire. The first gas lamp of Hill Street gave
a glow on the bath when set just there, and it was my
favourite place for reading. But I was so tired that it seemed a
long way from sofa to tub. There was a letter for George
Ogden on the mantelshelf.

'So I knew where you'd gone,' the wife continued, walking
back into the parlour, 'but I didn't know how you'd get back
without your pocket book.' The wife picked the coat up from
the floor and put it on the hook behind the door. Her face was
very brown from the sun; her eyes darker, hair lighter.

The wife said cocoa was waiting in the stove cup – the tin
cup – and that it 'ought to be just about right', which meant I

189

was to fetch it from the stove because it would be too hot for her hands. When I walked into the kitchen there was food set on the table: a boiled egg, a pork pie, a parkin, a bowl of peach halves in syrup. The wife sat down opposite, watching me start on the egg, which meant she had something to say. Water was steaming in the boiler.

'Do you want to know what happened?' I said, crossly.

'A man suffered an injury at the Crags,' she said, 'and you chased another man to Manchester.'

'The fellow that died,' I said, 'was Martin Lowther, a ticket inspector who was on the excursion when we hit the stone. And I didn't chase "a man", I chased the wrecker.' But I was starting to doubt it once again.

'Well,' the wife said presently, 'did you *catch* the man?'

'You've asked at last,' I said.

She sighed. 'Are you not going to eat your peach halves?' she said.

'No,' I said. 'No, I did not catch him, and, no, I do not mean to eat my peach halves. I do not care for them. When you've been hard at it, trying to catch a murderer, you don't want fruit.'

'What do you want?'

'A bottle of beer.'

She stood up and took the peach halves away to the sink. She was still wearing the holiday dress, but the holiday was over. She turned around and looked at me for a little while longer.

'I daresay,' I said, 'from your look, that you think when a fellow sees murder done, he should just let the killer stroll off.'

'I do not say that,' said the wife, and she continued to look at me.

I was thinking of railway tickets, and I was thinking of our lodger. 'Where's George?' I asked the wife.

'He was in earlier, then he went out.'

'What time?'

'Just as I got back.'

'Did you tell him what had happened?'

'That you'd gone haring off to Manchester without any money? No I did not.'

'What's that letter for him on the mantel?'

'How should I know?' said the wife, but after a short pause she added, 'It's from the Society for the Diffusion of Knowledge . . . It is to be hoped they put him straight on questions to do with the payment of rent.'

'Oh go on then,' I said. 'You mean to say something, so let's have it.'

'Well,' she said, moving to the table to clear up the rest of the pots, 'it's just this: he's not dead.'

'Who's not?' I said. 'The man who was killed? Lowther?'

'There was a doctor dancing up at the tea rooms, and he went down to him and said it was two broken legs . . .'

'But he wasn't moving,' I said.

'Nor would you be if you'd two smashed legs. The ambulance was sent for,' said the wife, 'and while it was coming the doctor talked to the man.'

'To Lowther?' I said.

'Whatever his name is . . . And he said he'd fallen.'

'Fallen?' I glanced down at the pea soup stain on my shirt; I thought of the chit given to me in the police station – they had never stopped thinking me a loony, and had meant to get me out of their city in double-quick time. The wife thought I was a crackerjack, too. If she could've handed me a one-way ticket to somewhere just then, I'm sure she would have done it.

I thought of myself as seen in the carriage glass: a little man.

A fellow who lived in Hebden Bridge, who happened to have been on a train that somebody had tried to stop, had suffered a fall at the place he lived. And I brought to mind once more that I had seen Lowther at the Joint station on Whit Sunday, at the very moment that he had decided to board our excursion, after waiting for the Leeds train and giving it up. Nobody could have banked on him making that decision; nobody could have known he'd be on our train. But with old Hind it was different: everyone knew he was aboard. It was his first train ride ever: a red letter day.

I was wrong over Lowther, just as I'd been wrong over the correct treatment of concussion cases. I ought to stick to firing engines, but I was filled with anxiety every time I did *that*.

I felt like somebody lying at the bottom of the sea.

'He tumbled off a rock that he'd been sitting on,' the wife continued.

'Why would Lowther be sitting on a rock?' I said, staring at the table edge.

'That spot is England's Alps, you said, and in the Alps, they climb.'

'But he's a bloody ticket inspector.'

'There's no need to start cursing just because you've been a juggins. Anyway, what's his job got to do with it?'

'Ticket inspectors', I said, 'don't generally go about climbing mountains. They make things hot for *them as haven't got railway tickets.*'

'The doctor said he'd been drinking wine too.'

'Now that I can credit,' I said.

The kitchen was too hot and too small. I pushed the chair back.

'You're all in,' said the wife. 'You should get in the tub and go to bed.'

'I'm off to go to the *pub*,' I said.

'Are you?' said the wife. 'Well, I would change that shirt.'

'They're not particular in the Evening Star,' I said.

She was on the edge of laughing, now.

'It is a definite fact,' I said, 'that . . .'

Something was a definite fact, but I was too tired to remember what.

'It is a definite fact,' I went on, 'that the man I chased was moving like greased lightning.'

'Well,' said the wife. 'Some people are close to an accident, and they don't like to be pestered to death over what they've seen. Or they think they might catch the blame if they hang about.'

'What rot,' I said.

'For all you know,' said the wife, 'he might have been running to catch his train.'

'Well, that beats all,' I said, and I was laughing now.

'Why does it?' said the wife, who was taking down her hair, letting the door-knocker fall.

'I expect there's a train every half hour going between Hebden Bridge and Manchester. Instead of half killing himself on the hottest day in memory, don't you think he'd stroll to the station for the next one?'

'I really don't know,' said the wife.

'No,' I said, 'and nor do I.'

'But it is a fact that he never touched the man found with broken legs.'

I suddenly thought of the Socialist Mission. Anybody could *say* anything. 'It is a fact,' I said, 'that Lowther *said* the fellow never touched him.'

The wife gave me a good steady look that I liked. I was back up from the bottom of the sea.

'Will you unhook this dress?' she said. 'I've had enough of it.'

When that was done, and the business that followed was done (after which the wife did not go off to do any family-stopping business), and I was lying in the tub with my *Railway Magazine* reading of the new goods yards in Dover, with the pages fluttering in the breeze that had finally started to come in through the window, and drinking a bottle of Bass that the wife had produced from the pantry, I said, 'We are not really at all alike, are we? One difference is that you were not on the engine, you know.'

'We have some points in common,' said the wife.

'What?'

'We both want to get on.'

I finished the beer, and the wife took the bottle away from me. She didn't mind my having a bath in front of the smart sorts in Hill Street, but would rather they didn't catch a glimpse of me drinking beer.

'When you get married,' I said some time later, but still in the bath, 'you think that's more or less it as far as knowing the other person's concerned . . . But it isn't really, is it?'

But the wife, in her petticoats, was curled up asleep on the sofa. She was full of surprises.

Chapter Nineteen

Two evenings later, on the Monday, I walked towards the Crossley Porter School and Orphanage all kitted out with the *Pearson's Book of Fun* under my arm, and a Farthing Everlasting Strip in my pocket. This would be my first social call of the evening; the second would take me to Halifax Infirmary, where John Ellerton had told me Lowther was laid up.

That day we'd taken an excursion to Skipton and back. Postal workers. It had been market day in Skipton, and the people had all been in the inns, and the animals all in the streets. I'd told Clive all about my adventures in Hebden and Manchester, not giving him my thoughts in detail, but just saying, 'Here's a fellow nearly catches it when the stone's put on the line between Salwick and Kirkham, then he has another close call not three weeks later . . . Rum, ain't it?'

Clive had been more concerned about keeping his boots clean, but in a Skipton pub he'd said, 'So you think it's the socialists again, do you?' and I'd answered, 'In a way it proves it can't have been that lot first time.'

'Why?' Clive had asked. 'Nobody's over-keen on ticket inspectors. When one of *them's* got at, you can't rule *anybody* out.'

I then told him what had become of old Hind, who'd been 'To-Day's Obituary' in that day's *Courier*. There wasn't much to it: 'The death occurred on Friday of Mr William Sinclair Hind, chairman of Hind's Mill. Mr Hind, who was ninety-nine, was being attended by doctors for his heart. In his earlier years, he was devoted to cricket.' That last part had been the only shock.

It was a hot, blue evening, and the orphanage looked like a castle in France, only black, of course, like everything in

Halifax. There was a garden to the front, and Savile Park in front of that. All the windows in the house were open, and, as I got close, I heard a voice saying: 'Give instances from the gospel of the times when our Lord . . .'

But gentle, like.

The garden was the kind that makes you feel riff-raff in working boots, even if you've been at the Erasmic Soap for the best part of half an hour, as I had. And even though it had likely been another fellow in working clothes – gaiters too, probably, *and* a clay pipe in his mouth – who'd made it all. Every flower-bed was a different colour and a different world. You'd look at one and think, that's the prettiest, with those giant orange flowers; then you'd look at another and see blue flowers, small but more of them, and you'd think, no, that one tops it, and so on. What all the beds had in common was a big stone urn in the middle.

Feeling like I'd climbed from the audience onto the stage, I stood at the top of the wide stone steps leading to the front door and rang the bell, which was set in an iron circle as big as a dinner plate. They went big with everything, the Crossleys.

The door was opened by a most unexpected person: a tiny, untidy woman who seemed to be just passing by. 'Oh, come in then,' she said.

I told her my business. She looked down at the package in my hands and said, 'That's all right, come along with me.'

She began leading me along a corridor, past rows of portraits. 'Our founders,' she said, putting out a small arm as she walked, and I marvelled at how founders are always bald men with beards no matter what it is they've founded.

'We've got plenty of nooks and crannies you know,' she said, after we'd turned a few corners.

But they were very *big* nooks and crannies.

As we walked, I could somehow tell the place was full of children, although I couldn't see any. It was a kind of trembling feeling, like when you have a mouse in your hand.

I was at last shown into a small wooden room marked

'VISITORS – BOYS' SIDE', which, if I'd been running the place, I would have shifted nearer the front door. In the office was a matron – a big woman with a happy face and pink cheeks that didn't go with her black dress, just as the garden did not go with the house. She fished my letter out of a drawer and her face fell into a frown as she read it, which set me wondering about the spelling, until I remembered that the wife had typed it.

'What day was your train smash?' she asked, putting the letter down.

I felt like saying: It wasn't *my* smash. Instead, I said, 'Whit Sunday.'

'Pentecost,' said the woman. I was quite certain she was about to say, Well you shouldn't be driving engines on such a day, but she looked at me, smiled, put the letter away.

'Good of you to bring the book,' said a voice from the doorway.

Turning around, I saw a big, brown, strong man who looked ready for anything. 'Matthew Ferry,' he said, shaking my hand.

'I thought I might read the boy a couple of riddles,' I said.

Matthew Ferry laughed. 'You've a hope.'

'He'll be having his supper,' said matron, 'so we won't bring him out quite yet. Would you like to come through for a cup of tea?'

Mr Ferry was now holding the door open for me, and we walked for another half minute before turning into a sort of parlour, with a scullery connected. There were a few attempts to make the parlour homely – green tab rugs on the floor, a red cloth on the table – but the empty fireplace was too big, and the ceiling was too high. On the walls were thin wooden crucifixes, with dried flowers tucked behind them, and I thought again of Whit Sunday: the Lord's day, and an extra special one at that. Maybe you *were* asking for all you got by running trains on that day. Come to that, wakes weeks had started out as religious in some way.

Mr Ferry began cleaning a pair of boots as the matron went through into the scullery. Very shortly after, she was calling over the sound of a singing kettle: 'Never smiles, that one you've come for.' She returned with a filled pot on a tray, and cups.

'Sarcastic disposition,' said the man, smiling and pausing in his boot-cleaning.

'Well, I believe he's precious careful not to be *seen* doing it,' the matron continued.

'A lot of them are like that at first. They don't think it's fit to be seen happy in a place like this. They sort of think they're in church all the time.'

'Or at a funeral,' said Mr Ferry, 'a funeral going on for years and years.' He seemed quite happy as he said this. 'Do you know what the boy wanted when he came here?' he asked.

'I don't,' I said.

'Fires lighting. Everywhere he went.'

'But it's been so hot,' I said.

'A fire reminded the boy of home,' said Matthew Ferry. He was going forty to the dozen at his boot, smiling down all the while at the glacé kid on the Nuggett's polish tin, who smiled back up at him. 'I had a long go at him a few days after he came in,' he continued, 'give him a chance to say whatever he might want to. I asked him about his mother but it was no go, and I had just one thing out of the boy.' He had stopped polishing. 'His mother', he told me, 'could make her eyes go crossed.'

'Well . . .' I said, and things went a bit quiet for a while.

They were not orphan's boots that he was cleaning. They were too big. And orphan boots would have come in bundles. No, these were Matthew Ferry's boots, and it struck me that a man would not be cleaning his own boots in front of a woman unless she was his wife – wife or sister, for they had the same high colour.

'Little bit of advice for you,' said Mr Ferry, who'd finished cleaning his boots and was putting the lid on the tin. 'When you see the lad, don't say: "I was sorry about your mother", because then you're going to have to say, "I was sorry about your father", "Sorry about your dog", "Sorry about you not getting your day in Blackpool", and so on till the cows come home.'

He had all the boy's misfortunes off by heart. No detail lacked.

'What did the boy's father die of?' I asked Mr Ferry.

'Heart gave out,' he said, quite brightly.

I realised I already knew that from Mary-Ann Roberts's letter. I picked up the cup of tea that Mrs Ferry had poured for me and took a sip, but it was too hot.

'He was in a similar line to yourself,' said Mr Ferry, folding his big arms, for the boots were now done.

'Engine man?' I said.

Mr Ferry picked up his teacup, poured some onto the saucer and blew – six shimmers, with the tea not allowed to come to rest in between each one.

'How many tons of coal do you have to lift in an ordinary day?' he asked.

'On a fifty mile run,' I said, 'it might come to . . . one.' I wanted to add: But there's more to the job than that.

The matron was talking to someone at the door, and it seemed that Arnold Dyson had been sent for. I put the book inside my coat, thinking to make a bit of a surprise out of giving it back.

'One ton?' said Mr Ferry. 'Now what would you say to firing the boiler in a mill?'

'Well, you know . . . It wouldn't suit.'

'Why not?' said Mr Ferry, smiling.

'Because a mill doesn't move.'

'It does not,' said Mr Ferry, standing up, 'even if you put six ton on the fires every working day, which is what Arnold Dyson's father was doing.'

'He was a boilerman?'

'That's it, fettling the boiler, but mainly shovelling coal and one day he just pegged out.'

199

'What mill was it?'

'Hind's. It's where he copped on with the mother.'

'Matthew!' cried the matron, 'we'll have less!'

He'd been grinning and glowing before, but this remark turned him up to boiling point and he gave out a laugh. 'We're talking of mills,' he said, brown face still beaming, 'so I'll use mill talk.' He picked up his tea and finished it in one go. 'I hear that lot are off to Blackpool again soon,' he said.

'Yes,' I said.

'Will you be firing the engine once again?'

I nodded back, trying to smile: 'Very likely.'

'Well I should keep an eye out!'

'When did the lad's father die?'

'Five years back. The boy could have come here then because fatherless will do for us, but his mother wanted to keep him. He was at board school in the morning, fended for himself until his mother came home in the afternoons. He would have gone on at the mill as a half-timer himself next year.'

'How old is he?'

'Ten,' said Mr Ferry, and there was Arnold Dyson, standing in the doorway.

His face said the same as before: railway accident. His hair said it, too – it was fighting against the Brilliantine that somebody had combed onto it. You could see a lot going on in his eyes, all of it bad. He wore a black suit with a big white collar, a rig-out meant for somebody who looked more like a child.

'You remember Mr Stringer,' said the matron to the boy.

I really thought she was about to add: The one who killed your mother.

Without waiting for an answer, which was just as well, for I do not think there would have been one, she was up and at him, brushing away crumbs from his coat. 'You muck-tub; you look a perfect fright,' she said, 'Bath bun . . . *plain* bun . . . *Somebody* ate a good tea.' Still brushing the boy's coat, the matron turned to me: 'Clarted with it, he is. Now you and Mr

Stringer here,' she said to the boy, 'are to take a turn about in the gardens.'

It was the first I'd heard of it.

Mr Ferry picked up his newspaper, saying, 'I think I'll come along,' which I was very glad of.

We walked back along the corridors, with Mr Ferry merrily asking about engines, and keeping the conversation going. The boy dragged behind. As we walked along a corridor, a door opened, and a great wave of children, all boys, all in their great black capes, swept towards us. There was no adult or master in sight, and as they swept by on either hand – all silent, but all *nearly* speaking – I half expected to see that they'd carried Arnold Dyson off with them. He was one of their own after all, and did not belong with us. But when I looked back he was still there.

Outside the front of the college, on the raised level that ran around the house, Mr Ferry leant against a stone urn full of flowers and began reading his newspaper.

I stood a few feet away with the boy, holding out *Pearson's Book of Fun*.

'This is yours,' I said. 'You left it on the train.'

No answer. He was looking out at the gardens like a little lord of the manor. Mr Ferry was making a lot of noise with his newspaper.

'Would you like me to read out some riddles?' I said.

'Read 'em to yourself,' said the boy.

'Come on now.' I opened the book at 'Some Riddles', and began reading the first one I struck: '"Why is a football round?"'

'Leave *off*,' said the boy.

'Leave off, *Mr Stringer*,' called Mr Ferry from behind his newspaper. 'Remember your manners.' I could not see Mr Ferry's face but somehow knew he was smiling over this.

I closed the book. 'Well then . . .' I said. I very much wanted the meeting to be over, being sure that at any moment the boy was going to accuse me of murdering his mother.

After a while longer of being stared at by him, I said: 'What did you do today?'

'Nowt.'

'Trigonometry first half of the morning,' called Mr Ferry from over by the urn, 'then Euclid. Afternoon: nature walk, composition, scripture.'

'Are you liking it here?' I said to the boy.

'I take as I find,' he said.

'If you would ever like to take a turn on one of the engines we have down at the shed I'm sure it could be sorted out.'

'What shed?'

'Sowerby Bridge shed. It's where the Halifax engines are mostly kept.'

'Why are they not kept at Halifax?' He sounded like the wife.

'It's all to do with history,' I said. 'The railways went to Sowerby Bridge before they came to Halifax, so the shed was put there.

'Well,' said Arnold Dyson, 'I wish they'd never come at all.'

I took off my cap and put it back on again, cursing myself. Of course most boys, like the son of Robinson, the light-suiting man sacked from Hind's Mill, were engine mad, but this one had the best of reasons not to be.

Mr Ferry seemed to be really taken up with his newspaper now.

'What's the name of your dog?' I asked Arnold Dyson. 'Reuben Booth, that's the guard on the train, the one that has it for safekeeping . . . He wants to know.'

'I'm not telling.'

'Why not?'

'Because then he'll be somebody else's dog.'

'But there's nothing else for it, is there?' I said. 'Reuben's a great hand with dogs, you know.'

'He's going to have to be,' said the boy. 'He's not too particular about getting bitten, I hope. Bob's a quarrelsome sort when he's –'

'That's his name is it? Bob?'

The boy looked away. 'Is not,' he said.

'I know a ticket clerk called Bob,' I said.

The boy turned and looked at the door of the college. 'So *what*?' he said to the door. He smeared his hand hard across his hair. Then he looked at his hand. He didn't like the Brilliantine. He put his hand through his hair again, harder.

A clock began to strike seven, and, all in a moment, Mr Ferry put down his newspaper, collected the boy, and took him back inside the college.

I stood on my own. I felt bad about Arnold Dyson because I'd tricked the dog's name out of him, and what was more, *Pearson's Book of Fun* was still in my hand.

Mr Ferry came back through the door towards me, saying: 'He's tough stuff, isn't he?'

'Well, I'm not a great hand at talking to kids.'

Mr Ferry nodded. 'Ticklish,' he said.

I remembered the Farthing Everlasting Strip, still in my pocket. I had made a poor fist of things all round: it had been crazy to offer Dyson a ride on the footplate. But Mr Ferry was still smiling at me with his newspaper folded under his arm, as if he knew all would come right in the end.

'Oh, while I think on,' he said, looking up at me, 'why *is* a football round?'

Chapter Twenty

It was only a little way across town from the Crossley Porter Orphanage to the other frightening mansion: the Infirmary. I walked from the one to the other across Savile Park, stopping at a drinking fountain on the way. All around me were children playing, jumping about in funny boots like little comedians. The killer had taken all that away from Dyson; the killer and me, working together. And now he was cut off from the world by a beautiful garden.

The garden in front of the Infirmary was not quite up to the same mark, although there were little clusters of people in bathchairs admiring it. I walked through the lodge and found myself in a wide, high room with lilac walls, and white, empty fireplaces. The nurses were in lilac and white too, criss-crossing underneath a sign reading 'ACCIDENT CASES' with an arrow beneath. I watched them for a while, liking the sound of their skirts – and there wasn't one not beautiful.

There were two bearded doctors laughing, and when they moved aside I saw a small woman, neither a doctor nor a nurse, standing behind a high desk and smiling across at me: 'Can I help you, sir?'

I pulled off my cap and walked towards her in noisy boots. 'I would like to see a Mr Martin Lowther. He would have come in on Saturday, I think, with two broken legs.'

'Ward Seven,' she said, without so much as a glance at a ledger or paper. 'Follow the signs.'

I walked along many bright, empty corridors with tall windows. A lot of glaziers had been here, and the windows gave on to gardens that *could* compare to the ones at the orphanage, with wide lawns and many strange-shaped hedges, like chess pieces. You might come round from breathing ether and, looking at these, not be quite sure which world you were in. It didn't look like any part of Halifax, and that was the fact.

I came to double doors that had the sign 'WARD 7' above them, and then the words, 'MRS BAILEY, MATRON'. I walked through the doors and there was a desk with a woman sitting at it: half nurse, half lady-clerk, and I did not like her face. You could have put over what it was like by just drawing a cross. She seemed to be signing, or making some kind of mark, on slips of paper.

'Excuse me,' I said, 'but I've come to see Mr Martin Lowther.'

'Well, you've come at visiting time,' she said, adding, as she glanced up at me, '. . . by accident or design.'

'It was by design,' I said.

'Mr Lowther is not at all well,' she said, 'and I don't think he'll see you.'

'Oh, but if you just once asked him . . .'

She sighed. 'What's the name?'

'Stringer,' I said. 'Jim Stringer, fireman of the Lancashire and Yorkshire Railway.'

'Is it necessary for him to know that last part?'

'It wouldn't hurt,' I said.

'But are you a friend of his, or family, or . . . what? I'll not have him disturbed over a work matter.'

I was about done with pretending to smile, so I gave it up, saying: 'You'll find that he'll see me.'

She stood up and went off into the ward, but not for long, and she came back grinning, so I knew it was a bad look-out. 'He'll not see you,' she said, 'I knew he wouldn't. Two gents came along not twenty minutes since; they gave me their names, just as you've done; I went in to ask and he turned them away as well. Taken very bad, he was, just at hearing they'd turned up.'

'What *were* the names?' I asked, and she answered before thinking about it: 'Mr Crocker and Mr Kilmartin.' She bit her lip directly after the words were out.

205

'Well, I shouldn't wonder he was taken poorly,' I said. 'Do you honestly think they're real names? Because if so, *think on* . . . What did the two of them look like?'

'I don't know, I'm sure,' she said, for she'd clammed up now.

'But you saw them, so you *do* know.'

The woman looked at me and said in a loud voice: 'Doctor Laing!' . . . Then, quieter, to me, 'I'm having you sent away from the hospital.'

The doors moved and Dr Laing was there. It was like shuffling a deck of cards. He was small and he was smiling. 'You would like to see Mr Lowther?'

'I would,' I said.

He turned to the nurse-clerk. 'What is the gentleman's name?' he asked.

'I don't recall,' she said, and I wondered whether she'd tried it on Lowther in the first place – not that it would have cut much ice.

Laing turned back to me, still smiling. 'You see, Mr Lowther has just got nicely off to sleep after being very upset.' And I could see now that this smile of his was more of a brick wall. '*Who* shall I say has called?' he said.

I thought of the names given by the two earlier fellows. 'Say that a friend came by,' I said, and, by doing that, I meant to set Lowther's mind at ease, but as I walked back out of the Infirmary it struck me that I'd likely done nothing of the sort, for, as far as I knew, Martin Lowther didn't *have* any friends.

PART TWO

Wakes

Chapter Twenty-one

In the week before Wakes we were mainly holding fire on the excursion trains, for it was the last time anyone would want to go away. After the Skipton run, we were back on the Rishworth branch for the Tuesday and Wednesday, with another Scarborough excursion booked for the Thursday.

In that week, Halifax was full of scuttling people, cancelling their orders for milk or newspapers, stocking up on straw hats and other summer goods, taking their money out of the banks. All pleasures were kept in check, the better to enjoy the jamboree coming up.

Halifax was living in the future, and every day the *Courier* contained 'The Wakes Outlook', giving reports on all the places that the townsfolk might be heading for in the coming week. At Rhyl, bowling, yachting and golfing were in full swing. At Penzance, the outlook was good for holidays; glass steady, wind from the north. At Yarmouth, the Winter Gardens stood ready to accommodate the people if it rained. Military bands were on the beach. Fine weather was almost sure at Douglas, Isle of Man, and as for Blackpool . . .

Blackpool, we were told day after day, was 'ready', and the *Courier* gave a list of the 'Principal Attractions' in the town. On the Tuesday I read, while rolling into Rishworth, that these included the Singing Simpsons at the Tower and the Palace, and 'Henry Clarke and Young Leonard' at the Seashell. He was a fine ventriloquist but I wondered why he'd been mentioned and not the other, grander one, Monsieur Maurice. Perhaps he would take his turn as a Principal Attraction another day. He was a regular bill-topper at the Seashell, after all.

But Monsieur Maurice certainly wasn't mentioned the next day, as I sat reading the *Courier* around the back of the Albert

Cigar Factory, with George Ogden waiting beside me.

We were kicking our heels, sitting on a wall at the loading bay while the narky little fellow who dished out the damaged cigars kicked around boxes in search of half a dozen 'A's for each of us, George having said he would stand me them.

He was a queer sort about money. He'd already asked for a rent reduction, and half the time I expected him to put the bleed on. Yet he'd paid me for the window. Whenever I thought about George and money, I thought about the missing tickets, and that led on to thinking about all the other business.

He was about five feet away from me, wiping his face with a little handkerchief. We'd met at the Joint and walked up together after our day's work. I hadn't seen him in a while, for he'd stuck to his usual habit of staying out late. 'Blessed hot,' he was saying now.

It was smoky, too. From the amount of black stuff tumbling upwards from the Albert chimney, they seemed to be at the highest pitch of cigar-making for that day.

'What's the blooming fellow up to?' George fretted. 'You wouldn't think it too taxing to find a dozen cigars in a cigar factory.'

'But it's substandard ones we're after,' I reminded him.

'The difficulty in this place', George said, 'would lay in finding any other kind.'

George seemed out of sorts. He went back to his pacing, I to the *Courier* and the Wakes Outlook.

'"A telegram from the Isle of Man today"', I read out loud, '"says if the weather is fair, the nights are as enjoyable as the day. This arises from the . . . "' I hesitated a little over the next word, '"pellucidity of the atmosphere and the play of light on the mountains and sea."'

'*Mountains!*' said George, turning about to face me. 'On the Isle of Man! That's obviously written by some fellow who's never seen the Pyrenees.'

'You've seen 'em yourself, have you?'

'I might run over there one day,' he said, standing still and running his hands up and down his marvellous waistcoat.

'What are you doing for Wakes?' I said.

'Why, I'll be slaving in the booking hall of course,' he said. 'But that's my style, you know. When the common herd are gallivanting about, I'm getting my head down for a bit of serious work.' He nodded at me to drive home his point: 'And vice versa,' he added.

I'd been kicking my boots against the wall, and suddenly a clod of soot from Sowerby Bridge shed fell down from one of them. We both looked at it.

'Things'll be pretty slow after the first couple of days,' I said. 'Everyone'll be gone by then.'

'Yes,' said George, 'but then it's all stock-taking and putting the records of the whole year straight.'

Here was my opportunity. 'Did those missing tickets ever turn up?'

'Missing tickets, old man?'

'It was you that told me of it.'

'You should be on the halls,' he went on. 'A Man of Marvellous Memory. But it comes back to me now . . . No, they never did show up, and the devil of trouble was caused by it. No end of bombardments from Knowles.'

The cigar fellow put his head out of his little office and called: 'I've got a dozen 'A's here.'

We began making for his little room.

'The tickets for the Joint are sent along from Manchester, aren't they?' I asked George.

'That's the idea, old man.'

'The tickets that went missing: were they singles or returns? And where were they for?'

George blinked a few times. 'Can't just remember,' he said. 'Gosh! I'll be forgetting me own name next!'

'Did you hear about what happened to Lowther, the ticket inspector?'

'Fell off one rock and smashed his legs on another, didn't he? Out at Hebden Bridge? In the *mountains* they've got there! Well, I expect the fellow was canned.'

'What makes you think so?'

'The poor fellow's famous for it. How do you think he got to be so glum? It always takes you like that in the end, you know.'

The 'A's were pushed over towards us. George took one of the cigars out of its box, and rolled it under his nose.

'Do you have a light?' he asked the little cigar man.

'No,' replied the cigar man, rather angrily, 'and I don't have the bob you owe me for those smokes either.'

George began fishing in his waistcoat.

'I was at Hebden Bridge with the wife and a friend of the wife,' I said. 'I had sight of what happened, and I thought he was pushed. I chased the fellow I thought did it all the way to Manchester. I couldn't see his face, but I'm sure he must have been connected with tickets in some way. Do you have any notion who it might have been?'

This was the facer.

But George simply turned to the cigar man, saying: '*Two* shillings. I'm paying for this gentleman's half dozen as well.' He paid over the money and turned to me: 'You chased him to Manchester!' he exclaimed.

And now I felt he was joshing, or wanting to seem to be. 'I chased him to Hebden station and got on the same train. But I lost him at Manchester Victoria.'

We'd walked back out into the loading bay by now. 'Well,' said George, 'ain't you the dark horse?'

'Who do you think might have wanted to crown Lowther?' I asked him.

George stopped in the loading bay and his eyes went wide: 'There's absolutely hundreds that would,' he said. 'The fellow was a regular bastard.'

'He was on the train when the stone was found on the line,' I said. 'I wondered whether that might have been somebody's first crack at him.'

He was on the point at once. 'As to that, nobody knew Lowther's movements beforehand. So no wrecker could have guessed he was going to be on that train, and it'd be a damned queer way of trying to kill him, wouldn't it? I mean, talk about going round the houses.'

I knew the first part of this to be true, and the second part seemed the soundest of good sense. 'You know,' I said, 'every time I look at the Wakes Outlook, I expect to read, "It is pleasing to report that no grindstones have been found on the lines going into the resort."'

'I'd say you were becoming rather overwrought about the matter,' said George, who had the cigar in his mouth. 'Anyway,' he went on, 'as I've already mentioned to you, chances are they were going for the train that came along *after* – the regular Blackpool service. Cheerio, old chap.'

I watched him walk away across the empty, sunlit yard that lay behind the cigar factory. I'd not yet mentioned to him about the Socialist Mission telegram to the *Courier*. It came to me that George had described himself as a socialist, but I couldn't see him being in with that show. Besides, I was a socialist myself, of sorts.

Come to that (and this was a new thought), from all that the wife said, Robinson, late of Hind's Mill, might even be counted a socialist, of a toffy kind.

'I'm obliged to you for the cigars!' I called to George, and he raised his hand in a backwards wave.

His going off like that quite took the fun away from having bought the 'A's. Maybe he was just tired after his day's work. He did look jiggered, and seemed to be dragging his large shadow across the wide, dusty yard.

I'd meant to take him along to the Evening Star for a pint, and I decided to head in that direction anyway. On reaching Horton Street, I looked on the old warehouse wall for the Socialist Mission poster advertising the 'MEETING TO DISCUSS QUESTIONS'.

It was gone.

Chapter Twenty-two

'Scarborough', I read in the *Courier* the following midday, is 'delightfully sunny. The town is to be seen in its best summer garb, the variegated blossoms making it a veritable garden city.'

Well, I would be seeing for myself in three hours' time, train wreckers permitting. For I could no longer think of a train line stretching away clear, especially not for the length of time involved in a life of firing and driving. That was a forty-year touch, and nobody's luck holds out that long. I was beginning to wonder whether I had the pluck for the job.

But today I was on show, so I ought to look the part at least.

The engine was number 1008, the very first of Mr Aspinall's radial tank engines, which ought to make a talking point for the Robinson boy. It was lately in from Bradford, and now waited alongside the reserve platform at the Joint, having just come over from York with six carriages. I would talk over a few points about the engine with the boy, and then it would be time for Scarborough. Clive was about, but kept coming and going, 'seeing to bits of business'. He had on brand new boots, laced up at the side, which he couldn't walk without looking at.

Departure time for Scarborough was 10.32, and Robinson and his young son came walking down the spare platform towards 1008 at 9.45, as arranged by the wife over the telephone from the Mill.

Peter Robinson was younger than I'd expected – might not have been more than about fifty. He wore round glasses and had a schoolboy look. The other Robinson had the schoolboy look in spades, for he *was* a schoolboy, although on a day off. He was small and also wore glasses, and a loose green suit made from what I took to be the famous light cloth. He looked very free in the get up, and ready to lift off, like a greenfly. It was queer that Robinson should have kitted out his boy in the stuff that had caused his own downfall. His own suit was of the common run: black and heavy.

'Good morning . . . Mr Stringer, is it?' Robinson called up.

He was a little la-di-da. Not an out-and-out toff, though. I gave the lad a hand up onto the footplate; his father introduced him to me as Lance.

'Now what do we have here?' said young Lance Robinson, which rather knocked me. He was a very confident lad, as different from Arnold Dyson as could be.

'It's one, zero, zero, eight,' I said, 'a tank engine with the two-four-two wheel formation, built by Mr Aspinall – who I'm sure you've heard of – at the company's works at Horwich. You might like a trip to Horwich one day. It's beautifully laid out, with a little narrow-gauge railway running alongside the full-sized ones, to fetch and carry all the parts.'

I was yammering on, being a little nervous with the boy's father on hand.

'You're not the driver, are you?' said the boy.

I shook my head. 'Fireman,' I said.

'But I suppose you know all the controls just as well as the driver?'

'It would be a poor show if I didn't,' I said.

The boy looked down on the spare platform at the Joint, where he'd just been standing. His father grinned up at him. The boy turned to me. 'Would you say that "alighting" was getting on a thing or getting off?' he asked.

'Lance,' his father called up, 'you know very well which it is.' Then Robinson called to me, saying, 'I'm much obliged to you for doing this, Mr Stringer. Can I leave you at the boy's mercy for ten minutes?'

'That'll be quite all right, sir,' I said, and Peter Robinson walked away towards the station buildings.

Watching him go, the boy seemed worried. Not about

himself, but about his father. 'He'll be all right,' he said. 'I expect he'll have a seltzer on the station and read his paper. Father takes the *Manchester Guardian*, you know. It's best for business. *The Times* is hardly circulated where we live in St Anne's. What paper do you read?'

'The *Halifax Courier*,' I said.

'My father was in business here in Halifax,' said the boy. 'He was a partner.'

This wasn't lad's talk. 'Yes,' I said, 'but we must get on if we're to learn all about the engine –'

'He had the notion that people would want light suiting –'

'Now this handle', I said, 'controls the cylinder cocks.'

'It wasn't one of his better ideas,' said the boy.

'The cylinder cocks', I went on, 'are most important because –'

'I'm wearing the light suiting just now,' said the boy.

'Well,' I said, 'it does look nice and light. Now if you look here –'

'It's rational,' said the boy, simply.

I nodded, saying: 'Perhaps we'd better start with the fire.'

'But people don't want it.'

'Well, I expect they will in time,' I said.

'But it'll be too late for Dad – I mean Father,' said the boy.

'The cylinder cocks', I said firmly, 'allow the steam into and out of the cylinders, and you must always remember to open them before moving the engine.'

'And what happens if you don't?'

'Then the piston would push the condensed water, which would knock the end out of the cylinder bore.'

The boy gave a little jump at this. 'I bet you'd catch it if you let that happen,' he said.

'Yes,' I said, 'you certainly would.'

'What *would* become of you if you let that happen?'

'If you were an engine man? And you let *that* happen?'

Lance Robinson nodded, eagerly asking, 'Would you be stood down?'

The kid was stuck on the question of people being sacked.

'It depends,' I said. 'It would depend what other daft things you'd done in the past. The shed superintendent would be down on you like a ton of coal though, no question of that. Now we come to the regulator,' I went on. 'There's a real art to controlling it, and the motto is –'

'What can a driver work his way up to?' said the boy.

'Well, most just stay driving,' I said. 'They like it, you see. But others go on to different things: traffic management in the company offices, engineering. There's lots you can put in for.'

'If a driver came to our house, would he come in at the tradesman's entrance?'

'Why would an engine driver go to your house?'

'Oh I don't know. Dad's train mad as well, you see. He's got hundreds of *Bradshaw's* all lined up in the dining room.'

I pictured again the grindstone on the line. I turned to the boy. '*Has* an engine driver ever been to your house?'

'Oh, I don't know,' said the boy. 'I shouldn't think so. What's that?'

He was pointing at the pressure gauge.

'That tells you the steam pressure,' I said, 'how much *pushing force* you've got.'

I had a case against Robinson in my head, of course, but until now it had looked rather sick. There'd been a pretty solid row at Hind's that had ended with him being stood down from the company – all just before the stone was put on the line. According to the wife, Peter Robinson owned a car, and a car had been racing along beside us that day. If it wasn't just hooligan's work, then the stone had been put on the line by someone who knew Hind's Mill, or someone who knew the railways, or better still both. And here was Robinson, coming up strongly on both counts.

The boy, Lance, was looking up at me.

'A working head of steam,' I said, 'on a fair-sized engine would generally be about two hundred pounds to the square inch. Now you need a very hot fire to get it up to that.'

'How hot?' asked the boy.

I told him to stand back, and I opened the fire door. The boy stepped further back when he felt the fire.

'Hotter than *that*,' I said, and I closed the fire door.

'Can I take another squint in there?' he said.

I liked the kid. He didn't look it, but he was game. I opened the door once again, and we watched the rolling, orange flames.

'It's just a different world,' said the kid, and whether he meant inside the fire or the engine-driving life I couldn't say.

'I wear spectacles as you can see,' said the boy. 'Would that stop me driving engines?'

'No,' I said. The true answer was 'yes', but it hardly mattered. The kid was far too posh ever to be on the footplate.

'Is it dangerous to work on engines?' he asked.

'Very,' I said, and I could not help trying a little fishing. 'There's wreckers,' I said, 'for one thing.'

'There was something put on a line at Whit,' said the boy. 'You had to clap the brake on and a lady was killed.'

'How do you know?' I asked, fast, but then I realised he might very *well* know.

'Because it was the mill where Father was a director – it was their Whit excursion to Blackpool.'

I now abandoned the engine-driving lesson. Careful questions were wanted, and I decided I would fare better with the kid if I did not let on that I'd been firing the engine on that occasion.

'Would you mind telling me what else you know about it?'

'It was reported in the Blackpool paper, which we see at St Anne's, being just a little way along the road, and Father cut out the article.'

'Did he point it out to you himself?'

'No, Agnes saw him reading it – saw him cutting it out too.'

'Agnes?'

'Our maid. We used to have two, but she's the only one left. We had a washerwoman on Mondays, and she's had to go too; and we had a gardener, and he's gone because the garden's gone. Well, we're selling the paddock at any rate. My pocket money's been cut down from half a crown a week to sixpence, but Father says there'll be a dividend for good schoolwork.'

I was thinking on. Robinson had certainly been hit hard by losing his place at Hind's.

'I'm fourteenth in Latin,' the boy was saying, and I didn't know whether that was supposed to be good or bad, but I nodded at him and smiled.

'He can do better than fourteenth at Latin,' came his father's voice from the platform. 'But how is he at engines?'

'He's not scared of the fire, sir,' I called down, 'so he's off to a very good start.'

'Call me Peter,' said Robinson, which as we both knew meant that from now on I would call him nothing at all.

The boy climbed down to his father, and I altered my plan. I would just *get* to it. 'I'd like to thank you for taking on my wife at Hind's,' I said.

'Anyone would have,' he said. 'It was one of the last things I did there, and one of the best. Lydia is a very fine young woman. There's a lot of steam in her, you know.'

'I know,' I said. 'It's none of my business,' I continued, leaving a pause where there should have been a 'sir', 'but did you happen to know that I was firing on the excursion when the trip was halted?'

Robinson moved the *Manchester Guardian* from being under his left arm to being under his right arm. 'No, I didn't,' he said, 'because I'd already started my paper war with the other two partners by then, and was cut off from all business. We were quite at loggerheads, Jim, with everything going through the lawyers, so you see I couldn't have gone off on a jolly with them.'

'The Whit excursion was your idea, as I understand it, sir?' And the 'sir' came out of nerves because I knew I was going in strong.

219

Robinson nodded. 'I can claim the credit for that, I think. There'd always been the Wakes Week trip of course, but I thought: it's fifty-five hours a week in the mill, fifty weeks a year. Why not have a respite at Whit as well, when the weather's warming up and the fun is just nicely getting going at Blackpool?' He smiled and moved the *Manchester Guardian* back to the arm it had been under before. 'Of course it *had* to be Blackpool,' he added.

Lance Robinson was by now holding his father's hand, and for some reason staring directly up at the glass canopy of the station roof.

'Do you have any ideas about the stone that was placed on the line, Jim?' said Robinson. 'I'm rather cut off out there at St Anne's. Nobody's been brought in for it, as I understand?'

'I do have a few ideas,' I said. 'Yes.'

'He thinks it was wreckers,' said the boy, still looking up.

Mr Robinson looked at me, wanting more. He touched his glasses.

'That's it,' I said.

'It puts me in a rage to think of it,' he said. 'What's the penalty for blocking the track?'

'They give it to you hot,' I said. 'It's penal servitude for life at the maximum.'

Now where that came from, I couldn't have said, but I knew it was right. 'And that's only for placing the obstruction,' I went on. 'If someone's killed it's a hanging matter, I suppose.'

'I knew the one that was killed,' said Robinson. 'Well, very slightly.'

'Margaret Dyson?'

He nodded. 'That's it. She was a good sort.'

He was not talking like a killer now, I had to admit. I found myself taking to the fellow, just as the wife had. Like his boy, he looked the milksop, but he had ideas and he put them into effect. He had become an enemy of the two Hinds, who'd pitched him out of the business, but not an enemy of the work people themselves. He seemed to be all *for* them.

'Thank you again for giving the boy a tour of the engine,' he said. 'Give my best regards to your wife, and I hope we meet again soon.'

I told him that I hoped so too, and waved to him and the boy, with my head buzzing.

Chapter Twenty-three

Ten minutes later Clive was walking towards 1008, and the damn carpet bag was in his hand again. He kept looking down at his boots as he got near. Before climbing up, he put his oil can on the footplate, and in my mind's eye it was the Bancroft's Hair Restorer that was being slammed down there.

He pulled himself up onto the footplate. New boots, poacher's pockets (with a copy of the *Courier* sticking out of one of them), kerchief crossed and held in place by . . . what? By nothing. Just like old Napoleon's. 'Don't look old,' said the slogan on the Bancroft's bottles, and Clive didn't, I had to agree.

'Who was the kid in the green coat?' Clive asked, as he stuffed the carpet bag in the locker.

I told him he was the son of a man who used to be a governor at Hind's Mill.

'Oh yes? In fancy dress was he?'

'That was light suiting,' I said, 'made by Hind's Mill. Well, it was for a while, until his old man was stood down over it.'

'I'm not surprised.'

'It's nice and cool to wear in the hot months.'

'What's the point of that?'

'Well, you know, coolness . . . in the hot months.'

Clive had finished stowing away the bag. He turned to me and frowned. 'In summer,' he said, 'you get hot, and that's all about it. A light suit's no good. It won't hold its shape.' He reached into his pocket and took out his copy of the *Courier*. But it wasn't the *Courier*. It was the York paper, the *Yorkshire Evening Press*. 'It was left on this engine this morning,' Clive explained. He was pointing at a short article, saying: 'Here's a turn up . . . I don't think.'

'Excursion Engine Driver Killed,' I read, and all the breath stopped on my lips.

> Mr Arthur Billington, who for many years had been employed as an engine driver at York by the North Eastern Railway, died yesterday of a head injury sustained while riding to York station on his bicycle. It is not clear what really happened. Some witnesses state that Mr Billington's bicycle simply capsized, others that he struck a pedestrian who was nowhere to be found after the event. Mr Billington was on his way to the locomotive shed at York, where he was booked to take a train carrying excursionists to Scarborough.

'It's the fucking wreckers again!' I said. 'They're out to get the Scarborough excursions as well as the Blackpool ones, and any bugger connected with them. There was the tree on the line before Malton, and now this . . .'

Clive, of course was having *none*. 'If that bloke Billington rode a push rod in the same way as he drove an engine, he was a liability to himself and others.' He was looking in his leather pocketbook, checking the time of departure.

I said: 'We're taking on a pilot from York, I suppose?'

He shook his head. 'I've just had a wire sent to say we'll do without.'

'But do you know the road?'

I was sounding rather old womanish, I knew, but I kept picturing Paul, the socialist missionary, stepping in front of the bicycle of Arthur Billington.

Everything, it seemed, was now put in my way to test my pluck, and to spoil what, in any other summer, could have been a happy prospect: a pleasant run to Scarborough, with no need to work the engine back, for we were to return 'on the cushions' once again.

We were put into platform four, where Knowles's blackboard announcing the excursion waited. The stationmaster himself, I noticed, was on platform three, speaking to one of his deputies and pointing to a weed growing down by the line.

'I would like to see lawnmower applied to that directly,' he was saying. 'And liberally, mind you. And anywhere else you see similar. You know where the bottle of the stuff's kept?'

We coupled up to a rake of six rattlers. I found Reuben Booth in the last one, asleep in his guard's part, which in looks was well below third class. He was sitting in a chair that had one arm broken off – probably chucked into the stove in those far-off days of cold. Reuben's gold coat was hanging over the back of the chair. His face disappeared into the grey-ness of his beard when he slept, but as soon as he heard my boots scrape over the dust on the floor of the van, he stood up, barking out: 'One hundred and fifty souls.'

The vacuum brake was tested, and we pulled away into the sun with half the hundred and fifty hanging out of the win-dows and Clive winding back the reverser, saying, 'There are some very well set-up lasses on this train,' for he'd had a good look up and down.

The sunshine, when we came out into it, was all golden slowness like treacle. We rolled along into the Beacon Hill Tunnel, with the coolness and the happy screams, then swept back out into the brightness.

After Bradford, Clive took an envelope from one of his poacher's pockets and passed it over. Inside was the medal. On one side of it was the company badge that was on the ten-ders of all the engines: the red rose of Lancashire and the white rose of Yorkshire, together with the shields of the Houses of Lancaster and York. On the reverse were the words 'Presented to C. Carter, engine driver, for extraordinary vigi-lance and promptitude in stopping his engine on June 11th, Whit Sunday, 1905.'

'It's a bobby dazzler, is that,' I said, handing it back, and thinking: they knocked that out in double-quick time.

Clive nodded. 'Mind you,' he said, putting the medal back in his pocket, 'I'd rather have had a day off.'

He'd said that before about the medal. It was as if he was a little embarrassed over it.

———◦———

It felt lonely to be going beyond York without a pilot, and I almost missed the shouting of the late Billington. We were feeling our way, so to speak, across foreign territory, and I had my eye out for every signal from then on, even the ones on Clive's side. The difficult signal spot was the one at Kirkham Abbey, as I knew from the last Scarborough run. And it was here that the branch had fallen. Again the name Kirkham Abbey made me nervous, putting me in mind of that other Kirkham, on the road to Blackpool where we'd come to grief.

We were flashing along at about fifty as we came up to the distant signal at Kirkham Abbey. It was off as before, so we kept on running.

'Now slow for the home,' I heard myself calling out to Clive, which was like something that might happen in a dream – a fireman giving orders to his driver. Clive didn't seem to mind though. That medal had been a real tonic for him, or maybe it was the new boots. He was looking down at these now as he reached up to the brake, but something was amiss with one of the boots – a dab of soot or a particle of coal lodged in the laces.

The broken buildings of the abbey shot into place alongside us: a great and grave thing, a giant tombstone in many instalments.

'Brake!' I yelled.

The movement from hand to boot was halted; the hand went up, brushing the brake handle as much as was needed. 'Keep your hair on,' said Clive.

'Sorry,' I said.

The home signal appeared, peeking from the trees. It was off – just as it ought to've been – and we rumbled over the

225

level crossing, where a motorcar stood waiting at the gate.

'You wait,' yelled Clive as we passed it by; 'it's us that'll be stopping for *them* before long!' He grinned at me, but I couldn't grin back, for I was fretting about whether I was up to the mark for an engine man.

As we crashed and rocked over the Xs into the excursion platforms, Clive said: 'You're all of a jump. Shall I stand you a pint?'

'But you've got your bag in the locker,' I said. 'Doesn't that mean you're sneaking off like before?'

We'd come to a stand now. Clive destroyed the vacuum while thinking over what I'd said. Then he decided to grin. 'I've time for a pint beforehand,' he said, eventually.

After a quick word with Reuben, who was heading directly back to the Joint, we ran the engine into the Scarborough shed. There were two fragments of yellow soap in the enginemen's lobby this time, so we were both able to get tolerably clean. Clive kept his carpet bag by him at all times.

We had a pint in a pub near the shed, and I was sitting there out of sorts, too hot, and wondering whether I'd be in a funk over obstacles on the line for the rest of my days. What bothered me especially was that next week was Wakes. *Would* we be given the Hind's excursion run once again? Then another thought came: would we be given the Highflyer for a second time?

Clive said, 'Sup up, we're off.'

'We?' I said.

'You want bucking up,' he said.

So we stepped out of the pub into the booming blue of the Scarborough day. The motor charabancs parked along the station were all shaking with their engines on, panting like horses. Looking down at his new boots, and with his carpet bag in his hand, Clive began to walk. I watched him go and he called out, 'Look sharp!' so I started to follow.

We didn't walk down the Valley Road, where Scarborough became the Garden City, but away from the sea and into some side streets that the sun didn't suit. We came to a row of dark shops selling gloomy things like sideboards, and one of the businesses was a tailor's.

Well, I ought to have guessed. There was a sign above the door, in small red letters: 'WINTERBOTTOM: CASH TAYLOR'. Clive pushed the door, and the bell rang very loudly, but Winterbottom was just on the other side of it, waiting. He stood up and a cricketing paper fell to the floor. He was a small, dark man with side whiskers which he for some reason wouldn't let meet to form a beard. His shop was small and so dark after the brightness of the day that blue smudges floated before my eyes as I looked about it.

'Good afternoon, gentlemen,' he said; then, recognising Clive: 'Mr Carter! Have you come in on an engine?'

'Nay,' said Clive. 'Walked it. All the way from Halifax!'

They both laughed at that. I knew right off that Clive and the tailor were thick with each other. Clive introduced me to Winterbottom, saying: 'This fellow needs a suit.'

'Working suit?' asked Winterbottom, half speaking to Clive and half to me.

'A Sunday suit,' said Clive, 'that'll come in for work later.'

'Wear it out,' said Winterbottom, 'then wear it *out!*'

'He always says that,' Clive said to me.

'To measure or ready-made?' asked Winterbottom.

'I can't run to tailoring,' I said straight away.

'Should be no trouble to fit off the peg,' said Winterbottom, eyeing me up and down: 'the greyhound breed!'

'That's another thing he always says,' said Clive, 'so don't get swell-headed.'

Winterbottom walked smartly towards a line of hanging black suits, then went clean through them and disappeared.

He came back a moment later with half a dozen suits over one arm. He let one of the coats – a blue one – dangle down. Clive shook his head at it, and Winterbottom let it fall to the floor, the trousers and waistcoat too. He held up another coat, biscuit coloured this one. It was the same coat as Clive's.

'Poacher's pockets!' I exclaimed, and felt foolish.

'Norfolk jacket,' said Winterbottom.

Clive was shaking his head. 'Won't do,' he said, which I thought rum, since it did very well for him.

The next coat Clive liked, and so did I. It was blue, of course, loose and comfortable-looking, and not too heavy. It came with turned-up trousers and there was a choice of two waistcoats to go with. Winterbottom held up the two: one had more pockets than the other – a lot more. It was a complicated sort of waistcoat, like George Ogden's.

'I'll try that one,' I said, pointing to it.

I went into the little changing room and when I came out Winterbottom was saying something to Clive and pointing me towards the mirror. He and Clive stood behind me, looking on, which stopped me looking at myself. So I put the whole thing on to them. 'What do you think?'

'Rather flattering, sir,' said Winterbottom.

I expected Clive to put in his motto with 'He always says that,' but he didn't. This was no joking matter. The suit *was* rather fetching. I could see myself driving engines in this, big ones at that, and meeting no obstructions as I did so. I could also see myself at the University of Liverpool, chatting to Mr Aspinall himself about railway matters.

'What weight is the cloth?' I asked.

'Give over,' said Clive, 'you barmpot.'

'Eighteen ounce,' said Winterbottom, 'a good summer weight.'

'I prefer this sort of light suiting,' I said.

'Quite so, sir,' said Winterbottom.

'Just out of interest,' I said, 'would you ever think of buying cloth as low as twelve ounces?'

'No,' said Winterbottom.

After a bit more fancying myself in the mirror, I asked the cost.

'Guinea suit,' said Winterbottom. 'I have a tie in brown that'll set it off to a tee,' he added, before disappearing once more into the line of coats.

'Tell him the lining feels a little rucked at the shoulder,' said Clive when he'd gone.

'But it isn't,' I said, 'well I don't think it is, any road.'

'No,' said Clive, 'but he'll know what you mean.'

'What *will* I mean?' I said.

'That you want a little off.'

'He feels it's a little caught under the shoulder,' said Clive when Winterbottom came back.

'A pound and sixpence,' said Winterbottom double-quick, before adding, 'It's already discounted, you know.' He then let a brown necktie dangle down.

'No . . .' I said. 'No thanks.' I certainly didn't want the necktie, but the question was the suit.

Winterbottom could see me thinking things over. 'Do you want it on HP?' he said.

'He's trying to work out what the missus'd say,' said Clive, grinning, and he had *that* right, although of course I wouldn't let on.

The wife wanted me to progress, and a good suit might come in there. She liked what was down-to-date, and turn-ups were the latest thing in trousers. Then again we were meant to be putting the coppers aside for the Special Piano.

I said I wasn't sure, that I would think on, and Winterbottom wasn't put out in the least. He just cut me off completely. Turning to Clive, he said something I couldn't quite catch, and pointed to the carpet bag.

I dawdled off to the changing room, trying to cotton on to what was being said, but all I heard was the word 'snowdrop'.

Five minutes later I was out in the street once more with Clive. 'You'll regret that,' he said. 'It did wonders for you.'

'I can always come back for it,' I said, but Clive wouldn't have it.

'It'll be gone in a flash,' he said. 'Top summer wear, that is.' He walked off with a wave of his free hand and I didn't have the brass neck to follow him this time. Before turning a corner he called back once more: 'Did wonders for you, that suit!'

I wandered back to the station and thought about taking the first train for Halifax, but I had a new sort of superstition about seeing the sea in a seaside town. If I didn't see it, there might be a stone placed on the line. So I walked down the Valley Road past the gardens in bloom. The same sort of plant came up over and again: a bush with long white flowers like railway signals. Wherever it grew, folk stood admiring it.

I turned to my left, and saw a giant white 'S', and it was the first letter of 'SNOWDROP LAUNDRY' – the words were painted on the wall of an end-terrace. A line of smoke came out of the chimney, but disappeared after a second, put to shame by the bright sea air.

That was where Clive had been heading with his bag. I wondered whether he was inside at that moment. I hung about outside the front door for a while, then gave it up and walked back towards the Valley Road and the sea view, feeling blue.

The sea didn't end, and so you felt useless looking at it. You could only do *little* things by comparison. George and Clive knew that, and the one little thing they did was cut a dash in the world. I had thought that driving and firing engines might be the thing, for it gave the freedom of flying, but I now could not think of the job without feelings of anxiety.

I turned away from the sea.

With all of Scarborough before me and the whole world in holiday mood, I could think of nothing to do but go back home.

I set off back up the Valley Road in my heavy boots, aiming for the station, thinking of Arthur Billington. In a holiday town, people go slowly towards the railway stations but they always come out of them fast, and so I was not surprised to see a pretty woman moving fast away from the railway station. I almost called out to her when it struck me that I knew her, but I buttoned my lip in time, for I did not know her at all, really, but had only seen her once at the Joint.

It was Emma Knowles, the stationmaster's beautiful wife.

Chapter Twenty-four

On the Friday before Wakes, Halifax was beginning to empty out. There was only one other man drinking in the Evening Star. The three lonely billiard balls were set out, but the chance of any sport seemed further off than ever. The *Courier* was bursting with late advertisements for wood and cane trunks, portmanteaus and other holiday goods.

Circumstances dictated a couple of pints after a very hot run that day – Southport and back. Southport was the second biggest holiday place after Blackpool. Taking a pull on my beer, I thought of Clive and Emma Knowles. What it totted up to was this: they had both been in Scarborough on the same day, and Scarborough held many people, especially now that all sunshine records were being broken.

Then I brought Blackpool into my mind's eye. Blackpool was waiting, and it was waiting for me.

I'd seen the notices for the coming Sunday and knew that the Hind's Mill Wakes excursion was to be taken there by Clive and myself. There'd been a fair chance it might be another crew, for almost all links were put onto excursions in Wakes, but in a way I was glad it had fallen to us. I wanted to see that line running clear across the Fylde with no obstructions placed, and the same folk as before riding behind.

I put the peg in after two, bought a bottle of Special Cola for the wife, and carried on up Horton Street, which was empty.

Towards the top of the street, I turned and doubled back towards the wall of the old warehouse. There was a new bill in place of the the Socialist Mission poster: 'All who suffer from the heat should add a few drops of Condy's Fluid to the Daily Bath.'

I thought of Emma Knowles in the bath as I passed by the open door of the Imperial. The fans were working away, spinning and rocking, but there were more waiters than toffs in there.

I walked fast to Back Hill Street so as to keep the Special Cola cool, and I was still moving fast as I stepped through the front door, so the shock of what I saw hit me with main force: a soot-clarted man on the floor wrestling with the continental stove. The wife was standing behind him with her arms hanging loose, and the strangest look on her face. There was a bottle of castor oil on the old mantelshelf, I noticed, as the sooty man on the floor said, 'How do.'

'You've caught on,' I said to the wife, 'you're pregnant?' I whispered because of the stove man, but with the word came the whole future, revealed all in a moment.

'Well, you needn't look like that,' said the wife.

'Like what? This is the way fellows always look when they get that kind of news.'

I took her through to the scullery, and, closing the door behind us, kissed her and handed over the bottle. 'It's going to have to be *Extra* Special Cola from now on,' I said.

'You feel all right about it then?' she said.

'Aye,' I said.

'Aye?' she said back, slowly.

'Not that it isn't a shock,' I said. 'I mean, so much for *How to Check Family Increase*.'

'Well,' she said, 'they say their methods are not perfect.'

'Do they now? They're right about that, at any rate.'

She was quiet, looking sideways. The man in the other room sounded as if he was clattering at the stove with a hammer. It was not a scientific business, getting those articles out.

'And I'll tell you this again for nothing,' I said. 'You're not going on the Hind's Mill excursion to Blackpool.'

She nodded very quietly, and I was just thinking that this was not like the wife at all, when she suddenly became her old self once more. 'I *am* going on the excursion to Blackpool,' she began, 'although only for one day. And why must I go to the Infirmary? I am not in the least infirm. Tomorrow I am to see a midwife recommended by the Guild. She's nearby and she has all the certificates. It will cost a shilling, and she will measure my pelvis.'

'Good,' I said. Why?'

'To make sure the baby will fit.'

'Well,' I said, 'it had *better* do. What happens if it won't? I mean it would be a rum go if it didn't, wouldn't you say?'

'At twenty-eight weeks,' said the wife, ignoring me, 'I will go up to the hospital and I will have regular checks after that to term. Meanwhile we must put away little bits of tea, sugar, and lay in little stores for the time. The Guild has lectures coming up on care of maternity, and I will go to those, and you might like to come along yourself.'

'I *might*.' I said.

'We will have a doctor at the birth, and as well as an ordinary fireplace instead of the stove, we must have another gas mantel put into the bedroom in case the baby comes at night and I tear, and need to be sown.'

'Bloody hell,' I said, and just then the stove man put his head around the door.

'It's out,' he said. 'Where do you want it?'

'Oh, in the yard,' said the wife.

He came back a moment later, lugging the stove, and we followed him into the yard. It was hotter out than in. The sky was ink and blue, with high streaks of black from the last chimneys working before Wakes. The wife was at the tub we'd got out there.

'The mint's starting to come up as well,' she said, bending over the tub.

'You shouldn't do that,' I said.

'What?'

'Bend over. And you're to keep your hands over your head whenever possible.'

'You barmpot,' said the wife. She was looking at the mint

233

again. 'They say it takes over the whole garden eventually.'

Just then the stove man let the stove fall, and it crashed onto its side next to the mangle and the outside privy.

'I don't think you have to worry too much on that score at any rate,' I said.

I looked at the stove. Now we would have a proper fireplace, which was safer for children if properly guarded, and would make the house more of a home. I paid the stove man and he went off. He would be back after a few weeks to put in a fireplace under the old mantel.

'Now you must look to your diet,' I said to the wife when the fellow had gone, and we were back inside the house. 'You're to eat plenty of vegetables and a lot of bone food – bread, you know, for the calcium – and on no account must you take intoxicants, which you don't do anyway of course, which reminds me, I wouldn't half like a bottle of beer. And you are to *sit down*,' I said, as I myself sat down on the sofa in the parlour, for the tremendous shock of the news was only now beginning to take hold.

Chapter Twenty-five

Wakes proper started on the Sunday.

The night before, I dreamt I was on an engine riding through open country that was half real and half a map. Preston was big capital letters lying spread over fields, then came the little villages of Salwick and Kirkham, with curly Ks in their names. On the very edge of the map was Blackpool with the capital letters again, these stretching out into the sea, which was nothing but a few squiggly lines, but dangerous all the same.

I woke at four, and so did the wife. She was excited about the Hind's trip. I tried again to talk her out of going, saying, 'It's all just skylarking, you know. You wouldn't care for it.'

'What do you take me for?' she said. Then we began to do something else, for stopping family increase could now go by the board.

Love-making eases anxieties, but not for long, and I was back to my old state of mind when, at half-past five in the morning, I wrote my name in the book that lay on its own table in John Ellerton's office at Sowerby Bridge shed.

It was not yet hot, and the weekly notices pinned to the wall were moving in the breeze from the open door. Every so often the breeze would increase, the door would bang, and a great surge of burning-coal smell and smoke would come in, for the engines were all being prepared outside, looking like a range of volcanoes. The usual timetables went to pot in Wakes. Half the normal trains in and out of Halifax didn't run, and the crews were put onto excursions instead.

Ellerton himself was at his high desk, drawing lines with a ruler in his fast and jolly way. He seemed to be enjoying the way the ruler worked, the perfect straightness of it over and over. The telegraph needle was clicking, but it must have been something safe to ignore, for he *was* ignoring it.

'You're in luck again over the Hind's,' he said, as he drew his lines.

'How's that?' I said. But I knew.

'Come along with me,' he said, and he stepped out from behind his desk, still holding his precious ruler. We walked out of the office and onto the barrow boards that crossed the tracks going into the shed.

It was a blue-grey morning. Night was going, but the engines around the shed were putting out their own darkness. I saw the Highflyer before John pointed at it with his ruler. Number 1418 – the very same beast as before: black but bright, the long, high boiler stretching out over the seven-foot driving wheels. It looked like an arrow in a bow, waiting to be fired. A cleaner with a long-handled brush walked carefully along the boiler frame, like a man on a mountain precipice. One long thin bootlace of smoke was winding out of the chimney.

'Where did that bastard come from?' I said.

John Ellerton laughed. 'It was fixed up at Horwich Works. Distant Control sent it down to us.'

'But why?'

'Well,' he said, 'why do they do anything? Orders from Manchester.'

'Who in Manchester?'

'Traffic manager – Outdoor Locomotive Office. Who else would it be?'

'What's his name?'

'Hasn't got a name,' said John, who was playing with his ruler, looking a little agitated at this bombardment. He wanted to get back to drawing straight lines.

'How's that?' I said.

'When I say "Traffic Manager" I mean Traffic Manager's *office*, and there's dozens in there.'

'The first time they sent us a Highflyer it was for Hind's Mill *Whit* excursion to Blackpool.'

John Ellerton nodded. A rush of tinsel sparks came spinning up from the Flyer's chimney.

'Now they send it for only the second time,' I went on, 'and it's Hind's Mill once again.'

Ellerton gave a big grin at this. 'What do you reckon's going on then?'

'I don't know.'

'Well,' said John, 'nor do I. Unless *nothing* is.'

'But what if someone's trying to get shot of that particular engine?'

'You're getting cranky in your old age,' said Ellerton.

'Has a grindstone gone missing from this yard lately?' I asked him.

John Ellerton just pulled a face.

We were at the front end of 1418 by now. Front bogey, guard plates . . . all good as new, as if nothing had happened. This was the virtue of blackness as a colour.

'Look here,' said John Ellerton, 'I put in for an engine for an excursion, they send me one. Manchester doesn't know it's for Hind's – they just want to keep all the engines working all the time. The Highflyers mostly work express, Liverpool to Manchester, but if it happens that one comes over to this side of the Pennines, they don't send it back light. They send it back on a job.'

I nodded, looking down. I knew for certain the wreckers would be back today, but I could say no more to Ellerton.

'You can put up some bloody good running in that engine. There's fellows would kill to be on it,' he added, and it was as near as he'd come to giving me an earwigging.

I saw Clive walking over the barrow boards towards us, carrying his snap tin and oil can, and looking down from time to time at his feet.

'Smart boots, he's got,' said Ellerton.

'They're new on,' I said, miserably. 'I believe he's bought them on the strength of his medal.'

Or was it on the strength of Emma Knowles?

237

With Clive still making his way across the front of the shed towards the engine, I climbed up onto the footplate just as the cleaner who'd lit the fire climbed down the other side. He, or somebody, had left an old *Courier* on the sandbox. There'd been a *Courier* left in exactly the same spot before our last run on 1418. I looked down at it: 'DONEGAL ELECTION, THIS DAY'S TELEGRAMS'. I opened the fire door and pitched it into the flames, where it whirled in a fiery circle, then disappeared. I turned to the locker and took out the ambulance box. There was the book again: *What to Do in an Emergency* by Dr N. Kenrick, F.R.S.E. This too I shied into the flames.

When Clive came up, I said, 'Rather queer, this business, en't it?'

'What's queer?'

'The two of us getting this engine again?'

Clive just shrugged. 'Luck of the draw,' he said, and began searching in his pocket for his leather book, where the time of departure from the Joint was written down. He wasn't bothered about where engines came from, only where he was taking them to.

'What's time of departure?' I asked him.

'Eight-nineteen,' he said. 'Ring a bell does it?'

It had been eight-nineteen last time.

We worked on for a while. Clive walked to the front of the engine to inspect the repair. Every so often there'd be a great bark of steam, like a gun going off, then more gunshot sounds and another engine would be out alongside us. Nothing would be left in the shed today, the first day of Wakes. Presently Clive walked off into the shed and came back with a kid who started putting the lozenge pattern on the buffer plates.

'She looks in fine fettle,' he said when the kid had finished and was walking away with Clive's tanner in his pocket.

'Will you be taking her a bit more steadily this time?' I asked as we both stood on the rails looking up at 1418.

'You're not in a funk are you?'

'I'll give you steam for whatever running you want,' I said, 'but if the wreckers were out to get someone from Hind's Mill, or *everyone* from Hind's Mill, then this'll be the day they'll try again.'

'If it comes to that, maybe they're out to get you,' he said, 'in which case you'll *never* rest easy.'

Or *you*, I thought.

I saw John Ellerton walking over to us again and he looked different. It was the first time I'd seen him not smiling or not ready to smile. He called up to us: 'You blokes,' he said. 'It's a bugger, is this, but I've just been speaking on the telephone to the fellow from the *Courier* – the reporter –'

'I bloody *knew* it,' I said. 'They've heard from the Socialist Mission again?'

Ellerton nodded, and even he looked pretty cut up. 'Now, he says the cops have not been able to dig up anything about this lot, and they're still of opinion it's a bluff.'

'But what did the message say?' I asked Ellerton.

Clive was looking down at his new boots.

'Bit of blather,' said Ellerton, 'but really just this: no excursions to run in Halifax Wakes.'

'But they will run, won't they?' I said.

'Of course they bloody will,' said Ellerton, and he turned on his heel.

Clive looked at me and grinned: 'That'll teach you to talk to strange blokes in pubs,' he said.

I shouted after Ellerton, 'Did they mention a fellow called Billington, an engine man killed at York?'

But I don't think he heard.

Chapter Twenty-six

At the Joint, originality was at a premium: everyone was doing the same as before. I wanted to shout out distracting things, to check the heavy programme of entraining and luggage loading.

We'd been put into platform three once more, where Knowles's blackboard again stood, reading: 'SPECIAL TRAIN, SUNDAY 9TH JULY, HIND'S MILL, WAKES WEEK EXCURSION TO BLACKPOOL', with masses of underlining beneath. Stationmaster Knowles was watching from the far end of the platform, the back end of the train.

To make things different, to give the kaleidoscope a shake, I jumped down from the footplate and took a turn along the platform, just as the first excursionists were climbing up. On my stroll, I struck other novelties. There were seven rattlers as before, but this time all third class. The Hinds, father and son, would not be coming along. And there was no Martin Lowther patrolling the train with a face like yesterday, ticket nippers at the ready. At the end of the train, I nodded to Knowles, who half nodded back then turned on his heel and walked off.

I looked back along to the engine. Clive was standing by it, in his special place, where he could be looked at and admired; glancing down sometimes at his new boots, then up at the waves of happy excursionists, keeping his eye out for the pretty ones as they came running over the footbridge, tumbling down the steps and searching out their compartments along the platform, all sporting their white rosettes. Another tea at the Tower was evidently in store.

There was a banging of doors, laughing and shouting. Two of the trippers were at the cream-biscuit machine once again, rattling the little metal drawers that should have opened and never did.

Some new posters of Blackpool had appeared along the platform: half a dozen all the same, with the beach looking like a mustard plaster, the Tower brighter, friendlier and not so frightening as when you were up close, and the slogan running along underneath: 'BLACKPOOL HOLDS PERENNIAL DELIGHTS'.

The luggage went into the place next to the guard's part, and here was another difference. Far more goods were for the van than before, this being a whole week away. Reuben Booth was in charge of the loading, or maybe he was just getting in the way of it. He had all on to check the boxes the porters were pitching in.

I walked back to 1418, and to Clive. Reuben was coming up, too.

'Five hundred and one souls . . . two hundred and twenty tons,' he said. The tonnage was the same as before, the extra Third in place of the First making no difference. The numbers were a little down. Well, not everybody could get away for a whole week. And then of course Margaret Dyson was dead, her boy in the orphanage.

Now Clive was giving me his special happy nod, meaning look at the doxies, and there was the wife, walking hand in hand along the platform with Cicely Braithwaite.

'It's the wife,' I said. 'I think I told you she'd got a start in the office at Hind's.'

'Which one's she?' Clive asked, double-quick.

'The beautiful one,' I said, 'what do you expect?'

'Well now,' he said, 'they're both rather handsome.'

'The one on the right,' I said, as the wife and Cicely stopped about three carriages down. They both wore the white rosettes.

The wife and Cicely spotted me, and gave a wave as they climbed up into their compartment.

'Will they not come and take a look at the engine?' asked Clive.

'No point asking the wife,' I said. 'She thinks all engines are mucky, smelly things.'

Clive frowned. There had been no takers at all so far for his fancily polished buffers. 'I hope you've explained to her that they're cleaned from top to bottom for about six hours at the start of every working day?'

'Oh yes,' I said; 'more than you can say for our house, that is.'

As the Hind's excursionists continued to climb aboard, I opened the firehole door and put on more coal. The wife was on the train now and, short of main force, there was nothing I could do about it. I knew it was not worth trying to persuade her to stay in Halifax. The Socialist Mission had not threatened this excursion in particular, and we were one of hundreds that would be leaving the Joint over the coming week. That was the argument she would employ.

I looked at the high-set, gleaming injector handles, the beautiful wide black numbers against the clear white background of the steam-pressure gauge, all so prettily set off by the bright red danger mark. To a fellow of the right sort, there could be no handsomer sight in the kingdom. There again the fire was a little thin to left and right, so I picked up my shovel, turned towards the tender and set to.

At eight-eighteen Clive was up next to me, moving the gear to full forward. I leant out to watch the starter signal, and . . . nothing happened. Perhaps they've thought better of sending us out after all. I looked away from the signal, looked back, and then it fell. Clive pulled the regulator (I got a whiff of the Bancroft's as he did so), and the engine gave its first mighty bark, like something being roused that doesn't want to be roused.

We started to roll, though.

We moved into the sight of the sun, and I turned once more to the tender and the coal. As the beats came faster they began to drown out the cheering of the excursionists, and that was all right by me, for I meant to trust my luck to the brightness of the day, and lose myself in the work.

We rolled, faster than I would have thought right, along the side of the branch canal, then *under* the branch canal, which brought on a short night-time, then into Milner Royd Tunnel, which made for a longer one.

Coming out of the tunnel Clive was at the reverser, notching up the great engine with his hair falling forward over his eyes. With the higher gear engaged, the rocking began, like the start of a dance, and it *was* the start of a dance, for our feet fell into the old way of counterbalancing. I thought of Mr Aspinall, sitting in his office in Manchester, and wondered whether he knew what he had let loose with this great mechanical greyhound.

Clive gave his two screams on the whistle as we passed the shed at Sowerby Bridge, and I swear that a horse pulling a dog cart up Town Hall Street was stopped by the shock of it. Clive was not known as a scorcher but maybe the habit was growing on him, for we went through Hebden Bridge clear twice as fast as we should've.

We climbed to Todmorden without noticing it was a climb at all. I could not see the church clock that was lit at night, nor (for we were going at such a lick) any of the churches that might have held it. This engine, I thought, makes churches disappear. I looked for the school with the huge cot in the window, the house with the birds circling above, but these things lived in a slower world and were not to be seen today.

Clive was at the gear again. He wanted 1418 faster, and all the signals did too, for every one of them was down as we galloped on over the Pennine Hills.

Crossing from Yorkshire to Lancashire was no more than jumping a ditch, and Blackburn might have been a village, for it was coming up and then it was gone, with not much in between save for a smudge of smoke.

This time there was no cause to stop at Preston, so those on board had all of thirty seconds to view the handsome new paintwork of that station. We were coming to the danger point now, Salwick and Kirkham, and Clive seemed in a hurry to get there, for he notched up once, twice, within the shadow of County Hall. Was he bent on suicide? No, the man was in the prime of life and making love in secret with the stationmaster's wife.

To put this from my mind I was throwing on coal, but Clive checked me with a funny look and shouted at me to get on the injector and put in more water. It went ill with me to move from coal to water. I wanted to stick at one thing, and wait. If all was well after Salwick and Kirkham, that would be the start of a whole new world. I would take a drink and have a beano with the wife in Blackpool, for I was to book off on arrival.

The signal box at Lea Green came and went. Harry Walker, the fellow in there, would be moving slowly between his levers, drinking tea. Maybe he'd given a wave. It didn't matter.

Salwick came up, more of a garden than a station, more of a graveyard than a station, and Clive was eyeing me. The engine was going at seventy, and neither one of us could properly stand.

I asked myself again how he could be so sure we were not to meet another wrecking attempt.

I laid my shovel against the firebox, forced my head out into the battering air and looked back. I saw the 8.36 from Halifax, the regular Blackpool express, a tiny train miles behind, crawling onto the fields of the Fylde.

I would not tell Clive to slow down, not even with the wife on board and her expecting. I was done with showing fear. I turned to the firehole, looked inside: the fire was shaking, every white-hot coal had been set jumping by the speed.

I stood upright again, and my shovel fell and began clanking over the footplate towards me like a thing gone live. Clive was standing back from the regulator, bowed down before it and pulling at the flaps of two of his pockets, the flaps of the poacher's pockets. He moved his hands slowly up towards his hair and put his head down and ran his hands through his hair, faster and faster. His hair was all there, but it might not be, so he had to make sure over and over again. He was looking at his boots as he did it, seeing how they were faring new-on, for really they should have been spared the black dust of the footplate. The best thing you can do with a pair of boots is not wear them. The best you can do with a railway engine is not drive it.

I looked through the spectacle glass and it was clean. I could see for miles along the line. Blackpool Tower, the tallest building in the country, and there it was: a tiny thing, ten miles off, jumping about in the corner of the glass, trying to come loose and move to the centre. Why had Clive got his medal? Well, it came in pretty handy, made it harder for Knowles to stand him down. There again, if Clive had copped on with Emma Knowles, the stationmaster might be expected to do a lot more than sack him. A *lot* more.

My eye went back to the spectacle glass, and I kept on staring hard at the clear track unrolling before us; I was challenging the track, and keeping with it for mile after mile. A sunbeam flew very far along it in a short time, and I almost gave a laugh at that. I turned away and looked again.

'Brakes!' I screamed, and Clive slashed at the vacuum handle as though killing something, which he was – killing the vacuum – and we began at once to slow . . . but *slowly*.

You can shout for brakes once if you're a fireman – once if there's no reason, I mean. With the engine finally at rest, and time moving once again, Clive turned to me and said: 'What was it?'

I had no answer.

I looked up at the spectacle glass and Clive looked there too. It was clean but for a single fleck of soot, dead centre.

'It might have been that,' I said, and I started to say I was sorry, but Clive checked me, saying: 'You were right to call out.'

I knew then he was one of the grandest fellows I'd ever met. It's rum. You know people for a while and you have them down for one thing, then they suddenly seem to *grow*.

I jumped down and looked along the train. Heads were coming out of the windows, but nobody was climbing down this time. We'd not had to use the reverser, so the train had stopped with a steadier motion. Yet a man in a cap called: 'That were a bit of a jar.' It was a lonely voice, floating over the fields.

'Anybody hurt?' I called.

'I'll consult!' he shouted, but he was already laughing. He ducked back into his compartment, then stuck his head back out. 'One here in desperate need . . .' he bawled.

I began walking fast along the trackside towards him, fretting over having burnt the medical book. 'In desperate need of what?'

'A nice glass of stout!' the excursionist called back. 'Nay, I'm only –' He ducked back in again. 'We're all in fine fettle here,' he said, coming out once more, 'but can tha get on? It's nigh on opening time, tha knows!'

I walked on fast; there were different flowers in the meadow from the time before: tall, purple ones. The wife was in the third carriage back from the engine. As I walked, the carriages were high above my head. It was like going along those old country lanes where the road has sunk and the hedges have gradually been lifted up: a feeling of being too small and kept in your place.

When I came to what I thought must be the right spot, I called up. It was Cicely Braithwaite who pulled down the window strap and looked out. She was laughing too. There was laughing gas running through the pipes on this train, but when she saw me her laughter caught.

'It's not the same going-on as before, is it?' she said.

I shook my head. 'You all right up there?'

The wife was at the window too, showing a face that had been laughing. '*Do* get on,' she said.

I looked along the line. The regular express was there behind in the distance, shaking in the heat, and so far off that at first I couldn't make out whether it was moving or not. But no. It was of course checked at the signal, and all my doing.

I looked up at the wife and grinned. 'When we get to Central, I'll meet you at the ticket gates,' I said.

She ducked back into the carriage as if I was just a spare part, standing down below the train where no person ought to be standing.

I turned to walk back to the engine.

'Ey!'

It was the wife, calling from the compartment; I turned while walking and she blew me a kiss. The holiday mood was certainly on her. At this rate, she'd be after a whole week in Blackpool.

Chapter Twenty-seven

In Central you could hardly breathe from the greenhouse heat burning through the canopies, and the press of people, and the nosebag smell, for the cab horses were at their dinner as we came in at just after eleven. A porter was standing on a stepladder, trying to put the excursionists into the right channels by a lot of shouting and waving of arms.

This was the busiest station in Europe.

We uncoupled and ran the engine to the shed, where everyone was too busy to think anything much of even a Highflyer coming in. Clive went off for a pint, while I legged it the quarter mile back to Central, where the wife was patiently waiting at the ticket gates.

'Did you notice we weren't wrecked?' she called over the noise of the crowd as I approached her.

Behind her at the gates was the ticket collector I'd seen the last time I'd been at Central, the one who'd thrown up the beer bottle. He was working now, collecting tickets but not looking at anyone who gave him one. His uniform still did not fit.

I kissed the wife. 'But we *did* have the stop,' I said, 'and in the exact same spot as before. Did nobody say anything in the carriage?'

The wife shook her head. She wanted to talk about something else. And I was glad to do it.

'Well how do you like Blackpool?' I said.

'So far,' she said, 'I've only seen the railway station.'

I caught up her hand and we pushed our way out of the station and into the blinding light of day. And you had never seen a day so full: tribes of excursionists going both ways on the Prom (they should have had an 'up' and 'down' as on the railways) with the trams trying to nudge their way through, and thousands more folk sitting on the sand, where all places were taken, although there were gangways left for the ice-cream carts.

The sea was doing all in its power to entertain: glittering and sending in pretty big waves, which came as a bonus on a day with hardly any wind. But the teams of Pierrots and Harlequins and the wandering ventriloquists were in competition with it.

I looked to the left and the right. Which way to go? What to show the wife first? I saw a woman's face coming towards me in the crowd. It was a smiling face under a bonnet, a normal Blackpool face. But when the face saw mine, the smile was checked. It was Mary-Ann Roberts. I hated her bonnet, I hated the way she had kept some of her prettiness, for that seemed to give importance to the question of whether she was smiling or not.

I hated most particularly the way she never did anything unexpected, like walking up to me and saying: You were not to know about the treatment of concussion cases. You are an engine man after all, and not a doctor. As I looked at her, she looked away.

I had brought her to Blackpool so that she could kill my enjoyment of the day.

We were now bang under the Tower, with the wife controlling events. We both looked at the top of it for a while, where the glass and iron palace was balanced. It was a marvellous sight, but I could only think of the stone on the line. We looked down and around, at the Ferris wheel over near the Winter Gardens, which was like a giant rosette. Then it was back to staring at the crowds, which went on for ever, like the sea. These people had all aimed for the bull's-eye, and they had all *hit* the bull's-eye. There was no point in thinking about the future or the past, this was the moment, and it just had to be carried on.

'What do you reckon?' I asked the wife.

She answered slowly: 'There's to be a free tea at the Tower in three hours' time, but first I want to take a turn on the flying machine.'

'Which one?' I said. 'I expect there's hundreds.'

'The Sir Hiram Maxim Flying Machines at the Pleasure Beach,' said the wife. 'I've read of them in the library. They're at Sand Hill.'

'That's south,' I said.

So we began going that way along the Prom. I kept looking over at the beach. I knew how things went with the Pierrot shows. Each one was like a little dream while it was happening, with perfect dainty people dancing to guitars. Then the Pierrots would come down from their little stands to start collecting the pennies, and the magic was gone. You'd be sorry for having watched, because it made you feel bad to pay them, and you felt a sight worse if you didn't. I looked beyond the crowds to the bathing machines wobbling down towards the water. There were teams of boys to control them and they were taking ten down at once, all in a line like a little landslide.

As we moved along the Prom we kept nearly colliding with people who wanted our money: the flowersellers, booksellers, quack doctors, all trying to stop you in your tracks by shouting at you.

As we walked, some amusements won out as the ones you really noticed, whether from numbers of sandwich men or quantities of posters, or through just being noticeable: the Royal Rumanian Band was on the North Pier all summer. You couldn't avoid knowing of that. And Beecham's Pills were to be had everywhere.

Presently, the machine came into view, high above the heads of the crowd: a wide-turning wheel, with the flying boats hanging from wires. As we watched, the wheel increased its speed and the flying boats flew further out and – which was the great thing – higher too. Every now and then there was a little snort of smoke from the centre of the wheel, but the thing was really almost silent, and turned like a weather vane or a windmill, all natural; and there was something of sailing about it too. Silent speed.

'It's beautiful,' I said to the wife, 'but aren't ladies in the family way supposed to avoid violent amusements?'

'Nothing violent about it,' said the wife, without looking at me.

So we joined the back of the queue. It was all sandy and dusty round about, like America. You were hard put to say where the beach ended. There was a carousel nearby bigger than the common run. It went anti-clockwise, which was the American way. I'd read of that somewhere. There were plenty of Yankees in Blackpool. Well, it was open house to all sorts.

There were several other rides on the go: a bicycle railway, a switchback, and over in the distance a waterfall coming down from a man-made mountain. A sign stood high up above the crowd: 'THE WATER CAVES OF THE WORLD', and hard by it was a giant banner: 'READ THE DAILY DESPATCH'.

Maxim's Flying Machine was looked after by big fellows in sailor suits, and when we were towards the front of the queue one of them stepped up and asked if we'd ridden on it before. 'You must not on any account try to stand up in the flying boat,' said the fellow. 'And you are to take off your hats.'

There was a notice about how this was all in aid of Sir Hiram Maxim and his attempt to fly a measured mile by powered flight, in a heaver-than-air craft, not a steerable balloon. There was a photograph of a real flying machine, and a photograph of a mile – well, a biggish field at any rate.

It was sixpence for the two of us. We climbed aboard our boat and the wheel started to turn. There was hurdy-gurdy music coming from somewhere, and I thought it was for the flying machine, but then another tune started up, far louder, and *this* was the one. It was a melody I'd heard before somewhere, but completely changed.

251

'This fellow Maxim must be out of his senses!' I shouted to the wife as we started to climb.

'Isn't it just wonderful!' she shouted back, and it *was*.

I liked it best when we were right out over the sea, when an extra bit of breeze would push you that bit higher and you felt you could float on for ever.

The boats gradually tipped, and at the highest point we were quite sideways – and silent, for there was nothing at all to be said.

When we climbed off, the wife, setting her hat back on her head, said: 'I feel just like I don't know what.'

We walked away from the machine hand in hand, and the wife said: 'That's set me up just nicely, that has, but I've done Blackpool now.'

We bought some treacle toffee, and it ought to have been the perfect day. Instead, I was suddenly furious that I could not bring before my mind's eye the face of the wrecker. Damn you, I thought, whoever you are.

'Why don't we go along to St Anne's,' I said, 'the next place along?'

'Where Mr Robinson lives?'

'That's it,' I said. I wanted to see that fellow again, though it would be hard to bring about. 'It's a nice run out there,' I said. 'I think they have a gas tram that takes you.'

But the gas tram I'd heard about was gone, long since removed from service. The ticket clerk at the Blackpool Southern Terminus, which was just a step from the Pleasure Beach, said passengers riding on it had found themselves not able to breathe on windless days. The tram to Lytham – which was the one that stopped at St Anne's – was electric now, like all the other Blackpool ones.

The ticket clerk shouted this to me, and he must have spent his whole life shouting, because that's how things went on around the Blackpool trams in the season. There was a fearful scramble to get on them, and the bells as they came up might have been the bells of a boxing match.

It was not quite so much of a scramble for the Lytham tram, though. Lytham and St Anne's were quieter resorts, and quieter types went out to them. We climbed onto the top deck when the tram came in. The steps were very high; they went up in a corkscrew, and 'HOVIS' was written very big on every one. The electric wires hung from what looked like ordinary lamp-posts that had grown arms.

The tram bowled along fast and high along the edge of the road, wobbling slightly, like a hoop being bowled, and in two minutes Blackpool was left behind. There were fields to our left, and dry grasses, sand dunes and the sea to our right. Sand had been blown onto the wide, white road. A long steamer was going by in the opposite direction.

'It's like Africa out here,' said the wife.

'Now I don't know about *that*,' I said.

Then the big gardens started coming up, and hotels all covered in ivy. We got off next to a miniature golf course. There was a low wall all around it made of dazzling white stones. As the wife and I stepped down from the tram, some smart sorts looked up from their game and stared at us.

'Do you think we passed muster?' asked the wife as we turned away from them in order to cross the road and reach the sea.

The beach was a startler. There were no fortune tellers or funfairs, but pretty banners stuck in the sand advertising shows by the Happy Valley Pierrots and the Jolly Tars, and there were three donkeys sleepwalking over the sand with children in sailor suits on their backs.

So this was Robinson's home. He'd done pretty well to get here, but now he'd lost all of his money because of the light suiting and the way he'd been treated by Hind, father and son.

We sat on the wall that divided the beach from the road.

'I bet they're all snobs round here,' said the wife.

'Aye,' I said.

'But I would like to live here.'

253

I looked at her.

'Well, I don't see why the snobs should have it all to themselves,' she said. 'And I've just had a vision of our little boy or girl skipping along the front.'

'Did you have a vision of our bank account at that time?' I asked her.

'I would come here,' she said, 'and I would get up a socialist club.'

'Oh they'd like that,' I said.

The three children were getting down from the donkeys. There were no more takers, and the donkey driver was getting out his pipe.

'I don't like that building on the pier though,' said the wife.

The pavilion on the pier *was* rather weird.

'I expect you'll be able to get it knocked down when you come here,' I said.

'You see how all the benches around it face away,' she said. 'That's so you don't have to look at it.'

I thought it more likely that this was so you could look out to sea. I then wondered again at how the train had not crashed this time, and how the wrecker or wreckers had left us alone. I felt grateful to them, which was the wrong feeling, I knew.

'Did you get a look at Clive,' I asked the wife, 'the driver of the engine?'

'I did, yes.'

'He's a handsome devil, wouldn't you say?'

'Yes,' she said, and then she laughed. 'Your face!' she said.

'Do you think we might pay a call on Robinson?' I said. 'He's rather keen on you, you know.'

The wife didn't seem to hear this; or she thought it a notion too daft to bother with. She was brushing sand off her skirt. 'Bustle up!' she called, and she was off across the wide, bright common that seemed to take up half of St Anne's-on-Sea, aiming for a pile of stones that were built up at its centre. She was a hundred yards ahead in no time and seemed too lonely, so I began running to catch her, when I saw beyond her a small boy seeming to spin backwards from behind the pile of stones. He was playing some secret backward-jumping game, and wearing a green suit. It was Lance Robinson.

He didn't know the wife, of course, but he knew me – and from a fair distance too, even though he was not wearing his spectacles.

'Oh hello,' he said as I came up close (the wife was looking at the stones in the background). 'The green's my home-from-home now that the paddock's gone. Have you come up from Blackpool?'

'I have that,' I said, and I called the wife over and introduced her to the boy.

It came out that the wife was working at Hind's, and the boy said: 'Cicely told me she had a new person working with her. I like Cicely. She's a brick, although Dad always used to say she wasn't a great hand at correspondence.'

The boy turned to me, and said: 'Cicely's awfully pretty, don't you think?'

'Well . . .' I said.

The wife, leaning against the stone, was making funny faces at me as if to say, Now what do we have *here*?

'Did you come along on the tram?' said the boy.

I nodded.

'It's smarter here, isn't it?' said the boy. 'It's nothing like Blackpool really, even though we're sort of tacked on to it. Our house is one of the first ones in St Anne's, and when we bought it, the Post Office had it down as Blackpool. Dad tries not to be snobby but he played merry hell over that, and he got it changed.'

Lance Robinson was doing his little backward dance on the grass. 'I'm not supposed to say that,' he said. 'Merry hell, I mean. I got it from our maid, the one that's gone. Would you like to come to tea?'

'Oh no,' said the wife immediately, and quite horrified.

'*Yes*,' I said. 'That's very kind of you.'

I wanted to see the Bradshaws that Robinson was supposed to keep lined up on his shelves. I wanted to see the fellow's motorcar, not that I could remember much of the one that had followed us to the Fylde, or the one that had frightened old Hind to death.

Lance Robinson turned and I began to follow him. The wife was fixed to the spot. But she followed along after a little while, and began chatting brightly enough to the boy: 'This is a lovely spot, isn't it? I don't think we can take tea, although it is awfully kind. Perhaps we'll just say a very quick hello to your father, who's a very pleasant gentleman . . . But we shan't come into the house.'

We were passing by an empty bandstand now, and stepping off the green. The boy wasn't used to walking with other people; he was going too fast, and his green coat was flying out behind him.

'It's the light suiting,' I whispered to the wife, as we followed the boy down a wide road of tall houses.

'I know,' said the wife. 'It's sad.'

I knew what she meant. At first I couldn't think of the word, but then it came to me. The boy had been put into clothes that made him a kind of experiment in motion – an experiment that had failed.

'Now listen,' the wife whispered, 'we are not to stay.'

'There was no stone on the line for Hind's today,' I said. 'Why not, do you suppose?'

'Oh give it an airing,' said the wife. 'I thought you'd finished with that.'

'I've got to work out why there was a stone before, and why there wasn't one this time. One difference from Whit was that the governors of the mill were not on the train: Hind and Hind Senior. Now think on: who would have wanted to see off the two Hinds? And who might already have done the job on the older one?'

The boy had come to a halt ahead of us. He stood at a turning leading into another wide white road of tall houses with exhibition gardens. He was putting on his glasses as we got near. 'I don't wear them outdoors,' he said, hooking them over his ears with his head down, 'but I'm supposed to.'

This meant we were drawing near.

'Father's not home,' said the boy, looking up.

The wife nodded, and I could see she was relieved.

'He's dreadfully worried,' said the boy.

There was a low fizzing in the street. All the gardens were full of bees.

'The police', said the boy, setting my heart thumping, 'have been here . . .'

Where? I thought. Which one is the house? They all looked like tall churches, and they were all joined together: a dark line of giants behind the gardens. You were really meant to see the gardens not the houses.

'How could you lose a mill?' asked the boy from behind his spectacles. 'Dad had one. He sold it, then went in with Hind's and now nothing's left and Mother won't pay calls because then people would have to come back, and they would see we only had one maid . . . If a mill came down to *me*,' the boy went on, 'I would sell it straight off and put the money in the Post Office.'

'You said about the police . . .' I reminded him.

'No, Jim,' said the wife, shaking her head.

'The Hind's Whit Excursion,' said Lance Robinson. 'They think Father tried to bring it off the line.'

I smartly took off my cap, because I was lost for any other way to react. I wondered whether the police had been working away all summer, like the bees, and whether I had not put them to it myself after what I'd said in the copper shop at Manchester during my funny turn. But it was no use trying to recall just what I *had* said then.

'Well, they're here again,' the boy said, and I knew the house. It was behind the boy, half a dozen along at the end of the road. A wagonette and horse stood outside. There was no motorcar in sight.

The colours in this place were all too high: the boy's green suit, the whiteness of the gateposts and road dust, the colours of the flowers in the gardens; and the pillar box in the middle of the road was red like none before. But the horse was black, and the wagonette was black.

'You must still come for tea,' said the boy.

When the strangeness started I could not say; the boy was walking on, and the wife was saying too loudly, 'Master Lance, Master Lance', as if just saying his name could change something. But the boy walked on and the front door of the house opened as he did so. He walked into it, and the wife turned on her heels and fled. A moment later, I turned and followed.

Chapter Twenty-eight

The tram raced back to Blackpool and seemed to fall into the welcoming arms of the crowd at the Southern Terminus. Blackpool was where the trams belonged.

As we got up from our seat, the wife pinned the white rosette back onto her dress and the quiet of the ride was over.

'I'm sure the boy has it all wrong, you know,' she said. 'The police will just have been asking Mr Robinson questions that might lead them to someone else. They asked you questions, didn't they?'

I nodded. She liked Robinson and didn't want him to be the wrecker, so I said nothing, but my thoughts were running along these lines: perhaps he put the stone on the track not so as to stop the train, but only to stop old man Hind's heart, give him such a shock that he pegged out, while he drove alongside in his motorcar to watch. When that failed, he'd tried again, with the motorcar as the weapon.

No. It was all loopy.

When the wife climbed down from the tram, she said, 'Now *where's* that Tower?' then, a second later, 'Oh!'

Blackpool Tower was the tallest building in England.

'Well,' she said, quite recovered and speaking in her special Yorkshire voice, 'I'm off for me tea.'

I arranged to meet her at six outside the main entrance to the Tower, and she disappeared into the crowd.

I remembered about an 'A' cigar that I'd put in my top pocket. I lit it and set off towards the Tower myself. Whether I was pressing against the flow of the crowd or going along with it I couldn't have said; sometimes one, sometimes the other. Inside ten seconds I saw two other fellows smoking big cigars. Blackpool was that sort of place. Down on the beach the crowd was especially thick and you'd see a white arm waved or the top of a pointed hat, and this was a Pierrot show going on.

I was alongside the Tower now – the wife was inside and below, taking tea in the basement.

Music was coming at me from about a dozen different places, and the jangle of it was like those contraptions they have in pubs: the polyphons, which turn very prettily, but never quite seem to play what you'd call a tune. I crossed over the Prom and leant against the railings looking out to sea for a while. There was something about the sea that made you breathe deeply. I smoked my cigar and thought about Robinson: he had lost everything over the summer suiting, and it was the old man who'd been most particularly set against him. Of that I was now certain.

I looked down, and there on the beach, giving a show, was a ventriloquist with a figure on his knee. It was the good ventriloquist from the Seashell, Henry Clarke, and the doll was . . . what was the name? Leonard. Young Leonard.

There were steps to the beach nearby. It was hard going, walking over the hot sand in my boots, and I fretted that the turn would end by the time I got to it.

'By gum it's hot work this, you know,' Henry Clarke was saying to the little crowd when I reached the spot. 'My head's fairly throbbing, and I'm starting to sweat all over.'

I was at the back of three rows of kids, but Clarke's voice carried pretty well. He was sitting on a folding stool. There was a bottle propped in the sand before him, with a few coppers placed inside to show that's what it was for. Underneath the bottle were some papers, and I knew what these were: handbills for the Seaside Surprises at the Seashell Music Hall.

'It's not quite polite to speak of "sweating" you know,' Henry Clarke was saying to Young Leonard. 'Now let's all hear you say the word "perspiring".'

Leonard looked up quite suddenly then stared around at all the children, his eyes seeming to get wider by the second, but they *couldn't* do that, so it was just something about the face.

'Oh come on now, you know you're awfully good at talking when you've a mind to be. Leonard, I would like to hear you say: "Around the ragged rock, the ragged rascal ran."'

Leonard looked at Henry Clarke, then out at all of us. 'So would I,' Leonard said, sounding very glum.

It was all daft stuff but it was real too, and that's why it was funny.

Henry Clarke's folding stool suddenly slipped in the sand, and it was his turn to pull a funny face. This seemed to bring the show to an end, and some of the kids went forward to put money into the bottle.

I put in a penny myself and picked up one of the papers. At the top of the page was Henry Clarke's name. Above it there was nothing. The name of the other ventriloquist, Monsieur Maurice, appeared down below.

'The bill's changed,' I said.

Henry Clarke looked at me with his pleasant face. Leonard was still on his knee. Clarke smiled, perhaps nodding slightly, but saying nothing. He wasn't about to start putting on swank.

One of the kids was pointing at the figure. 'What's he?' he said. The kid was eating a penny lick.

Clarke smiled again. 'Why, this is Leonard,' he said.

Leonard suddenly smiled too, and looked at the boy, who jumped back. It was like electricity.

'He's got a good face,' said another of the kids.

'He has lots of faces really,' said Henry Clarke. 'He has what we call his "By Jove, you don't say!" face.'

And those words were now spelled out in the face of Leonard, just as clearly as if they'd been written.

'And he has his . . . well, what we call his "thinking it over" face.'

Now the dummy was all thoughtfulness, nodding gente-like.

'Sometimes,' said Clarke, 'he even comes to a conclusion!'

At this, a great look of surprise and happiness appeared on Leonard's face, so that he beamed like the glacé kid on the boot-polish tins.

'He's not living though, is he?' said a very little kid, and it was as if he knew the truth but wanted to make quite sure.

'He is not,' said Henry Clarke, which was the kindly answer I thought.

He tipped the dummy forwards and slid the head out of the neck. Leonard's head was just as lifelike as before, but now we all saw that it was on a long pole, with levers and wires attached.

'Superior Professional Movement,' said Henry Clarke, and he winked at me, for this was grown-up stuff. 'Most figures have a set-up called something similar but Leonard's works are more superior and professional than most. His mouth and eyes move at the same time. That's not so out of the common, but it's the *way* they move. You see, the leather around his nose and eyes . . . It's very supple, and the levers draw it in just the right way . . .'

He gave us a few more expressions of Leonard's, and it was like watching a musician play his instrument.

'Did you make him?' asked one of the kids.

'Oh I'm not nearly clever enough to do that. Leonard was made by a Mr Pardoe, who lived in Manchester and worked under the name of Zack. He passed on some years ago.'

'Why?' asked one of the kids.

'Why . . . did he pass on?' asked Henry Clarke.

'Why did he go round calling himself Zack?'

'Oh well, people in the show business often go in for fancy names, you know. I think it's because it makes it easier for people to remember them.'

The world was then put back to rights, as the neck was slid back into the body. As some of the kids walked up to have a closer look at Leonard, I was thinking of Monsieur Maurice, or – what was his real name? – Morris Connell. He'd been moved down the bill because he wasn't up to snuff, which was like an engine man moving from an express link down to local goods. There would be no coming back from that.

So here were two men who'd lost everything: Robinson and Connell.

As I looked at Henry Clarke, I made the leap, and he saw something progress in me, for he pointed and said, 'Question, sir?'

'Were you playing at the Seashell Music Hall at Whitsuntide?'

'Yes,' he replied, 'I was here for Whit Week in the Seaside Surprises.' He smiled at me as he said the name.

'When did that Whit Week show begin?'

'Why, on the Monday of Whit Week,' he said.

He was too much of a gent to tell me to simmer down.

'You'd been at the Palace in Halifax not long before, hadn't you?' I said. 'On a run that was extended?'

He nodded.

'Did you come over here by train from Halifax?'

'I have done, yes. I'm on the go all the time, and the Seashell only keeps me here odd weeks.'

'No, but I mean before that very week. Did you travel up on Whit Sunday from Halifax?'

Even the smile of Henry Clarke was beginning to fade under this bombardment. He looked up at the sky. Leonard lay dead on his lap. There was nothing in the sky but blue, yet he found what he was looking for.

'Why, I believe I did, yes.'

'On the eight thirty-six express from Halifax?'

He was shaking his head before I'd finished. 'No, no, I have it wrong. I did play at the Palace in Halifax before Whit, you're right over that, and then I had a day or two free in the town. Later on, I had to go and see . . . Mr Wood . . . Mr Wood at . . . at Burnley on a business matter. And so I came here to Blackpool from *Burnley*, and it was on the *Monday* that I came, not the Sunday. Why do you ask all this, if you don't mind?'

The kids had all faded away by now and I felt a chump. 'I just thought I might have seen you on that train,' I said, which sounded pretty sick, but was all I could come up with. 'I work on the railways, you see.'

Henry Clarke nodded.

'Fireman,' I said, 'with the Lancashire and Yorkshire. The name's Jim Stringer. Jim Stringer from Halifax,' I added, and I moved forward and shook his hand.

The poor fellow still looked a bit flummoxed.

'I have a boy who's mad on ventriloquism,' I lied.

Henry Clarke smiled, which was about all he could do.

As I walked back over the sand, I thought: it *might* be true. I might have a boy. And he might be keen on ventriloquism one day.

I climbed back up to the Prom, and the further I walked from Henry Clarke, the crazier my late notion seemed. This had been it: Monsieur Maurice had placed the stone on the line to stop the 8.36, knowing his rival, Henry Clarke, was riding on that train, and not realising our excursion would hit that spot first.

I was going nuts.

But when I looked back at the beach, Henry Clarke was staring after me and frowning.

<hr>

The wife was coming out of the Tower buildings and laughing with Cicely, who coloured up very nicely when she saw me. She was about to go off to the company house she was staying at with some of the others from the mill, including one fellow with a bushy moustache who would seem to dart towards her whenever the crowd was after swirling her away. I wondered if the two of them had clicked over tea or before.

By the time the wife and I started back towards Central station, the evening gulls were in full cry.

'Noisy brutes aren't they?' said the wife, as the line of cabs outside the station came into view.

'Are you jealous of them because they can stay?'

'The gulls, you mean, or the lot from Hind's?'

'Well,' I said, 'both.'

'I wouldn't want a whole week here, but I wouldn't mind staying for a couple more hours, just for a walk along the sands.'

'We can do that if you like,' I said.

'Let's not,' said the wife, 'it's train time now.'

Chapter Twenty-nine

Having grafted through fourteen-hour turns on the Monday and Tuesday of Wakes Week, taking such folk as had not already got away to spots round about Halifax, I found myself with a day's leave on the Wednesday.

I woke early, and the sound of the Horton Street tram floated up to our bedroom as usual – steel fighting stone at high speed – but this time there seemed to be something freer and wilder about the noise, for there was nobody at all about to muffle its racket.

The wife left for Hind's at seven, and I heard George Ogden clattering down the back steps a little later. Towards eight, I was drinking tea and eating bread and butter next to the window looking down into Hill Street while reading over yesterday's *Courier*. There was no news of any smashes.

There was not a soul to be seen out, and by 8.15 it hit me that the baker's van had not even troubled to appear. But the heat was rising steadily in the empty street, as if trying to force the folk left in town out of their houses.

It was getting on for eleven when I put on my Sunday suit and set off for a turn about Halifax.

Back Hill Street was empty, and so were the alleys and snickets beyond: no sound of marbles rattling along gutters, no footballs bouncing down the alleys or screaming kids giving chase. Also, there was more sky than usual: no washing on the lines! I came to Horton Street and a tram flew past, like a stone that someone had pitched at the Joint. The only one aboard was the driver.

I strolled over to the Palace Theatre.

Morris Connell – Monsieur Maurice – was back and still topping the bill here, even if no longer doing so in Blackpool.

But who would want to go to the theatre in Halifax in Wakes? And in this weather?

As soon as I set foot in Commercial Street, I heard the jangling of a barrel organ, like a man walking down a street kicking bottles and somehow making a tune of it. The barrel-organ man was getting on for being the only person in the street. He was right outside the Post Office. As I walked towards him, a fellow came out of the Halifax and Huddersfield Bank, hurrying towards me with a kind of secret smile on his face. He knew this Wakes show was a queer going-on, though not really worth speaking of, for it did happen every year after all.

I looked inside the bank as I passed: at one clerk, sitting under the coloured sunlight that came through the stained glass.

As I walked, it was hard to tell whether the shops were open or closed. You had to walk right up to them to find out. The fishmonger's in Silver Street was closed, and looked as though it had been for years. Well, everybody had gone to where the fish came from.

I found myself walking over to Northgate. I wanted to see whether the New Zealand cheeses were in the window of the Maypole Dairy. They were there all right: fresh cheese, fresh plants, electric fans revolving above them. The door was propped open and, for the first time, I walked in rather than just looking on.

The place smelt so much of heat and cheese that I could hardly breathe, yet there was a nice old fellow smiling behind the counter. I asked him to parcel me up a bit of something cheap, and he said he'd knock a penny off since it was Wakes.

'Not going away yourself?' I asked him.

'Oh yes,' he said, 'I'll be in Blackpool Wednesday until Sunday. I never miss, you know.'

I bought a couple of bread rolls, a bottle of beer and a bottle of Special Cola at the grocer's two doors down, then walked over to People's Park, seeing not more than half a dozen folk all the while. In the park they were a little in the holiday way.

267

There was a helter-skelter tower near the bandstand, and half a dozen children around it. I had my pick of the benches, so I made for one near the fountain, which gave out coolness, and here it struck me that there was something different about the day apart from the want of people: clean air. You saw things *faster* than usual.

Presently I stood up and made for Horton Street. Sugden was there, dreaming outside the Crown with his ice-cream cart as usual.

'You should be in the park!' I called to him. 'There's a few about up there!'

'Righto,' he said, 'I'll think on.'

But I knew he wouldn't be straying too far from the Crown. Sugden's trouble was that if it was hot enough for folk to want penny licks, it was hot enough for *him* to want a glass of beer.

My steps fell in with the beating of exhaust steam as I neared the Joint. Two trains were pulling out at the same time: one was going 'up', one 'down'. It made a nice balance, like two ends of a reef knot being pulled. As the sound of the engines faded, the Joint fell quiet: a lot of excursions had gone and a lot would shortly be coming back, but just at present we were in the eye of the storm, so to speak.

Approaching Hind's Mill at the top of the Beacon, I saw that all the doors were open, as if they were giving the place an airing. I walked straight into the main doors, and the first surprise was the clocking-off machine: it was lying on its side in bits.

I walked on, into the weaving hall. The looms were still and silent, with not a soul to be seen.

I moved along a line of looms. They looked both old and new: knock-kneed somehow, but dangerous. I put my hand into one of the looms, thinking: if this loom starts up now, I'll lose this hand. It was a crazy thing to do.

It was cool in the weaving room; I kicked at some blue fluff that floated in the sleepy white light.

You'd think there'd be some stay-behinds, but no; the place was quite deserted. Well, there had to be somebody about, for the front doors had been open.

I walked clean through the weaving hall and found the wife's office. The door and the bob-hole were both shut tight, so I knocked. No answer. I pushed at the door and walked in, closing the door after me. The wife was expecting me at about this time. Where was she?

I was going off Wakes by the second. I wanted everything back to normal. Putting the little buffet of bread and cheese down on one of the high stools, I spotted the *Kelly's* directory I'd seen in this office before. It was lying open. I picked it up and saw that it was the *Kelly's* for 'Yorkshire – Western Division'. I put it down.

There's nothing about this room to show that my wife works here, I thought. The typewriter was set on one of the desks, and I thought: well, it's nothing more than the wife's own loom.

I then spotted a whole row of *Kelly's*. I took down the one for 'Lancashire – Eastern Division', then searched out a pencil and made a note of an address.

The next item to catch my eye was an envelope lying next to the typewriter. 'Rly Accident' was hand-written in the top corner. It was not the wife's writing.

I picked up the envelope and pulled out the first paper just as the door flew open.

It was the wife, carrying more papers. She came over and kissed me. It was rather exciting to be kissed in an office.

'I'll swing for that maintenance man,' she said.

'What's up?' I said.

'Oh,' she said. 'Certificates for this and that. He wants all the ones I haven't got.'

I looked down at the paper in my hand. It was a copy of Major Harrison's draft report into the smash.

'What's the telephone number at this place?' I asked the wife.

'Four,' she said, '*Halifax* four.'

'I'll try to remember that,' I said.

'You must make a note of it somewhere. Of course, the Dean Clough Mills are number one.'

'Cheese,' I said, pointing to the stores I'd brought along, 'from the Maypole Dairy.'

'It's beautiful,' she said, looking inside the bag.

I didn't think you were supposed to say that about cheese.

'We could eat it by the mill pond,' she said. 'Just ten minutes. We've a lot on today, with maintenance and inspections.'

So we walked out and had our dinner by the mill pond, with Halifax in the sun below us, and nothing for once between it and the sky.

When we'd put down most of the food and drink, the wife said: 'That's me done,' and we walked back inside. But as soon as we were through the door, the wife said, 'Blast, telephone,' lifted up her skirts, and began making fast towards the office. I followed on behind.

I stood in the doorway as the wife picked up the instrument, said, 'Hello, Hind's Mill,' very briskly. But something was said the other end that checked her.

She put the instrument back in its place. 'Peter Robinson's dead,' she said. 'That was his solicitor.'

'*How* is he dead?'

'He *jumped*,' said the wife.

'How do you mean "He *jumped*"?'

I remember thinking: By God, he's bloody well jumped off Blackpool Tower, and then being a little disappointed when the wife said: 'He jumped off the pier at St Anne's . . . In the light suiting . . . Only he'd put stones in the pockets . . . So it *wasn't* light.'

The wife looked at me with a kind of rising wonderment, but then she just sighed and said, 'Oh it was *such* a mistake.'

I thought of Lance Robinson. He wore spectacles like his father, and these were now a kind of memorial of his father. I wondered whether it was the loss of money that had driven

Robinson to his jump, or the questioning by the police over the stone on the line. Had I put the police in his way by what I said during my strange turn in Manchester? I could not remember.

I followed the wife, who was walking towards the weaving hall saying, 'I am to tell the director.'

'Hind?' I said, following. 'Is he about?'

We burst into the weaving room and Hind was there, walking between two lines of looms. In my mind's eye he was out on the Fylde, coming along the track towards the stone on the line, a fellow whose feelings you couldn't make out.

The stale man. He owned a mill, and he was used to owning a mill, and he was tired of owning a mill. He was quite correct in his black and white clothes; he had just enough hair to be going on with. His face was biggish but for no reason, and his age was anything from fifty to seventy. I couldn't see him on a yacht off Llandudno, drinking champagne.

The wife said, 'I've just spoken on the telephone with Mr Robinson's solicitor, sir, and he gave me some terrible news: Mr Robinson is dead. It appears he has committed suicide.'

Hind looked at the two of us. 'The poor soul,' he said. 'And so soon after Father.'

There was no clue to be had from the man. Every word had the same force as every other word. He set off walking again, heading in the direction we'd just come from: towards the back doors of the weaving room.

The wife said: 'That's the old sod who did for Robinson.'

I'd never heard her curse before. She was looking up, and there was a painting on the wall – a new painting, or newly put up. It was Old Hind, with one strand of hair going over his white, gone-from-the-world head. I could see that the fellow was very likely a bastard, but it was the wrecker who was to blame, for this and for everything.

Chapter Thirty

The next day, Thursday of Wakes, we were booked for another run out to Southport and back. Most of those on the train had already had time away elsewhere earlier in the week and were light-headed with holidayness. There'd been some bottle-throwing from the windows.

All this skylarking, all this life . . . and Robinson lying dead after drinking his fill of the Irish Sea.

During the day the questions had picked up speed and rolled into a blur: had I put the police on to Robinson or would they have questioned him anyway? And was that the reason he jumped off the pier, or was it the loss of his fortune?

After the Southport turn, I'd taken a pint with Clive in Sowerby Bridge and was later than usual going back up Horton Street. The wife, I knew, was being kept late at Hind's by the summer stock-taking, so I was in a fair way for a call at the Evening Star.

I took my pint while reading the *Courier*, which had not been published the first three days of Wakes. It was back, but thinner than usual. I looked for news of Robinson's death, but there was nothing. Newspapers, I knew, waited for the inquests, and the reports always ended the same way: 'A verdict of Suicide while of unsound mind was recorded.' It was hard to imagine Robinson, with his specs and his brainy looks fitting that bill.

I had my two pints then pushed on up the street with my coat over my shoulder. Walking past the Imperial, I looked through the window, and there in the jungly darkness sat George Ogden. He was at his supper, and enjoying it so much that he seemed to be singing at the same time as eating, moving his hands in the air and fluttering his fingers in between mouthfuls.

His eye caught mine and he froze for a moment, like a bio-scope broken down; then he stood, with his napkin still at his throat, and signalled me for me to come in. A waiter saw him do so and strode up to the door, taking guard.

'Might I just come in for a moment?' I said, which was not the right way at all of going about it.

'Of course you might, sir,' said the waiter, and there was a bit of sauce, I thought, in the way he threw back that word 'might'.

I pulled my cap off my head. I almost handed it to him, and he almost took it, but we both thought better of it in time.

I walked over to George, feeling for the first time the blast of those fans on my hair. The place was only a quarter full: frock coats and wine glasses; Halifax swells with their legs stretched out, showing me the sharp creases in their trousers. Nobody looked up at me, in that steady world of wine drinking, as I walked across to the beaming face of George Ogden. But I couldn't help notice how my boots did not make any play with the lights and how my trousers just flopped like cloth tubes.

George was still standing. There was no food and drink on his face, but it was all only just *inside* it, and he glistened like a ripe red apple.

'Hello, Features,' he said, putting out his hand and pointing to the empty chair opposite his own.

'Having a bit of a blow-out?' I said.

The waiter, walking past, heard me say that and going by the face he pulled didn't much like the sound of it.

'Spot of supper, that's all,' said George.

'You do yourself pretty well.'

George looked down at his plate. 'It was potted shrimps to start, and this is steak and kidney pudding. Well, it *was*. I've a mind to finish off with wine jelly and brandied peaches, then the coffee and cheese, of course. Now the wine carafe's empty, I see . . .'

George was waving for the waiter.

273

'Some sound wine for the two of us,' he said and he winked. 'You *will* join me in a glass.'

'I've just had a couple of pints down the hill,' I said.

'Beer?'

I nodded. It would hardly be anything else. 'You wouldn't like to settle up and go back there with me, I suppose?' I said.

'I will not drink those apron washings,' said George.

The waiter came over and George said: 'Another of these please,' waving the carafe.

'Could I have a glass of beer,' I interjected.

The maps of India seemed to come up onto George's cheeks, but faded into the general rosiness pretty quickly. 'Will you run to a beer for a good fellow like this one?' George asked the waiter.

It seemed that the fellow could, but that he would be putting himself to a fair bit of trouble in the process.

'I've been able to pull the string,' said George when the waiter had gone, 'but it really is quite amazing the airs they put on here.'

Then he suddenly asked: 'You ever been to London?'

'I lived there for a while,' I said, 'Waterloo way.'

'South, en't it?' said George.

'It is in the Southern Division,' I said, proudly.

'Ever get up to the Cri?'

'The Cri?'

'The Criterion, I mean.'

'What is it? Music hall?'

'Leave off,' said George. 'I don't hold with those places at all. No, the Cri is rather a select bar and restaurant . . . Mind your eye!' he said, for the waiter was coming up to us, swirling down a silver tray with another of the queer wine containers and a glass of beer. The beer had too much froth and looked like an ice cream; tasted all right though.

George was saying something to the waiter, thanking him for going out of his way with the beer and asking for his pudding. He seemed born to it all, I had to admit.

'What does your dad do, George?' I asked.

'Dad? Oh he's in the potty house.'

'That's a good 'un,' I said, taking another pull on the beer.

'No,' said George, 'honour bright. Dad was a solicitor in a small way of business . . .'

'Where?'

'York,' said George. 'Near there at any rate.'

'*Where* near there?'

'Well,' said George, 'ever heard of a spot called Bishop-thorpe?'

'Can't say I have. Well anyway,' I went on, 'I'm very sorry to hear it, George.'

He was frowning perhaps, and I wondered whether I had found the limit of his cheerfulness, but he put his napkin to his face, wiped his mouth, and when the action was done he was smiling again.

'It's quite all right, old man. Dad was always a little blue, and then he just got bluer and bluer, and . . . well, they call it a hospital, you know. The Garden Hospital. It's a pretty name . . . Just going to drain off, old man.'

He stood up, and walked off to the Gentlemen's. He came back, not walking but rolling, full of himself all over again.

'Question for question, Mr Stringer,' he said, sitting down.

'That's fair do's,' I said, and I waited.

'Your Mrs Stringer, she's a regular beauty, you know.'

I wished he would stop saying that.

'How's she liking it at her mill?'

'Getting on all right,' I said.

'Do you know her movements this weekend?'

He must have seen the look coming over my face – and it was a look of horror – for he quickly put in: 'It's only that I must pay the rent, you understand.'

I wanted to keep George Ogden away from the wife, even in his talk. I said, quite sharply: 'She should be back home by now. You can come along with me and pay it directly.'

'I may be kept here a little late with brandy and a cigar,' he said. 'Second matter,' he went on, sipping wine. 'Any news of Lowther?'

I sat back. 'Curious question,' I said. 'How the devil should I know?'

George frowned.

'Tickets, after all,' I went on; 'it's your line of country, isn't it?'

'No, no,' said George. 'We *sell*'em, he *inspects*'em, or did. It's quite different. I'm pig-ignorant when it comes to the inspecting side.'

George's pudding came, and he set to.

His trouble was that he was not ignorant of anything. He had brains to spare – brains not used up in the booking office at the Joint.

As George put down his peaches it didn't seem right to watch, and my eyes began to rove over the restaurant. I caught sight of our waiter, and was glad to see he was looking at George and not me. The look in that waiter's eye said: now, can this gentry come up to the chalk as far as the bill is concerned? I too was wondering about George's pocketbook. How could he afford brandied peaches and all the rest on a booking clerk's wages?

I was certain there'd be a to-do over the bill and wanted to be off before it happened, but first, I needed to use the Gentlemen's.

Well, there was a fellow *lived* in there: he had a desk, a chair and a little stack of newspapers to be going on with. He passed you a towel when you'd washed your hands, and you put a penny in a silver bowl by the sink.

When I came back, the beaming smile on George's face was turned up to full. A sovereign was lying on top of a folded paper that I took to be the bill, and a glass of brandy and a big cigar were waiting at my place. The cigar was longer even than the 'A's I'd had the week before from the Albert Factory. I looked at the cigar band and there was a beautiful picture of a tropical scene: a whole other world, half an inch square.

'I've taken the liberty of laying in stores,' said George.

A lighted match was before me. I lit the cigar, drew on it. It was tighter, more complicated somehow than the 'A's and 'B's: more to it all round. I sipped the brandy, once, twice, and by degrees my suit became just my suit and nothing to be ashamed of. I checked on the waiters again and none were looking our way.

'Not so bad is it after all?' said George.

'I shouldn't let you stand me all this.'

'Nonsense,' said George, and he just smiled at me for a long time. It was pleasant in a way, because he was a good smiler, but I thought: What's he fishing for? Trouble was, I wouldn't trust myself not to give it, even though it couldn't be a good thing.

He leant forwards and began talking railways: about how the Lanky had its faults but was a great show really; how it had carried twenty-six millions of tons of freight in the year before; how its freight engines lit up the nights across Yorkshire and Lancashire; how it was, all in all, a fine place to make your corner.

'I see you in Manchester,' he said to me quite suddenly.

'Manchester Victoria?' I said, to stretch out the moment of pleasure.

'I picture you as part of the brass,' he said. 'At first, I thought: railway police. That's the thing for Jim Stringer, on account of his great stickability; his wanting to *know*. You've showed me that over this stone on the line business . . .'

'I still mean to get to the bottom of that,' I said, trying to look gravely at George, but not succeeding and feeling foolish in the attempt.

'But I now feel you have the steam to go further,' George went on.

I knew it was all daft talk, but I was carried along with it. 'But I'm not the right sort, am I?' I said. 'You know that very well.'

'Not a johnny, you mean? I wouldn't worry over that. You have a gentlemanly way of going on, pleasant looks. I don't say you wouldn't benefit from a new suit, but fate intended you for a fortunate man, Jim Stringer.'

Why would anybody say that if they did not think it true? Why?

I told George about my visit to Winterbottom, the Scarborough tailor, and early on he began to shake his head.

'You must not buy off the peg,' he said. 'Of course it'd make no odds up on the footplate, but in the offices at Victoria you'd be found out.'

'Shabbiness is a false economy,' I said, nodding, just as if I was already there in those offices at Manchester.

'You have it,' said George, and he fell back to smiling at me for a long time.

Another brandy came along for me, and a quarter of an hour later I floated out of the Imperial on a wave of beer, brandy and cigar smoke, leaving George behind for what he called his 'nightcap'. I was canned, and I was looking forward to the cold night air of Halifax. But of course when I came out into Horton Street the air was still warm, and another trick was in store, for all the buildings seemed to lift and turn so as to let me see them in a new way.

Chapter Thirty-one

The next day, the Friday of Wakes, the Hind's Mill lot came back from Blackpool, but it wasn't Clive and me that brought them in. Instead, we were running specials from Hebden Bridge into the Joint, which was no distance at all, and I felt sorry for those who'd only been able to get as far away as Hebden in their only week off during the year, pretty spot though it was. It was like a prison breakaway that had not come off.

That evening at seven I was coming back up from the Joint with my shadow stretched out before me as long as a railway carriage, but the heat of the day still at my back. I was quite done in, and the sun had gone from being a daily marvel to plain hard work.

My shadow reached and touched from time to time the boots of a tired man in black plodding up the hill under a black bowler. He stopped for a while at Sugden's ice-cream cart, but Sugden was not about, and there was no boy holding the pony. The fellow looked very agitated waiting there, and for a moment I thought he was going to try making enquiry of the white pony which was letting the man know, by certain sideways glances, that it would rather be left alone.

As I came up to the man, I saw that it was Bob the booking-office clerk. Or was it that other rather half-baked chap, Dick? Was it the one who had the same name as Arnold Dyson's dog, or was it the one that could write with both hands?

It was the second: Dick.

'If you want a penny lick,' I said, 'you'd best go in the Crown. That's where you'll find Sugden.'

Dick seemed a bit embarrassed at being caught wanting an ice cream, and pulled at the ends of his stiff collar. 'Well, you know,' he said, 'anything for coolness.'

'How do you fancy a pint in the Evening Star?' I said.

I was in no hurry to get home, since the wife would be out again, I knew. She was taking Cicely Braithwaite to a meeting of the Co-operative Women's Guild. This had been fixed up and put off several times, on account (I guessed) of Cicely not being over-keen on going.

Dick was looking me up and down: rather nervous of the working man, in his holed clothes and with his stink of yellow soap. But he voted yes. 'You've talked me into it, old man,' he said.

We walked in past the red billiards table, which he looked at long and hard. 'It's a good make,' he said.

'Do you play?' I asked him.

'Not really. I can generally see when a shot's on, but I can't make it myself.' He laughed nervously.

'But you can write with two hands,' I said.

'Yes, I can that,' he replied, and he sounded a little more Yorkshire, and a little happier now. Maybe it was the sight of the pint of Ramsden's I was passing his way.

He took his first go at the beer and I let him talk cricket for a while, and then we took another glass each and I thought: Well, I'm sorry for you, mate, but now the bombardment must begin.

It was one facer after another, but he took it pretty well, and the airs and graces that go with ink-spilling work gradually fell away.

'Do you remember when I stepped into your office that time, and George spoke of some tickets going missing?'

He nodded. He was looking at the beer barrels behind the bar. 'There was a pretty solid row over that,' he said.

'Why?'

'Well,' he said. 'Tickets going missing . . . It's the next worse thing to money being taken.'

'So Knowles was down on you?'

'Like I don't know what,' said Dick. 'We all thought we'd be sacked. Sacked or reduced over it anyway.'

'And that would be because the tickets went from your office?'

'That's just it,' said Dick. 'Did they? The tickets always come in from Manchester. That's where they're all printed up. They come in by train with a lad riding along of them. Now the lad says he brought this particular load up. Some of them were third-class returns to Liverpool. Not so many of those. Maybe just one block of two hundred and fifty, and then there were a good many more of another sort.'

'What sort?'

'Blackpool singles,' he said.

'That's it,' I said, and he looked at me strangely.

'Firsts, seconds and thirds,' Dick went on. 'Hundreds of pounds' worth. I worked out the exact figure once, but I've forgotten it now. The lad who rode with them from Manchester says he brought them up and left them in the office. He admits it was a busy sort of time when he did it; we say we never had them. You know how it turned out, don't you?'

'No,' I said.

'In the end, we were the ones believed, and some poor fellow in the despatch office at Manchester was stood down, and they're talking about bringing a prosecution for theft against him.'

'What did he look like, that fellow?'

'What did he look like? I don't know. I've never clapped eyes on him. He'd been in bother with the coppers once before, though, so that was him out.'

'Will you take another Ramsden's?' I asked Dick.

He passed me his glass. 'I swear on a hundred bibles I never saw those tickets,' he said.

'What about anyone else in the booking office? What about Bob?'

Dick shook his head.

'Now,' I said, 'what about George?'

Dick shook his head again, and then, as I handed him his fresh pint, tried a laugh that didn't come off. 'He's a caution, isn't he? Old George. Lodges with you, I hear?'

'Just while he looks about for a mansion of his own,' I said.

'We can't all be born into the nobility,' said Dick, 'but old George . . . He don't seem to know that.'

'If you'd had those Blackpool tickets away,' I said, 'how could you sell them?'

Dick was on the point right away. He wanted this chat as much as I did myself. 'If you were a booking-office clerk,' he said, 'you could sell them through the window. You wouldn't record the sale, and you'd pocket the brass.'

'But those tickets might be inspected on the train, and they're bound to be collected the other end. Besides, everyone's going to be on the look out for the missing numbers.'

'That's why you'd have to be off your head to try it,' said Dick. 'I mean, you might hope to get pally with as many of the ticket-checking and -collecting fellows as you could, but it wouldn't half take some doing. Of course, you *would* have the brass to pay them off.'

'But anyone you tried to bring into it who cut up rough . . .'

Dick was nodding. 'They might split,' he said, 'then you'd be in dead lumber.'

And it was just then that I heard the last sound you'd ever expect in the Evening Star. I turned about, and the billiard balls were rolling, but the fellow who'd made the shot was already through the door and gone. I walked out into Horton Street and there was nobody to be seen. But there again, the Imperial was the next place along, and its door was forever open to those who felt themselves the right sort.

———◦———

When I came home the wife was talking in low tones to Cicely Braithwaite. The two of them were sitting on the sofa and leaning forwards, holding hands. I knew what had happened: the wife had told Cicely that she was expecting.

I kissed the wife and nodded at Cicely. 'Is our lodger about?' I asked the wife.

'I've not seen him,' she said, and she didn't seem too happy about the subject being brought up.

'Lecture went off all right, did it?'

It was Cicely who answered. 'Oh it was such a lovely hall: green and white with electric light, and bright fustian curtains, ha'penny teas and buns . . .'

'And the talk that was given?' I said.

Cicely had begun to frown. 'It was ever so good,' she said, but she was well into her frown by now.

'What was the subject?'

'"The Municipal Duties of Co-operative Women",' said the wife, rather crossly. 'Mrs Duggan was not quite at her sparkling best.'

'Oh she *wasn't*, love, was she?' Cicely eagerly put in. 'Not that I've ever heard her before. You know, I was thinking all the while what a lovely place it would be for a dance.'

I left them to it, stepping through into the scullery for my usual scrub down at the boiler.

Through the closed door I could hear the wife saying: 'I just *knew*. You change, you know . . . *here*.'

'Well you did look peaky, love,' Cicely was saying, 'and to be honest, I did wonder . . .' The wife said something I couldn't catch, then Cicely said: 'Raspberry leaf tea – you must have it. And something else Lydia, dear: you must not raise your arms above your head too much.'

In the scullery, I laughed at that.

It must have been getting on for ten o'clock when Cicely quit the house, whereupon the wife and I went to bed. We had all the windows open, and it was as if there was no town at all outside.

I couldn't sleep, and at midnight I heard the chimes from the parish church, going on for ever and mingling with the clanging of the boots of George Ogden on the outside stairs. I heard him open his door and step into his bedroom. There was no sound at all for five minutes or so. Then he started moving about in his room, and I believed he was still doing so when the two o'clock chimes came, at about which hour I finally fell asleep.

Chapter Thirty-two

The Saturday of Wakes, I was with Clive on the Rishworth branch from five in the morning. The afternoon I had off.

Arriving back at the Joint from Sowerby Bridge shed, I walked to the booking office. Bob was at the window.

'Is George in?' I asked him.

He shook his head. 'Day off.'

I walked up Horton Street and did not stop at the Evening Star.

I wanted a normal sort of Saturday, with the town packed to bursting, the pubs with all their doors propped open, the trams flying about and the shop goods set on trestles in front of the windows so you couldn't help notice all the bargains going. But it was just the silent streets, with the sun hanging above and every tram looking like a runaway.

At three o'clock I reached Back Hill Street. The wife wasn't in: she was off seeing the midwife she'd been put on to by the Maternity Branch of the Co-operative Women's Guild.

I sat on the sofa in the parlour with a book of the wife's: it was by Charlotte Brontë, and I couldn't get on with it, but I had determined to read and wait for a while, so I finally took up one of my old *Railway Magazine*s and started an article on joint stations. The first was the Tri-junct at Derby, shared by the North Midland, the Midland Counties and the Birmingham & Derby Junction Railway. It was madness: three stationmasters. But then they all became the Midland Railway, so the station was no longer joint. There was no mention of *Halifax* Joint, which was rather disappointing – sort of made you feel like you didn't exist.

There was then an article on joint *lines* . . .

I heard the parish clock strike the half hour, and could wait no longer. I walked up by the inside stairs to George Ogden's bedroom. In case he was asleep inside, I knocked on the door, then I *clattered* on the door. Hearing nothing, I opened it and walked in.

The room was a jumble of dead plants and unread books. You could tell they were unread just by looking at them, just by the silence that surrounded them. All he'd done was set them in piles, but the piles had fallen over. The sunshine coming through the window was rolling gently over the dead plants, as if to say: well, I did my bit for you lot, you know.

I reached for the first of the books, *Letters of Descartes*, and there inside it was the wife's neatly typed-out contract for regulation of payment of rent, notice periods and so on. I picked up the next: *Hazlitt: Essays*. Inside was a tiny blue flower, dried out and itself turned almost to paper. I brushed it away and caught up the next volume, the biggest of all: *Don Quixote*.

There suddenly came a great crashing at the front door. It was not knocking but an attempt to bring it down, so it could hardly be the postman, early with the evening delivery.

I dashed down, and there at the front door was a scruffy man with a big head and big boots, turning and looking about the street. Next to him was a small man with fair hair, light, white beard, wide pale-blue eyes and a beer bottle in his hand. It was a big one, and it was broken, too.

As soon as I opened the door, this fellow passed this bottle to the taller one and, looking away towards Hill Street, said, 'Give him something for himself.'

'Is it a delivery?' I said, and the broken bottle hit the side of my head. I was up and at the bottle man and got one good one in, but then he did a leap and put his whole weight into his boot and his whole boot into my stomach. I was now down on the floor in the parlour, and the fair-haired one was sitting on the sofa with my copy of the *Railway Magazine*, taking my place in all particulars.

This was Cornstalk, the ticket collector I'd seen at Blackpool Central after my night with Clive at the Seashell, and then again while meeting the wife. He was the one who'd thrown the beer bottle in the air; the one who looked not like a railwayman but an angel gone to pot. I sat up on the floor as best I could, and there was a flowing free coolness on the side of my head. I slid my fingers over the skin on the side of my head and they moved through wetness, and then they were *under* skin. I slid my fingers back down through the blood and the skin fell; I moved them up once more and it rose again. It was a simple mechanism, like a letterbox, a shortcut to the inside of my head. The feel of it stopped me moving.

'Some Notable Joint Stations', Cornstalk was saying, and even as he was speaking he was tearing the pages. He stood up so as to make a better fist of the ripping, saying, not to me but his mate with the boots, 'I don't go much on this paper, you know.'

'What is it, Don?' asked Boots.

'Fucking *Railway Magazine*, Max,' said the fair-haired kid. 'I don't care for it because it always seems to remind me of fucking railways. Ask him "Where's George?"'

Max, the boot specialist, turned to me. I was still sitting on the floor. There was a warm sound in my head.

'Where's . . .'

He had many teeth, all white but assorted shapes and sizes; all strangers to each other. He smelt of old meat.

'. . . George?' I said. 'He's gone.'

'What's that? He's a fucking *gonner* you say?' said Max, leaning down over me.

'We fucking know *that*,' said Don to Max.

'He's gone,' I said again. 'What do you want him for?'

'Owes us brass,' said Max, who was taking from his pocket a bag of something. White powder. He held it out to me.

'Stick your finger in,' he said.

My blood was starting to stick my collar to my neck. I pulled the collar away. 'Did you two cunts put the stone on the line?' I asked Max, who was still holding out the white bag.

'Did we fucking *what*?' he said, and I knew they hadn't.

Don continued tearing up the *Railway Magazine*, fighting with it over at the sofa. His face was going pink, which made his eyes seem bluer, his beard whiter.

'Take a lick of this fucking sherbert,' Max said, moving the bag closer to my face. He said *sure bert*, drawing it out. His head was too long. It looked like something you saw on its own in a museum.

I could feel the blood a long way south inside my shirt now, heading down in force towards my belt.

'Did *George* put the stone on the line?' I asked.

Max still didn't seem to cotton on to what I was saying, but Don did, and, looking over to Max, he said: 'Doesn't sound like one of his strokes, does it?'

But Max had only one idea in his head. '*Sure bert*,' he said again, and the bag was right under my nose.

'I don't want any fucking sherbet,' I said.

'Are you sure about it?' he said, and I stood up and swung at him, missing, and falling over. He kicked me in the belly and I was down again, couldn't breathe, could only bleed.

'I want to put this lot on the fire now,' said Don, the angel gone to pot, who was standing at the sofa with the remnants of the month's *Railway Magazine* all around him. 'I want to get a fire going and I want to get this lot on.'

'There is no fireplace, Don,' said Max.

'Jesus Christ, you're right,' said Don, looking at the hole in the floor.

The wife would be back very soon. If there was trouble of any sort with the examination, if her pelvis was too small, she might be kept late. But the wife was strong and perfectly built.

I saw now that Max, holding that powder of his, wore gloves. On a day of this heat they were not required. Max picked some of the powder from the bag and threw a little of it towards me. It hung in the hot dark air of the parlour like stars. I rolled back away from it.

'That's it,' said Max, leaning over me with his horse's head,

'You do right. Quicklime, see. Be the blind home for the rest of your days, mate: half fare on the fucking trams, basket weaving and chair caning . . . riding that long push bike with all the other fucking blind blokes. *You've* fucking seen 'em . . .' He leant forward again, roaring: '*En't* yer? Six of the buggers to one bike, and all blind as fucking bats.'

'No, Max,' said Don, who'd sat back down on the sofa, with his hands in his pockets. 'The one at the front can see. Tell him: we know Ogden's done a shit. Now where's he gone?'

'I don't know.'

Don was frowning on the sofa, with his legs wide apart, looking down at his pointed boots.

'He's the landlord though . . .'

'George has flitted,' I said.

'Now that *does* sound like him,' said Don, standing up, and he nearly looked at me this time. Then he said, 'Put his fucking lights out with the quicklime. One eye, any road.'

Max's horse's head fell forwards and changed. He was looking down at the bag of lime and the change in his face was a grin. He punched his gloved hand into the bag, and there was a clatter at the door. Two letters came floating through and I wondered if my eyes would last to see them land. I rolled away again from Max as he threw the lime. I stood up and swung the coal scuttle at his head, and he was flying at me, boots first.

Don was at the door saying, 'Letter for George,' and then he gave a chuckle as he opened and read it. 'It's from his ma,' he said. 'She's expecting to see him tomorrow at her place. No wait, *today*, at seven.'

'Has she put down the address?' asked Max, after putting me down again with another kick.

'She has that,' said Don. 'People generally do in letters, you know, Max.' He put the letter in his pocket, saying, '54 New Clarence Road, Bradford.'

With that they were out of the door, and a second later it was the wife who was standing there.

'Who were those loafers just coming out of the house?' the wife asked, but the breath went out of her when she saw me sitting on the floor with the wonderfully clean and straight split at my temple, and the bag of quicklime spilled alongside me.

'I know that address,' I said, all in a daze, 'I know the address on the letter.'

<hr/>

As the wife was bandaging my head with one of her petticoats, I said, 'How was your pelvis?'

'Never mind that,' she said, 'what about all this?'

'It was all railway business,' I said, for it *had* been: railway ticket business.

She was looking at the old mantel. 'The gold cross has gone,' she said.

I looked up at our marriage lines, at the place where the gold cross wasn't. 'It will be put straight soon.'

'It *will*,' said the wife. 'It will be put straight and it will be over, this and all railway business.'

This was the second time there'd been scrapping in her house over trains. The first time was down in London.

By writing to her son, George's mother had accidentally saved me, but what was she accidentally bringing on herself? I then remembered about the address: 54 New Clarence Road, Bradford, was the place George told me you wrote to in order to obtain biscuits if the machine at the Joint failed.

I saw the second letter on the floor, the one that had arrived with the letter from George's mother. Holding the petticoat to my head, I picked it up and put it into my coat pocket.

We then walked across Halifax to the Infirmary, a place I had been sure I would not be returning to until the wife was twenty-eight weeks gone, and maybe not even then. We struck barely anybody on the way.

This time, I followed the sign for 'ACCIDENT CASES', and I was the only one, so I was taken directly through for sewing.

Chapter Thirty-three

As the stitches were put in, I asked the doctor whether concussion cases ought to be kept lying down or raised up. He gave a great sigh and said, 'It depends,' and I was happy with that.

Each stitch was like a little star made of silk. Iodine was painted over the top, and it was stinging under the bandage as I walked back through the Infirmary grounds with the wife.

'I don't know what's going forward,' she said, 'but you are to speak to the police.'

'Yes,' I said, taking the second letter from my coat pocket. It was franked 'Blackpool', and had been forwarded to Back Hill Street from the Joint station. It was from Henry Clarke, the good ventriloquist.

'Dear Mr Stringer,' I read,

On the sands at Blackpool recently you made enquiry as to whether I had been on a particular train, namely the 8.36 Halifax to Blackpool Express on Whit Sunday last. I told you that I had not been, but there seemed something rather familiar about those details.

On returning, directly afterwards, to my dressing room at the Seashell Music Hall, and looking in my diary, and at certain documents in my pocket book, I remembered that my ventriloquial figure, Young Leonard, was sent in his travelling basket as luggage in advance on that very train.

Forgive me for writing but I am fairly burning up with curiosity as to why you should have made your enquiry, and I admit that I cannot put from my mind a feeling of anxiety. If my figure were to become lost or damaged, I would very soon become destitute, and it is always with the greatest reluctance that I entrust my 'boy' to the care of the railways. Leonard's basket is marked about with 'fragile', 'this side uppermost', and every label going, but it is always such a relief when he is returned to my own safekeeping. Might I close, then, by asking you outright why you put your question. I do so in every confidence that, as a conscientious employee of the railway company, you will have sought the information in my own best interests.

Please do write to me here at the Seashell, Mr Stringer.

Yours respectfully,

Henry Clarke

I stopped amid the tired flowers of the Infirmary gardens and turned to the wife. Suddenly, all was newness. 'I am going off to the Palace Theatre,' I said.

'No,' she said.

But I knew that she would not argue with an invalid, and I set off at a lick for the centre of Halifax, calling back to the wife: 'Don't touch the white stuff in the bag on the floor of the parlour – it's quicklime.'

Had the terrible ventriloquist Monsieur Maurice tried to wreck the 8.36, only to find his stone in the way of our special train pulled by the Flyer? And had he done it in order to kill something that was already dead?

Young Leonard, the very lifelike figure, was a winner in the halls and could not be built again because his maker, the man in Manchester with the queer, short name that I could not bring to mind, was dead.

Young Leonard had been the making of Henry Clarke, and in a roundabout way the undoing of Monsieur Maurice.

As I pounded on, I saw that Halifax was a little busier by now. What had been the chances of the guard's van, or the guard's part of a carriage where the luggage was kept, being blasted to smithereens in our smash? No more than fair. And what were the chances of a ventriloquist's doll, heavily protected in a well-made travelling basket, being ripped apart in that smash?

You'd get long odds against that. You'd have to be clean out of your senses to try it. But there again train wreckers *were* clean out of their senses.

That summer the world was full of old men sweating in livery, and one of them stood outside the stage door of the Palace Theatre, where Monsieur Maurice was top of the bill for Wakes Week. I didn't know the exact time, but I did know we were not far off the first performance of the evening.

'How do,' I said to the guard on the stage door, who said nothing back but stared at my bandage, I supposed because I looked like a Hindoo. 'I'd like to have a word with Monsieur Maurice,' I said.

'Best write him a letter,' said the door guard.

'I mean . . . Morris Connell,' I said.

'Acquainted with the gentleman, are you?'

'We've met before,' I said.

'What do you want to see him for?'

'Just . . . shake him by the hand, like,' I said. 'I'm a student of ventriloquism.'

'Follow me,' said the door guard, and he led me into the back of the theatre, past all those hot, empty gaslit spaces that must exist for the shows to go on. There was a very strong smell that was completely new on me. A tiny cat followed behind us for a bit of the way, and, through one doorway, I glimpsed a fellow wearing trousers and boots but no shirt. He was plucking at a banjo. His eyes were blackened with make-up, and as he turned to stare after me I seemed to see right into his mind.

We came to a door with a little slate attached to it. On the slate were chalked the letters 'MM', and the word 'KNOCK'. Livery knocked, and the door was opened by Monsieur Maurice.

'Fellow wants a word, Mr Connell,' said Livery. 'Student of ventriloquism.'

293

Monsieur Maurice nodded at the doorkeeper, who went away with the ventriloquist looking after him.

'Time was when a fellow like that would have said "sir",' said Monsieur Maurice. He closed the door and fell to staring at my bandage.

I put out my hand. 'Jim Stringer,' I said.

He didn't give his name; everybody knew it after all.

He was not in his stage costume, but wore an ordinary blue suit. His fancy beard and moustache looked just as they did on stage, though, with the moustache stretching out wide, like the yardarm of a sailing ship.

The dressing room was painted green. There was a looking glass with electric lights running all across the top of it, which put me in mind of Blackpool. But the lights only lit the mirror. In shadows at the back of the room was a long couch, and the walking swell figure with the moon head was stretched out on it. The thing looked about right lying down – what could be more natural than taking a breather between shows? It was a better hand at lying down than walking at any rate. Behind the couch was a closed door.

Monsieur Maurice took a drink from a glass of something strange-coloured that was on his dressing table. 'Student of the art, are you?' he said, and he looked me over. He did not seem to recognise me from our earlier meeting, but it was hard to say. 'Lesson number one, take care of the vocal chords.'

He looked at the concoction in the glass and I thought: the fellow's canned. That's why he's let me in.

'Now I must be careful as regards you students,' he said. He folded his arms and looked at me.

'Why?'

'I call it brain stealing . . . Had most of my best ideas imitated over the years.'

'I just really came along to say how much I enjoyed your performances, and especially the walking, which I hold to be the hardest thing of all to pull off.'

He nodded and nearly smiled. 'I sometimes wonder if there's any call for it these days,' he said. 'Lately, we've had a steady run of stars in the art who go for the knee figures: the smaller sort of doll, sitting there on the knee. They're all right in their way, but they're just comic turns really. I prefer the walking and the business with a row of figures. Ventriloquism ought to be a spectacle to be wondered at rather than just laughed at.'

'I agree,' I said.

As he picked up his drink and took another pull at it, a strange vapour came across to me from the glass. The stuff was yellow and bits of it lingered on his moustache, shining there in the gloomy room. Behind him lay the figure: sleeping so very deeply, with its head like a big toe expanded to giant size.

'And of course, the younger chaps have all given up the distant voice,' he went on.

There was a pause, and a sizzling sound came from the direction of the figure stretched out on the couch. It took me a moment to realise that something was happening to Monsieur Maurice's lips behind the moustache.

'Frying fish, do you see?' he said, at which the noise stopped. 'Of course the beauty of the distant voice is that one can have an act without going to the expense of buying a figure. Do you have one of your own as yet?'

'No,' I said, 'although I am putting a little away every week in hopes of getting one. I am thinking of going for one of the knee figures I must admit, simply on account of those particular ones being so much cheaper . . . I rather like Young Leonard, you know, Mr Henry Clarke's schoolboy figure.'

Monsieur Maurice sighed, but that's all he did.

'That doll has a good saucy face,' I said.

Monsieur Maurice glanced backwards at the blank, sleeping moonface of his own walking figure. 'Sauciness is all the fashion now,' he said. 'And the poor ventriloquist is merely the butt of the jokes made by the figure.'

'Yes,' I said, 'but of course it's the ventriloquist himself who's making the jokes.'

Monsieur Maurice was frowning at me. 'Of course it is,' he said.

'Henry Clarke's all right if you like that sort of ventriloquism,' I said.

'Yes,' said Monsieur Maurice with another sigh, another sip of his strange cordial. 'Yes he is. We've been sharing bills at Blackpool, and they've lately put him top, over me.'

He looked down and looked up and there was a heaviness in his eyes.

'Henry Clarke's a pleasant fellow,' said Monsieur Maurice, 'but why do you think they would put him up to top of the bill?'

I could see that he really wanted to know.

'I couldn't say,' I said, 'I work on the railways. I'm pretty often firing trains to Blackpool . . .'

There was no flicker in the face of Monsieur Maurice, just a deepening sadness.

'For this reason,' I went on, 'I am pretty often *in* Blackpool, and I saw you on at the Seashell only a few weeks ago. All I can say is that I thought you a good deal better than Henry Clarke, who's more of a droll, as you say.'

'By Jove, did you?' said Monsieur Maurice, and he brightened a little. 'I sometimes feel,' he said, 'as I walk across the stage with the figure, that if there ever was another cry of . . .' He began to shake his head. 'I don't quite follow,' I said.

'Oh, at the Seashell once . . . There was a big fellow sitting on the front row . . . Blackpool's a vulgar sort of place as I expect you know, and all the vulgarity had come together in this fellow, who was with his girl because . . . Well, you know, they're never alone, the ones that call out.'

'What did he call?'

Monsieur Maurice looked down at his empty glass, then at the door at the back of the room, and I heard the fish frying once again; more fish this time, in hotter oil, and now with words mixed in: 'Monsieur Maurice, Monsieur Maurice . . .'

He turned back to me, and said: 'I am being called from that door.'

I looked at the dead figure and the door behind.

'Front-of-house business,' said Monsieur Maurice; 'I really must attend to it; I am so grateful for your interest.'

He bundled me out through the other door, and I was back in Horton Street, double-quick time, with a very choice expression on my face.

Monsieur Maurice had not put the stone on the line. The world was moving away from him at a great rate, which he knew; and he also knew there was nothing to be done about it. I was thinking of the vulgar fellow who had called out the word that Monsieur Maurice had not been able to bring himself to repeat. I doubted that it would have been anything out of the way. 'Rubbish!' – that would probably have been it. Or 'Get off!' I could imagine George Ogden giving such a cry.

And nobody went alone to Blackpool, as Monsieur Maurice had almost said.

I began to run.

Chapter Thirty-four

As I ran, I glanced back, seeing a line of people trooping steadily up Horton Street with boxes and bags in the evening sun, and I thought: it's finished. They're coming back.

On walking into the house, I saw the wife sitting on the sofa.

'Where's the bag of quicklime?' I said.

'We're shot of it,' she said.

I should have known not to ask her to leave it alone.

'What did they bring it for?' she asked, looking at the bandage on my head.

'Put the frighteners on,' I said.

'How?'

'Made out they were going to dash it into my eyes.'

'Was one of them the man you chased to Manchester?'

'No. It's all connected with Lowther, though. They visited him at the Infirmary, or tried to. Couldn't get in, but the names they gave damn near finished him off.'

'Well that's as clear as mud,' said the wife.

'Now they're after George,' I said. 'He's not been back, has he?'

'No.'

'He's flitted,' I said.

I climbed the stairs to George's room once again and opened *Don Quixote*. Inside it was a photograph of George. He was in his high collar and fancy waistcoat as usual, but was sitting inside a flying boat. You could tell he was off the ground, for his hair had all been knocked to one side by the wind.

The wife was looking over my shoulder. 'It's the flying machine at Blackpool,' she said.

She was looking all around the room now, saying, 'Why

298

ever did he not water these plants?'

I turned the photograph over. On the back were the words, 'I told you there was nothing to it, silly C. Love from Big G.'

I caught up some fragments of dried flowers, which I'd scattered about the room and were on the very point of becoming nothing at all. 'What's this?' I asked the wife.

'Forget-me-not.'

'When do forget-me-nots come out?'

'I forget,' said the wife, and then she laughed, saying: 'All I know is they're Cicely Braithwaite's particular favourites.' Then she stopped laughing.

I looked at the wife, then around the room. There was something else besides the books. Curtains, damask curtains, thrown anyhow onto the floor under the window.

'They're so viewsome,' I said in an under-breath. It was the strange saying that Cicely had come out with on seeing the forget-me-nots at Hardcastle Crags.

The picture came into my mind of George running in order to get his letter posted in the box on the tram. He'd said the letter was to his best girl, and that she was out in Oldham. What better way to get rid of the whole question of a sweet-heart? The young lady's out at Oldham. There's something about the word 'Oldham' that checks *all* questions.

'Is Cicely walking out with anyone that you know of?' I asked the wife.

'She is not,' said the wife.

'And was she keeping company at all before?'

'There was someone before I knew her. But she had to chuck him over.'

'The name was never mentioned?'

The wife shook her head. 'If you ask me she's rather sweet on Michael Hardcastle.'

'The traveller for Hind's?' I said.

The wife nodded.

Cicely had mentioned him on my first visit to the Mill, and coloured up as she did so. I thought of the man trying to keep next to Cicely in the crowd under the Blackpool Tower when the Hind's lot had come spilling out after their tea. Was that the fellow? 'Do you know where she lives, off hand?' I said.

'I don't,' said the wife. 'Somewhere over Savile Park way. The address is written down at the Mill, of course, but you'd have to wait until Monday for that.'

'There's no way round it?' I said.

'Not short of marching through the streets bawling out her name,' said the wife.

'I must speak with her,' I said.

'What you're trying to make out,' said the wife, 'is that George Ogden wanted to wreck the train so as to kill Michael Hardcastle?'

'He was *on* the Whit excursion then was he?'

The wife nodded. 'On both excursions,' she said.

'No,' I said, 'I don't think that was his reason.'

'Well you're right there,' said the wife, 'because nobody could have known there was anything going between them back at Whitsuntide – they barely knew it themselves.'

'I think it's odds-on he was out to get Cicely,' I said.

'Oh,' said the wife, and she sat down on the truckle bed.

'But how will you ever prove it? And what would you do if you could prove it?'

'Put salt on him,' I said.

'But still we don't *know*, do we?'

'Oh no,' I said. 'It's all just thinking on. Did you never mention to Cicely that you had a lodger here called George Ogden?'

The wife went red, which you didn't often see.

I looked out of the window, and down: at Halifax. The sky was dark blue. The gaslights were all coming on, and more of them inside the houses than for the past six days. The strange thing was that, even though it was getting on for seven o'clock, I was breaking out in a sweat. Wakes was over, but the glass was rising still.

300

'You know I'm not over-proud of taking in lodgers,' said the wife, at last.

'Well, I'm off now,' I said.

'Off where?'

'Down to the Joint. I've to catch a train.'

Chapter Thirty-five

The clock was striking seven as I half ran down Horton Street, against the waves of excursionists that were rolling up towards me. The next day, Sunday, I had a six o'clock go on with Clive. We were to collect from Southport twice over, and the turn would be a bugger: a ten-hour touch at least.

As I ran, I didn't know exactly *why* I was running. I wasn't really trying to catch a train; I was trying to catch the station, more like.

Seven o'clock had gone, so I had missed the chance to see whether George had kept his engagement with his mother at 54 New Clarence Road, Bradford. He wasn't a great one for keeping his word, and he'd had a lot on, what with being hounded by Don and Max. I wondered why he had given the address of his mother as being the address of the cream-biscuit-machine factory when I'd first gone up to the cigar factory with him. Most likely because he didn't write off for replacements, as he'd said, but stole the deliveries as they came in. There was a biscuit scheme as well as a ticket scheme, but the ticket scheme was the bigger one. Then again, it wasn't railway tickets that had made George Ogden a killer.

If George *had* been at 54 New Clarence Road in Bradford, he might be lying dead at this very moment, or be a hospital case at least. Why did Don and Max want him?

They were in on the ticket scheme with him.

It wasn't so hard to tease it all out. Don, the little, clever fellow, the angelic-looking one who was a tough nonetheless . . . He was a ticket collector at Blackpool, although he hated the work. His job would be to put his hands on as many as possible of the stolen Blackpool singles that had been sold on illegally by George at the Joint. Those, when collected, would be put out of sight of the ticket brass, or the auditors, or whoever it was checked over spent tickets.

Max, the big-headed fellow, the mate of Don's . . . Well, I wasn't quite sure where he came in.

As I sped on past the empty warehouse in Horton Street, I saw that a new bill had been pasted over 'CONDY'S BATH FLUID', which had in turn replaced 'A MEETING TO DISCUSS QUESTIONS'. I caught a glimpse of the new one as I went flashing past: 'A DIRIGIBLE FLIGHT', I read and, underneath, 'Balloon v. Motor Car'.

Down at the Joint, the trains were coming in at a great rate, and the excursionists were climbing out, looking red in the face and morngy. There were stacks of bags and boxes like little mountains here and there on the platform. All the porters' faces were shining with sweat in the white and green gaslight. I dashed about without a ticket, and then I heard a shout go up from one of the deputy stationmasters. The shout was 'Preston train!' and my plan was made. I ran along to it and climbed up, bumping into a ticket inspector immediately. He was miserable all right, just like all that sort, but he let me buy a ticket off him. It was not a ticket for Preston, though. I was only going to change there. The ticket I bought was for a place a couple of stops beyond: Kirkham.

The stone had stopped the Highflyer between Salwick and Kirkham, the two villages in the fields before Blackpool. If George had been the wrecker, he would have needed to get the stone to the line. He would have needed a turn-out of some sort. In my last visit to the wife's office at Hind's Mill, I had looked in the 'Trades' part of the *Kelly's* directory for East Lancs, searching for fly proprietors, jobmasters or livery-stable keepers at Salwick or Kirkham, and had turned one up at Kirkham. I'd made a note of the address in my pocket book, but the name was easy enough to remember: The Wrong Way Inn.

———◦———

There wasn't much to Kirkham: shadowy, empty cattle pens near the station, and the place had one mill to its name. The Wrong Way Inn was at the end of Wrong Way Lane: a dusty track between tall hedges that were fairly seething with life in the darkness. Big red berries glowed in the hot night; moths and small mysterious flying things swooped about before me.

The Wrong Way Inn looked like a mansion given over to the hoi polloi. There were fires blazing in all the rooms. There was an arch going clean through the front of the inn, and this led to a courtyard with stables and a hot, sweet, hay smell and all kinds of carts and carriages about the place. The horses were just dark movements inside the stalls. A fat man was standing in the middle of all. He wore a leather apron and had a very red nose – the colour of something that by rights should have been part of his insides not his outsides. I knew right away that he was a horseman or jobmaster, happier to be out with his nags than inside the inn.

I stood before him for a second, trying not to look at his nose, while he looked at my bandage.

'What are you after then mate?' he said.

'I'm not quite certain,' I said.

'I see. Want the whole stable trotted out, do you?' He smiled, which came as a relief. I think it went in my favour that I was not canned, for sobriety must have been at a premium during Saturday nights at the Wrong Way Inn.

'I'm a fireman on the Lanky,' I began; 'the Lancashire and Yorkshire Railway, I mean.'

His smile fell a little at that. Horsemen did not as a rule like railways any more than railwaymen liked motorcars.

'Railway business is it, then?'

I nodded. 'I wondered if you might be able to say whether somebody had hired a dog cart or something of that kind on Whit Sunday last.'

'Oh aye?'

'I have a notion of who it might have been,' I went on. 'He

304

would've been a youngish fellow, quite well turned out, with a very particular sort of waistcoat. He was also quite . . .'

I looked at the horseman. He wasn't half fat.

'He was quite, ah . . . well, quite a chubby sort,' I said.

The jobmaster grinned. 'Well, you know what they say,' he chuckled, 'fat and happy!'

'He tried to wreck the engine I was firing along the stretch just near here.'

That checked the horseman's good humour.

'He did it by placing a grindstone on the line.'

'Jesus Christ, did he?' said the jobmaster, and he turned about in a circle as though looking for somebody or something. When he was facing me again, he said: 'A fellow we had here a few weeks back . . . I don't say it was Whit because I don't recall, and I wasn't the one looking after him . . . He was seen to by a lad who's not here presently. Now this character took a pony and cart for the day, and he had a grindstone off us 'n' all. The bloody thing was lying about in the yard here. Too bloody smooth, you see? No use to man nor beast, but the lad as works here let this fellow have it for a bob, helped him load it up too.'

'Well then,' I said.

'You make out the bloody thing was used to wreck a train?'

'It was an attempt,' I said. 'It didn't come off, but we had to clap the brakes on so hard that a lass on the train tumbled over in a carriage and was killed. Have you not had the coppers here, asking questions?'

'We have not.'

'And would the lad remember this grindstone fellow? Would he make a witness, I mean, if it came to it?'

'I'm bloody certain he would. He was full of it afterwards. Acted like a lord, the bloke did. Then off he went, with his little pony and worn-out grindstone.'

I nodded.

'Where's this bloke now?' asked the jobmaster.

'That's just it,' I said. 'I've no notion.'

Chapter Thirty-six

Sunday, we had the Southport turns to work.

We ran the first engine out there empty, and came back with umpteen chuffed-off excursionists. Then we did the same again. The engine – which was a rotten steamer – would only go right when the fire was just so. It was another unbreathable day and I'd taken off the bandage. When Clive asked about the stitches, I said I'd fallen, which he did not believe, but it was simpler than starting on a story that was not yet finished.

Clive, as usual, was looking the very glass of form, and I wondered again about what he'd been up to in Scarborough, and whether he was making love to the stationmaster's wife, but if my notions about George were right, it hardly mattered.

As we booked off at Sowerby Bridge, Clive said: 'See you tomorrow at six,' for that was the time of our go-on. I nodded back, but I knew he'd be booking on alone.

◄○►

The next morning I walked to Hind's Mill with the wife.

The whole of the town was going back to work and the mood was black. We fell in with the Hind's lot inside the tunnel that runs under the Joint. It was filled with the sound of clanging clogs, but no voices. Before clocking on, there was Halifax's steepest hill to be climbed in roasting heat, for the sun didn't know the holidays had ended.

Cicely Braithwaite's was the first happy face I saw. She was sitting on the wall by the mill pond waiting for the buzzer to go, and when she spotted the wife, she called, 'Clog on, Lydia! I've so much to tell you about goings-on at Blackpool!'

But when she saw me, her face turned puzzled.

The wife said: 'Cicely, my husband would like to ask you something.'

Not 'Jim' but 'my husband'. It was the kind of talk you come out with when there's been a death. Well, there *had* been a death – three, all told.

I knew the wife would have worked out the wording beforehand. It was her way of saying: I have nothing to do with this myself, her way of trying to keep up a friendship that my questions were well-nigh certain to end.

I said, 'Cicely, was a fellow called George Ogden courting you?' I looked up at the mill chimney: the smoke was already racing out of it and Cicely was going from white to red. I felt bad about the effect the question had on her, then glad about it, then bad again.

'He did,' she said, standing up. 'He *was*, I mean. How do you know him?' It was a new, sharper Cicely: the weaver-turned-clerk. It's not so easy to make that jump after all.

'He was our lodger,' I said.

The wife was standing by the water in the background.

'Only he's flitted,' I went on.

Cicely looked at me straight, then the buzzer went. It was as if all the steam available at that moment had been put through the one tiny whistle. The doors were rolled open and Hind's Mill began to suck in its people.

I waited. Cicely and the wife waited too.

'Well, *I* flitted from *him*,' said Cicely when the racket had stopped and the people were all inside.

'Did you go to Blackpool with him?'

'Oh, he didn't hold with Blackpool. Too common by a long way. But yes, we went, and it was one of the best days we had.'

'Did you take a picture of him on the flying boats?'

'You've turned it up, have you?'

'It was left behind in this room.'

'I wouldn't go on myself. He went up. George had pluck, and

he could be the most charming fellow, you know. Afterwards, we drunk Champagne in the Winter Gardens.' She gave me a look that said: bet you've not done that.

'I think he put the stone on the line,' I said.

'Now you fuck off,' said Cicely Braithwaite.

The wife came up but Cicely put her arm up: just one movement, like a signal. The three of us were alone by the mill pond now, with Halifax working beneath us in the heat.

'You don't believe he did, then?' I said.

And there it ended. Cicely turned, the wife took her into the mill, and I set off back down towards Halifax.

But when I was no more than half a minute down the hill, I looked back at the front doors of the mill. Cicely was standing before them, just as though the mill was her own home. She was looking at me, and as I walked back up towards her, she walked down to meet me. She took off her bonnet and said: 'I'd finished with George. He was up to something crooked at the station and that's what brought it on. He accepted that we were finished, but he said I was not to go to Blackpool without him. I said he was nuts. He *is* nuts, you know.'

'I know.'

'But he loved me.'

That knocked me; I hadn't expected it to be said.

'That's perhaps *why* he did,' said Cicely, and tears and laughter nearly came together in an instant. But instead she said, 'George told me he would stop the excursion.'

'You're a witness to that, you know,' I said.

'I am,' said Cicely. 'I've thought about it and I will say what must be said. He's written to me since,' she said. 'Threats. I will not have that. But I still don't believe he tried to cause a train smash, you know.'

'Where's he now?'

'Well,' she said, 'is he not at work down there?'

She pointed at the Joint.

This I had not considered. He'd flitted from Back Hill Street

308

and was being chased for brass by Don and Max. But what harm could come to him in the booking office?

'I'm off to look,' I said.

———◄○►———

At the Joint, Dick and Bob were both at the window. Two clerks for the price of one, arguing over a ledger.

'Is George in?' I asked Bob. 'I want to see him most particularly.'

'George!' said Bob. 'We're out with that idle so-and-so. He's not turned up, left us short-handed on one of the busiest days . . . but hold on a moment, he lives with you. Have *you* not seen him? What's going off?'

All these questions, like a little summer fly going round and round my head. But Dick was looking at me with a steady eye. We'd had our chat at the Evening Star, and I knew he had an inkling.

'He's flitted,' I said to Bob. 'Owes back rent.'

I turned to Dick. 'Where's he gone, mate? Any ideas?'

'I'll tell you what,' said Dick, 'wherever it is, he wouldn't buy his ticket here, now, would he?'

This was a joint station, and my eyes went over towards the next-door ticket window, the one operated by the Great Northern.

Dick shook his head. 'They know him there 'n' all,' he said.

'Everyone knows George,' said Bob.

'He may have bought it at the next stop along,' said Dick.

I nodded. Sowerby Bridge.

'Let's have a ticket for Sowerby Bridge then, Dick,' I said.

Half a minute later I had in my hand a third-class single to Sowerby Bridge. I looked at the ticket and I looked at Dick. It was number 6521. A nothing number in a run of ten thousand.

Trains from the Joint to Sowerby Bridge are ten a penny. I was aboard one in no time, and climbed off it dead opposite the little booking office at Sowerby Bridge station. I could see the shed in the distance, smoking away in the sun.

I'd thought that Dick and Bob were your regulation booking-office types, but this fellow before me took the bun: hair all moved over to one side with Brilliantine; titchy, thick, scientific-looking specs.

'How do,' I said.

The Sowerby Bridge booking-office clerk said nothing. I'd never struck this fellow before because I usually just relied on folk knowing me on my runs between Sowerby Bridge and the Joint. And if it came to it, there was always the footplate pass in my pocket.

'Have you sold a ticket lately to a big fellow in a fancy waistcoat?' I asked him.

'If I had done,' he said, 'it would be my business, wouldn't it?'

'It's just that he might have done a murder.'

'Police matter then,' he said.

There were two layers of glass between us: the clerk's specs and the ticket-office window.

'What do you reckon?' I said.

Still nothing.

I took out my pocket book.

'I have an interesting sort of railway ticket here,' I said.

'What's interesting about it?' he said.

And I knew I had him.

'The number,' I said.

'Four zeroes, I suppose it is,' said the ticket clerk. 'I buy them for myself when they come up, if they're not too pricey.'

I held up at the window the third-class single to Todmorden that George had given me.

'One, two, three, four,' said the ticket clerk, reading the number. 'Third class . . .'

'What do you reckon?' I said again.

'Fair do's,' said the clerk. 'I'll give you thruppence for it.'

'It's yours gratis,' I said, 'if you answer the question.'

'I forget,' he said.

'You forget what?'

'The question.'

'A big fellow,' I said, 'running to fat; lot of hair; fancy waistcoat. Acts like a lord.' I was still holding up the ticket.

'I did strike a fellow like him,' said the clerk.

'When?'

'Forty-five minutes ago.'

'Where was he off to?'

'Goole.'

I nodded. Step on at Goole for the Continent.

'When's next Goole train?' I said.

'Half an hour,' said the ticket clerk.

I handed over the interesting ticket to the clerk, and had a third-class single to Goole off him in return. I did not look at the number.

Chapter Thirty-seven

All morning there'd been something amiss; all bloody *summer* there had been, and, as the train for Goole pulled out of Sowerby Bridge station, the answer came: blue blackness in the sky.

I had never been to Goole, but I knew it to be an inland port. The barges used the canals that went out from it – and there were any number of those. The sea-going ships came and went by the Humber Estuary, which by the time it reached Goole was called the river Ouse.

So the steamships went out into a *river*, and they could only do it when the tide was right.

The eastward ride to Goole was a two-hour touch, taking me right across Yorkshire. The rain was stalled in the blackness at Sowerby Bridge; skies were clear again over Wakefield, but our little train struck storm conditions once more at Pontefract, where the black ink was spilling across the sky. Here I leant out of the window as the guard was giving the 'right away', and one big raindrop was blown into my face.

The first lightning flash happened just as Goole appeared, and it seemed to bounce the whole town into my view.

Lightning is the *real* light, and all was revealed in an instant: the frightening black and red water tower, the tall coal hoists like factories on legs that could roll back and forth, and one of them seemed to be *walking* through the port in that bright, white moment, but no: that was the coal hoist that floated. I saw the sailing ships, plenty of those – the masts and yardarms made tall crucifixes – and the steamships too, with their backward-sloping funnels. Most would be of the Lanky's own fleet.

The station was only a few hundred yards from the docks. As I stepped through the ticket gate, the wind made the sound of a motorcar – a motorcar far off but gigantic. The rain was flying in the wind; the bookseller outside the station had an oilcloth over all his wares.

'Batten down the hatches,' he said to me as I passed by.

I stopped beyond the station for a moment, looking at the docks. Goole was not like a town, but more like a giant *system*, with the moving cranes going one way and the trains running a different way, and the houses hard by the docks with sea water rolling before them instead of roads. The lightning came again from out over the Humber, like the blue lines you might see in the whites of a woman's eye, in the *corner* of the eye, almost out of sight.

And then the lightning came again, from a different side of the seaway, as if the light was blown by the wind.

I walked on into the docks. The first thing I struck was a church that stood in the centre of the low dock buildings, like the hub of a wheel. The flag on the steeple was having a rare old time of it. I saw that the clock was lit by lightning-coloured gas.

The time was midday – midday in summer and the town was dark, with gas lamps lit all across the docks.

I walked on, and the water that should have been down there in the docks was up and at me, and there was a sharpness to the wetness. There were half a dozen docks before me, each like a town square filled with water. At one dock close by, two men were winding wheels on opposite sides of a small pump. A white tube, shining in the rain, came from the pump and hung down over the dock wall into the water, and I thought: there's a man down there on the end of that. Well, he was out of the rain at any rate.

Over the road from where I stood were two warehouses with a pub crammed between them. Along from the warehouses was a building that looked like a chapel, but was not. The wide doorway was propped open. Above it was a carving

313

of two small galleons bobbing about on a sea, and, above these, a flagpole flew the seagoing version of the Lancashire and Yorkshire Railway badge. It was the shipping office for the Lanky.

The place was stifling: long lines of men in bowlers and steaming Ulsters stood queuing for tickets. The two blokes giving out the tickets at a long table were both smoking pipes. It took a long time for any man to get his ticket, for it was all a lot of fishing in pocket books, presentation of passports, checking of same; and finally the issuing of tickets that looked like little books, with each page needing to be stamped.

Behind the ticket clerks was a wide painting showing the fleet of Lanky steamers, each in its own bit of sea, and all set in a circle going around a sort of gravestone on which were two columns headed 'CONTINENTAL PORTS' and 'DAYS OF SAILING'. Today was Monday. On Monday there were sailings to Amsterdam, Antwerp, Ghent, Hamburg, Rotterdam. All ships conveyed merchandise, but would take passengers too – it was ten bob to most places.

I walked up alongside one of the fellows in the queue. 'What time are the ships going off today?' I asked him.

'Four o'clock.'

He'd answered without looking at me. He looked like a criminal. Every man jack of them in that queue looked as if he was escaping from somebody or something. And then I noticed a copper standing in the corner of the room, and for the first time I was set thinking about what I would do if I tracked down George. Up to then I'd just been dreaming of saying to him: 'I know you did it, you fucking rotter.'

I don't know exactly why, but I never tried asking the ticket clerks in the shipping office whether they'd sold a ticket to a fellow with the particular looks of George Ogden. It was something about the length of the queue, and the way the blokes silently smoked as they tore and stamped the dockets. I knew it would be like talking to a wall.

Then there was the copper.

I could put the whole matter in his hands. But no, not yet. It would be Manchester all over again if I did that.

I walked out of the shipping office and the storm was still there. I watched the rain hitting the sea like a quarrel and streaming through the circles of light around the gas lamps. The two men were still winding the wheels on the small pump connected to the air tube. And something being done in the docks was sending an underwater-bell sound floating over Goole.

I walked into one terraced street, turned into another. Between two houses was a shop with a wide black iron panel fixed to its front. Pressed into the iron was the shape of three balls, as if three iron balls had been hurled there when the iron was hot. I saw the remains of gold paint in the hollows, and below, also driven into the iron, the words 'HARPER BROTHERS. MONEY ADVANCED ON PICTURES, BRONZES, VIOLINS & C & C.'

I stared at this place, and George Ogden walked out of its door holding a little case.

I was over the road from him and along a little. I shouted out and he ran directly around the corner with his funny, wobbling run. But it served him well enough because, as I stepped forward, I slipped on the slimy kerbstone, dashing the back of my head on the cobbles. I put my hand directly up to the wound that had been sewn. It was not torn. Then I hared around the corner, striking a long, empty street, dead straight. It ended in lines of railway wagons. As I watched, the nearest line of wagons jangled into life, and the words 'TRANSHIPMENT', 'COAL FACTORS AND EXPORTERS', 'TRAN-SHIPMENT', 'COAL FACTORS AND EXPORTERS', over and again in alternation, were dragged across the end of the street.

There was a little hotel. I hurried along to it and burst through the front door. It was full of very dry people in strange hats, and all smoking cigars. I was in the public bar and for a moment thought my hearing had gone west, for

315

they were all speaking words I could not make out. They were all foreigners.

I came out of there double-quick and ducked into the next place. It was a little watery fishmonger's, with things floating in pails of cloudy water, but most of the fish already sold and the owner swabbing down the floor.

'You've not seen a fellow come by this way, have you?'

The fishmonger shook his head.

I gave it up. Back into the rain; back into Goole town.

George was in Goole at any rate, and he would only be leaving the town on a boat, and the boats could not set sail just yet.

So I walked about for an eternity in the blackness and the rain, keeping my eyes skinned. I must have stood for half an hour in front of a butcher's, with a line of dead rabbits over my head holding the rain off. Presently, I turned back to the docks, where the black water looked as though it was being beaten by hammers. There might have been getting on for half a dozen steamships loading. Horses were being walked up onto one of them, but it was mainly coal that was going in. As I looked on, a coal barge came by, snaking through the docks with smaller barges towed behind, all heaped with coal. I thought of the swan at Hebden Bridge, with the signets following behind in a line.

I found myself after a while back in the place near the church, bang outside the Lanky shipping office once again. I looked up at the flag, the little galleons carved over the door. Right over the road was the pub I'd spotted before. It also had two galleons on show – these on the pub sign. They were friendly-looking little ships, but the pub was just a white room, heaving with sea-going blokes. There was nothing on the wall but gas flares with no mantels, giving out a bright white light. Everybody was supping, and everybody was smoking, for what else do you do while waiting for your ship to leave? There were bags and portmanteaus all over the floor, and the fashion was to stand there swigging your ale with your foot placed on top of your bag, so as to stop it being carried away.

I pushed my way through to the bar, trying to avoid the hazards of the luggage pieces, and asked for a glass of ale from the barman, who was small and rough-looking, like his pub. Just as he passed the beer over, I saw something red in the far corner of the room: the redness of a glass of wine, the one glass of wine being drunk in that room.

Well, it was George Ogden drinking it.

As I moved over to him with my own glass in my hand, one of the big fellows waiting for transhipment knocked against Ogden, and half the wine was down his fancy waistcoat. When I got over to him, he was trying to rub it away, saying to himself, 'Just need a little something in a bottle to furbish it up.'

'It's all up, George,' I said.

He was not wearing his stiff collar. He was wearing the white shirt as usual, but he had on no collar at all and I saw his neck for the first time. There was a fair amount of it.

He closed his eyes for a second, as if he could magic me away by the power of his mind. But then he looked back. 'Hello, old man,' he said, putting his hand inside his coat and taking out a pocket book. He handed me a pawn-shop ticket and a banknote. 'Look, old sort,' he said, 'the fellow in that pawn shop's as tight as Kelsey's Nuts. He let me have a sovereign for the gold cross, and I'm now giving you the ticket and ten shillings. You'll have the balance directly I get myself straightened out.'

I put down my glass of ale on the nearest table, took hold of his shirt and pitched him against the wall. He bounced back off it. The blokes around us barely moved – it was a normal sort of event in this place.

'Careful, old sort,' George said presently, 'I will not be slighted.'

'Let's have it,' I said. 'Tell me about the tickets first.'

'Had a few away, that's all,' he said. 'Just a lark, really. I began by thinking it rather a pretty little scheme.'

317

'You needed help with it though.'

'Ha!' said George, 'and that's where things got a little tangled. I'll tell you what, old boy: you wouldn't believe – good chap like yourself – the vagabonds they've got on the ticket-collecting side over at Blackpool.'

'Don was one of them,' I said.

'Well I'm blowed!' said George, who was now getting back to something like himself. 'You've happened on that gentry, have you? Very nasty piece of goods indeed.'

'And his pal, Max, is a sight worse,' I said.

George blew out his cheeks. 'You're not wrong there either.'

'Where did he come into it? I asked. 'Max, I mean. He's not a ticket collector, is he?'

'Well now, Max . . .' said George. 'He was on hand just in case anyone should stumble over the scheme and then . . . well, how can I put it, old man? He *is* rather scarifying. I mean, Queensbury Rules don't enter into it with that particular chap, and that I can promise you.'

'You're waiting for a boat,' I said, ignoring this. 'Where are you off?'

'Holland, old man.'

In my mind's eye I saw George Ogden in Holland, wearing big trousers with patches sewn on, sticking his fat finger in the hole in the dyke.

'Thought I'd try my luck in Amsterdam,' he was saying. 'Now you wouldn't crack on, old man, would you? We've had some rare old larks, the two of us. I'll be honest, I liked your company. But could I ask you a question, old man? Why should you be up there, day in, day out, working for slave wages in all weathers, getting burnt, bashed about the head – I see you have stitches in – when many stupider fellows are sitting back in their offices and barely lifting a finger for twice what you're on? I only wonder because I saw you in the restaurant and you were like a cat on hot bricks, and it's not right that you should be. You must have a *scheme*, old man, otherwise your life will be quite wasted. Would you care for a refill?'

'No.'

Over the heads of the crowd in the bright, white room I saw the helmet of a copper. It was the one I'd seen over the way, in the shipping office. He was standing by the door, chatting to a bloke who looked as though he ought to be *arrested* by the copper, not passing the time of day with him.

'I had a sweetheart once,' George continued. 'Oh, she'd go for the salt with her knife as soon as *wink*. Well, I checked that in no time and schooled her in speech a little: "Six *year*", she would say, and I would say "No, sweet, six *years*". Now, she didn't like it one bit, but I kept at it. Started on the mill floor, that one did. I'm not ashamed to say it, old man: I was stepping out with a factory girl, but I put her up to going for the office, and it was the proudest moment of my life when she went typewriter in the same concern. And why do you think I bothered? Because she had brains, and I would *not* have them wasted, and I would not have her slighted. It was my duty to keep the wind off that girl, and I tried and I tried, and in the end, old man, you see, I failed.'

I was not really listening to George. I was thinking of Margaret Dyson and how, as I had picked her up, the life had spilled out of her.

'You're the same in some respects, you know,' George was saying, 'but you have your Mrs Stringer, and she will keep you up to the mark, old man, believe me.'

The doctor's words came back: 'I will go further, and say that if it is a delicate person you are dealing with . . .'

'Oh, whether you like it or *not*,' George Ogden was saying, 'believe me. And you *will* like it, for you're an intelligent fellow.'

'To put him or her suddenly upright may cost your patient his or her life.'

'And I knew, I just *knew*, old sort, that I could never keep anything back from you,' George Ogden was saying, 'and I'm really awfully sorry for trying.'

319

'Speaking of that,' I said, 'your dad's not in the nutty house at all, is he?'

George gave a laugh, and what was vexing was that it was a real laugh. 'He is not, old man! Though he should be, and I only wish the bastard *were* locked away. Why, Dad was a butcher, just like your old man, from what I gather. I say, did yours put little lumps of suet on the scales so as to give short change?'

'No,' I said.

'I don't want to talk about my pa any more, if it's all the same.'

'You clapped eyes on your mother lately?'

'No,' said Ogden. 'Why do you ask? She doesn't live with Dad any more on account of his being so . . .' He frowned, adding: 'I did have an arrangement to go and see Mother, but what with one thing and another . . .'

'Why'd you put the grindstone on the line?'

He was shaking his head at this right from the off. 'Now just a moment,' he said, 'I know as little of that as the new-born babe. I realise you thought it might have been part of some plan to do for Lowther, the ticket inspector, because of what happened to him later, but you see, old sort, Lowther was in with us on the ticket scheme. I sounded the fellow out, in a roundabout way, and he jumped at it. Lanky wages, you see: they make desperate men of the best of us.'

He looked at me, nodding for quite a while.

'Now I happen to know', he went on, 'that Lowther came to grief, over in those Hebden Crags, at the hands of a rather angry fellow from Ticket Despatch in Manchester.'

'The one who lost his job over the missing tickets?'

'That's him. I wouldn't have had it happen for worlds, you know, that a fellow should lose his position over the business, let alone another ending up with two busted legs.'

'You put the stone on the line,' I said, 'not because of the ticket business, but because you wanted to kill Cicely Braithwaite, who'd thrown you over.'

'If I could just . . .' said George. His hand was moving.

'Or at best you wanted to scare the bloody daylights out of her.'

George's hand was in his waistcoat and the clasp knife was in his hand, the one he used to slice the ends off his cigars. I saw it there, shaking in his fat hand, and I saw on the handle a picture of Blackpool Tower.

There came a great yell and a tug from behind on my coat.

I almost fell backwards at the yank that was given, and in that instant I saw the empty space where George had been standing and heard the barman roaring: 'You've not paid me for the fucking ale!'

'For Christ's sake!' I shouted, putting coins into his hands, 'you daft fucking cunt!' and I was fighting my way over the bags and through the crowd, after George, or the copper, but the copper who'd walked in had gone. In fact, half the lot that had been in the pub no longer were, and when I stumbled out into the street I saw why. Clear skies: the blueness seemed to go up and up, and all was order and good sense once more in the port of Goole, with happier-looking folk all about the place and the steamships not just steaming but moving.

All across the docks, I could see fellows walking in circles, pushing wooden spars attached to turning poles. The tide had risen to the correct level and the lock gates were being opened. Two of the steamers were already out on the Humber, moving with no sign of effort over the wide, bright water.

I ran into the docks, looking for a copper, or looking for George. Had he loved Cicely Braithwaite, or tried to control her? They were the same thing. At any rate, I wanted to see him swing.

I dashed back and forth as the big blokes turned their circles and one lock gate after another opened, bringing a gentle rushing sound, the ringing of bells on the boats, and shouts back and forth between the boats and the docks.

321

This was the moment of freedom for those sea captains and they all wanted to be off and away. In amongst all the ship business I saw the diver, the iron man, up from underwater, sitting on a chair at the top of the dock wall near to me. With his two attendants standing by, next to the pump that was now still, he looked like a strange sort of king from another world, with his great iron boots that could have been gold, his white suit that could have been silk, and the great brass head. As I peered closer, I saw the face of an ordinary man staring through the window at the side of it.

'Where's the Holland boat?' I shouted to a man throwing a rope onto a moving steamship.

'Ouse Dock!' he shouted, and pointed over to a ship still in dock but steaming hard; there were horses on its deck in pens, and blokes working away before it, one on either side, turning the wheels that controlled the dock.

From behind me, George Ogden appeared with his tumbling run. He leapt a pile of ropes and stumbled, but still he had ten yards on me as I began pounding after him. He was making for the boat that was about to leave Ouse Dock.

The iron man was standing up once again and moving towards the top of an iron ladder that led down into the water. His attendants helped him all the way, as if he was an invalid. The breathing tube trailed behind. As I leapt the coil of ropes that George had leapt a moment before, I saw that the three were in George's path. I saw him try to leap the air tube, but his boot caught, pulling the pump over. I saw the pump topple and the iron man turn with a sort of slow shock, and . . . I couldn't see George.

Beyond, at Ouse Dock, I saw the lock gates moving, with water moving *on* them: two mobile waterfalls, swinging away from one another. The boat was a Lanky boat. Its name was written big on the side: *Equity*.

I looked again at the iron man, now alone on the dock. His two attendants were climbing down the iron ladder. They were both clinging on to the top of it and shouting things I couldn't take in, but as I got up to the top of the ladder, one dropped into the water, reluctant, like, and then the other. The last man that could help bring George up was the one that was dressed for diving, all togged up to sink.

I looked down. The assistants had been under and were up again now, moving the water with their hands, as if it was long grass they'd accidentally dropped something into.

I looked up again at the *Equity*, moving through the lock gates with a clear, confident rumbling of the engine, the horses all looking forward, with their manes streaming backwards in the direction of the funnel smoke. The sky, cleaned out by the storm, was light blue with a gleam of gold. The long grass in the meadows either side of the waterway was all blowing gently to the right. There was a church out on one of the banks with a pretty sort of barn near that, and you saw that Goole was not so great and terrifying a machine after all if you could be out of it and into country so fast.

As I watched, and the iron man's attendants roared in the water, the steamship moved into a turn in the centre of the channel, like a dancer; the horses were turning too, under the spinning smoke that was hanging over the shining water, hesitating.

PART THREE

After

Chapter Thirty-eight

I took the train with the wife to Hebden Bridge. From there we walked – not to the Crags this time but to a high pasture out towards Mytholmroyd, the route along the lanes being indicated by smaller copies of the Horton Street poster that had read 'A DIRIGIBLE FLIGHT' and 'Balloon v. Motor Car'.

The hill tops and the parts of the fields that were for some mysterious reason colder than others were still covered in snow. In other spots, the ground was showing through again in unexpected shades. The sky was the colour of iron, and such daylight as there was seemed somehow begrudged. The trees were black and still.

As we followed the signs, the cold made steam engines of the wife and me. I liked to talk in this weather, just to see the clouds come rolling from my mouth.

'There's hardly a breath of breeze,' I said.

'That's good for the aeronauts,' said the wife. 'They don't sail in excessive wind.'

The jaunt was the wife's idea. She'd seen the poster in Horton Street and it had set her reading anything she could lay her hands on to do with aeronautics. It seemed to be one of the funny ways pregnancy had taken her.

'I can see that wind might cause trouble for the free balloons,' I said, 'but the dirigible pilots are able to steer, aren't they?'

'Somewhat,' said the wife.

She didn't want to talk; she wanted to reach the flying ground. In her hand were two Farthing Everlasting Strips.

We continued on. The wife wore her overcoat, but I'd made do with my work suit, which came into its own in freezing temperatures. It was the middle of October, and summer was already far beyond imagining.

327

'Just look at all that silk,' said the wife, sounding rather jealous, as we walked through the gateway into the flying ground.

Two of the three so-named free balloons were already inflated and were being held down by teams of shouting men. They looked like upside-down onions, and were onion colour too: silvery brown. A third balloon was being inflated from tanks resting on a cart, and, as the gas went in, it was just like seeing a big-headed man slowly raising his head from his pillow.

The three motorcars that were to give chase waited in the corner of the field with their own shouting attendants, all heavily muffled up. A corps of cyclists would also be following along, and this lot were pedalling in circles in the field, trying to keep warm.

There were not as many spectators as I'd expected, so it was pretty easy to pick out old Reuben Booth. He wore an overcoat that seemed very black, like a night without stars, and then it came to me that this was his own overcoat and not the one he wore for work, so there was no gold on it. Next to him stood Arnold Dyson in his Crossley Porter cape, with the Irish terrier, Bob, alongside. All three stood close together but silent, looking on.

As I led the wife over towards the little group, I watched the dog. Every time a little more of the gas went into the balloon, Bob would inch forwards, eagerness increasing.

I nodded at Reuben. 'How do,' I said.

'How do,' said Reuben.

The boy Dyson wore the same face as before: a sort of knot. Every so often, though, he would pat the dog, which he was holding by a string, and his features would relax for a moment as he did so. The lad was quite taken with the balloons, anyone could see that. Mr Ferry had written to us from the orphanage to say that the boy's interests lay in that direction.

A man in a long coat was in the centre of the field, shouting through a loud-hailer. He seemed to be pointing to one man in particular of all those holding on to the balloons, and this fellow, it was given out, was the Chief of Aeronautics.

I introduced the wife to the boy, and he just gave a grunt, as I'd warned her he would do. That was when the Farthing Everlasting Strips came out. When they were put into his hands, Dyson looked up at Reuben, who winked and said: 'Tha's a lucky beggar, en't tha?'

Then the first balloon went up.

In no time at all, the people riding in the basket were higher than the top of Blackpool Tower, and looking down on us and waving as best they could in their thick coats.

They're waving to show us they're not scared, I thought, even if they are. The next two went up in very short order, skimming over the fields in exactly the same direction, for of course it was the breeze – such as there was – that had taken charge. Their tailing ropes bashed the same hedge in the same place, sending up sprays of snow on both occasions.

There came another burst of shouting from the man with the loud-hailer, and the cars and bicycles went off, but how they hoped to give chase I could not say for, upon turning through the gate, they were immediately required to follow a lane that took them in the opposite direction to the balloons.

'I don't get it,' I said to Reuben.

'Rum,' said Reuben, looking after the motorcars.

'Now, where's the dirigible?' I asked, for that was the bill topper, the steerable balloon.

'Yonder,' said Reuben, tipping his head.

They were bringing it across the field towards us. It must have been in another field to start with, stowed away behind a hedge, out of sight.

'More silk,' I said to the wife, and I realised I'd interrupted a conversation of sorts between her and the boy.

The dirigible balloon, or airship, was half inflated, and so was half floating. There was a line of men underneath it, and I couldn't make out whether they were holding the thing up or holding it down. Directly beneath the balloon was a wooden frame, inside which sat the aeronaut, who looked like a hero already, the way he was being carried aloft. At one end of the frame was a propeller; at the other end was fixed a rudder (which was the important article). It was not a regular balloon shape. Instead, it was horizontal – a big cigar.

The loud-hailer man was now telling us all about the aeronaut, who by all accounts had been practically born in mid-air. Last winter, he had flown somewhere to somewhere in fog. His training, we were told, was a jolly good dinner; he smoked and drank in moderation, and the only thing he did to excess was fly. The engine in his craft, the loud-hailer man continued, was controlled by wires; this would be a short flight, but still the aeronaut would be quite lost to sight for most of it; he would be flying in a circle and returning within half an hour to this very field.

But I didn't want to know about the aeronaut. I wanted to know about my mate on what had become once more the relief link, Clive Carter.

'Reuben,' I said, 'you know those Scarborough runs we had this summer?'

'Aye,' he said.

'Clive disappeared both times with a bag.'

Reuben nodded.

'What was going off?'

As we looked on, the dirigible was placed on wooden supports while a team of men started pulling the gas cart nearer.

Reuben's mouth was opening behind that worn-out grey beard. He meant to speak, so I leant close, for the air was filled with the sound of the rushing gas and the shouting of the loud-hailer man.

Reuben's words came with shaky breaths and shaky clouds of steam. 'Eighteen seventy-five,' he said; 'that were when I had my start . . . Midland Railway.'

'As train guard?'

Reuben shook his head. 'Carpenter,' he said; 'Settle to Carlisle stretch.'

'It's famous,' I said. 'Gave the Midland its line to Glasgow. But they had hell-on building of it, by all accounts.'

'Ribblehead Viaduct . . .' said Reuben.

'That bugger was the highest of the lot,' I said.

'That were me . . . day in, day out . . .' Reuben was shaking his head. 'Never was such a wild spot . . .'

'It was all navvies,' I said. 'Very tough sorts.'

'Couldn't half sup, though,' said Reuben, and he stood there in the freezing field smiling for a while.

'Would you take a drink back then, Reuben?' I said.

He shook his head. 'I were *Chapel*.' Then he smiled again. 'I were a great hand at . . . harmonium.'

I laughed at this, for I thought it might be the right thing to do.

As the attendants sent the gas from the tanks through long sleeves of silk into the dirigible, I watched as the craft changed by degrees from a 'B' cigar into an 'A'.

'The Ribblehead Viaduct,' I said; 'I've read a good deal about it. They built it up with wooden piers first of all.'

'That's it,' said Reuben. 'Timber framing below, stone going in up top . . . Could never make out how it could stand without rocking.'

I nodded.

'March twenty-first, eighteen seventy-five . . .' Reuben was saying, as the attendants seemed to just lift the dirigible off its supports, and *put* it into the air.

'Crane they had up top,' said Reuben as we both watched the dirigible, 'well, it suffered a mishap, like . . .'

The aeronaut, sitting in his frame under the big cigar, was yanking on a long wire.

'Sling chain broke,' Reuben was saying; 'let go a block of stone, size of . . .'

The tiny engine of the dirigible was going at last.

'Size of what, Reuben?'

The dirigible was going up; circling and swooping but certainly going up all the same, and not in quite the same direction as the free balloons, which *proved* it was being directed by the aeronaut.

'Six and half ton,' Reuben said, nodding.

'And it crowned you?' I said. 'No, it can't have done, else you wouldn't be standing here talking.'

'I'll tell tha summat,' said Reuben. 'It had me cap clean off.'

We looked up at the sky where the dirigible was turning like a weathervane; then I remembered why our chat had begun in the first place.

'But where does Clive come into all this?' I asked. 'And all the Scarborough goings on?'

Reuben was nodding. 'Come March twenty-first any year,' Reuben said, 'I'll celebrate, like.'

'Understandable, that,' I said.

The dirigible was nearly gone from sight.

'March twenty-first, nineteen hundred,' said Reuben. 'Now that were twenty-five *year* after . . .'

'And you were in Scarborough with Clive?'

Reuben nodded.

'He said we were to take a drink . . . Grand Hotel, he said . . . Nowt else would do, on account of it being such a near thing, like . . .'

'Bloody hell,' I said.

'So we took oursens off up there,' Reuben continued. 'Trouble is . . .' He turned to me, and he was smiling again. 'They're most particular as to costume.'

'They wouldn't let you in,' I said.

'They would not.'

'It's a bloody disgrace,' I said.

'Didn't bother me,' said Reuben. 'Clive though . . . proper riled, he were.'

'I *have* it,' I said. 'Ever since then Clive's been going into the Grand whenever he has a run to Scarborough?'

Reuben nodded.

'So in that bag of his,' I went on, 'he had all the proper togs?'

Reuben nodded again.

'Frock coat,' Reuben said, 'and all that carry on . . . Goes off beforehand to a little spot off the Valley Road . . . whatsname . . . Snowdrop . . . aye.'

'Snowdrop Laundry,' I said. 'I knew that much.'

'They've a steam press there,' said Reuben, 'but you've to pitch up at a certain time to be sure it'll be working, like.'

'That's where he was hurrying off to then,' I said. 'To the laundry, then to the Grand. I suppose he didn't want it known.'

Reuben nodded.

'I can just picture him,' I said, 'acting all la-di-da . . . Well, I'm sure he looked the part, any road . . . And here's me thinking he'd clicked with Emma Knowles.'

Reuben was still nodding.

The sky was changing and you could see the serious stuff coming: darkness and colder snow.

'Stationmaster's missus . . .' Reuben was saying.

'Crazy notion,' I said, looking up at the sky for any sign of the dirigible coming back. I noticed that Reuben was looking at me with a smile buried ever so deep.

'Hold on,' I said. 'He never *is*, is he?'

But Reuben was now gazing up at the sky, along with most of the spectators.

'He's late,' said some fellow standing close by.

The master of ceremonies was waiting, loud-hailer at his side. Arnold Dyson, the wife and the dog, Bob, were in a line looking up.

The Chief of Aeronautics was in the middle of the field, looking down. His arms were folded.

With all Reuben had said, more strangeness was put into the weird summer I'd had of it. I thought back to the lifting of the stone from the line and all the things that had come out from underneath, so to speak.

I fell to thinking of Monsieur Maurice. He'd been connected to the stone on the line only in my mind. The upshot was that he'd thought me a fan, and I was glad of that, at least.

333

Monsieur Maurice had topped the bill once more at the Palace, but for only one night – late September, it would have been – and the notable event had been written up in the *Courier*, under the heading: 'RETIREMENT OF A FAMOUS VENTRILOQUIST'. Monsieur Maurice, I'd read, had resolved finally to take in hand his small garden in Sussex.

It would have been at about the same time that the order for great quantities of the light suiting had arrived from Italy. It had been the wife's notion to send out the particulars, and she had received thanks, of sorts, from the younger Hind. It was all too late for Peter Robinson, of course, and the wife had asked me: 'Why couldn't Hind Senior have died instead?', and that while stepping out of Halifax Parish Church.

Who'd murdered old Hind? Nobody. And the same went for Arthur Billington.

As far as I knew, the Halifax coppers were still looking out for the Socialist Mission.

The long-haired fellow, Paul, was now to me like something in a dream, and his governor, Alan Cowan, last heard of in Dunfermline, was like a dream dreamed *inside* a dream.

Well, I was Paul's one chance of having the Mission written up in the newspapers as something to be reckoned with. And as far as that went, I'd done all the work for him, apart from a bit of stone throwing. Paul had pitched the stone through the excursion-office window, I was sure of that, but whether he'd burst our bedroom window . . . I didn't really believe it. It might have been George trying to father the blame for the wrecking onto the socialists, but he would have had all-on to get back into his room and let me see him there a moment later. No, I believed it was Don and Max, who'd done it to warn George over the money owed. Although, of course, they'd got the wrong bedroom. I'd not seen either of them again, at Central or anywhere, and another ticket collector at that station had told me Don had been stood down long since, and taken himself off to London.

The light was quite gone now, and the blackness of the sky was coming down to meet the blackness of the trees. I was cold, and fancied that I could detect every one of the burn-holes in my work suit. But I was proud to have a suit full of burn-holes, and proud once again to be an engine man. The great thing was to make speed, and then to give it to others, for it gave folk *time*, and it gave them *life*.

Looking up once again, I still could not see the aeronaut. Nothing moved in the sky, but somehow the greyness was mixing with the blackness. It would certainly snow again, and the weather brought to mind an interesting article I'd read that very morning in the *Railway Magazine*, under the heading: 'Fighting the Snow on a Canadian Railway'. 'British railroadmen', I'd read, 'have a limited conception generally of what excessive snow can do . . .' Well, it could be that we were about to find out, for extremes of temperature seemed to be all the rage in 1905.

I was thinking back to the summer once more, and the strongest picture in my mind's eye, the one with the strongest, brightest after-storm colours, was that of the Lanky steam-boat, *Equity*, rocking on the Humber, heading slowly out to Holland, and down by one passenger.

I'd not read the report of the inquest when it had appeared in the *Courier* a week later, but I'd had the notion of writing to Peter Robinson's solicitors telling the tale of the funny fellow, George Ogden, and mentioning that, since he'd put the stone on the line, their late client could have had nothing to do with the matter. That would have been a comfort to the boy, Lance. But, as the wife said, a letter of that kind would have made things hot for Cicely, who by rights ought to have spoken up earlier.

The Chief of Aeronautics had taken out his pocket watch.

A fellow I didn't know, who was standing nearby, turned to somebody in our little group of watchers, and said, 'I reckon he's been dashed to death.'

I watched the wife as she stared upwards. She was waiting for much more than the airship, of course.

A movement caught my eye – the loud-hailer going to the lips of the master of ceremonies; and there in the corner of the dark sky, tiny, but quite all right, was the dirigible.

I looked over to Arnold Dyson and saw that he was smiling.

The fellow with the loud-hailer was going forty to the dozen once again, giving us more credentials of the aeronaut. The fellow, it appeared, had three daughters; he was to be the principal attraction somewhere on Wednesday next. He valued his airship at no less than £3,000.

The attendants were all gathering to receive the airship.

The wife was next to me. 'Well, I hope they don't mean to *catch* it,' she said.

Arnold Dyson was alongside the wife and grinning up at me, just as though he'd been all smiles from the very start.

'She's all right, your missus,' he said.

'She is that,' I said.

'She can make her eyes go crossed, you know.'

I looked at the wife, but she was miles away, gazing up at the airship.

'*Can* she?' I said.

Rose

and the
Silver Ghost

HOLLY WEBB

sourcebooks
jabberwocky

Published by Sourcebooks Jabberwocky, an imprint of Sourcebooks, Inc.
P.O. Box 4410, Naperville, Illinois 60567-4410
(630) 961-3900
Fax: (630) 961-2168
www.jabberwockykids.com

Originally published in 2011 in the United Kingdom by Orchard Books, an imprint of Hachette Children's Books.

Library of Congress Cataloging-in-Publication data is on file with the publisher.

Source of Production: Versa Press-USA, East Peoria, IL
Date of Production: January 2015
Run Number: 5003105

Printed and bound in the United States in America.
VP 10 9 8 7 6 5 4 3 2 1

Also by Holly Webb

Rose

Rose and the Lost Princess

Rose and the Magician's Mask

For Jon

One

"A ND ONE, TWO, THREE, and one, two, three, and—twirl, girl!"

Rose sighed and twirled obediently. The last time she'd danced had been in a Venetian ballroom lit by candles hanging in huge crystal wheels from the ceiling. She had been surrounded by masked society ladies and by the music, which swept her around in a whirl of silvery chimes.

The thin tinkling of the piano couldn't send her feet circling like that Venetian orchestra had a few weeks before. And Bella refused to obey Miss Fell's strict instructions on the polite steps of the quadrille. She kept adding fancy footwork, and Miss Fell did not approve. Even the jauntiest tune was dismal when the piano stopped every four bars while the pianist hissed with horror.

Rose half closed her eyes, remembering soft, white fur gloves instead of Bella's thin, hot hands.

"Rose! Not you as well! *Chassé!* Oh, stop it, stop

it. I cannot stand the pair of you any longer. Tell one of the maids I shall take tea and a piece of lavender shortbread in my room." Miss Fell sprang up from the piano stool with remarkable energy for one so elderly, and strode—as much as she ever did anything so unladylike—out of the room.

Rose sank onto a small gilt chair and shook her head. "Mrs. Jones will have a fit. I'm almost certain there's no lavender shortbread in the kitchen. She'll have Sarah making holes in the plain kind with a pin and sticking the lavender in."

"You'd think Miss Fell would know that, as she's such a powerful magician," Bella said thoughtfully, chasséing perfectly across the polished floorboards and settling onto the windowsill beside Rose's chair.

"You would, wouldn't you?"

The two girls exchanged glances, and Rose looked down at the floor, smiling a little. Only a few months before, she had been an orphanage brat. The first time she met Bella, she had been laying the fire in the younger girl's bedroom. Rose had moved from the orphanage to become the lowliest maid in the house of Bella's father, Aloysius Fountain, a powerful magician who worked as an adviser to the king. But then Mr. Fountain's apprentice, the insufferable Freddie, had discovered that Rose could do magic too, and everything had changed. Dancing lessons—however horrible—were a world away.

Miss Fell had been living in Mr. Fountain's house with them ever since they returned from Venice, where they'd traveled to defeat the crazed magician Gossamer. Miss Fell wasn't anything as humble as a governess, but she *had* taken over Bella's lessons and insisted that Rose attend too. She also taught Freddie some subjects, but he had taken to developing interesting illnesses on his days for etiquette and genealogy.

Mr. Fountain had intended to find a new governess for Bella anyway, as she had finally driven off Miss Anstruther, her last long-suffering governess, just before they left for Venice. Bella's magic was now starting to show—and she couldn't control it properly. Rose rather suspected that Bella didn't want to because it was more fun that way. Unfortunately, Bella's magic was also immensely strong.

No one had quite realized *how* strong until they landed at Dover two weeks before. As Mr. Fountain had predicted, the Venetian ship hardly stayed in port long enough for them to disembark. The captain seemed to have little need of favorable winds, and the spell-laden sails filled and swelled despite the stillness in the air.

Rose and the others were left abandoned at the dock, something that happened to Mr. Fountain very rarely. It was terribly cold, and Rose felt desolate, looking at the gray water and grayer sky. It was surely about to snow again, which would at least cover the dirty slush

3

around their feet. Their adventure in Venice had been dangerous and frightening and almost fatal—but it had been exciting too, while coming home was just dismal. Tattered recruiting posters were pasted on every wall, and the war with the Talish Empire seemed to have grown nearer and more certain while they were away.

Bella had huddled against Rose, moaning, her hands snuggled inside her huge, white fur muff and her blue eyes enormous in her pinched, cold face. "I want a carriage!" she whimpered. "I'm frozen. Papa, summon a carriage. I want to go home!"

"I want, I want," Freddie muttered. "Don't worry, sir. I'll run to the inn and fetch one. Sit on that post, why don't you?" He ushered the master over to the iron post, worriedly eyeing the area of Mr. Fountain's waistcoat where the magician had been stabbed. Bill, one of the young servant boys, helped Freddie to ease Mr. Fountain down. "And don't let Bella work you into one of her tantrums. If anything's going to bring about a relapse, it'll be that."

"Thank you, Frederick." Mr. Fountain sighed wearily. The cold seemed to affect his spirits in the same way it ruined Bella's.

"I'm not having a tantrum!" Bella smacked Freddie on the arm. "I won't be spoken of in that horrid way. Apologize! Papa, make him!"

"Bella dear!" Miss Fell frowned haughtily. "Ladylike manners, if you please."

"I'm not a lady. I'm only eight, and I'm cold, and I want to go ho-*oome*!" The last word extended into an eerie wail, and Rose put her hands to her ears as they began to throb, pain pulsing through them with the wobble in Bella's voice.

There were startled cries from the deck of the ship anchored nearest to them, a tall clipper, as the masts started to shake. The sailors fell to the deck, wrapping their arms around their heads.

"Bella, stop it… Please…" Rose whispered. There was no chance that Bella would hear her. How was she doing it? She had always had a piercing scream—Miss Anstruther had left Mr. Fountain's employ after Bella had made her ears bleed. But nothing like this.

A break in the dreadful battering of sound let Rose open her eyes, but the silence was only due to a catch in Bella's throat. The wailing would start again in moments. A horrified glance around showed Rose that the others were clutching their heads as she was. Bill was on the ground, pulling his jacket over his ears, and Mr. Fountain drooped limply on his perch. Freddie was trying to hold Mr. Fountain up, his face buried in the master's shoulder as he tried to protect himself.

Bella's father! She was killing him! Rose took a deter-mined step toward Bella, who seemed to be affected by the sound herself. She was lying in the snow, curled into a little ball, still uttering that unearthly noise.

"Bella!" Rose pulled urgently at Bella's shoulder, then

5

cried out herself. Taking even one hand away from her ears was agony. "Bella, you have to stop! *Bella!*" Suddenly angry, Rose resorted to Mrs. Jones's remedy for hysterical housemaids and smacked Bella across the face.

The screaming stopped rather abruptly, and Bella uncurled and looked up at Rose, her hand to her cheek. "Did you *hit* me?"

Rose took a cautious step back. "Yes," she admitted, wondering if she should run. But Bella looked more confused than angry.

"Why?" she murmured, rubbing her cheek. Rose could see the red mark across Bella's pale skin, but she didn't feel guilty.

"Look!" she snarled, hauling Bella up. Rose wasn't frightened anymore. Now she was furious. How could Bella not know what she'd done?

Bella sagged in Rose's arms and looked around at the others. Mr. Fountain's cat, Gus, was slumped on the cobbles, his fur trailing in the dirty ice. As the girls watched, his tail flickered, and he licked a paw weakly.

"You did that, Bella!" Rose snapped. "Because you had a stupid, selfish little girl's tantrum. You can't do that anymore."

"But I didn't mean to…" Bella whispered weakly. Then she ran to stand in front of her father, laying a hand on his sleeve. Freddie was kneeling by him still, and there was a thin trickle of blood running down the boy's neck from his ear, staining his starched collar.

"Oh, Papa! I didn't mean to hurt you." Bella glanced up at Rose with wide blue eyes, the whites showing all around the blue. "Did I do that to Freddie? The blood?"

Rose nodded and saw the expression on Bella's face change. The fear shifting slightly into thoughtfulness. Perhaps even a little pride.

"Yes. And it's horrible!" Rose hissed.

Bella nodded guiltily.

"Please don't do that again," Freddie muttered, shaking his head as though he felt dizzy. "Sir? Sir? Are you all right?"

"Mmm. Tell me, Frederick. Dear boy. Was that Bella?"

Freddie hesitated, not sure whether he might send the master into heart failure by admitting that it had all been Bella's doing.

"Yes, then." Mr. Fountain sighed. "I really should have found her a better governess."

"She doesn't need a governess. She needs a cell!" Miss Fell swept across the snow toward them. Her hat was on crooked, and she seemed old and angry.

Bella was trying hard to look innocent, as though it was all just an unfortunate misunderstanding, but when no one seemed to appreciate the careful fluttering of her eyelashes, she lapsed into a sulk.

There was an ominous creaking sound from above them. Rose looked up slowly, reluctantly, as though if she didn't look, it might not happen.

"The mast!" Freddie muttered, staring with her.

"She broke the mast! I don't believe it. Sir, we have to move. Please, you have to get up!"

The foremast of the clipper, a solid lump of wood taller than a tree, was swaying above them. Bella's screaming had splintered it fatally.

"The sailors..." Rose whispered. "It'll hit them—they're all unconscious on the deck. We recovered faster because we know magic. Bill's still collapsed too. Look."

"Don't just stand there gaping and whining, you silly girl," Miss Fell snapped. "Help. And you too, Isabella, since this is all due to your ridiculous behavior. Frederick, see to your master. And the cat and the servant boy." She marched briskly toward the ship's gangplank and swept up it, her plum-colored coat trailing over the wood. The girls scurried after her.

"Why are we going toward it?" Bella whimpered. "We should be going *away*..." But she stopped when Miss Fell and Rose turned remarkably similar glares on her.

Miss Fell threaded her way delicately between the unconscious sailors, pulling the skirts of her coat away from them. Bella and Rose trailed behind her, staring up at the hypnotic swaying of the mast. Rose felt herself drawn toward it, wondering which way it would fall.

"Put your hands on it," Miss Fell commanded. "Isabella, stop playacting. This is your ridiculous spoiled-child mess." She snatched Bella's hand and pressed it against the dark wood of the mast. Rose followed, wincing as she felt the tearing shudders running through the timber.

"It's going to fall on us," she muttered. "Bella, if I get squashed, I will kill you."

Bella snickered, but stopped quickly when Miss Fell glared at her again.

"I don't work with wood." Miss Fell sounded frustrated. She was gripping the wooden mast as if she was trying to push her fingertips into it, but it was iron hard, cured by the salty sea winds.

Rose pressed her fingers against the polished wood, feeling for a hold, but it was no use. She hissed crossly and felt Miss Fell's eyes on her, just a moment's glance.

Ever since they first met Miss Fell in Venice, she had been looking at Rose oddly, and she kept dropping strange little hints. She seemed convinced that Rose must belong to one of the old magical families. Bella was certain of this too. Rose kept finding Bella staring, her nose wrinkled in a delicate little frown as though she were trying to catch a scent.

"I can't get inside the wood," Rose told Miss Fell apologetically. "It's too dead. The sails maybe? Could we do something to those?"

The old magician gave a thoughtful little nod.

"Our magic is very similar, I think, Rose… Agh!"

With a shrieking crack, the mast suddenly listed to one side, sending Bella careening into Rose. Rose fell back but was hooked upward by something seizing her

9

coat collar. An invisible something, a spell that Miss Fell had conjured up to catch her. At the same time, the sixty-foot mast suddenly exploded—very gently—into a cloud of powdery dust.

Gaping, Rose steadied herself and dragged Bella upright. "I thought you said you didn't work with wood, ma'am," she murmured admiringly, looking around the deck of the ship, now heaped with little drifts of sawdust.

Miss Fell's lips pursed in a dissatisfied expression. "I don't. I dislike merely—*blasting* things. No finesse. No delicacy. So uncouth."

Rose nodded and brushed the dust off Bella's bonnet. It would be rather lovely, she thought, to know one's magic well enough to actually decide what sort of spell to use, rather than just having to grab whatever happened to be passing through one's head, as she seemed to. She shivered a little.

She knew that Miss Fell was an incredibly strong magician—she had watched her heal Mr. Fountain of a fatal stab wound in their fight against the mad magician Gossamer—but this was different. That solid slab of wood was simply gone, and the feathers on Miss Fell's bonnet hadn't even twitched. It was pure power, and now that Rose had time to think, it was frightening. So frightening that Rose wanted to be able to do it too.

"I think perhaps now we should go to an inn," Miss

Fell said, twitching dust out of the folds of her coat. "Rather tiresome to have to explain to these good fellows why one of their masts has disappeared."

"Woodworm? Very hungry weevils?" Bella suggested, but Miss Fell ignored her majestically.

As they reached the dock, Bill was stumbling up from the ground, but Gus was still stretched out in the dirt, his whiskers trembling.

Rose hurried down from the gangplank to pick him up, lovingly wiping the grayish slush from his fur with her handkerchief.

"That girl...is a menace..." Gus moaned. "I'm *dirty*. I need to wash..."

"Can't you just glamour it away?" Rose suggested helpfully.

Gus rolled his eyes, one blue and one orange, at her in disgust. "Don't be stupid, Rose. If I glamour myself sky blue, I'm still white underneath! The dirt would still be there. I can feel it! Ugh!"

"What did she do?" Bill's eyes were rolling, and he staggered as he tried to walk toward Rose. Bella's screams seemed to have left his ears ringing. "Is she one of you now, then? Mrs. Jones'll quit—she always swore she wouldn't stay when Miss Bella was bringing the house down around her ears."

Rose put an arm around his shoulders to hold him still and sighed. "Mrs. Jones was right about that. I think if Bella had gone on longer, she could have toppled a house." She shook her head disgustedly. "And not a hair out of place. Look at her! How did she find the one clean spot in the harbor to lie in?"

* * *

Mr. Fountain had been horrified by Bella's screaming fit at Dover Harbor. He had blamed himself for allowing Bella to run wild instead of insisting she stay at home in London with a proper governess. And then he had begged Miss Fell to take Bella on as her apprentice in the same way he had taken Freddie into his house for training.

When he suggested this in their private parlor at the grand Dover inn, Rose thought Bella was about to have another fit of hysterics. She had turned an unearthly white and seemed hardly able to speak. Despite her awful behavior, Bella loved her father dearly and clearly couldn't bear the thought of being parted from him. Mr. Fountain didn't seem particularly happy about the idea either. His mustache was drooping, which made him look like a depressed walrus.

"Please…" Bella whispered.

Miss Fell, seated in the best armchair, her back ramrod straight and her hands resting on her silver-headed cane, regarded Bella thoughtfully. "She certainly needs to be taught," she agreed, although Rose thought she sounded somewhat reluctant. "But I do not think my household would be particularly suitable. My London residence has been shut up for some years, for a start. I shall be staying in a hotel while I engage new servants. All most unsettling. Not the place for a young girl." But her eyes rested on Rose as she spoke.

Mr. Fountain watched her, his eyes thoughtful. "A hotel is a most soulless place," he suggested delicately.

Miss Fell stared back at him, her sharp nose making her look hawklike. She inclined her head very, very slightly.

"Would you not be more comfortable if you came to stay with us?"

Freddie's head whipped around at this, and his eyes widened in horror. He'd had enough of Miss Fell's old-fashioned ideas on the upbringing of children and apprentices.

"How very gracious…" purred Miss Fell. "And then, of course, I would not only be able to teach dear little Isabella, but also Rose. And even Frederick." Her eyes closed for the merest fraction of a second as she contemplated that thought.

But Rose was quite sure that this was what Miss Fell had intended all along. She descended on the Fountain house in a mass of expensive luggage. Of course, Mr. Fountain had not thought to inform his housekeeper that he was bringing home a houseguest. He simply expected Miss Bridges to deal with the consequences. In fact, Rose mused, Bella's selfish habits were inherited from her father—he merely managed to make them seem rather less obnoxious by adding a great deal of charm. Perhaps rich people were all inconsiderate, having never known anything else? Rose wrinkled her nose thoughtfully.

Luckily, Miss Bridges and Miss Fell seemed to like one another. Rose suspected that Miss Bridges would have liked anybody who was prepared to educate Bella—or at least try. It also helped that Miss Fell had made a special visit to the kitchens and had been so gracious to Mrs. Jones about the orange syllabub she served at supper the first night that the cook didn't quit after all.

Although, if Miss Fell kept asking for lavender shortbread, Mrs. Jones might reconsider, of course.

Rose sighed and shrugged the thoughts away. She sometimes thought that she would never understand people who had been born with money. "I'll go down to the kitchens. Wish me luck. If Mrs. Jones is in one of her moods, I'll be having bread and butter for supper, without the butter."

Luckily for Rose, when she reached the kitchen, Mrs. Jones was hidden behind her newspaper with a cup of tea at her side, sighing heavily. "Dreadful. Dreadful," she kept muttering, as she rustled the pages.

"Another murder?" Rose whispered to Bill, who was drinking his tea out of his saucer, since no one else was in the kitchen and Mrs. Jones couldn't see him from behind the paper.

Bill shook his head and slurped. "War," he muttered, eyeing the edges of the newspaper.

"Oh…" Rose sighed. The war with Talis had escalated over the last few weeks, and they had arrived back to find London papered with still more recruiting posters and columns of soldiers marching through the streets. They frightened Rose when she was out on errands. Somehow she saw those bright uniforms splashed with mud…and other worse things. Then she would blink, and again the cloth would only be red with dye. It made her feel sick.

What would happen if the Talish emperor did as everyone said he meant to, and there was an invasion? Would there really be fighting in the streets? Rose kept telling herself that Mr. Fountain and the other magicians would never let it happen. But the emperor had magicians of his own. Lord Venn had even worked for him for a while. The plot to steal Princess Jane had been a subtle ploy to gain the emperor's trust. Who was to say that another powerful magician wasn't directing the Talish forces now?

Rose stared at the words screaming from the cramped type of the newspaper. *Cannon. Seventh Light Infantry. Treaties dissolved. Undue provocation…*

Her new life in the Fountain house was so wonderfully precious, and the bands of soldiers seemed to be marching over it in their heavy black boots.

"Those Talish. Traitors!" The newspaper shook aggressively.

Rose crossed her fingers behind her back for luck and cooed, "Mrs. Jones...would we by any chance happen to have lavender shortbread?"

Mrs. Jones's eyebrows appeared over the top of the newspaper. "That woman will be the death of me," she sighed. "There's a porcelain jar of dried lavender in the larder, Rose. Fetch it for me, there's a dear. And next time"— she eyed Rose sternly—"next time, try to encourage her to want something that you know I already have. Use that dratted magic stuff."

She gave a slight shudder as she said it, but Rose still stared at the cook over her shoulder as she went to the larder. Mrs. Jones detested magic and kept the kitchen doors sealed against it by some ancient rituals of her own, which Rose suspected were just as magical in their way as Mr. Fountain's spells. Mrs. Jones usually pretended not to know that Rose could do magic too.

"Miss Fell would see straight through me, Mrs. Jones," Rose told her, as she came back with the heavy blue-white jar. "She can make spells with her little finger that I couldn't do if I tried with all of me for a week."

Mrs. Jones folded up her paper and smoothed it out with little thumps of her fat hands, as though she were squashing away things she didn't want to see. "She seems like such a nice, proper lady," she murmured, then pulled the lid off the lavender jar with a sharp jerk.

"Looks like nasty little dead beetles," Bill said disgustedly as he peered into the jar. "And the smell! She's going to eat that stuff?"

"It's a lovely smell!" Rose said, glancing at him in surprise. It made her think of drawers full of clean, pressed linens. Miss Fell herself smelled of lavender, Rose realized. She probably kept bags of it to freshen her lace collars and cuffs, but Rose couldn't help wondering if Miss Fell's fondness for lavender shortbread scented her from the inside out.

"How are we going to put the lavender in the biscuits?" Rose asked anxiously. She had forgotten it was Sarah the kitchen maid's afternoon out, and she wasn't sure she was up to inserting lavender into shortbread herself.

Mrs. Jones sniffed. "Lavender icing. It may not be exactly what madam ordered, but she'll have to deal with it. We can't all cheat."

Rose gave a brisk nod. "I only hope it puts her in a sweeter mood. She's supposed to be teaching us painting in watercolors later on, and after the dancing lesson we've just had…"

"You're good at pictures," Bill pointed out, but Rose sighed.

"Not painting them. Mine just happen when I'm talking, and I don't mean them to. Sorry, Mrs. Jones," she added automatically. Mention of magic was not usually allowed in the kitchen either.

"Watercolors are very suitable for a young lady, Rose," the cook told her approvingly as she whisked a bowlful of icing.

"I'm not a young lady," Rose pointed out, pursing her lips.

"But you could be, dear. Most girls would bite your hand off for the chances you're getting. Learning Latin and all that. Mind you, we'll be lucky if we're not all speaking Talish this time next year."

"You can't say you aren't a young lady, anyway," Bill put in, sneaking a fingerful of icing while Mrs. Jones examined the lavender. "You don't know."

"Oh, don't you start," Rose told him witheringly. "You're like the girls at St. Bridget's, all sure they're really little lost princesses."

"But you might be!" Bill protested. "All that... *strangeness* had to come from somewhere, didn't it?"

"It's just an accident," Rose muttered. But she didn't sound sure. Before she came to work at Mr. Fountain's house, Rose had spent so long in the orphanage refusing to imagine that she had a family that she found it desperately hard to think about her history now. She wasn't sure she wanted to find the people who had thrown her away—for that was what they'd done. They hadn't even bothered to deliver her to the orphanage, simply abandoned her in a church-yard—in a fish basket, to add insult to injury. Why would she ever want to know them?

* * *

"What are we painting today?" Bella asked rather un-
enthusiastically, swooshing her brush around in a water glass.

Miss Fell frowned. "Isabella dear. Don't splash.
Today I have found a painting for you to copy."
She brought a cardboard folder over to the schoolroom table and untied the ribbons. The watercolor
inside was of a large house built of white marble, like
some ancient temple, and surrounded by perfectly
green gardens.

Rose's shoulders slumped a little. At least in their
earlier lessons, they had painted flowers and one of the
china ornaments from the drawing room. Copying
another picture seemed so dull.

"Try to match the colors," Miss Fell instructed
them. "See the delicacy of line? Light washes, girls, no
heavy-handed brushstrokes." She sighed and gently
stroked a finger down the paper.

Rose wondered why Miss Fell kept the painting
tucked away in a folder instead of having it framed to
go on her wall. It was clear that she loved it.

Rose dipped her brush into the water and tried to
enjoy watching the color spread across the paper. But it
all seemed so silly! She was no pampered little rich girl,
being groomed for a society match. Why on earth was
she bothering with this?

The answer was simple, of course. Because she wouldn't dare refuse, although she was rather hoping that Bella might do it for her.

But Bella was doodling happily in a mixture of green and pink streaks, the odd tree shape appearing here and there. Rose glanced over at Miss Fell, who was staring out the schoolroom window at the square, twisting a lavender-scented handkerchief between her fingers.

Irritably, Rose sketched in the line of the columns along the front of the house. They formed a pretty terrace, where the daughters of the family were likely allowed to stroll. *They probably didn't go anywhere else*, Rose thought bitterly, *constrained in corsets so they could walk only a few steps among the peacocks.* Perhaps she had been better off in the orphanage after all. *But a magician's daughter wouldn't be so hemmed in*, she admitted, spying Bella now mixing paint directly into her paint water to make tornado swirls. Delicate mists of color sank through the water—until it turned an ugly purplish-brown. No one could stop Bella from doing what she wanted.

And not me either, she told herself, half looking at the watercolor and painting without thinking. A pattern grew under her fingers, coils and swirls and feathery shapes, and the peacocks stalked slowly through her thoughts.

"What is that?" A papery whisper pulled Rose out of the strange, dreamy state she'd been in, and she jerked, streaking red paint across her sketch. Miss Fell was standing over her, the handkerchief now pressed to her lips.

"Oh—I'm sorry, ma'am, I didn't mean to…" Then Rose trailed off, looking down at her painting. The house was still there, but the composition had changed entirely. Now a young girl was walking through the scene, heading away from them toward the house, a shawl trailing from her elbows. She had one hand stretched out with a piece of bread to feed the peacocks, and they walked beside her, their tails trailing along the ground like her long shawl. The feathers seemed to grow into the intricate pattern of the fabric, as though she was wearing them too.

"That's—that's not in the picture," Rose stammered.

Bella leaned over from her side of the table to examine Rose's work. "How did you paint that?" she asked wide-eyed. "Rose, last week your bouquet of snowdrops looked like tree trunks. And who is she?"

"How did you know her?" Miss Fell asked, her voice still strange. "You can't have known her! What did you do?"

When Rose simply gaped at her, the old lady seized Rose's chin in her hand and pulled her face around, turning it so she could look into Rose's eyes.

"I didn't! I didn't do anything! I was thinking and not paying attention, and it just happened. I don't think I painted it at all," Rose added, shamefaced.

Miss Fell let go of her and clutched the back of a

21

chair, as though she needed it to stay standing. Rose and Bella stared at her, wondering what on earth was wrong, and whether they should do anything. This wasn't like Miss Anstruther's fainting fits. Rose was sure she could see the old lady's bones as she clung to the chair, and she was trembling.

"Miss Fell?" she asked hesitantly. "Ma'am? Should we fetch you a—a cordial? Or some smelling salts?"

"Useless quackery," the old lady snapped, seeming to come to herself all of a sudden. "Make sure that you wash those brushes properly, girls. I have a slight headache, and I shall be going to lie down."

But she tottered from the room, actually leaning on her cane instead of using it as part of her harmless-old-lady disguise as she usually did. As the door swung shut behind Miss Fell, Bella raised her eyebrows at Rose.

"*Slight headache*, my foot," she pointed out.

Rose nodded and picked up her sheet of watercolor paper. "Who is this?" she asked, staring down at the girl in the picture and tracing the interlocking pattern of the paisley shawl. "I don't remember her. How could I? I can't see her face properly, but I'm sure I've never met her. There's something, though…"

Bella frowned at the painting too. "She isn't all that much older than us," she pointed out. Rose rolled her eyes without Bella seeing. Bella hated being the youngest in the house and refused to admit that Rose was older than she was. Rose didn't actually know how old she was, but she was reasonably certain she was at least ten or eleven. Bella was only eight. But Bella was right—this girl was young.

"Perhaps fifteen or sixteen?" Rose suggested.

"She has a tolerable figure," Bella pronounced. "But I don't think her hair is naturally that fair. Probably it's the same color as yours, and she put lemon juice on it."

"Or maybe I just painted it the wrong color," Rose said.

"Oh, don't be so silly," Bella snapped. "You only held the brush. This was a spell. Miss Fell knew it too, and more than she was saying." Bella's eyes were fixed on the strange sideways portrait, as though she was willing the girl to turn around. "It was something to do with you and that house—and her."

Two

YOU MEAN, SHE REALLY is still working? As a servant?" Miss Fell's fluting voice filled the word with horror.

"Well, yes." Mr. Fountain looked uncomfortable, glancing at Rose as though he hoped she might rescue him.

"In between her lessons?" Miss Fell went on, glaring at Rose. "She is an apprentice. How can she possibly be a maid as well?"

"I'm used to working, ma'am," Rose murmured.

"Be quiet, Rose." Gus walked along the back of the chaise longue and wafted his tail over her mouth. Rose tried to argue and found she couldn't—her mouth felt as though it had been stuffed with hair. She swiped at Gus's tail and glared angrily at him, but he only purred, his eyes smug. "She is ridiculously stubborn, and I have been telling her for months that she can't be a magician's apprentice *and* a housemaid."

Rose hadn't realized that Miss Fell thought she was

an apprentice and nothing else. She had lain awake through the night, hearing the city bells tolling hour after hour, as she wondered and worried about the girl in her painting. Then she had dragged herself out of bed at six to lay the fires. She had been laying Miss Fell's bedroom fire when she stupidly dropped the fire irons in the grate.

The clumsy crash of the irons had woken the old lady, who had been remarkably patient with the careless servant in front of her until she discovered who it was. Miss Fell had swathed herself immediately in a lace-trimmed robe and summoned Mr. Fountain and a tea tray to the drawing room. Gus hadn't been summoned—he had arrived out of incurable nosiness.

When they returned from Venice, Rose had been unsure what she was supposed to be. While they were away, she had definitely been a young lady—she had danced at a palace ball, for starters. Little Venetian servant girls had lit the fire in her bedroom, and to her shame, she had even stayed asleep while they did it.

But back at Mr. Fountain's house, there had been the flurry of finding a room for Miss Fell and dusting it and hanging the curtains for the bed and fussing until everything was perfect. So Rose had found herself putting her beautiful, silver lace dancing dress on a hook in her tiny bedroom in the attic, feeling quite sure she would never wear it again. And then she had run down to the kitchens to soothe Mrs. Jones's panic about how to produce a suitable supper for the master and his guest, when (she claimed) there was only a haddock in the house, and that was past its best.

How could Rose possibly have refused to help? As she stared now at Miss Fell's disapproving face, she imagined a similar expression on her own as she told Miss Bridges that she was not a servant now and would not be ordered around. Rose hadn't joined the family at supper—which wasn't haddock, of course—although Mrs. Jones swore that she was ashamed to send it upstairs.

"But I *am* a maid," she whispered. "That's why I came here. Miss Bridges took me out of the orphanage, ma'am. I can't forget that."

Miss Fell's eyes glinted like flints. "You must. You are no longer a servant." She stared thoughtfully at Rose. "It's much easier to be a housemaid, isn't it, Rose?"

Rose gasped. She was willing to bet Miss Fell had never scrubbed steps or cleaned a grate. How on earth would she know? Did she think maids spent all their time gossiping in the kitchens?

"She's right."

Rose flinched as Gus delicately pricked her hand with one extended claw. She glared at him. She much, much preferred him as a dance partner, as he had been in Venice, she decided.

"It may be hard work, but someone is always telling you what to do. You have a list to run the errands, or you just do the same backbreaking chores every morning. You never have to think." The silvery-white cat swiped his whiskers across her cheek affectionately. Their tips felt like tiny dancing feet. "No difficult decisions to make. You can be lazy."

Rose stared down at her lap, where her hands were tightly folded. Callused, dry-skinned hands, which Bella kept being rude about. But Rose couldn't stand the thought of raw-chicken-skin gloves, however much Bella swore they would make her skin pretty and soft again. She stretched out her fingers, eyeing the roughened patches.

Was that what it was? That she didn't want to give up a life where she only had to follow orders? She had always had marked hands, for as long as she could remember, because she had worked at the orphanage. They all had; even the littlest ones could carry washing. Rose had been proud of working and delighted with her wages. Since she'd become an apprentice, Mr. Fountain had paid her the same allowance he gave Freddie, but that didn't feel quite the same.

"Freddie always has dirty hands too," Gus told her helpfully. "Covered in ink and who knows what else."

Rose sighed. "But who will do my work?" she asked miserably. "Already they're stretched belowstairs, with me having so many lessons."

"Can your housekeeper not engage another maid?" Miss Fell asked. "Or even two. Really, the house seems to be run on a skeleton staff as it is."

Mr. Fountain sighed. "I suppose so. I dislike new people in the house. It feels different." He twirled his mustache irritably around one finger. His magnificent scarlet brocade dressing gown clashed horribly with the mauve armchair he was sitting in, and he looked generally grumpy and very tired. He was spending even longer than usual at the palace, being dragged into meetings about military strategy and war defenses, and he hated it. "I will speak to Miss Bridges."

"What will I do when I don't have lessons?" Rose's voice was small. "I could help in the kitchens anyway, couldn't I?"

"Of course not!" snapped Miss Fell. "I am trying to get you out of the kitchens, child. You should be in the schoolroom or the workroom. Or you may sit in your own bedroom, of course. You should practice your sewing. That would be very suitable."

Gus gave a short, purring laugh. "Sitting cross-legged on her bed like a tailor, ma'am? She sleeps in a garret. No chair and only a hook for her clothes."

Miss Fell closed her eyes and shuddered slightly. "Of course. Well, there's no shortage of rooms. I will speak to Miss Bridges about this myself. Perhaps the room opposite mine?" She asked Mr. Fountain out of courtesy, but it was plain that she expected him to do as he was told.

"But I like my room, the one I have now." Rose faltered, aware that she was sounding stubborn and silly.

Miss Fell hardly glanced at her. "You are a young lady, Rose. You are being educated. It's hardly appropriate for you to be living in an—an attic."

Rose gulped back a sob. Her precious first maid's place had gone, and now her little room as well. It was all very well to say that she would have a proper bedroom now, one that suited her station in life, but that attic room had been the very first place that was hers. The first clothes that had been only ever hers hung on those hooks. Her eyelashes fluttered miserably. She supposed she would have to get rid of the clothes too. In her strange, unhappy mood, she forgot how delighted she had been with the new dress from Venice, and smoothed her too-short dark wool dress lovingly over her knees.

Why was she so frightened by all this? It wasn't that she didn't want to be an apprentice. But giving up her other life as a maid seemed so final. It had been there waiting if everything went wrong, she supposed. She could go back to the kitchens and the way things were before. Rose ground her teeth. The *safe* way things were before. Gus and Miss Fell were right, even though she hated to admit it.

But she really didn't see why she had to give up her little bedroom. "I don't need to move, ma'am," she protested politely. "I'll practice my sewing in the schoolroom, I promise."

Miss Fell's eyes skewered Rose like daggers. "It is not appropriate!" she hissed. "Not for a…" She stopped herself sharply, her bony, knobby fingers clenching into her palms.

"A what?" Rose asked, confused. Somehow she could feel that Miss Fell had almost said something terribly important, and it was there, just waiting to be dragged into the open, if only she could catch hold of it. She stared hungrily at the old lady, but Miss Fell was sitting calmly, her hands folded around the old silver mirror that she carried in her reticule.

"For a young lady," Miss Fell repeated, each word falling into the room, hard-edged.

Mr. Fountain sighed and nodded. "I'm sorry, Rose." Rose wasn't sure whether he was apologizing for not treating her like a proper apprentice before or for letting Miss Fell turn her life upside down now. She suspected he wasn't sure either.

She sniffed pathetically, and Gus clawed her again. "Stop it," he murmured. "Such self-pity. Disgusting. Ask for a new dress, and stop being so feeble."

"I shall speak to Miss Bridges after breakfast. A meal which *you* will eat in the dining room, Rose," Miss Fell pronounced, and she walked regally out of the room.

* * *

"The room on the other side of my room?" Bella asked, whispering to Rose over her boiled egg.

Rose nodded. Exactly what she needed: Bella

running in and out of her bedroom all the time. Bella had never seen Rose's attic room—she had probably never gone beyond where the stair carpets stopped, as servants didn't need carpet.

Rose smiled into her porridge, wondering whether Bella could possibly be a worse neighbor than Susan, the other housemaid, who couldn't stand Rose. But then her eyes filled with tears suddenly. She wouldn't miss Susan; of course she wouldn't. The girl had spent weeks torturing her. It would be a pleasure never to see that sharp-featured, sulky face again. But it also meant that Rose wouldn't see Mrs. Jones or Sarah or her dear friend Bill—or only in passing in the corridors, and they wouldn't be allowed to talk. That wasn't going to happen, Rose told herself. She jabbed her spoon into the porridge angrily, striking a ringing chime from the delicate porcelain.

Miss Fell looked up sharply. She had taken most of her meals in her room since she arrived, only attending occasional family dinners, and she hadn't realized that Rose's absence meant she was eating in the kitchens. This morning Miss Fell had appeared promptly for breakfast, in severe plum-colored silk with an ivory walking stick. She meant to see that her instructions were being obeyed. She frowned disapprovingly at the lapse of manners, but perhaps the stiff set of Rose's shoulders discouraged her from commenting.

"Oh, *good*," Bella murmured sweetly, and Rose

31

shuddered. Bella sounded altogether too happy about the idea.

"It will be delightful for you, Isabella, to have Rose close by," Miss Fell pronounced.

Freddie smirked and trod on Rose's foot. "Notice she says it that way, not the other way around," he muttered. "Good luck." Rose kicked him hard in the ankle and went back to eating her porridge with an angelic expression that she had usefully learned from Bella.

Eating at the long dining-room table felt odd. She had eaten with the family in Venice, but that was abroad, where things were obviously different. Now she couldn't help feeling as though someone might shout at her for sitting down.

She had personally polished the silver teapot that stood in front of her—it was a beast to polish, with all those fiddly little bits around the lid. She kept wanting to smack Freddie for reading a cheap horror comic under the table. If he didn't pay attention, he was going to drop bacon grease on the tablecloth, and it was impossible to get grease stains out of linen.

But she was actually drinking out of a cup from the Meissen breakfast service, Rose reminded herself. The tablecloth wasn't for her to worry about anymore. Her fingers felt like sausages around the cup's delicate handle.

Miss Fell finished the meager triangle of toast that had been her breakfast and stood up. "Isabella and Rose, we will discuss etiquette and the proper spells for managing a well-run household at eleven o'clock sharp in my room. I shall go and speak to Miss Bridges about your new accommodations, Rose."

"Why does she want me to change rooms so much?" Rose murmured half to herself as the last whisper of Miss Fell's silken train died away.

"Don't you want to?" Freddie asked, looking up from his comic in surprise. "I mean, I could see why you'd want to stay as far away from Bella as possible, but the room you have now… It's more like a cupboard, Rose."

"I know. And I suppose I'd like to have a bigger room. It's just odd." Rose glanced over at Mr. Fountain, but he was deep in a book and appeared not to be listening. "It feels odd. I–I liked being half and half. I'm not a lady, and I can't see how I ever will be!"

Gus licked the last drops out of a bowl of cream. "Miss Fell does seem fairly sure that you are or should be already," he murmured thickly.

"She's very set on it," Rose agreed in a gloomy voice. It hadn't taken any of them long to learn that whatever Miss Fell was set on tended to happen rather fast.

"I wonder why?" Bella mused, licking egg yolk off a little silver spoon with the tip of her tongue. "Why does she mind so much?" She flicked a curious sideways glance at Rose.

"She's just like that," Freddie shrugged. "She wants things her way, that's all."

Bella shook her head. "I don't think so." She dug her

spoon into the egg again, perfectly aware that almost everyone around the table was now staring at her while she diligently scraped around, finding the last little bits.

"Oh, pick it up and lick it!" Gus snapped. "What are you talking about? What do you know that we don't?" His whiskers quivered with irritation.

Bella smirked. "I watch, that's all. I've seen how Miss Fell looks at Rose. And there was the painting, of course..."

Freddie pushed his chair back with a screech. "We all know Rose is the most talented apprentice magician ever. Let's not go over it again." He stomped out, slamming the door loudly enough to shake Mr. Fountain out of his book.

"More tea?" he asked vaguely, waving his cup at Rose.

Rose filled it, waited until the master was safely back in a world of his own, and then stared at Bella and Gus. "What was that?" she demanded, jerking her head at the door.

"He's jealous." Gus shrugged. "You take to spells more easily than he does, or so he thinks. It's true that Miss Fell doesn't seem very interested in teaching him. He feels slighted."

"It's only because he's a boy!" Rose sighed. "She's like Miss Bridges. She only likes tidy people, and he's always knocking things over. He doesn't want her teaching him anyway; he's always trying to get out of her etiquette lessons."

Gus snorted. "Etiquette. He doesn't care about that. The woman is one of the most powerful magicians of the age! That's what Freddie wants, her secrets. He's an ambitious boy. And she's giving them to you instead."

"Oh." Rose sounded doubtful. Despite Miss Fell's obvious power, so far all their new mistress had done was criticize Rose's embroidery—and practically collapse in a painting lesson. Rose did not feel that she was being taught secret, powerful spells. She raised one eyebrow at Bella, who looked equally unconvinced.

"I expect she'll get to that. Maybe we need to be able to sew properly first." Bella sighed. "But anyway, Rose, that wasn't what I meant at all. I mean, you may be good at spells, but you certainly aren't as good as I intend to be." She smirked smugly. "I think Miss Fell is interested in you for quite a different reason."

She paused, clearly waiting to be begged, but Rose wasn't in the mood. She was still turning over the strange news that Freddie was jealous of her talent. He had been impressed when she first used her magic, impressed and furious that he had been shown up by a servant, but Rose had thought that had worn off by now. "Oh, stop being so silly, Bella. If you want to tell, tell. Otherwise I have to go and study that diagram of curtseys before our lesson."

Bella pouted, but she couldn't resist. "Oh, Rose, it's obvious. She knows who you are."

She sat back, looking proud of herself, and took a

delicate bite of toast. But she was peering sideways at Rose to see how she took the news.

Rose put her hands in her lap, wrapped around each other to stop them from shaking. She had suspected as much, but the idea seemed so much more real when Bella said it out loud. "Why wouldn't she just tell me?" she whispered.

"I don't know…" Bella said thoughtfully. "Maybe she isn't quite sure? It would be cruel to tell you if she wasn't certain. Or perhaps she thinks you aren't ready to know. It might be such an awful truth that it would send you screaming mad." Bella crunched more toast. "Yes, it's probably that."

"She has to tell me." Rose sat up straighter. "If she knows who I am, she has no right to hide that from me! She has to tell!"

Gus snickered. "Remember what I said about one of the most powerful magicians of the age? I don't think she has to do anything."

"Shut up, Gus." Rose stared at Bella, her eyes narrowed. "Exactly what did you see to make you think she knows? Did she say something?"

Bella blinked a little nervously. She hadn't seen Rose like this before, and she was frightening. "She looks at you…Rose. She…she looks *like* you. Now, the way you're glaring at me, you look like her. I think you're a Fell. And she knows."

Gus surged up from the pile of cushions on his chair

and picked his way swiftly through the breakfast things until he was nose to nose with Rose. "A Fell. Well, goodness me. The child could have said something useful, for once. A Fell child in an orphanage. That would be a surprise." He sat down, wrapping his tail around himself thoughtfully and still staring at Rose. "Why would a child from one of the most feared and respected magical families in the world end up in an orphanage, Bella?"

"I don't know." Bella shrugged. "But you think I'm right, don't you?"

"Possibly. Possibly." Gus purred with satisfaction. "This really is turning out to be a most interesting day."

"It isn't just an interesting thing to talk about over breakfast!" Rose hissed at him. "This is important! How are we going to find out if we're right?"

"You could ask her," Gus suggested.

Rose shuddered. "No. She'd just give me one of her looks and tell me my petticoat was showing. If it were that simple, she'd have told me already, wouldn't she?"

"I'm all out of ideas, then." Gus yawned, deliberately widely. "Time for a nap, I think."

"I'll help," Bella suggested hopefully. "Please, Rose. It was me that told you. Let me help."

Rose nodded reluctantly. Bella was right. She was the one who had noticed. It wouldn't be fair to shut her out now. "Can you think of anything?" she asked.

Bella frowned. "Nothing very clever," she admitted.

"But I wonder if we could search her room. There must be something in there. Old letters, perhaps. Some clue to who you are."

Rose swallowed, but her mouth still felt dry. She'd had a horrible feeling that Bella would say something like that.

"Hesitating to say it for the third time, but *one of the most powerful magicians of our age*. Hmm? I think not the best person to burglarize." Gus jumped off the dining table, hitting the polished floorboards with a solid thump, and strolled out of the door, his tail tip whisking happily. Rose stared after him, wondering who he was going to tell.

* * *

"Simple persuasion spells can be very useful, but in general, servants and magic do not mix," Miss Fell continued. She was sitting in a wing chair by the window of her room, where she taught Rose and Bella most of their lessons. They were perched on footstools in front of her chair, trying to concentrate on the proper management of servants.

Rose couldn't help feeling that she knew rather more about servants than Miss Fell ever would. Between that and trying to look for clues without Miss Fell noticing, she was finding the lesson hard to attend to. It didn't help that she had to keep elbowing

Bella, who had no idea of discretion and kept turning around to stare at anything that looked like it might be useful in their search.

For once, Miss Fell was not sitting bolt upright. She looked tired—which Rose couldn't help feeling was her fault. The old lady didn't usually come downstairs for breakfast, preferring to take a tray in her room. By accidentally waking her this morning, Rose had added several hours to Miss Fell's day.

As she tried to concentrate on the old lady's flutey voice, Rose wondered how old Miss Fell really was. Rose had had some experience with glamours, but she had no sense that Miss Fell was using one. She just was one of those people who always looked perfect, even in her nightgown. Even now, only the purple shadows under her eyes and her slightly huddled position in the chair showed that she was weary. She was holding her pretty silver-framed mirror in her gnarled hands again, and she stroked it as she talked, gently running her fingers around the delicate frame.

"Rose dear, pay attention," Miss Fell scolded. "And don't frown like that, child! You will have wrinkles before you're twenty if you sit and scowl. Really, direct sunlight and excessive facial expressions"—Rose had to think for a moment before she decided this probably meant smiling was outlawed as well—"are the ruination of the complexion. Don't frown, and never let me see either of you in the sun without a parasol. Rose,

39

you are *still* frowning! Here, dear, look." She handed Rose the silver mirror. "Just look at the creases between your eyebrows. Disastrous."

Rose felt a strange little skip of frightened excitement as she took the mirror and smiled sadly at her own anxious face in the tarnished glass. She nodded obediently at Miss Fell and tried hard to flatten out her forehead, but it seemed to want to crease.

She was handing the mirror back when it happened. The face seemed to come sliding out of the frame, as though the glass had been pulled sideways. Rose thought for a moment that some strange fault in the old glass had twisted her own reflection about. She had seen what was called a haunted mirror in the magicians' supply shop where she ran errands for Mr. Fountain. The younger Mr. Sowerby had shown her one that made her jump at seeing her reflection all stretched out. But this was more than just old glass. The face was hers but not. It was her but *older*, and how could that be, unless the glass had some strange glamour spell on it? There was something else dragging at the corners of her memory too, a certainty that she had seen this face somewhere else.

Rose tore her eyes away from the girl staring back at her and looked up at Miss Fell, her mouth open to ask. But the old lady hadn't noticed what had happened and was still lecturing Rose on the perils of scowling. Miss Fell simply held out her hand for the mirror and laid it back in her lap. She gave no sign that she expected Rose to have seen anything odd.

Which left Rose wondering: was she the only one who saw strange faces in that glass?

* * *

"What was it?" Bella demanded, a little while later. As soon as they had been dismissed by Miss Fell, she had hauled Rose along to her own bedroom and practically shoved her into the window seat. "Come on, Rose! The mirror, what did it do?"

"Did you see it?" Rose asked her sharply.

"No!" Bella smacked a cushion crossly. "I knew it; there was something. You went the strangest color. What happened? Was it one of your strange pictures? Oh, was it something about the war? I saw a paper on Papa's desk which said that the Talish are most definitely making plans to invade. It said one of their plans is to fly across in huge balloons, but I can't believe that's true."

Rose shook her head. "Nothing like that. Nothing—grand. It's only that I looked in the mirror and it wasn't my face looking back at me. I've seen odd things in mirrors before, but only when I was *supposed* to," Rose muttered. "When we were scrying to find out what had happened to Maisie, and I saw Miss Sparrow. I asked the mirror to tell me that time, though. This was something different. I think that face is always in the mirror."

"Who was it? Was she pretty? Was it someone you knew? Oh, Rose, stop sitting there like a lemon and tell me!"

"Bella, I think it might have been...my mother," Rose whispered.

Bella's mouth fell open, and for once, she was speechless. She stared at Rose, mouth and eyes circles of amazement.

Bella looks like the queen's Pekingese dog with her eyes like that, Rose thought vaguely. Her brain was behaving like a butterfly, flitting from thought to thought and back again, and refusing to stay on the important things. Until she'd told Bella, she'd hardly dared say it to herself, but she was almost sure that she was right.

Bella got over her amazement quickly and moved on to curiosity. "How do you know? Did she look like you? And was it just her face, or do you think she could see you back? Is she inside that mirror?" Bella wrinkled her nose in disgust.

Rose frowned. "No. It was only her face. She didn't move, and her eyes didn't seem to see anyone. I only saw her for a moment, but she wasn't alive. Or anything like that. It was more as though she used to look into that mirror, and it kept the memory of her."

"I don't see why Miss Fell would have a mirror with your mother in it," Bella objected. Then her eyes brightened with the excitement of scandal. "Maybe it was your mother's mirror and Miss Fell stole it! We really have to find out about this properly, Rose. It's just so exciting."

Rose sighed. She knew she probably couldn't discover the truth on her own, but she wished Bella wasn't quite so eager. This wasn't one of those silly novels full of castles and dungeons and beautiful heroines that Bella's governess, Miss Anstruther, used to hide in the schoolroom ink cupboard. Bella couldn't seem to see that it was real. And just because Rose hadn't fainted dead away—gracefully, of course, like one of the idiot girls in the books—didn't mean she wasn't upset. She had just seen her mother. It couldn't be the first time she had ever seen her, but it felt like it. Everything had changed.

"I don't know what we're going to do," Rose muttered. "But Miss Fell isn't going to tell me. That's clear, or she would have done it by now. So I need to find out myself. I'm not giving up!" she told Bella sharply. But then her shoulders slumped. "Though I might as well, since I can't think of anything. The mirror is the only clue we have."

"We don't have it," Bella pointed out, and Rose clicked her tongue irritably.

"You know I meant…" She trailed off. "What if we did?" Her voice was scared, and she looked at Bella wide-eyed.

"You want us to steal it?" Bella asked hopefully. "But what about what Gus said?"

Rose folded her arms, her face grim. "If Miss Fell is actually my long-lost relative, then she probably won't kill me. Probably. She might kill you."

"No, because then she would have to deal with Papa, and he's one of the most powerful magicians of the age too," Bella said sunnily.

Rose nodded. "I suppose it's good that she's making me change rooms. It'll be easier to get into her room from this floor than it would be from the attic."

"What shall we do with the mirror when we've got it?" Bella's eyes were sparkling. She'd skipped over the difficult part as usual, Rose noticed. "Because whatever we do, Rose, we'll have to do it quickly. Miss Fell's bound to see it's gone when she gets up. She always uses it to put her hairpins in, haven't you noticed? She always picks it up when she's putting the ones that have fallen out back in."

Rose shivered. "So we'll have to creep into her room twice, so we can put it back as well. And she wakes easily. I know she does. I woke her this morning, and I hardly clanged the fire irons at all."

Bella smiled delightedly. "I know a spell we can use to be quiet. I was reading one of those strange old books in the workroom, the one with the cover that looks like squashed lizard."

"Ugh. I haven't touched that one," Rose admitted.

"It looks so horrid that I always think it's going to be full of poisonings and disgusting things to do in grave-yards at the full moon. Is it?"

"Of course it isn't. Think, Rose. Anything like that would be on the high shelves in Papa's study."

Rose blinked. She hadn't thought of it that way, but now she rather wished that Bella hadn't been so sure that her father had that sort of books. She wondered how often he used them.

"It's actually a collection of useful spells you can make from everyday ingredients. Things that you can find around the house. We need the Silent Slippers spell." Bella looked proud of herself, but she was also eyeing Rose sideways.

"What?"

"It does have some ingredients you won't like." Bella edged back a little over the coverlet, as though she didn't want to be too close to Rose. "The slippers are mostly made of spell, but the magic's woven into something real—something very soft and quiet…"

Rose stared at her in a panicky way. "What, Bella? Please, you're giving me palpitations!"

"We have to harvest rather a lot of cobwebs," Bella admitted.

"Oh." Rose smiled in relief. "No."

"You can't just say no!"

"Yes, I can, because I just did. I won't do it, Bella. You know I can't bear spiders."

"I don't know why on earth not. Honestly, I'm the one who was brought up to be a young lady. I'm supposed to be screeching on a chair while you catch the spiders in a jam jar, Rose!"

"Please don't." Rose put her hand over her mouth. "I shall be sick on your silk bedcover."

"Really? Just because of jam jars?"

Rose watched Bella file this information away for future use. The huge blue eyes were clear and innocent again in seconds, and Bella smiled. "Well, I shall do it then. But this is an extremely big favor, Rose. You'd better remember that."

Rose nodded wearily. There was very little danger of Bella letting her forget.

Three

ROSE ENLISTED BILL TO help Bella on her cobweb hunt. The maids spent a great deal of time making sure that the family's part of the house had not so much as a strand of a cobweb. Rose had always had to do this with a very long brush, and sometimes with her eyes closed. Somehow, if she couldn't see the possible spider, it wasn't there. Susan would brush them down with her fingers, but even the thought of it made Rose gag. That awful gummy, smooth stickiness—how could Susan stand it?

The spell called for "several hanks of fresh cobweb" which Rose thought was remarkably vague. How many were several? And how much was a hank? To find even one cobweb, they would have to go out to the stables in the mews at the back of the house. Bill escorted the girls politely through the kitchens where all the staff stood frozen, watching them. Rose stared pleadingly at Mrs. Jones.

The news of her permanent promotion to young

lady had traveled very swiftly, Rose realized. There was a small pile in the middle of the kitchen table—her workbasket and the pinafore Miss Bridges had made her to put over her uniform if she had to be presentable. All the things she had left belowstairs.

"I will have them sent up to your new room, Rose," Miss Bridges said gently, and Rose nodded. Thank goodness no one had called her "miss." She might have cried.

Rose waited outside the tack room, ignoring the stableboys snickering at her, while Bella and Bill went hunting spiders. She stood there shivering in the January cold and trying not to nibble her nails while she worried about burglarizing Miss Fell's bedroom.

"I do like this spell." Bella had suddenly appeared beside her, looking even smugger than usual.

Rose jumped, and the stableboys hooted with laughter. Had Bella done the spell already, to be able to move so quietly? Rose glanced down at Bella's feet, but they looked perfectly normal.

Her hands, though, were draped with silver-gray web, and she wasn't even wearing gloves. She waved the webs at Rose. "I think I might try breeding spiders in the schoolroom, Rose, so we can always have a supply."

Rose slapped her hands across her mouth and moaned.

"She's gone green!" one of the stableboys pointed out with interest.

"Find her a bowl, mate," the other one advised Bill. Bill's response was to grab Rose around the shoulders, run her back through the mews to the kitchens, and shove her in front of the scullery sink—where for once Sarah wasn't doing any washing up.

Rose leaned on the white china sink, her head swimming, and tried to stay on her feet. Even though she was a young lady now, she refused to faint.

"She did that on purpose," she moaned to Bill, who was hovering anxiously next to her.

Bill shook his head. "Nope. She's just excited about the spiders' webs and this clever spell thing. Sorry!" he added quickly, as Rose lurched toward the sink again.

"I don't think I'm actually going to be sick—but her hands—she was covered... Ugh..."

"I didn't mean to upset you, Rose." Bella's voice was husky, and she sounded guilty.

"Don't show me them again," Rose gasped, wheeling around so as not to see Bella by the scullery door.

"I won't. It's all right. I've hidden them in my handkerchief. And I washed my hands in the horse trough. I'm sorry, I really am. I didn't think. I was pleased because we'd gotten such a lot, and I was excited about the spell."

Rose dared a look at Bella and saw that she was staring at the stone floor, looking guilty.

"I wanted to help you. I was so pleased that it was going to work," she whispered. "Rose, are you going to be able to wear the spell slippers?"

Rose was silent for a moment, gulping. "Will it still look like cobweb?" she asked.

"There isn't a picture in the book—we could ask them not to, I should think. Would it be all right if they were just a different color? Would pink cobweb slippers make you sick?"

"I honestly don't know!" Rose half laughed. Then she shook her head. "They'll have to do. I won't give up over something so silly."

"You could find a different spell, couldn't you?" Bill asked.

Bella sighed. "I could only think of this one. We could try, but it might take weeks, and we can hardly ask Miss Fell if she happens to know a good spell for sneaking around, can we?"

* * *

Later that afternoon, the two girls sat on the floor of Rose's new bedroom. It would have been easier to do the spell in the workroom, but Freddie was in there, and he was still sulking. But sitting on the floor wasn't a hardship. The rug they were curled up on was worth more than Rose's yearly wage, she was fairly sure. In her old room, there was hardly enough floor space to open the door, let alone to put down a rug.

Rose had her eyes closed, because even with one of Bella's handkerchiefs over them, the cobwebs seemed to move and shimmer and crawl. "Do you need me to do anything?" she muttered.

"No, I don't think so." Bella sounded so excited. She had done very few spells so far—or at least very few spells on purpose.

Rose sat tensely and heard Bella riffling through the pages of the spell book and then tapping the paper thoughtfully with a fingernail. All the sounds seemed clearer and louder now that she couldn't see. There was a rustle of fine linen, and shivers crawled up Rose's spine, like the spiders she couldn't chase out of her mind.

Bella whispered and muttered to herself, and Rose heard only odd words. Even Bella's voice sounded spidery and soft. Rose was desperate to leap up and race out of the room, but she didn't dare disturb the spell. If it went wrong, who knew what would happen? Spiders in slippers might invade her brand-new bedroom. The thought of cobwebs on the heavy plum velvet curtains made her feel sick.

"Put your foot out!" Bella told her sharply. "Quickly, Rose. I can't hold it like this for long!"

Rose's eyes snapped open without her meaning them to. She stared at her foot, pale in a white cotton-knit stocking, and forced herself to stretch it out toward Bella's hands.

What Bella was holding looked like a hairnet, a pale-pink silk one. It glistened, and Rose tried not to flinch as Bella draped it over her foot.

"Now the other one."

Rose's feet felt light as thistledown—as light as

51

cobweb. It looked like she was wearing delicate, jeweled, pink slippers—but they were only spider silk, beaded with dots of Bella's magic. Bella must have added a hint of glamour spell to change the color and make the slippers look like pretty shoes, if anyone should see. It was very clever, deceitful magic. Rose was beginning to think Bella took after her father.

"We won't make a sound while we're wearing them," Bella told her proudly, twisting to admire her own feet. "Aren't they *pretty*? I wonder how long they last."

A soft paw reached out and gently batted the pale-pink mesh. "Pretty but fragile," Gus commented. "Only the one night, I should think."

Rose stared at him sternly. "I shut that door myself."

"Did you?" Gus yawned, showing a mouthful of sparkling white needles. "Really. How interesting. And this is relevant how, Rose dear?"

"How did you get in? It's still shut. You can't walk through doors, can you?"

"No. Well, I could, but why bother when there's a perfectly good chimney and a flue system that links the whole house?"

Rose and Bella turned around to stare at the fireplace. The fire was lit, only a small blaze, glowing gently and sending pleasant warmth into the room.

Gus was now licking one of his front paws and smoothing it around his ears luxuriously, his eyes blissfully closed.

"Next time I'll just leave the door open," Rose whispered. "I mean it, Gus. Please don't do that again." Gus opened one eye, the amber one, and leaned across to swipe his tongue over Rose's fingers. "Dear little Rose." He rubbed his paw around his ears one last time and got up, stalking over to the fire. He stared into it, dangling his whiskers dangerously close to the glowing coals.

Bella jumped up, looking ready to grab him away from the fire, but he glared at her, and she hung back. "You'll burn your whiskers," she protested. "Think how awful you'd look if you were all singed."

Gus sighed. "Neither of you has any faith in me." Before they could stop him, he put one paw up on the grate, murmured, "A lot of dust here, Rose. Most unsatisfactory work," and leaped into the middle of the fire.

Bella shrieked and Rose would have done the same, but she felt as though the air had been knocked out of her, and she had no breath to scream.

Gus sat there for a moment with the flames swirling around him, looking mildly bored. Then he strolled back out onto the hearth rug, where he examined his paws carefully. Rose peered at them too, but they looked exactly the same as before, the pads a delicate apricot pink.

"Can you teach us that?" Bella asked eagerly.

Gus smirked. "When you've grown a tail, Bella,

come back and ask again. Rose, you cannot keep me out with a door."

Rose shook her head. "I wasn't trying to. But—we're planning to do something you told us was stupid. We thought we should plan it privately. Freddie's been fuming in the workroom since he stormed out at breakfast, and we can hardly use the schoolroom in case Miss Fell walks in on us."

"So what are you after?" Gus sat down in between the two girls, his whiskers glittering with excitement.

"Her silver hand mirror. She has it with her most of the time, so we think we'll have to do it tonight," Rose explained.

Gus leaned forward, his shoulders heaving so convulsively that Rose wondered if something was wrong.

"Are you coughing up a hairball?" Bella asked in disgust.

Gus glared at her. "I was laughing," he pointed out coldly, "at you being so blindly stupid. Do you actually think you'll get away with it?"

"We haven't a choice, and Bella's made us these silence-spell slippers. We're going, whatever you say about it," Rose snapped.

"Oh good. Well, I shall come too, just for the amusement value." He sprang onto the end of Rose's bed. "Be quiet now, children. I shall need to sleep if we're going gallivanting all night." Then he curled himself into a perfect white ball with his nose tucked under his tail so that they couldn't see his eyes to argue with him.

"Oh!" Rose huffed crossly. "He really is impossible. I didn't ask him to come!"

"But he'll probably be useful, if he can stop himself from laughing at us," Bella pointed out.

Gus's tail twitched, and they couldn't tell if he was laughing or cross, so they decided to finish plotting in Bella's room instead.

* * *

"I don't want to wear my nightgown," Bella hissed. "I was going to wear my black velvet dress, the one I had for Uncle Dolph's funeral. It's perfect for going burgling in."

Rose flinched. "Don't use that word."

"Stealing? Trespassing? Looting?"

"Ssshhh!" Rose crammed her knuckles in her mouth and nibbled them. "Don't go on about it, or I might back out. That would be an awful waste of a spell, wouldn't it?"

"If you back out, I shall go without you," Bella retorted. "This is the most fun we've had since we came back from Venice."

"I'm not backing out. But, Bella, please just wear your nightgown. Then if she wakes up, we can pretend to be sleepwalking."

"Both of you at the same time?" Gus asked.

"Oh, don't you start!" Rose begged wearily. She

was feeling terribly guilty at the thought of stealing a valuable mirror, and she had frightened herself quite enough already creeping along the dark corridor to Bella's room. The difficult part had been tiptoeing past the particularly forbidding door behind which Miss Fell was sleeping—or so they hoped. If she'd woken up in the middle of the night and decided to read for a while, they were lost. As Rose had crept along, she'd been convinced that the ornaments on the little tables in the alcoves were all staring at her, and one of the paintings had definitely snickered.

"Or we could both have heard a suspicious and frightening noise." Bella nodded, twisting her face into a scared-little-girl look and wringing her hands together. "Yes, I see." She stroked the black velvet dress regretfully but closed her wardrobe door. "Shall we go, then?"

Rose smoothed the front of her nightgown nervously and nodded. "We should get on with it. Do you have the slippers?"

Bella produced them from under her pillow with a flourish. They sparkled invitingly, but they slid onto Rose's feet with a slightly sticky eagerness that made her shudder. Still, they worked—Bella tried leaping on the creaky board two feet to the right of her dressing table, and there wasn't a sound.

Rose picked up her candle, and the girls padded out into the corridor with Gus sliding around their feet silently. They paused outside Miss Fell's door and stared at the handle uncertainly. Moonlight was shining through the tall window at the end of the corridor, gilding the brass doorknob so that it seemed to ripple and shimmer.

"Open it!" Gus purred gently, nudging Rose's leg. "Go on!"

"What if she's still awake?" Rose hissed. "She always says she hardly sleeps."

Bella immediately assumed her scared face. "Don't worry, Rose. I will cry. You know how good I am at it."

Rose grasped the handle and turned it, gently pushing the door open. Miss Fell's candle was extinguished, and a pitifully small figure lay under a mound of quilts in the huge bed. Without her corsets and huge silken skirts, she was a tiny old lady.

"Look!" Bella breathed. "On her nightstand!"

Next to the bed, the mirror glimmered in the faint candlelight, and Rose stole closer to snatch it up. She paused, her fingers hovering over it as she watched Miss Fell sleep, wheezing gently in a nest of lace-edged pillows. It all seemed too easy. What if the mirror was enchanted against theft? What if it screamed as soon as she picked it up?

Rose grasped the handle, waiting for the metal to bite her back or some strange spell to knock her to the ground. She was almost disappointed when nothing happened. It was only a mirror, and it did nothing.

She grabbed it up and whirled around in the spell-slippers, shooing Bella and Gus out of the room.

They rushed silently across the corridor, giggling and panting and throwing themselves into a heap on Bella's bed, as pent-up nerves took over.

Eventually, Rose stopped shaking and laughing, and stared down at the mirror lying on Bella's pillow. It looked unhelpfully plain.

"Now we have the rest of the night to work out why it's so special," she murmured.

Four

J HE MIRROR WAS VERY pretty, made of silver that had been polished so many times that it was almost silky. It was oval with a handle, and the silver frame had a pattern of roses molded all around it like a garland. Several of the roses were so worn away that they were more like shadows on the silver. Rose stroked the pattern, smiling. If she had been born the young lady that everyone now wanted her to be, she would have been given something like this. Perhaps with a brush that matched, specially chosen for a little Rose. But Miss Fell's name was Hepzibah, so that didn't quite fit.

"Look into it!" Gus hissed, peering over her arm. She had told him about the strange vision she'd had from the mirror before. "You might see her again."

Rose swallowed nervously and held the mirror out in front of her. She had a right to be anxious, she told herself firmly. She might be about to find a vital clue to the mystery of her abandonment. Within the next few minutes, she might even have a family.

But then she bit her lip and stared determinedly into the slightly dull glass. That wasn't true. How could she ever have a family, whatever she found in the mirror? A proper family would never have left her in the first place. She might get relatives, but that was about it.

She had been expecting to see the same odd reflection, the older version of herself. Instead, her own face stared back at her, worried and heavily shadowed by the flickering candles. Behind her in the mirror lurked a blue-eyed child and a highly curious cat.

"I can't see anything strange," Bella complained.

"It looks like any old glass," Gus agreed, pushing his nose around Rose's elbow and gazing into the mirror. A well-groomed white face looked back at him, and he twitched his whiskers at himself admiringly. "What did you do the first time to make it show you its secret?"

"Nothing." Rose shook her head. "Really nothing. I saw myself at first, and I only caught a glimpse of her as I gave the mirror back. She just came sliding out of the frame toward me, somehow."

"So she's in the back of the mirror," Gus muttered, sniffing at it. "I can't smell a secret catch, but it may be very well hidden."

"What do you mean, she's in the back of it?" Rose's hands shook without her meaning them to. She didn't want the thing touching her if it had someone inside it.

"A lock of hair is all I meant," Gus snapped. "Or a letter. In a secret compartment. Something that holds a memory of the girl, and it made you see her. Stop being so fussy and feeble, Rose."

"Oh!" Rose nodded in relief. "Yes." She had seen the locket that Mrs. Jones wore all the time, tucked neatly under her apron, and every so often when they had stopped work for a cup of tea, Mrs. Jones would draw it out and polish it on the corner of the apron. She had shown Rose how it opened with a tiny spring, and inside was a woven lock of sadly faded light-brown hair. The hair of baby Maria Rose, the tiny daughter that Mrs. Jones had lost to the cholera so many years ago. This mirror could well have something similar inside it. Perhaps that was why Miss Fell loved it so much. Because it held the memory of someone she had loved.

"The lock of hair could even have belonged to one of her suitors," Bella suggested dreamily. "He died before they could marry—how tragic!"

Rose raised an eyebrow at her. She sometimes suspected that Bella had read quite a few of those books Miss Anstruther stashed in the ink cupboard.

Bella went pink. "Well, it might be true!" she protested.

Gus was still sniffing at the mirror and even licking at the rose garlands with the tip of his shocking pink tongue. "I'm sure there's something inside," he muttered. "Lay the mirror on the bed, Rose."

Rose laid it down obediently, and Gus crouched in front of it, his shoulders sticking up sharply and his tail lashing from side to side. Eventually he extended one paw and raked a claw around the edge of the glass. Then he sat back smugly and blew on the mirror.

"Tip it up," he told Rose, and she did, rather gingerly, turning the handle of the mirror so that the glass faced the coverlet.

With a splintering chime, the mirror-glass fell out onto the bed. Rose gulped and lifted the frame back up, unsure what she would see inside. Her sensible instincts told her it would be the bare metal of the back of the mirror, or perhaps a silken lining bedding down a lock of hair. But the dark and the late hour and the flickering candles were screaming that it would be something horrible, like a finger bone, or that some disgusting apparition was already clambering and seeping out onto Bella's bed.

In reality, it was something completely different. Hanging out of the mirror frame was a piece of paper, the thick, expensive woven kind that Miss Fell had given them for their painting lessons. On it was a portrait, a watercolor, perhaps by the same hand as the sketch of the house that Miss Fell had given them to copy only yesterday.

"That's who I saw!" Rose squeaked, tugging the portrait gently out of the frame. "I'm sure it is." She picked up the glass front of the mirror, and held it and the painting side by side, looking from one to the other.

"Uncanny…" Gus purred, dangling his whiskers over

the painted face. "The spitting image of you. But five—maybe six years older? That hairstyle is out of date too."

"I can see why you thought she was your mother," Bella breathed. "Is there anything written on the back?" Rose turned the paper over with trembling fingers and traced the faded pencil inscription.

For my dearest Hepzibah, a portrait to remember me by on our travels. With all my love, Miranda Fell

"Miranda Fell! *That's* Miranda Fell?" Bella squealed excitedly. "Oh, of course. I should have known!"

"Why? What do you know about her?" Rose seized Bella's wrist and shook her a little. "Bella, don't tease me. Who is she?"

"Ow! Shhh, stop it, Rose. Do you want to wake everyone up?" Bella cradled her arm tenderly and glared. "And don't shake me. I was about to tell you."

"Please, Bella," Rose begged her, stroking the painted face. "I want to know."

Bella put her own hand over Rose's and traced the line of the face. "You know who the Fells are, don't you?"

"Gus said this morning that they were one of the most powerful magical families in the world."

"They were once," Gus put in reprovingly. "Sadly lacking now, of course. Living on their past glories, I should say."

"Well, yes, that's what I'm about to tell her! Don't interrupt, Gus!" Bella glared. "Miranda Fell was the only daughter of the family, the only child even. The heir. All the money was to come to her, and that huge house up in Derbyshire. She was incredibly beautiful, so they say"—Bella looked critically at the painting, and then at Rose—"and wonderfully strong at magic. She had everything she could ever want." Bella glanced back and forth between Rose and Gus, her eyes sparkling. "But she threw it all away! She disappeared, and apparently she ran off with the gardener's boy. Or at least, he disappeared too, so one can't help but come to conclusions."

"Of course one can't," Gus muttered. "Ran away with the gardener's boy. What a lot of nonsense."

"It isn't!" Bella glared at him in outrage. "It's what everyone says happened! My aunts still talk about it. It was the most enormous scandal."

"They talk about that sort of thing in front of you?" Gus wrinkled his white-furred muzzle in disgust.

Bella blushed, her cheeks staining the faintest pink. "Of course not." Then she shook her curls defensively and scowled. "But if I happened to be hidden behind the drawing-room sofa… No one ever tells me anything. I have to listen! I remember them talking about it, and they did say it was the garden boy."

"Hmf. Whenever a young lady disappears, it's always the gardener. No imagination." Gus swished his tail disapprovingly. "I remember thinking so at the time."

"When?" Rose whispered.

Bella and Gus stared at her, and Bella's eyes widened. Gus straightened his whiskers, as though he saw how important a question this was. He glanced at Bella, who wrinkled her nose, and then they looked back at Rose together.

"It was about eleven years ago, Rose child," Gus murmured, and Bella nodded, twirling one of her golden curls around her finger.

"Where did they go? Did anyone ever say in all the stories?" Rose stared down at the painted girl so she could not see them exchanging worried looks over her head.

Bella nodded and swallowed. "Her parents searched the whole country for her. They found the coachman from the stagecoach, and they paid all the passengers to talk. Miranda and the boy went to London, Rose. They came here."

* * *

It all fit. Like one of those strange jigsaw puzzles that Bella had in the schoolroom, maps and pictures all cut up. But there was a huge hole in the middle of the scene, and Bella hadn't any more pieces, not even hiding under her chair or knocked behind a cupboard like they usually were.

"But then what happened?" Rose asked. "Didn't her parents find out any more?"

Bella shook her head. "They simply vanished. The Fells had investigators all over London. But they never found even a sniff of them."

"So we don't know if—if…" Rose trailed off. She couldn't say it, even now.

Gus nosed her cheek gently, his whiskers fizzing lovingly against her cheek. "If they had a daughter and lost her, dearest one?"

"Mmm. Or left her." Rose brushed the sleeve of her nightgown over her eyes.

"Something must have happened to make them leave you," Bella protested. "Or—well, they could be dead, Rose." She looked up at Rose anxiously as she said it.

Rose nodded. She had always rather hoped her parents were dead, since that would at least mean they hadn't given her away in a fish basket. But the thought seemed dreadful now, when she felt as though she was chasing a trail at last, following the clues toward her birth. The image in the mirror had drawn her so much closer to that girl, Miranda Fell, who might have been her mother. Seeing her picture made Rose feel as though Miranda had died only a few days before, just barely slipping out of Rose's clutches.

"They probably are dead," she agreed quietly. "But I still wish I knew how it all happened." She gave a bitter little laugh. "I can't stop. Two days ago I didn't know anything, and now I'm getting greedy. Now that I've seen her." Rose shook her head. "And the gardener's boy. I can't feel the same about him, somehow, and it isn't fair." She rubbed at the rough edge of the paper. "I don't suppose there's a painting of him."

Gus brushed his whiskers over the painting again. "This painting obviously has a strong link to Miranda, or you'd never have seen her in the mirror. If we put it back in its hiding place, we could use the mirror to scry. To find out what happened. Then you might even see him, if we do it well enough."

Rose looked doubtful. "Would that work? I mean, the painting must have been done before Miranda ran away, mustn't it?"

Deep wrinkles of thought appeared above Gus's eyes, furrowing his white fur. "Yes…but it might not make any difference. We have to hope so, anyway. And we need to be quick. Look." He nodded toward the window. "It isn't long till dawn."

Rose glanced at the lightening sky. Very soon they would have to take the mirror back. This was their only chance. She slipped the painting back into its hiding place. Feeling silly but trying not to care, she quickly kissed her fingers and stroked them across that sweetly smiling face. Then she pressed the glass carefully back over the top and gazed at her reflection. It looked just the same as before, but perhaps a little more tired. Not like someone who might have a mother and a father now. Surely something that important would have made her look different.

"Rose." Bella pulled her sleeve gently. "Rose, come on. We haven't any time."

Urgency had slipped into Bella's voice, even though she was trying to be patient, and Rose nodded apologetically. She had to stop thinking about things. But her middle-of-the-night mind kept worrying over so many strange little thoughts. Would her mother like her new dress from Venice? Would her mother like *her*?

"Look into it properly," Gus commanded. "Rose, concentrate or I shall bite you, and a cat's mouth is a hotbed of dirt and disease." He sounded quite proud of that. He nudged the mirror up in front of her face with his nose and then peered into the glass hopefully with her.

Rose cupped her hands around the back of the mirror and balanced it on her knees, cradling it carefully. Bella scrambled up on the bed next to her and pulled the comforter around their shoulders, so that they sat huddled together, staring into the tiny circle of glass.

What Rose saw there was dark—but surely darker than it should have been. It wasn't only flat, reflected night; it was the dark that comes before a vision, and Rose felt her heartbeat start to race.

A faint mist appeared in the darkness, threading

its way toward them from the back of the mirror—wherever that was. It felt so odd. Rose could feel the edges of the molding pressing into her fingers as she held the mirror. But a dark tunnel in it extended back miles. Looking at it made her feel dizzy, as though she were floating off down that black path, through the backs of her own hands and somewhere out past Bella's bedroom wall.

"Rose! *Rose!*"

"What? I'm doing it. You wanted me to look and I am. Can't you see?" Rose muttered, narrowing her eyes and trying to see what that strange mist meant.

There was a frightened little moan, and Bella put her hand across the glass, severing Rose's link with the mirror.

"What did you do that for?" Rose hissed. "I had something!"

"Did you indeed?" a cold voice inquired. "Something other than the mirror you stole from my room?"

Rose finally looked away from the glass and swallowed. Miss Fell was standing at the end of the bed, looking somehow taller than usual, as though fury had inflated her.

"Oh." Rose ran her fingers over the back of the mirror, hating the thought of giving it back. "We're sorry," she murmured, unsure what else to say. But "sorry" was no good when her hands wouldn't let go of the mirror.

"You stole," Miss Fell repeated, her voice splintery cold.

"We—we didn't really want to," Rose babbled. "But we couldn't think of any other way to find out, and…" She trailed off into silence. There was no excuse.

"To find out what?"

Rose swallowed again. Her mouth felt dry and sticky. How could she ask Miss Fell if they were related when she had just stolen from her?

"It was you, Isabella, wasn't it? Passing on little secrets? Whispering?" Miss Fell seemed to glide as she came closer, and Bella shrank back against Rose, her eyes dark with fear.

"I didn't mean to—I only told her—I thought she ought to know! She looks so like you, and you kept watching her… What are you going to do?" Bella's voice was squeaking, higher and higher, and Rose gasped as she realized what was about to happen. Bella was losing control and falling into hysterics, which meant she was going to scream.

The noise began as a keening wail. Bella's eyes were still fixed on Miss Fell, but Rose thought Bella hardly saw her. There was only blankness behind the blue of Bella's eyes, as though she had hidden away inside her own head, shutting everyone out with that terrible screaming.

"Stop her!" Rose snarled at Miss Fell, as Bella trembled and twisted in Rose's arms. "It's you that's making her do this. She's frightened. Tell her you won't hurt her, that you're not angry! Oh, ow…"

"Too late, I think." Gus's ears were laid back flat against his skull, and his whiskers were bristling.

Miss Fell's anger had subsided, and the glassy look of fury had left her eyes. Now she looked slightly worried. Considering that she rarely allowed her emotions to show on her face, Rose reckoned this meant that Miss Fell was very worried indeed.

"How did you stop her last time?" the old lady demanded, clicking her fingers in front of Bella's glazed eyes. Miss Fell's shoulders were shaking with the effort, but she did not cover her ears.

Out of pride and anger, Rose didn't cover hers either. She wanted to. She was desperate to wrap her arms around her head and screw her eyes shut tight, in case any more of the agonizing sound crept in through her eyelids, but she didn't. Instead she held Bella tight, letting the eerie sound shake them together. It was like being buffeted by furious waves, those great walls of jade-green water that had slammed against the ship on their journey home from Venice.

"I hit her, but I don't think it would work again. She's gone further this time. She isn't really there," Rose gasped.

Miss Fell placed her hands gently on either side of Bella's face and peered at her. "You're right. We have to bring her back to make her stop."

The door slammed open just then, revealing Mr. Fountain leaning on Freddie's shoulder and looking horrified. Freddie had a striped scarf wound around his head, but it didn't seem to be working. He was sheet white and looked sickened.

"Bella! Bella, stop! What on earth has happened to her?" her father demanded. "*Bella!*"

Rose ignored him. The ebb and flow of the sound around her was still making her think of the sea journey, and Freddie's greenish pallor had given her the merest hint of an idea.

She wrapped her arms even tighter around Bella, squeezing her closed, and laid her face against Bella's, feeling the feverish heat of the little girl's skin. Rose closed her eyes and let herself rock with the noise, riding it. The bed was a flimsy raft, and they were shipwrecked on the sound, dragged to the top of each enormous wave and flung mercilessly back down.

She had never tried to use her moving pictures inside anyone else's head before, but if anything would break Bella out of her fit, it would be this. She was dreadfully seasick and had spent a large part of both their sea journeys curled up, moaning in her bunk. No one could scream and be sick at the same time, Rose was fairly sure.

Bella broke in mid-scream, the uncontrollable trembling giving way to coughs and splutters and a horrified whimper.

"Get a bowl!" Gus growled at Miss Fell, who was watching fixedly, the back of her hand pressed to her lips. "Oh, Rose, stop it. You have me doing it too!" He slunk over the side of the bed and underneath, and could be heard coughing wretchedly into the chamber pot.

Miss Fell thrust a bowl of scented rose petals in front of Bella and retired to a safe distance, looking pale.

"A most effective hallucination," she murmured, sinking onto a chair.

Bella moaned weakly and looked around her bedroom. "We were out at sea," she muttered. "Why is everyone here?" Then she pressed her hand guiltily against her mouth. "Oh! The mirror. Did I scream?"

"You did indeed," her father told her grimly. "I must go and reassure the servants. Thank you, Freddie. I can walk now." He wrapped his dressing gown around himself tightly, glared at Bella, and stalked out of the room.

Bella stared after him miserably, so much unhappiness floating out of her that even Freddie was moved to sit down on the bed and pat her hand. "What happened?" he muttered.

"The girls have stolen a mirror from my room, Frederick." Miss Fell's voice had lost the coldness, but Freddie still gaped at her, and then swung around to stare at Rose and Bella.

"Are you two mad?" he asked.

"Indeed." Miss Fell sighed. "No. I am being unfair. Presumably, Rose, you felt you had no other choice."

"What?" Freddie muttered, looking cross. "I shouldn't quarrel with you two. I miss things."

Bella managed a wan smirk, but Rose hardly even heard him. "Will you tell us?" she whispered, her eyes fixed beseechingly on Miss Fell.

"I think I must." Miss Fell gazed unseeingly at the curtained window. "Yes, I think I must."

Five

M ISS FELL TURNED BACK to look at them at last. "Give me the mirror, child," she half whispered. "Please."

Rose scrambled out from underneath Bella and picked up the mirror, which she had dropped among the pillows. Shyly she padded across the rug and handed it to Miss Fell.

The old lady caught Rose's wrist as she came close, pulling her gently toward her. "Sit with me," she begged, and Rose settled on the arm of the chair like a rag doll. Miss Fell had the sort of voice that made one want to obey.

"I have to apologize." Miss Fell still held Rose's hand, and she patted it gently as she spoke. Rose nodded politely, unsure how to answer. She could see Bella and Freddie edging toward the side of Bella's bed, wanting to be closer, to hear what was about to happen. Even Gus came crawling out from under the trailing bedclothes, his whiskers drooping. He sat at Miss Fell's feet, washing furiously.

"How much have you worked out?" Miss Fell looked up at Rose, her dark eyes gentler than Rose had ever seen them.

"Bella…" Rose halted, unsure if Miss Fell would be angry again. She couldn't face another bout of Bella's hysterics.

"Isabella is a clever little girl," Miss Fell said dryly. "Too clever for her own good. You remembered the rumors about Miranda, didn't you?"

Bella nodded. "And you do look alike…" she whispered. "Just every so often."

"I saw her picture in the mirror," Rose explained. "When you gave it to me to look at my frown lines. It wasn't me in the glass, but it was so like me. After that…we had to take it. Steal it, I mean," she added shamefacedly. "I had to know who she was."

Miss Fell nodded. "As anyone would who had been left in such circumstances. Oh, dear Rose. I think Miranda must have been your mother. I can't know, of course. I never saw her again after that strange day when she gave me the painting. If only she had said! I would have helped. She never even sent word that she was safe. I suppose she was too afraid that the message would be traced."

"She was your sister?" Rose's tongue seemed to fumble over the words.

"You flatter me, dear. My niece. Your mother was my brother's child. Miranda Fell." She hooked a delicately pointed fingernail under the side of the glass and pulled it out, revealing the painting. "Yes, she is so very like you."

"Did she run away with the gardener's boy?" Bella asked curiously. "Gus told us that was nonsense, but Aunt Fay said she did."

Miss Fell's eyebrows drew together haughtily. "Your Aunt Fay, Isabella Fountain, is a gossip and a flirt and gallivants with her footmen. And I'm quite certain that story wasn't meant for your ears, miss." Then she nodded very slightly. "Unfortunately, in this instance, she had the story right. Except that he was one of the under-gardeners. A most handsome young man and a good worker. John Garnet, he was called."

"You didn't know?" Rose murmured. John Garnet. Her father. The name sounded…good. A solid, honest name.

"No. They must have been so careful. I suppose she knew even at the start that it would never have been permitted. Oh, I knew something was different, and I suspected that she might be pining for someone, but I assumed it was one of the boys she had met in London. She had been presented for her first season, you see."

Rose nodded, although she had very little idea what that really meant.

Miss Fell was staring at her again, searching her face. "Seeing you in Venice, I told myself it was just a chance resemblance. Some strange quirk of nature. But when I heard your history, I couldn't help but wonder. Perhaps I should have said something then, but I wasn't sure, not at all. And you seemed contented, Rose. I wondered if you were better off without the truth—such as it is."

"I wanted to be." Rose picked at the lace cuff of her nightgown. "I'd always thought I was happy not knowing, but the magic seemed to make everything different. I wanted to know where it had come from, all this strangeness."

"When I gave you that painting of Fell Hall…"— Miss Fell closed her eyes—"it was a test. My curiosity got the better of me, Rose. I couldn't resist seeing what would happen. I thought almost certainly nothing. You had never been there, after all, so why should you react? And then you painted her. Miranda loved those peacocks. She would wander up and down the lawn for hours, slipping them crumbs. She called that wrap her peacock shawl and swore that its patterns were feathers." She sighed. "I still don't know how you did it."

"I didn't," Rose muttered. "It just happened."

"Unconscious magic can be the strongest of all. At any rate, it proved to me who you are. I shouldn't have reacted the way I did, but then I never went back, you see. I haven't been to Fell Hall in eleven years."

"Whyever not?" Freddie demanded in surprise and then looked guilty. "Sorry, ma'am, I didn't mean…"

Miss Fell gave him a very small smile. "I quarreled

with my brother, Frederick." She patted Rose's hand again, but this time it felt almost like a warning. "When your grandfather, my brother, found out that Miranda had run away with a servant, he disowned her. He changed his will and left everything to a charity that provides meat for stray cats."

Gus coughed appreciatively. Miss Fell nodded. "Quite. But this was not in a spirit of generosity or out of any love for your race, my dear. He was purely furious. He was ashamed that a daughter of his would have done such a thing, and then that she had the gall to hide so well that he couldn't find her and drag her back. I tried to dissuade him, but he made it very clear that Miranda would not be welcome there ever again, and that if I persisted in taking her side, neither would I." She sighed.

"And so I left. I had my own money from my mother, so I came to live in London, and I traveled, and I looked for her wherever I went. I was almost grateful to Miranda, when I wasn't furious with her for disappearing without telling me. I had always longed to go abroad, but Fell Hall… Well, it has some strange magic of its own. Leaving it can be very difficult. Which only proves, Rose, how much your mother must have loved that boy."

Rose nodded. "I wish I knew what happened. It must all have gone wrong."

"Horribly wrong." Miss Fell sighed. "I had always

hoped I might find her again, you know. Even that she might find me. But Miranda wasn't the sort of person to abandon a child, Rose. That's why it was so strange for me to see you. I was so excited to think that you might be Miranda's daughter. But at the same time, you were an orphan, which meant that Miranda was dead, and somehow I'd never quite brought myself to believe that. I was sure I would have known or felt it somehow. Instead I'd always convinced myself that she was just living hidden away somewhere, and one day she would come back."

"I'm sorry," Rose murmured, feeling stricken.

"Oh, Rose! None of this is your fault—and I feel as if I have Miranda reincarnated, which is an amazing gift." She smiled and stroked Rose's hair. "Seeing you, even your grandfather would have relented, I think."

"Would have?" Freddie asked before Rose could. He was lying on Bella's bed now with his chin on his hands, listening avidly, as if this were some exciting bedtime story.

"He died. A few years ago, and your grandmother too, Rose. I'm sorry. I'm afraid I must be your only close relative."

"My—my great-aunt?" Rose stammered, hardly sure if she dared to suggest it.

"Yes." Miss Fell smiled at her.

"So who lives at Fell Hall now?" Freddie asked, breaking into the strange little silence.

Miss Fell shook her head. "No one. There was a huge fight about the inheritance. Some distant cousins objected to the cats' meat people and contested the will. They thought they should have Fell Hall." She gave a grim little smile. "The court agreed that your grandfather had behaved out of spite, but the case didn't turn out the way my cousins expected. I had been gone long enough that Cousin Magnus had forgotten I existed. The court ruled that the house belonged to me."

"But you've still never been back?" Freddie gaped at her.

"Close your mouth, boy. You'll catch flies," Miss Fell told him tartly.

Freddie shut his mouth with a snap, but he was still staring at her, and she sighed. "I would always be thinking of Miranda. I didn't want to go back. I have a steward there, and he keeps the house with a skeleton staff, but I am afraid the old place is probably rather ramshackle now."

Rose smiled to herself. She was willing to bet that a skeleton staff meant at least twenty people, and ramshackle just that they weren't keeping all the silver polished.

"You should have this, Rose." Miss Fell stroked the roses around the edge of the mirror, then closed her eyes for a second and handed it quickly to Rose.

Rose held it, wide-eyed. "It's yours…"

"It was your mother's first. I gave it to her, in fact.

For her twelfth birthday, with a jewelry box to match.
She loved it."

"But didn't she take it with her? Could she not
take anything at all?" Rose imagined Miranda heading out into the night—somehow she was sure her
mother had gone at night—with only the clothes she
was wearing.

"They decided she must have had a small bag, but
she couldn't pack properly. It would have been too
obvious. And oddly enough, Rose, she did take this
mirror with her. She left the jewelry box. That's in my
room too, but you missed it on your little spying mission, my dears." Miss Fell's eyes glinted as Rose tensed
beside her, but then Rose saw that it was the brightness of tears. "It was brought back to me by a friend
who saw it in a jeweler's shop. He recognized the Fell
emblem on the back, you see?"

Miss Fell turned the mirror over in Rose's hands to
show them, and Rose frowned. She hadn't noticed a
crest or a coat of arms. But Miss Fell was pointing to
the engraved rose garlands. Cleverly twisted into one of
them was a tiny mouse, its tail wrapped around a rose
stem, and its little, sharp-eyed face peering out from
between the thorns. "The mouse in the roses is the sign
of the Fells. Some strange dream that one of our ances-
tors had long ago, I think."

Rose ran her finger over the little mouse, smiling. It
seemed a more suitable emblem for her family than a

proud lion or a griffin or some such fabled beast. She felt at home with a mouse.

"I knew that things must be very wrong when he handed it to me." Miss Fell's voice was threadlike. "She wouldn't have given it up easily." She struggled up out of the chair, looking suddenly exhausted. "I am going back to bed. I would appreciate it, dear ones, if you could manage not to produce any more disasters until late morning. Perhaps even after lunch."

Rose and Bella nodded guiltily, and then Rose suddenly had to strangle the most enormous yawn. Miss Fell had very strict ideas on young ladies yawning. One simply didn't.

"I am coming to sleep on your bed, Rose," Gus announced. "I approve of your new bedroom very much, although I wouldn't personally have chosen that odd violet shade for the curtains. But in general, a much more fitting place for me to sleep." He wove himself around her ankles as she walked wearily to the door. "I will guard the mirror for you, if you like. Or are you going to sleep holding it?" He stared up at her, his mismatched eyes bright and knowing, and Rose blushed scarlet.

* * *

"If I ever fight with you again, Rose, you must remind me of all this," Freddie muttered.

83

They were sitting in the workroom with a plate of toast that Rose had begged from Mrs. Jones, since they had all slept through breakfast. Bella and Rose were explaining to Freddie about everything that had happened since they found the painting. Gus was apparently asleep in front of the fire, but his tail twitched irritably every time he disagreed with the girls' storytelling.

"I can't believe you're a Fell." Freddie shook his head. "That's like magical royalty, Rose. One of the Fells back in Tudor times had a pet dragon, or so everyone says."

There was a disgusted sniff from the hearth rug, and Freddie glared. "They do say it! Just because you don't believe in dragons, it doesn't mean I can't. And I do."

"Stop talking fairy tales and do something useful with that mirror." Gus stretched himself paw by paw as he uncoiled from the mat.

Rose blinked. She had the mirror on the table in front of her, at a safe distance from the toast. She hadn't wanted to leave it in her room. "Such as what?"

"Scry in it, of course! Have you forgotten what you borrowed it for?"

"But we don't need to now. Miss Fell told us about my mother." Rose frowned at Gus, who had jumped onto the table and was sniffing thoughtfully at the mirror again.

"You did start to see something in it." Bella, who had been playing idly with a crust of toast, sat up straight, her eyes eager. "You said so, while Miss Fell was being so frightening. In fact, it was interesting enough that you didn't even notice her."

Rose nodded. "A strange black tunnel. I think someone was about to come out of it." She shuddered. "Or something, perhaps. It could have been anything."

"If we all do it together, we're even more likely to make it work," Freddie suggested, fingering the silver roses. "Don't you think?"

"Let Rose hold it," Gus told him. "She is the one with the family connection. You and Bella can hold her and lend her the strength of your magic."

Rose nodded. Family connection—Gus had said. It made her heart jitter in a strange way. It wasn't family in the sense she had thought of it—it was more like history. A very distant relative with a pet dragon. A link to a family house. Even if the house was about to fall down because her grandfather had been so furious with her mother. "I still don't know what we're actually looking for," she said, sounding rather dazed.

"A glimpse into the past," Gus suggested. "We want to know what happened."

"This mirror was your mother's, so maybe we can scry for her." Bella sounded a little hesitant.

"*Can* you scry for ghosts?" Freddie asked Gus.

"Freddie! I was trying to be tactful!" Bella scolded.

"Everyone is so sure she's dead," Rose murmured, stroking the mirror.

There was a silence that no one wanted to break. Eventually Gus nudged her hand with his muzzle. It felt whisker bristly. "You heard your great-aunt. She sounded quite sure."

"I know. I know my mother must be dead." Rose smiled, biting her lip, and then looked away from them all. "I know it's stupid. I'm chasing rainbows, wanting her still to be alive. It just seems so unfair that we've found out all about her, and I can't even talk to her. Unless—unless she's a ghost. I don't think I want to talk to a ghost..." she added in a whisper.

"Then maybe we shouldn't do this." Freddie folded his arms, looking suddenly older brotherly.

The girls stared at him in surprise.

He shrugged, turning pink with embarrassment. "It seems bad form to summon up a ghost, especially if you're going to get all upset about it, Rose. I mean, we're dragging this spirit up from somewhere and she might be busy, and then to have you crying all over her..."

Gus snorted. "Busy!"

"Well, what do ghosts do?" Freddie shrugged. "I've never met one."

Bella looked at him with her head cocked to one side. "Are you scared?"

Freddie started to deny it furiously, but Rose just shuddered. "I am. I don't think I'd be scared of just any ghost—I've seen so many strange things since I came here. But this ghost actually belongs to me, and that's

86

scary." She gripped the edges of the mirror frame tightly, forcing herself not to put it down and walk quickly out of the room. "I don't think it's scarier than the spiders' webs, though. So we should do it. Do we have to do anything special if we think we might be summoning a ghost?" she asked Gus, her voice squeaking at the edges.

Gus frowned at the glass. "I think we should be a little careful about what we invite into the house. We're opening a door, in a way." He was kneading his front paws against the tabletop in the way he did when he was anxious.

"Practically the first time I met you," Rose said, "you'd opened a door in this very room, and you were fighting off a mist monster—and don't tell me not to call it that, Freddie!"

Gus, for once, looked embarrassed. "That was research…" he muttered. "Freddie encouraged me. And that just means you know how dangerous it is to go around summoning things."

Rose sniffed. She had in fact sent off the mist monster, or elemental spirit or whatever it was called, by thumping it on the nose, which it hadn't expected. But when she and Freddie and Bella had been trapped by a crazed magician who wanted to use their blood for a spell, Freddie had summoned up the mist monster again and it had devoured Miss Sparrow in what looked like a couple of smallish gulps. Gus was right. They did need to be careful.

"Well, if something bad was coming, you'd smell it, wouldn't you?" she asked. "Or it would make your whiskers go all tingly."

"Oh, I'm not saying we shouldn't do it," Gus told her airily. "I just like you to be properly aware of what you're doing, that's all."

"So that you can rescue us when we do it wrong?" Freddie raised his eyebrows.

"Indeed." Gus gave him a slit-eyed smirk. "Or not. Anyway, Rose, no. Just do what you were doing before."

Rose shrugged. "All I did was look."

"Then look again." Gus was starting to sound impatient. "And look carefully. Be watchful."

Rose shivered, but she gripped the mirror frame tightly and felt Freddie and Bella draw closer, leaning over her shoulders to stare in too. There was the distracting aroma of buttered toast.

Rose concentrated hard on the glass, pleading with it inside her head. *Tell us what happened. I want to see. I want to know why—why she left me. But not a ghost, please. Unless there's nothing else...*

The blackness took longer to settle into the mirror this time, perhaps because they were all weary. But at last the glass clouded, like paint settling into clear water, and turned a murky black. Rose's shoulders tensed, sensing that something was approaching. The blackness seemed to be tunneling back, heading away to some strange place. Now the odd silvery mist that Rose had seen before was flowing toward them through the dark. As it came closer, Rose's breath caught in her throat, and she had to force herself to start breathing again. It was a figure.

Her mother's ghost.

Six

ROSE LET OUT A muffled, gasping sob and almost dropped the mirror. Only Freddie grabbing it saved them from losing the vision entirely. As it was, the figure in the mirror seemed to recoil, cowering back into the darkness and darting anxious glances this way and that, as though she wasn't sure she was doing the right thing.

"Rose, stop it!" Freddie snapped. "Pull yourself together. We nearly lost it there."

Rose gulped. How could Freddie be so cruel? "She's dead. She is, after all. That's a ghost, isn't it? So my mother is dead. I don't think I can bear to talk to the ghost of my mother. I thought I could do it, but I can't!"

"Then you'll never know what happened. Which is worse?" Gus was standing on Freddie's shoulders, hissing in her face, and Rose wept, turning away from them and from the silver figure in the mirror.

"I don't know, I don't know!"

"Ssshhh!" Bella poked Rose in the ribs. "Stop squabbling, all of you, and look. I don't think that's anyone's mother, Rose. That's a little girl."

Rose looked back around slowly. She wouldn't have put it past Bella to try to trick her into looking so that she couldn't pull away.

But Bella was right. Lingering in front of them, just inside the mirror frame, as though she didn't dare climb out into the room, was a ghost girl. She actually looked older than Bella herself—Rose's age, or even a little more. But Bella would never admit how young she was.

"She doesn't look anything like you or the portrait of Miranda," Bella pointed out. "As much as one can tell, when she's all silvery gray. Do you think that's because she's been living in a silver mirror?" Then she nudged Rose's shoulder. "You'd better talk to her, Rose. She's staring at you."

She was, her eyes round with wonder and fear and deep confusion.

Rose swallowed. "Who are you?" she asked quietly, trying not to sound too accusing. She felt accusing—she wanted to demand what this girl was doing coming out of her mother's mirror.

The ghost blinked, her washed-out features seeming to frown. "Eliza. I'm Eliza. Don't you know me, Miss Miranda?"

"Rose, she thinks you're your own mother!" Bella hissed excitedly. "She must have known her."

"I'm—I'm not Miranda," Rose stammered, and the ghost girl leaned closer, pressing up against the mirror glass, frowning and peering at her.

"Miss Miranda? Maybe—maybe you're not. You look like her, but I haven't seen her in such a long time." She pulled away from the glass and rubbed her hands over her face as though she was confused. "I don't understand. Who are you? You're too young to be Miss Miranda, I think. Unless…I don't understand," she repeated wearily.

"You're a ghost. Do you understand that?" Gus asked suddenly, and the girl jumped, pressing her hands over her heart.

"Mercy me!"

"Your heart isn't racing, however much you may want it to," Gus pointed out. "Think. You're a ghost, aren't you?'

"Don't be cruel to her," Rose whispered, feeling rather shocked. Gus was being dreadfully callous.

"She'll be no use to us until she understands what she is." Gus didn't even turn and look back. "What are you?"

The little figure drooped sadly and nodded. "A ghost. A dead thing, sir."

"Gus, this is mean!" Rose hissed.

"Do you want to know what happened to your mother, or not?" Gus snapped, his whiskers vibrating with irritation. "Don't be so soft. The dead are dead, and if she doesn't understand where she is in time, she can't show us what happened, can she?"

"I still don't see why you have to talk to her as if she's a slave!" Rose stopped and frowned slightly at him. "Unless…you're afraid of her, aren't you? Is this why you kept uttering all those dire warnings about doors?"

"Shut up." Gus's shoulder bones were sticking out of his fur, and his tail was fluffed out like a bottle brush. "You dislike spiders; I dislike the dead. They play tricks. That's all there is to it. Now talk to this one, so we can send it away."

"Don't send me away," the little silvery figure pleaded. "I'll be good. I'll tell you what you want to know. Please."

"Who are you, please?" Rose asked very politely, trying to counteract Gus's rude treatment of the little ghost.

"Eliza Lampton, miss," the ghost told her promptly. She wrung her wispy hands nervously and cocked her head to one side. "If you're not Miss Miranda, miss, might you be so good as to tell me who you are? You look the very spit of her, miss, when she was a good bit younger, that is."

Rose glanced quickly at Gus, suddenly unsure whether telling one's name to ghosts was dangerous, but he was sitting on Freddie's shoulder watching like a disapproving statue. Feeling absurdly shy, she explained, "My name is Rose. I don't have a surname, not a proper one. I came from an orphanage, St. Bridget's. But I think—I don't know for certain—I think I may be your Miss Miranda's daughter. Oh! Don't do that. Please, don't go!"

The silvery girl was drawing backward away from them, her hands over her mouth and her eyes huge in that pale face surrounded by strange, dark, wet-looking hair. She was muttering something behind her hands, and Rose had to lean forward to catch what she was saying. It felt as if she was reaching into the dark tunnel.

"I remember! I remember!" The ghost sat down in the darkness and wrapped herself around her knees.

"I remember it all…" she whispered at last, looking up at them as though she was the one who was haunted, and not them at all.

"Can you come out of the mirror?" Rose asked her suddenly. She wanted the poor little thing to come out and sit with them. Perhaps even to hold her hand, while she told them the story.

The ghost shook her head. "I don't think so, miss. Not yet, anyway. I've been in here a while. I'm tied." She sat up and stretched out her hands to either side. To Rose it looked as though she was stretching her fingers into nothing, but clearly she could feel the darkness pressing against her. "Besides…" She glanced nervously at Gus. Clearly she liked the look of him as little as he liked her.

"Keep her shut away in there," Gus muttered. "Then we're all safe. Her as well."

Rose glared at him. "Eliza, how did you know my mother?"

Eliza wriggled closer to them and stared out at Rose. "I was her maid, miss."

Rose nodded slowly. She should have expected it, she supposed. A grand young lady like Miranda Fell would, of course, have a personal maid. There was a strange sort of symmetry to it as well, that she should find her mother's maid. Rose's life had been far more like Eliza's than her mother's.

"I went with her, miss, when she ran away with John Garnet—him that was your father, miss."

Rose gasped. "Did you? No one told us that. So you know what happened? Why they left me? You know why I ended up at St. Bridget's?" In her eagerness to hear, she reached out her hand to Eliza, wanting to touch the little kneeling figure, to show her how important this was. Her hand slipped into the darkness inside the mirror, and she yelped at the sudden cold.

"Come back!" Gus hissed, and he raked his claws over her wrist. Rose pulled her hand back sharply and sucked the long scratches, glaring at him. "What did you do that for?" she mumbled.

"Who knows where you would have ended up, stupid girl? Be careful! What did I say to you before we started this?"

"But she isn't some horrible thing we're opening a door to," Rose argued back.

95

"We don't know what she is. She may have been Eliza Lampton once, but who's to say she hasn't changed? Don't touch her, for all our sakes!" Gus stared suspiciously into the mirror, and the ghost stared back, looking anxious.

"Stop squabbling!" Bella leaned closer to the mirror. "Eliza, will you tell us about Miss Miranda? How she ran away, and what happened after?" She didn't say please, and her tone was imperious, but it seemed to be what Eliza was used to. She nodded eagerly, looking almost relieved. She was used to orders.

"Yes, miss." She closed her eyes, remembering. "Miss Miranda asked me to help her pack. She swore me to secrecy." There was pride in her voice. "She told me the master would never let her and John Garnet be together, and they were running off to London to get married. She'd had a fight with the master, you see. We all heard the shouting, all us servants. Miss Miranda wanted me to fetch her a carpetbag, or some such, out of the attics. She couldn't go up there without people noticing, you see."

"She must have trusted you," Rose murmured.

Eliza nodded proudly. "And she never put a spell on me, miss, even though she could have. She knew I'd not tell her secrets. So I fetched her a bag, and I fetched one for myself and all. I told her I was going with her. Well, she tried to say no, and she was that embarrassed, poor dear, because she had to tell me she'd not be able to pay my wages any longer. She knew the master would cut her off without a penny, mean old skinflint that he was. She'd be living on what John Garnet could earn for them, and he'd have no references from the master, would he? So it would be a laborer's wages, if they were lucky."

"But she was a magician! Couldn't she use her magic?" Bella sounded disgusted.

Eliza shook her head. "She didn't know how to do much that was useful with it, miss. It didn't cook the dinner or wash the clothes, and she couldn't do any of her grand spells, in case the spies her father had put after them found out, you see? She used to make a lovely warm fire, though, I'll say that."

"Where did you go when you got to London?" Freddie asked curiously.

"Some nasty low place close by Covent Garden." Eliza sniffed. "Miss Miranda didn't like it, but she didn't say a thing. She was good like that, and she didn't want to hurt his feelings. It was all they could afford, 'specially since they'd had to buy a marriage license with his savings."

Rose nodded thoughtfully. She could imagine her mother's life after her elopement much more easily than the pampered existence she'd had before. Rose had never lived in the London slums herself, but many of the other girls at St. Bridget's had arrived half-grown after their families were wiped out by hunger or some terrible sickness that had spread through the city. They had hated being confined to an orphanage, but they'd regarded three meals a day (even if mostly cabbage) and an outfit of clean clothes that almost fit as the height of luxury.

"Did he get a job?" she asked. "My—father?"

Eliza nodded. "As a porter, miss. Unloading the carts bringing the fruit and vegetables to the market. They were so pleased. It was a cruel, hard job, but he was used to working out in the open air, from being a gardener. And soon enough we worked out that she was having you, and she was going around in a dream world. I'd never seen her that happy, never."

Rose found she was smiling. "They wanted me, then?" she whispered.

"Wanted you?" Eliza snorted. "You'd think a baby was something that had never happened before. Your father, he made you a cradle out of fruit boxes, and the toys he carved! A Noah's ark with all the animals, all lined up, waiting. She even sewed for you, miss! And for Miss Miranda, that wasn't usual. She hated sewing. Mind you, she was cheating, I'm sure. She could never have made those little dresses without a spell to speed the sewing."

Bella looked envious. "I want that spell," she whispered.

"It was almost the only magic she did while they were living there, miss, that and keeping the fire going. She was sure her father still had his spies out, and she

98

didn't want to get caught. And she never said, but I think she was sick of it, anyway. Magic reminded her of her family, you see, and the way they'd cut her off. All the magicians she knew, they all thought she was mad, she said. She didn't want anything to do with them or their magic."

"What about Miss Fell? Miss Hepzibah Fell, I mean?" Rose asked. "We know her—now, in our time. She didn't cut Miranda off, did she?" Rose gripped the mirror frame tightly.

Eliza smiled. "No. Miss Miranda said she wished she could tell her aunt where she was going, but Miss Hepzibah was right under her brother's thumb. He'd have it out of her faster than a greased rabbit, Miss Miranda reckoned, and he'd make her life a misery doing it. Miss Hepzibah was safer not knowing."

Rose drew in a shaky breath of relief. She hadn't known how important it was for that to be true. Even though Miss Fell had been lying to her, or at least not telling her the truth, for ages, Rose desperately wanted to be able to trust her. But her grandfather sounded fearsome, if he was someone who could terrorize Miss Fell.

Bella was frowning thoughtfully. "I wonder if it was Miranda leaving that made Miss Fell so...well, you know. Stiff spined. She said she fought with your grandfather and left because she was so angry. That doesn't sound like the same person Eliza's talking about. I can't imagine Miss Fell under anyone's thumb now, can you?"

Rose let out a nervous giggle at the thought, but then she nodded. "I think my mother did her a favor."

"What went wrong?" Gus leaned in closer to the mirror from Freddie's shoulder. His ears were laid back, and he looked and sounded fierce.

Eliza darted back as though he'd aimed a blow at her, and Rose wondered if he had by magic. She gave him a stern glare, and he gazed coldly back. Rose shuffled her feet, embarrassed. Sometimes she forgot that Gus was probably a great deal older than she was, and certainly a great deal better at magic.

"Wrong?" Eliza quavered. "Oh! He died, sir."

"Oh!" Rose whispered. "John Garnet? My father died?" For a few moments it had been such a lovely story that she had almost seen it, the little room warm with firelight. The cradle ready, and the line of little wooden animals watching over it. Hints of it, little glints, had moved in the mirror behind Eliza, she was sure. Now there was only darkness again.

Eliza nodded. "It was a horse, miss. One of the cart horses, with a load of cabbages. Trampled, he was. It was awful. I thought Miss Miranda would die herself, she was that stricken. He'd made a little mouse for the ark the night before. The size of a fingernail, it was. She sat there holding it and crying because there was only one instead of two."

"She'd left everything to marry him, and he was gone, just like that," Rose murmured. "I would be too. Cabbages!" she added with a choking gasp of horrified laughter. "I'm surprised it wasn't fish," she sobbed.

"Oh, there, miss…" Eliza wrung her silvery hands and then stretched out toward the glass nervously, dabbing at it with her fingers as if she wanted to reach through and touch Rose. "It's only vegetables at Covent Garden. Oh, I can't, I can't… You!" she hissed at Bella. "Put your arms around her! Miss, I mean," she added hastily.

Bella did as she was told, patting Rose a little awkwardly, and even Gus stepped from Freddie's shoulder to hers and nudged her cheek. Freddie took a step backward and offered Rose his handkerchief from a safe distance.

"So what did she do?" Rose whispered sniffily at last. "She can't have gone back. Did she die too?"

Eliza shuffled regretfully, winding her fingers into the strings of her apron. Clearly she didn't want to say.

"Tell me!" Rose snapped, and felt guilty when the little ghost's eyes went round and fearful, though not as guilty as she'd thought she would.

"She used her magic, miss. She had to. You were well on the way, so she couldn't do anything heavy like. She didn't want to—she thought her father would find out and come after her. But she didn't have a choice. She sent me to put a little card up in the window of the Three Bells, the pub down the street. *Any Tasks Undertaken*, it said. *Discretion our watchword. No love potions*. Miss Miranda said those would probably make our fortune, but she couldn't bear it."

"Did he find you then? Mr. Fell?" Freddie asked. He was so fascinated that he'd forgotten to avoid tearful girls and had crept close to the mirror again.

Eliza shivered. "No."

Freddie drew in an excited, anxious breath. "But someone did?" he guessed, leaning close to hear Eliza whisper.

"It were all right at first," the little servant muttered. "She did little things. Found a lady's lost lapdog. Found an old man's will for his son, when he'd died and not said where he'd hidden it. But then she started to get known, you see? She was getting a reputation. And this shifty-eyed man came. He wanted her to look at some gold coins and see if they were real or forgeries. He said someone had used them to pay him." She shivered again. "And if they did, I feel sorry for them, I truly do."

"The coins were fake?" Gus asked with a professional sort of interest. Mr. Fountain had made his fortune as the country's only successful alchemist. Gus, as his familiar, clearly regarded this as research. He had stopped being quite so unpleasant.

Eliza nodded. "Very clever fakes, Miss Miranda said. With a spell on them to make them even better."

"Hmf." Gus considered this, his eyes hooded.

"When Miss Miranda told the man, I could see he weren't happy," Eliza whispered, her eyes dark with the memory of fear. "I couldn't tell if what he'd said was the truth, or whether he'd made those coins himself, and he just wanted to see if she could tell."

"You think he was the counterfeiter?" Gus demanded sharply, and Eliza nodded very slightly.

"I thought so. Miss Miranda was just glad he paid her in the real kind. She was past caring, poor thing." Eliza eyed Rose almost accusingly. "Made her life a proper misery those last few months, you did."

Rose nodded mutely, unsure if she should apologize. It was the strangest conversation.

"It was the very next day that he came." Now Eliza was visibly trembling. It made her strange silvery skin shimmer all over, and she wrapped her arms around her chest, as if trying to hold herself still.

Rose found herself trembling too. "He?" she whispered.

"The counterfeiter told him. He must have. Miss Miranda was on his turf, see? He came, and he had the card from the Three Bells's window. He said we didn't need it any longer, and somehow, when he said it, I knew it was true. He had the gift. He could make you believe anything, Pike could."

"Pike? That was his name?" Bella sounded contemptuous, but Eliza frowned at her.

"One of the stableboys told me once what a pike

is—I'd never known before. Great big river fish, all grayish green and spotted. They lie in wait for the smaller fish, hanging still in the water, hardly even twitching their fins. And then a poor little fish swims past, and the pike leaps on it and swallows it whole with its huge teeth. They're so crazed, sometimes they try to eat a fish that's as big as they are and die trying. Nasty, evil things."

"They taste nice, though." Gus's bright pink tongue stuck out of his mouth for just a second, and his eyes misted with the memory.

"Stop it, Gus. He likes fish," Rose said apologetically. "Did Pike bewitch Miranda too?"

Eliza shook her head thoughtfully. "Not at first. It took him a lot longer to catch her. She was sitting there, watching him drink tea, and she had a look on her face, same sort of look as that one had just now"—she pointed to Bella—"like she thought he was common. And when he started saying that she was on his territory, she just laughed.

"But she was so tired, what with the baby and grieving for Mr. John. He went on and on and on at her. She didn't see what he was doing. She was such an innocent, you see. All the time he was wrapping her in layers and layers of magic. Like a spider wrapping up a fly. The more he talked, the weaker she got, like he was drawing the strength out of her, sucking out her insides."

"Ugh." Bella shuddered.

Eliza nodded and leaned closer to the glass again. "And when she was all drained out, he sent his magic into her. She was like a puppet, dancing on strings." She sighed. "I couldn't tell her. I could see it, but he wouldn't let me tell her. I couldn't move, let alone speak. I just sat there in the corner, and she thought I was being a good, quiet servant, but all the time I was raging and screaming inside!"

"What did he do to her?" Rose begged, her nails digging into her palms, sure that she was about to hear how her mother had died.

Eliza laughed sadly. "He told her to pack. She only had her little carpetbag and another bundle of the baby clothes. He had her walking out of the door, and I was still sitting there on the stool in the corner. But then she stopped. She didn't see me, but she knew something was wrong. She knew I was missing. Even though he had her all wrapped up in a spell, she remembered me." The pride in the little ghost's voice was pitiful. "She made him stop and bring me too."

Gus twitched his whiskers. "You *wanted* to go? To be kidnapped by this powerful underworld magician?"

Eliza simply stared at him. "Where else would I go? Miss Miranda knew I didn't have anywhere else. I couldn't have gone home, even if I could find the fare for the stage coach from somewhere. And I would have had to go somewhere a decent girl wouldn't think of, mind you. No, if I'd have gone home, my dad would have sent me right away again. My family lived in a cottage on the Fell Hall lands; their home belonged to Mr. Fell. If they'd taken me back after the way I'd run off with Miss Miranda, my whole family would have been out. We'd all have been in the poorhouse. I burned my bridges when I went with her, Mr. Cat."

Gus laid his ears back a little at that, but he didn't complain. Rose could see that as much as he disliked ghosts, he was developing a grudging respect for this one and her loyalty.

"That's how Miss Miranda Fell and me, we joined the Pike gang." Eliza giggled, but she didn't sound as though she really thought it was funny. "The most bloodthirsty gang of murdering thieves you're ever likely to meet."

"She didn't—she didn't work for them?" Rose asked, her voice horrified.

Eliza sighed irritably, a puff of chilly, silvery not-breath smudging the mirror glass. "Of course she did! She hadn't a choice! Do you not understand anything? They made her do it. I cleaned and cooked and ran errands and did what I was told, and Miss Miranda did the same. She did what she was told." Her shoulders drooped. "If it makes you feel any better, miss, I don't think she ever actually killed anybody."

Rose gasped. "You don't *think*?" She shivered, and her fingers seemed to grow cold and dead. And she dropped the mirror.

Seven

"CATCH IT!" BELLA SQUEALED, and Rose stared at her hands in dismay. She had no feeling in her fingers—it was as if they didn't belong to her anymore. The mirror seemed to spin as it headed for the floor, and a thin, despairing wail floated up.

"Oh, no, no…" Rose moaned, as it hit the floor with a thud.

Bella snatched the mirror up. "Eliza's not there, but it isn't broken!" she cried thankfully. "Oh, Miss Fell would have killed us. Rose, what were you doing?"

"My mother was working for a bad magician! For a gang of murderers! That's probably how I ended up in the orphanage, Bella. Someone fought back and killed her. She was a criminal!" Rose stared down at her fingers. They felt just like they usually did, and she clenched them, digging her nails into her palms. She could feel that. She dug in harder, watching red half-moons flower on her skin. It hurt, which was good, because she felt as though things had changed so much in the last two minutes that it might not have.

Through all her time at St. Bridget's, she had assumed her parents were simply too poor to keep her. She had never, somehow, thought that they might be anything but honest. "My fingers stopped working before. When Eliza said…"

"She did say she didn't think your mother killed anyone," Freddie reminded her helpfully.

Rose glared at him. "Oh, wonderful! Not quite a murderer's daughter, then!"

Freddie sighed. "She didn't have a choice, Rose. You heard what Eliza said—she was bound into a spell. It sounded like a very clever one too. She wasn't used to dealing with other magicians, was she? Not if she'd lived most of her life in the wilds of Derbyshire, with what sounds to me like a mad family. He got her good and proper."

Rose nodded. She set the mirror down in front of her and gazed at it, her chin on her hands. She hoped that being dropped hadn't hurt Eliza. "It's what Mr. Fountain said would happen to me," she told them very quietly.

Freddie blinked. "What?"

Gus was eyeing her sympathetically. "You see now that he was right, don't you?" he asked gently.

"What did Papa say?" Bella sounded indignant. She disliked it when other people knew more about her father than she did.

"When everyone in the kitchens hated me, I was going to run away. Ssh!" She held up a hand as Freddie and Bella both started to talk at once. "I never even tried. Your father stopped me, Bella. Him and Gus. I was going to try to make a living for myself the same way my mother tried to, finding things. Helping people. It seemed such a good idea!" She laughed hollowly. "Gus said someone would cut me up and throw me in the river in a whole set of sacks. Or that I'd be made to work for someone awful. Like Miranda was."

"I can't believe you were going to run away!" Bella burst out. "You never told me!"

"You hardly ever talked to me then, except to complain that your dresses weren't properly ironed," Rose pointed out. "Nobody talked to me; that was the point. Even Freddie was being standoffish because he didn't want to share being an apprentice with me."

"I'm sure I was not." Freddie scowled. "Or only a little, Rose, anyway."

"I hated it here. I can't believe the same thing almost happened twice." She smiled sadly. "Perhaps I am like her."

"But *you* have people to watch out for you." Gus tickled her cheek with his whiskers. "We would not let that happen to you, Rose. We didn't. Like we said then, we're responsible for you. Even though we know who your parents are now, you are still Aloysius's apprentice, and we will always be bound together. We

109

would not let a backstreet magician steal one of our children away." He sniffed disgustedly.

"Think yourself lucky, Rose. Those Fells. Obsessed with birth and history and lineage, but not with people. They should not have let your mother out of their hands. Although…"—his whiskers shimmered thoughtfully—"it's highly possible that the girl had more fun in the year she had living in the London slums than she ever did walled up in a drafty mansion in Derbyshire."

Rose giggled in spite of herself. "I wouldn't let Miss Fell hear you say things like that. She'd have you turned into fur gloves."

Gus gave her a sharp look before obviously deciding that this counted as nervous exhaustion and not insolence to cats. "Miss Fell might even admit the same. She said it herself—she could not leave the Fell house until she was so angry she made a clean break from the family. I suspect she is infinitely happier for it." He thumped Rose's arm with his lead weight of a tail. "Now, find that girl ghost again. I want to know what happened next, even if you don't."

Rose nodded and picked up the mirror a little gingerly, in case the strange thing happened to her fingers again. "I do want to know, I suppose… Oh, of course I want to. I want to know every last detail, but I'm not sure I want to actually hear how she died. I just want to *know*." She looked around and saw that Bella and Freddie were frowning, and Gus was giving her the look of an impatient cat, his tail slightly twitching.

"Just look into the mirror, Rose dear," he purred, unsheathing his claws very slightly.

Rose sighed. "Sorry." She stared into the dark glass, searching for Eliza, but only her own face stared back. The silvery ghost girl had gone entirely. "She isn't coming back." Her voice had risen slightly in panic.

Bella peered at the glass. "Just do what you did last time."

"I did!" Rose snapped. "Nothing's happening."

"Maybe you scared her away, dropping it like that," Freddie said, tapping thoughtfully at the glass with one finger.

Rose shook her head. "I can't have. I didn't drop it that hard, did I?" she asked them pleadingly.

Bella shrugged. "It looks like you must have." Freddie nodded. "It might have felt to Eliza like you did it on purpose," he pointed out.

Rose stared into the mirror again, straining her eyes and her mind, but the glass remained obstinately glass. What if Eliza never came back? "No..." she whispered. "Please, Eliza, I need to talk to you. I have to know how it ended!"

Gus looked down at the glass and hissed thoughtfully. "Perhaps it didn't..."

Rose dragged her eyes away from the mirror glass and frowned wearily at him. "What do you mean?"

Gus went on staring at the mirror, his tail flicking faster now. But he seemed to be angry with himself, for once. "We could have been wrong. I've heard of the Pike gang. Notorious lot. Very savage. Mixed up in the opium trade too, I think…" He closed his eyes in a slow blink and then looked up at Rose. "They're still there. So why shouldn't she be?"

Rose felt the chair suddenly swing beneath her—as though a rug had been pulled out from underneath it.

"Rose!" Bella caught her hands and rubbed them. "She's like ice. Rose, wake up!"

Rose shook herself. Gus's words had seemed to send her into a dream—that confused state where nothing is ever certain. The strangest things happen, but no one cares. She swallowed tightly and whispered, "But you said…you all said it. That I was being silly, wishing she were still alive."

Gus wrapped his tail firmly around his paws and stared off sideways into the shadowy corners of the room. Clearly he hated having to contradict himself. "All I'm saying is, it may not be as much of a certainty as we thought," he growled. "So look in the mirror, girl."

Rose snatched it up. Perhaps Eliza had just been shocked when the mirror fell. Surely now they would see her, edging toward them through the mist…

But there was nothing in the glass, not even the slightest silvery shimmer. Rose sat back, staring down at her hands. How could she have been so stupid and dropped the mirror? "What am I going to do?" she whispered, more to herself than to the others.

"Miss Fell might be able to help," Freddie suggested reluctantly. "She must have known Eliza if she was your mother's maid while she lived at Fell Hall. Maybe she could summon her for us."

Bella sniffed. "I wouldn't come if I were a ghost and she summoned me."

Freddie shuddered. "Knowing her, you wouldn't have a choice."

But Rose shook her head. "I don't think that would be a good idea. You saw how much it upset Miss Fell to talk about my mother. What if we tell her all this and raise her hopes, and then we can't find her?" She swallowed. "Or worse, if the gang did kill her, and Miss Fell has to find that out. It would almost be worse for Miss Fell than it would be for me. I've never even met my mother. Well, not since I was a baby."

"Shouldn't you be calling Miss Fell, Great-Aunt Hepzibah?" Freddie pointed out with a sweet smile, but Rose shuddered.

"No. It would feel too…familiar."

"She is your family!" Freddie teased, but Bella interrupted him.

"We should tell Papa instead."

Gus nodded. "Indeed. The sooner the better. He may even know more about the Pike gang. He has several times consulted for the police, after all." He jumped off the table and looked back up at Rose. "And bring the mirror. He may also be able to compel that girl to come back and speak to us." He was heading for the door, his tail waving grandly, so he didn't see Rose clutch the mirror tightly to herself.

Rose didn't want Eliza compelled! She would tell Mr. Fountain so, she resolved. It was her mirror now, after all, and her mother they were trying to find. He wouldn't make her force Eliza out, surely?

But when they trooped down the main stairs—something that still made Rose's stomach lurch, as she had only been allowed on those stairs to clean them when she was a servant—they saw Mr. Fountain fighting his way into his stylish caped overcoat. The front door was open, and Rose could just see Bill hurrying off across the square, presumably to fetch the master a hansom cab.

"Is everything all right, sir?" Freddie asked.

"Another dratted summons to the palace!" Mr. Fountain snapped irritably. Officially his post was that of a magical adviser to the Treasury—which meant that he made gold—but as he was the only magician the king trusted, he tended to be called in for everything.

"I'm going to have to start getting things wrong—being indispensable is remarkably boring. The Talish really are mounting another invasion, apparently. They've been building more ships in secret. Oh, and that's military intelligence, so don't tell anyone."

A battered, black horse cab drew up outside the house, with Bill hanging on grimly behind. Mr. Fountain eyed the cab despairingly, and Bill shrugged and rolled his eyes as he ran up the steps.

"You said to be quick, sir!" he protested. "Matter of life and death, you said. It goes, don't it?"

"Does it?" Mr. Fountain muttered. "I wouldn't count on it. Behave, all of you. I may not be back for dinner." He sighed. "Or breakfast."

He climbed into the cab, which wobbled worryingly when he slammed the door and then raced away, leaving the children staring at each other in the hall.

"Well, that spoils that plan then," Freddie muttered. "Are you sure you don't want to talk to Miss Fell about it, Rose?"

"I don't think giving the houseguest a heart attack counts as behaving," Rose pointed out.

"What did you want Mr. Fountain for?" Bill asked, keeping an eye on the green baize door to the servants' quarters, in case anyone popped out to tell him off for fraternizing with the upstairs children.

"Oh! He might know!" Bella exclaimed, pointing at Bill in what Miss Fell would have called a most unmannerly fashion.

Freddie nodded. "Of course! He knows everything that happens in the square. He talks to all the other boys, the lads from the stables, the delivery boys. Don't you?"

"That's only around here. Just because we came from orphanages, it doesn't mean we rub shoulders with thieves' gangs!" Rose pointed out. "I didn't know anything about the Pike gang, did I?"

"Here, don't you go getting mixed up with them!" Bill snapped, his eyes widening worriedly.

Bella smiled smugly at Rose. "I told you. He does know who they are."

"Do you really?" Rose asked. "You're supposed to be respectable!"

Bill shrugged. "Only gossip from the stables and some of my mates from St. Bartholomew's."

"Do you know where we could find them?" Rose begged, grabbing his arm excitedly.

"No, I do not, and if I did, I wouldn't tell you! Are you asking to get chopped up into sausage patties?"

"Ugh, they don't, do they?" Bella asked with horrified fascination.

Bill folded his arms grandly. "So they say. Hey, Rose, what's the matter? What's she gone that color for?"

"Her mother. She was a magician, kidnapped and forced to work for the Pike gang," Freddie explained, putting a hand on the small of Rose's back to hold her up. "Rose is…upset. It may have been her mother, um, mixing the sausage."

Gus, who was in Rose's arms, patted a fat paw firmly against her cheek. "Don't faint! You'll drop me. If you really want to find her, you have to accept that you might not like what you find. Though, really, Frederick, a little tact!"

"Your *mother*?" Bill whispered, staring at Rose.

She nodded. "And it may be that she's still alive… Miss Fell thought she was—Oh, I forgot. You don't know. Miss Fell is my great-aunt."

"That old tabby upstairs?" Bill gaped at her.

"Yes. Miss Fell thinks she would have known if my mother was dead. They were very close. So she might still be there, Bill, with this Pike gang. I have to find out, don't you see?"

Bill nodded slowly. "But I still don't know where they hide out, Rose. And I'm not really sure I want to go asking either." He shivered. "That Pike—by all accounts he's some sort of monster."

"Eliza said he was a very strong magician," Rose agreed. "He bound my mother in a spell to make her work for him."

Bill looked lost. "Who's Eliza?"

"Oh, bring him upstairs and explain it all to him!" Gus snapped. "It's beneath my dignity to hang around in hallways. If he's missed, you can tell them Bella wanted her bedroom furniture moved, and then she didn't like it and he had to move it back again." He leaped from Rose's arms to land with a graceful thump halfway up the stairs. "Come along."

* * *

Even once Bill understood everything that had been going on, he still maintained he couldn't tell them how to find the Pike gang's hideout, however much they begged. He agreed to make very, very discreet inquiries among old friends from the orphanage, but that was all.

"I don't want my ears cut off, Rose," he pointed out as he left the workroom.

Rose sighed. "I don't know who else to ask."

Gus was sitting on the table, washing his ears thoroughly. "So defeatist," he murmured dismissively.

"So how would you do it, clever paws?" Freddie demanded, and Gus wrapped his tail around his paws and glared at him, narrow eyed.

"All right, all right, I apologize," Freddie said hurriedly. "But really, I don't see how we can find out any more about the gang."

"Bribe the cats," Gus told them all smugly. "Even a common alley cat knows exactly what's happening in his territory."

"How?" Rose frowned.

Gus shook his head, sweeping his wonderful whiskers to and fro. "Really, Rose dear. What do cats do all day?"

"Sleep!" Freddie snorted.

"Exactly. But usually with at least one eye open, and in a place where we have a panoramic view of our territory and everyone who comes in or out of it. Why the governments of every independent state in the known world have not instituted a Feline Intelligence Bureau, I do not know. Paid in fish—kippers, perhaps, and smoked salmon for the lieutenant grade. Simple."

"FIB," Freddie snorted. "And that's what it would be. All cats lie, Gus. They're known for it."

Gus's whiskers gave an irritable twitch. "Only because we're so bored."

"Don't they need to be magical cats? How would they tell us things?" Rose frowned.

"Any cat could pass on messages. With its eyes closed and all its whiskers stuck together with fish glue. Is it our fault if you don't understand?" He sighed. "I will translate. But I will require lobster for this, Rose. You understand?"

* * *

Gus slipped out of the house to speak to his "associates," as he called them. Rose hadn't realized that he spent time with the other cats in the square, but he assured her as he perched on the windowsill that there were several, and some of them were quite aristocratic. "Lady Ponsonby in the corner house has a Siamese. Strange creature. I showed you him once, do you remember, when we were discussing glamours?"

Rose laughed. "Oh, yes! The cream-colored cat with black paws. The thin one."

Gus glared at her frostily. "Who is doing whom a favor, Rose?"

"Too thin," Rose added hurriedly. "You are a—a majestic size."

"Hmmm." Gus leaped lightly from the sill to the floor below—very lightly, considering that he really was rather a plump cat.

He was back a few hours later, yawning and demanding sardines, which Rose had to steal from the kitchens for him.

"So what happens now?" she asked him eagerly, watching him lick the plate down to the pattern.

Gus gave the plate one last careful sweep and stretched out his front paws luxuriously before starting to wash. "We wait," he told her in between swipes around his ears. "Think, Rose. All I have done is ask them to look."

"But how long will it take?" Rose half wailed.

"I have no idea," Gus said, stretching out one hind leg in a way that suggested the conversation was closed.

Rose glared at him and considered slamming the door, but her new room was so full of lovely, precious things that she couldn't bear to, in case she broke something. She had already broken the magic of her mother's mirror, she thought sadly. Her new room had a dressing table with a pretty mirror of its own, but she had laid the silver mirror there too. She sat on the delicately carved chair and stroked the silver frame, rubbing it between her fingers. *Like Aladdin trying to call the genie from the lamp*, she thought, remembering the battered little book of fairy tales from the orphanage. But there was no puff of smoke, and Eliza didn't appear.

"Oh, there you are. We have a lesson with your great-aunt. Had you forgotten?" Bella caught Rose's hand and towed her along the passage to Miss Fell's room.

"I wish you wouldn't call her that," Rose muttered as Bella knocked on the door. She tucked the mirror into the large pocket of her pinafore. If Eliza came back, Rose didn't want her to find herself abandoned.

"She is. You have to get used to it." Bella turned the door handle as they heard the faint voice inside telling them to enter.

Miss Fell was staring out the window as they went in, and she beckoned them over with a thin hand.

"Look at that."

Bella and Rose stood by the window, peering out and trying to see what the old lady was watching. The only movement in the square was a few houses away. A boy in uniform, just getting onto his horse and waving to a group of girls who were crowded on the front steps of the house.

"What? Alfred Madely?" Bella asked. "He's a twit, and his sisters are worse. But he did rescue my kite from a tree in the garden once." She frowned. "I didn't know he had joined the army."

Miss Fell nodded. "A Guards regiment, see the smart red uniform? Poor child."

"He's at least seventeen," Bella pointed out. "Not really a child, ma'am."

"He'll be lucky if he sees his eighteenth birthday." Miss Fell sighed. "So many years lost. All those stolen centuries."

"But…we're winning the war, aren't we?" Rose asked. "Mrs. Jones's newspaper is always saying we've had a successful battle. We sank two Talish ships. That was in the paper yesterday."

"They are driving us back to the coast, Rose. Soon the battles will be here instead."

Bella nodded. "Papa was called to the palace, Miss Fell. The Talish are planning another invasion. But… it won't really happen, will it? The navy will fight them off. They won't ever be able to land, surely."

Rose shook her head firmly. She couldn't imagine London full of Talish soldiers. It was unthinkable. Surely Miss Fell was weaving this out of panic and memories of the huge sea battle eight years ago when the Talish had last tried to invade. This invasion threat was all just smoke and mirrors, and it would die down again, like it always did. Wouldn't it?

Miss Fell sighed. "The invasion won't happen if your father can help it, Isabella. But sooner or later there will have to be a decisive action. A battle that turns the tide of the war once and for all." She watched

Alfred Madely trotting out of the square on his glossy horse, his spurs jingling. "I hope it comes soon. Before your father and the others are worn out and all those eager children are dead."

Rose shivered. She felt almost guilty. The country was at war, and everywhere in the streets there was a strange mixed feeling of excitement and fear. Alfred Madely's sisters had been full of laughter and kisses as they waved him off, but once he turned the corner, they had clung to each other, crying.

Rose couldn't worry about it, not the way she should. Too much of her mind was taken up with thoughts of her mother.

* * *

"I don't believe it," Freddie muttered. "Everyone knows cats would lie as soon as look at you. This Ginger probably made it all up."

Gus stalked majestically along the table and stared down at Freddie. He was a master at glamours, and Rose suspected he might have employed a subtle one as he walked—he wasn't normally that big, was he? He looked like a small white bear.

"Not you!" Freddie stammered.

"I will vouch personally for the honesty of my associates," Gus hissed. "Would you like to discuss this further?"

"No! Thank you!" Freddie said, backing down.

"Quite," Gus replied witheringly. "Now would you like to know what Ginger found out? After only a day, might I add."

They were sitting in the workroom, where Gus had summoned them, his whiskers glittering with smug pride. Rose nodded—because she was too scared and excited to get any words out.

"Pike and his gang use a warehouse down by the river as their base. Ginger knew exactly who we meant. They've been there for years. Pike and an odd, shambling fellow who seems to be his right-hand man. And then a couple of others. Never more than four or five of them, Ginger thinks. The warehouse looks abandoned, but behind the crumbling front, there's a whole warren of rooms. Most of them full of stolen property, apparently."

"Did he know about my mother?" Rose blurted out hopefully. "Had he seen her?"

Gus frowned and shook his head. "No. But he's never actually been inside. He spends most of his time hanging around the fishermen. He's never had that much interest in Pike and his gang—no food involved, you see." His whiskers quivered irritably. "This is the problem with alley cats. Everything has to be about the next meal. No sense of adventure, no nose for information unless it's leading to fish."

Freddie gave a little snort that sounded like,

"Lobster?" and Gus glared at him again. "Very amusing. I like fish, yes. But food is not my be-all and end-all. Don't despair, Rose. Your mother could still be there, tucked away inside. She's a valuable thing, remember."

Rose managed to smile gratefully at him, but inside her stomach was jumping. What did this mean now? What were they going to do?

"Can we go and look?" she asked quietly.

Gus shook his head regretfully. "We would be too conspicuous."

"Oh, for heaven's sake! We're all magicians!" Freddie shouted. "Can't we use that hiding spell the master taught us in Venice?"

Gus twitched his tail crossly. "None of you are up to maintaining that spell long enough."

"Gus, we know that spell backwards!" Bella protested. "Of course we can. Especially the three of us together and with you there. Although, Rose, I think we should take Bill with us."

"I could protect you," Freddie said jealously.

"You can do spells," Bella agreed. "But when it comes to simply thumping someone, I'm afraid Bill is better at it than you are."

Freddie scowled, which only made him look like an enraged white mouse and rather supported Bella's point.

Gus gave a doubtful little sniff. "Show me the spell,"

he commanded, sitting up straight on the table and staring at them critically.

Glancing at each other, Rose, Freddie, and Bella caught hands and closed their eyes. Bella, in the middle, simply added to the power as the other two waved their free hands in a complicated gesture, at the same time picturing the images Mr. Fountain had taught them. Misty silence, deep water, veils of protection. Around them a strange bubble of air suddenly appeared—visible to those outside it only as a slight shimmer, something that tugged at the corner of the eye, to be dismissed as just a shadow or the flight of a small bird.

Inside the disguise spell, Rose opened her eyes. She could see the room as usual, although the colors were dimmed slightly. Inside, she and Bella and Freddie seemed to have turned a strange pale silvery color. Rose half laughed, realizing that they looked very much like Eliza had. She could feel the weight of the mirror, dragging down her pocket. Even though there was no sign of Eliza whenever she looked, she couldn't bear to leave it in her room.

Outside, she could see Gus prowling around their spell, testing it with his whiskers and an occasional flick of his tail.

"Mmm. Acceptable. But how long can you keep it up, hmmm?" He slid inside the bubble with them and leaped suddenly onto Freddie's shoulder. The bubble of the spell distinctly wobbled. "And can you keep it up when you are distracted, hmmm?" He climbed very carefully onto the top of Freddie's head and hung down over his face, peering into Freddie's eyes upside down.

"Ow! That's my scalp you're digging your claws into!" Freddie hissed. "And don't tickle me with your whiskers! Agh!"

"It's a test, Freddie. Concentrate!" Rose murmured anxiously, pouring more of her own strength into the spell to make up for Freddie being distracted. "Gus, that isn't fair. No one else is going to climb on his head and dangle their whiskers in his face."

"They might do several worse things," Gus pointed out. "Such as gutting you with a dirty fish knife."

"No, they won't, because they won't see us in the first place. The spell works, doesn't it?" Bella said sweetly. "Even with you attempting to scalp Freddie?"

"Hmf." Gus released his claws and slid gracefully back down to Freddie's shoulder. "I suppose. And I will be there too. Very well, I will take you."

The spell bubble flew apart as Rose let go of Bella and hugged Gus delightedly. She only stopped when she realized that Freddie and Bella were giving her a horrified look, and that she could feel Gus's tail twitching. The twitch seemed to echo all through him. "I'm sorry," she said hastily, putting him down very gently on the table.

Gus gave her a regal nod. "I should think so. You

must think before you act, Rose. Particularly when we are investigating gangs of murderous thieves."

But his fur wasn't standing on end in the slightest, and Rose couldn't help suspecting he had rather liked it.

"So. Send for that boy, and let us go." Gus's tail gave a demanding little flick, as though he expected Bill to appear from thin air.

"Now?" Rose gasped.

Gus stared at her. "Of course now! Why wait? It's the middle of the morning. Not dark for hours. What are we waiting for?"

"I–I don't know," Rose admitted. "I just hadn't thought...*now*..."

"Rose, are you changing your mind?" Gus asked her wearily. The word *again* was strongly hinted in his voice.

"No! No, I just wasn't quite ready. But I am now." Rose nodded firmly and slid her hand around the cool weight of the mirror in her pocket. She would make herself ready. She had to.

* * *

"Down here? Really?" Bella asked distastefully, and Gus glared at her from Rose's arms. They were already inside the spell—before they had cast it, Gus had hidden in her scarf, as he was rather startling to passersby.

"Yes, really. What, you'd like your criminals to live on a better class of street?" he asked.

"It's just so dirty," Bella complained, lifting one delicate foot and inspecting her boot anxiously.

"Probably means we're getting close then," Bill muttered. "Still can't believe you talked me into this, Rosie. Following a cat to the Pike hideout? I must have let that house get to my head."

They hadn't walked far. It seemed as if they had only gone a few streets beyond the shops where Rose was used to running errands for Mrs. Jones.

"Are we really so close?" she asked, looking around. Gus nodded, and she felt the truth settle like a heavy weight inside her. How could she have lived this close to her mother's prison for so long and not known? St. Bridget's, the orphanage, was even closer—only a few minutes' walk, she guessed.

"Someone's coming!" Freddie said sharply.

"Shh, don't panic. They can't see us." Gus peered ahead. "I can't see anyone. Where?"

"There!" Freddie hissed. "And whoever it is can see us. They're making straight for the spell!"

"Drat it, it must be one of the gang. I thought Eliza said only the leader was a magician." Gus wriggled out of Rose's arms and jumped down to the dirty stones. "Ugh. Be ready to run."

"No!" Rose breathed. "It's Eliza! Look!"

The ghost girl was hurrying toward them, looking

anxious. The faint bleaching of the colors outside the spell had made it harder to see what she was from a distance, but now her silvery color was obvious.

"Tsk. I shall make a note to the master that this spell does not work on ghosts," Gus growled.

"You came back!" Rose reached out to touch Eliza and then drew back again, unsure if she could. But Eliza laid a soft, transparent, silvery hand on Rose's arm. "You shouldn't be here, miss!"

"How did you get out of the mirror?" Freddie demanded.

Rose stroked Eliza's hand very carefully. If she'd told herself it wasn't there, her fingers would have brushed straight through to her own sleeve. Eliza felt like a cold, silvery breath blown against her cheek.

"I thought we'd lost you," Rose murmured. "I've been carrying the mirror with me everywhere and calling, but you never came."

The little ghost's fingers seemed to become more solid under Rose's gloved hand. Eliza ducked her head shyly, but Rose could see that she was smiling. "I didn't know where I was, miss. I was jolted out of the mirror somehow."

"But how?" Freddie looked at her, frowning. "You'd been tied to it all that time. Was it because Rose dropped it?"

Eliza blinked. "It was talking with you, sir. I think it strengthened me."

"Wonderful," Gus muttered.

"When I told you, miss, about your father. I wanted to come out then to help you. You looked so like her! But I didn't quite dare. I'd been there so long. It got comfortable."

"But where have you been since?"

Eliza shook her head, the damp locks of her hair flying. "I dunno, miss. That house, it's full of strangeness. I got turned about, and there's things floating…"

"Lord knows what she's interfered with!" Gus's tail lashed from side to side, and Eliza shrank back.

"I didn't touch nothing, Mr. Cat. It were the same at Fell Hall. We knew not to touch, us servants. But then you went out, miss, and you took the mirror. So I tried to follow you, but it isn't easy. I'm not used to being out. I got lost, and then I felt him too. Pike! You mustn't be around here, miss! It isn't safe. You shouldn't be here," Eliza repeated. "You're too close to the gang."

"We meant to be," Rose told her. "We want to find my mother. If—if she's still there…" she added in a whisper. She meant, *If she's still alive.*

"You can't! You can't! It's far too dangerous!" Eliza's eyes darkened in horror.

"But if she's still there, caught by his spell, how can I leave her?" Rose caught Eliza's hands and shivered at the strange, soft ghost-touch. "Please! You loved her too, didn't you? Don't you want to see her get away?"

"Of course! But I don't want them catching you." Eliza gulped, her face twisting with fright, and then hissed, "Don't you see? That's how I died! I tried to stop them from taking you!"

"Oh." Rose stared at the little ghost, lost for words.

"Come on!" Eliza tugged her, her hands patting and pulling at Rose's own. Her fingers seemed to sink into Rose's skin, and Rose followed her more to stop the horrid sensation than from any strength of Eliza's.

Eliza led them further down the murky alleyway to the edge of the river. The tide was out, and a vast expanse of mud stretched out before them. The silvery ghost pattered down a set of rotting steps and out across the mud, and they followed her gingerly to an old boat, lying upside down on the mud like some strange old shell. "Sit in here. We'll be hidden. I'll explain."

There were several pieces of old packing cases under the boat, as though this was a common haunt for someone, but even they were slimed and dirty with river water and weed, and Bella clearly couldn't stand the thought of sitting on them.

"Oh, Bella, stop it," Rose hissed. "Your papa will buy you a new coat if you flutter your eyelashes at him. Just sit down! I want to hear, and you do too."

Closing her eyes in disgust, Bella did as she was told, and Eliza began to tell her story.

Eight

Y OUR MOTHER HAD ALMOST forgotten her previous life," Eliza explained. "She was so deep in the spell that Pike had put on her that she couldn't even remember who she was. Every so often she'd catch a glimpse—I reminded her of the way things used to be. But most of the time she thought she'd lived in the old Beloved's Import & Export warehouse forever. That's the name of the building where Pike has his headquarters," she explained. "I don't know when those Beloveds last used it, but there's a big, faded old sign on the water side."

Rose glanced back toward the building. It was a misty, grim February day, but she thought she could just see the sign Eliza meant. It was lopsided, and the wall it was hanging on didn't look much better.

"Why didn't you go to the police if you weren't under this spell?" Bill asked. "Didn't they let you out?"

Eliza shook her head, her eyes widening in horror. "You don't know what they'd do! I saw them! I saw them while we was there—they cut one lad's tongue out for blabbing about a shipment, and he weren't much older than you! Besides, Miss Miranda was doing Pike's dirty work for him. I couldn't go telling. They'd have hung her too. If the police had ever caught them, which they wouldn't have." She sniffed dismissively. "Pike never got caught. That's what he had Miss Miranda for. He wrapped her up in that spell and stole the magic out of her to make him stronger."

Gus frowned. "That doesn't sound right. Wouldn't her magic fight against his own if he used it against her will? He must be a strange sort of magician."

Eliza shrugged. Clearly she didn't know and hardly cared. "She was lucky she had me to look after her. She wouldn't even have remembered to eat if I hadn't made her, and she needed to, with you, miss. Not that they gave us much. Reckon they thought she lived on air, and she did, some of the time, when I couldn't wake her from the spells to have a little something.

"But then when she was near her time with you, miss, she started to break out of his magic. More and more, she was almost herself. She said you wriggled worse than a squirming cat, and you kicked her, and that kept waking her up out of the magic, you see. She was worried, I could tell, about what was going to happen—how she'd look after you in that place. But at the same time, she could see that having you was going to make it harder for Pike to make her do what he wanted. Already you were breaking his hold on her. That's why she named you the way she did, when you were born."

"What? What did she call me?" Rose was crouching on the mudflats in front of Eliza, stretching out her hands, trying to make her tell.

"Hope. That's your name, miss. Hope Garnet. You were her hope of keeping herself herself, if you see what I mean."

Rose nodded, but then she sat back on a piece of packing case. "It didn't work, though. She didn't escape."

Eliza shook her head, her eyes half closing with remembered grief. "She was worth too much to them, miss. And so were you. It was all right for the first few months. Miss Miranda—not that I should call her that, but I still can't think of her as anything else—she was careful not to let them see how much in control of her magic she was getting. She couldn't risk them finding out and Pike recasting the spell. She was working her way out gradually, like. But then he came to see her one day, and he was watching you. You'd learned to crawl, miss, and I made you a rag doll. You played with it all the time." Eliza sniffed a laugh.

"You used to carry it around in your mouth while you were crawling. Usually, Miss Miranda would try to hide you away when he came, make sure you were sleeping or get me to take you out to see the water, wrapped up in a shawl. He turned up unexpected that day, and she could see him eyeing you. He knew what you were. Your father might not have had magic, miss, but your mother had enough that it was bound to be bubbling over in you." She shook her head.

"That was it. Once she saw him looking at you like that, as though you were something valuable, something he could make money out of, she knew her time was gone. She hadn't managed to drag herself out of the spell enough to escape, and she wasn't going to have you trapped there too. She didn't want you growing up as their little tame magician, never knowing right from wrong. You'd have been a monster, miss."

Eliza nibbled on her knuckles and eyed Rose anxiously. "That's why she did it, miss. You do see, don't you? It wasn't that she didn't want you, not at all. You were saving her, and even if you hadn't been, she adored you. That's why you had to go. She couldn't bear to see you made into one of them." Eliza looked down at her transparent, battered boots, and then sharply up again at Rose. "She thought you'd be better off dead."

Rose gasped, a tiny, shocked noise that seemed to echo around the wooden ribs of the boat, and Bill put his arm around her, staring angrily at Eliza.

"You would have been!" Eliza snarled fiercely. "You don't know what they're like, what they would have made of you!" She folded her arms, glaring at Rose. "Don't you dare think ill of her. She couldn't do it. She said if she'd really loved you properly, she could have. She was angry with herself for not being strong enough. I took you to the churchyard instead. So that someone would find you and take you away, look after you and keep you away from Pike."

"Why there? That churchyard?" Rose whispered faintly.

Eliza shrugged. "Because it was close. I didn't have long, miss, before someone would notice I'd gone. I put you in the old fish basket I used when they sometimes let me go to the market. Miss Miranda liked a bit of fruit, and they used to let me out to buy it for her, if Pike was feeling generous."

Rose nodded. She had always assumed the basket meant her real parents had something to do with fish. "Didn't she have anything to leave with me?" she asked wistfully. "Even a note?"

Eliza shook her head. "We thought about it, leaving a note. But all she could have done was use it to send you back to her family, and she thought that would be worse than useless. She said they'd fling you into an orphanage, and you'd probably be better off there anyway."

"She should have written a note to Miss Fell," Bella said critically.

"No, she never saw Miss Fell the way she is now," Rose reminded her. "When Miranda left Fell Hall, her aunt was still under my grandfather's thumb. She was the dear aunt that Miranda wouldn't tell she was running away, in case it got her into trouble."

Eliza was nodding vigorously. "Exactly, miss. So

she decided, no note." She was silent for a moment, wringing her hands over and over, as though she was trying to wash off some dreadful stain. "But she did give me something for you, miss." She looked up, her eyes pleading. "And I'd never have taken it if I weren't so hungry. But it was silver! I knew I could get so much for it that I couldn't bear to just leave it there in the basket with you."

"What was it?" Bella demanded. "A ring? A necklace?"

Rose was staring at Eliza, shaking her head. "No. Of course. It was the mirror." She slipped a hand into the inside pocket of her coat—she had unstitched it enough that she could slide the mirror in. It was the only thing she had of her mother's, and it had seemed important to bring it with them. She stroked the metal roses gently.

Eliza gave a reluctant nod. "She said that she loved it, and she wanted you to have something that she loved. Something special. She thought maybe one day you'd get to understand the meaning of the little mouse on the back, and you'd be able to trace your family. But it wouldn't be obvious to just anyone. Only when you were old enough to know you came from a magical family, then you might be able to use it as a clue."

She darted an anxious glance at Rose, clearly afraid of what she might say. But Rose only nodded. "What happened?"

"I took it to a pawnshop." Eliza wiped her ragged

sleeve across her mouth, as though the thought of it still frightened her. "I was stupid," she added in a whisper. "I was in a hurry. I had to get back before they missed me! So I went to a pawnshop I'd seen before on the way to the market."

"Too close." Bill shook his head, and Eliza looked at him gratefully.

"Too close," she echoed. "They knew who I was. One of Pike's. I shouldn't have been in there with anything precious to sell. Old Mr. Green, he knew he'd get on the right side of Pike if he dragged me back." She laughed bitterly. "Pike even let him keep the mirror, he was that grateful!"

Rose swallowed. "What did they do?" she whispered. "Is that how you…?"

Eliza stared at them all, her back ramrod straight with pride. "I wouldn't tell. I'd promised Miss Miranda I'd get you away. I let her down. If only I'd done as she said and left the mirror in the basket, they'd never have known what happened to you. Miss Miranda was going to tell them you'd died of the typhus. So I wasn't having them going and finding you. I wouldn't tell."

Rose reached out one hand and tried to stroke Eliza's damp, rat's-tail hair. "They drowned you, didn't they?"

Eliza smiled, an odd, proud little smile. "Right here, miss. Pike held me under himself. It was high tide, then, of course."

Everyone was silent for a moment, their eyes

flicking nervously around the battered boat, trying not to imagine.

Bill swallowed. "And we're going to barge into this chap's hideout?"

Rose shook her head. "You should go back. But I have to try. If she's there, I can't leave her. Not after…" She trailed off and waved a hand at Eliza.

No one said anything, but Bella sneaked an arm around her waist, and Gus purred. Bill and Freddie shifted closer on their boxes. They were all coming with her, she knew. Four children and a cat huddled together under the battered little boat, staring at a ghost child.

"Then after that you haunted the mirror?" Freddie asked at last.

"It was because of the mirror I died," Eliza explained. "I stole it, didn't I? I think that's how it works, anyhow."

"You've been stuck inside it all this time?" Bella shuddered.

"Not so much in it, miss…" Eliza frowned. "Just tied to it somehow. It was like a door, but I couldn't open it. You opened it and called me out." She looked at Rose, her eyes thoughtful. "What are you here for, miss?"

Rose blinked. "To find her, of course. I have to rescue her. She'd rather have died than let me grow up there. You said so! So how can I leave her? She's my mother!"

"You have to." Eliza shook her head firmly. "She

couldn't get away from Pike, so how will you be able to do it? Besides, miss…" She hesitated. "Pike could have done away with her, for all we know…"

"I have to know for certain," Rose told her through gritted teeth.

"I still don't see how you think you can get in there!" Eliza cried, sounding almost angry.

"We'll sneak in," Freddie told her. "We're invisible under this spell. Pike might be able to see us, but if he's the only magician, the rest of the gang won't. We sneak in and rescue her."

Eliza stared at them doubtfully, twitching her head from side to side as she tried to see the spell. "I can't tell no difference," she objected.

"It's there," Freddie assured her. "And we can do other things too."

"Can you show us the best way to get in?" Rose pleaded.

Eliza wrinkled her nose. "I can try. I'm still not that good at moving about, but I can tell you what it was like back then. Might all have changed by now," she muttered dubiously. "Whenever there's a wrecked boat, they steal the timbers and build another little room in there. Proper rabbit warren, it is." She shrugged and laughed. "Can't do me any harm, I suppose. They can't drown me again. But you're not to let yourselves get caught!

"They'll kill you as soon as look at you. Pike's a

monster, and that other one, Jake..." She shuddered. "He's almost worse. He smokes the opium himself, and he's more like a ghost than I am. He never says nothing, and his eyes burn." She frowned. "Or maybe they won't kill you. If you're all magicians like Miss Miranda, they'll keep you, and that's worse."

"I'm not," Bill growled. "They'll drown me."

Freddie gave him a disgusted look. "Run home then."

Bill snorted. "No chance. I'm not leaving you looking after this pair. Let's just not get caught, right?"

"I'll show you the way in I used to know," Eliza suggested. "Make sure your spell is working." She crept out of the boat and stood up, brushing down her water-streaked skirts and looking around. "No one's moving outside," she muttered. "Let's go."

They followed her, threading across the mudflats to a broken stone wall, just under the warehouse. The stones had fallen apart enough that it was relatively easy to climb up onto the wall, where there was a narrow causeway around the side of the building.

Eliza led them as they crept around the building to a window. It had been boarded up with several old pieces of wood, and Eliza sniffed. "They haven't mended it. Didn't think they would have done. Push that bit, and it'll slide over. This is the way I used to take you out to see the water, miss. Come along in, but quietly."

Bill held the piece of wood aside, and Eliza disappeared, reappearing as a beckoning hand from inside the gap. Rose and the others scrambled in, naturally lining up along the inner wall, pressing themselves back against the stones. No one wanted to go further in. They seemed to be in a storeroom of some kind, lined with packing cases, mostly battered and water stained.

"Stolen cargo," Eliza said wisely. She beckoned again from the door of the little room. "Come on. Miss Miranda's room used to be this way. Your spell is still working, is it?" She was looking at them doubtfully, as though she didn't really believe in the magic.

Rose, Bella, and Freddie took hands again for a moment to boost the strength of the spell before they followed Eliza, creeping along a narrow passage. It really was built out of parts of old boats, Rose realized, as she ran her fingers over sea-worn timbers scattered with ancient barnacles. A strange, sharp-nosed face sticking out over a doorway made them all jump, until they realized it was part of an old ship's figurehead, the paint long peeled away, leaving the face a weary gray.

"Here," Eliza whispered. "This is where they kept her. And you, miss."

The doorway was low, and there was no door in it—perhaps her mother wasn't trusted enough to have a door to hide behind, Rose wondered—so they could see in as they gathered around the entrance to the room.

Eliza pressed herself against the doorframe, so close that they could see the splintered timbers through her.

"That's her…" she whispered. "Still here!" Her whispery little voice cracked with tears, as she stared into the room. "All this time…"

"She's there?" Rose felt strangely reluctant to look. She'd been imagining the girl from the painting, which she saw was stupid now. That girl would never have survived in here. Whoever was in that room, it wasn't the pretty child Miss Fell had loved, or even her father's stolen sweetheart or Hope's doting mother.

But Gus was leaning forward in her arms, his whiskers twitching with interest as he peered around the tiny room.

She had to see.

"Be careful," Freddie reminded her in a whisper. "She's strong, remember. She might be able to see us, even through the spell."

Rose stepped further in, brushing against Eliza and feeling that strange faint chill again. There was very little to see. Rose's mother—if that was who it was, Rose couldn't tell—was sitting curled up on a low, narrow bed, leaning the side of her face against the wooden wall. All Rose could really tell was that her mother's hair was a little lighter than her own and that her woolen dress was faded and worn. Rose longed to go and tap her on the shoulder and shake her out of that sad lethargy, but she couldn't quite bring herself to do it. Not yet.

"Sshh. Someone's coming. I can hear them talking." Eliza flitted anxiously in front of her.

Two men were walking down the passage, muttering to each other. The children whisked inside the tiny room and then drew back against the wall, flattening themselves against the timbers. The spell would stop most people from seeing or hearing them if they were careful to whisper, but they were still *there* and fatally obvious to anyone who brushed past too close. The two men shambled up to the doorway and paused just inside without noticing them.

They didn't look like murderers. The most noticeable thing about them was that they both had very fine mustaches—not smartly curled ones like Mr. Fountain's pride and joy, but brisk, fat ones like nailbrushes. Rose was so nervous that it made her want to giggle. The second man's hair was a dull grayish brown, and it made him look as though he was wearing a dead mouse under his nose.

"Pike has a mustache," Eliza whispered. "The rest of the gang copy him."

"Mrs. Garnet, ma'am." The man's voice was strangely nervous, which made Rose and Freddie exchange a surprised glance. But then, Rose realized, it wasn't that odd. These two weren't magicians. They were like the servants at the Fountain house, forced to live with magic and not really liking it. Rose's mother was the strange, unpredictable one they had to depend on for the spells they needed. Probably the only thing they could say for her was that she was less frightening than Pike.

The figure curled on the bed shook a little and uncoiled slowly.

Rose caught her breath, her heart suddenly beating in sickening thumps. She could feel the others, even Gus, looking at her mother and then glancing back at her, back and forth, trying to see how similar they really were. She couldn't tell. Miranda still had a faint look of the painting in the back of the mirror, but she had changed so much. Her face was milk pale—which was hardly surprising. Had she really been shut up in here for longer than Rose had been alive?

"You have her eyes," Gus purred softly. "Look. I can see you in her. We can bring her out. Somehow we will…"

Rose swallowed and shook and brushed her cheek gratefully against the glittering warmth of his fur.

The woman on the bed nodded at the two men wearily, and even that seemed like an effort. It was as though every move she made was fighting against the spell that bound her.

Eliza's face was scrunched up and horrified. "He must have doubled the spell after he discovered what we done," she breathed in Rose's ear. "This is much worse than it used to be. She can hardly move."

"How can she possibly do magic like that?" Rose whispered back. "It's like she's piled down with chains."

Eliza shook her head. "No. That's the way he made the spell. If she's working for him, the spell lifts off her somehow. She's free—she's only free when she's working for the gang. I think Pike hoped that would break her, so in the end she'd choose to join them, but it can't have worked."

Rose nodded proudly to herself. Her mother might be working for the gang, but only because she was forced. She hadn't lapsed. But the strength of that spell was terribly daunting. How would they ever get her out of it?

The man with the dead-mouse mustache took his cap off and stood twisting it in front of him. "Mr. Pike says, ma'am, you're to make us look like this." He handed over a piece of paper with a rough drawing, but it was hard to see what it was from where they were squashed against the wall.

"What is it?" Rose clenched her nails into her palms.

"I'll look. They won't see me, miss. Only you can, because you have got the mirror." Eliza flitted across to peer over his shoulder. "Footmen's livery," she whispered to Rose. "She's changing them so they're disguised for robbing a house."

Rose nodded. It made sense. Having a tame magician must make the gang one of the most successful in London, despite their tumbledown quarters. But she still didn't understand why Pike didn't just do all this himself. Unless the gang was so huge that he was doing it too. She shivered at the thought.

"She saw." Gus's ears had flattened against his skull.

"What?" Rose stared at him anxiously.

"Miranda. She saw Eliza when she went to look at the paper. I saw her eyes move."

"Are you sure?" Freddie muttered, next to Rose.

Gus half closed his eyes. "I am a cat. I am a natural predator, even without the magic. I can tell when a mouse has an itch behind its ear. Of course I'm sure, idiot boy."

"What's she going to do?" Freddie whispered, gazing wide-eyed at Miranda. "I thought only we could see Eliza. Can your mother see us through the spell, do you think?"

"She shouldn't be able to. We should be invisible to everyone. Not ghosts, but then we never had one to test it on…" Gus stepped onto Rose's shoulders, standing with his front paws on one shoulder and back paws on the other. His paws felt like little rocks pressing into her, and she could feel his heart beating against her ear. He stretched his nose out toward the three figures around the bed, his whiskers flickering around his muzzle as he searched the air. "No. No, I don't think she can. And I don't think she can truly see Eliza either, not unless Eliza wants her to. But she knows there's something."

Miranda raised her hands toward the two men, and Rose saw them flinch. They must be truly terrified of Pike to let themselves be enchanted when they hated it so much.

The glamour spell seemed to stretch them— footmen had to be at least six feet tall, and preferably, if there were two in a house, they had to match. The spell changed their clothes as well, the dirty grayish fabrics flooding with bloodred and suddenly sparkling with golden braid and polished buttons. They wore white stockings too, which Rose privately thought was a mistake on her mother's part, because unless the stockings had been especially bespelled to avoid mud, they would not be white by the time the men got out of that horrid alleyway. But she supposed the men would just have to make do—the white stockings were what the footmen at the palace had worn, and those same buckled shoes. They must be going to rob a truly grand house, for they looked as though they would earn at least thirty pounds each a year, and who knew how much that grand livery would cost.

Freddie shot Rose an admiring glance. They knew how difficult it was to maintain one glamour, let alone two, and on such unwilling subjects. "She's very strong," he whispered, and Rose nodded, feeling absurdly proud.

The two men surveyed each other, looking somewhat disgusted, and then nodded their thanks to Rose's mother. Gus gave them a disparaging stare as they tramped past in the heavy buckled shoes. One of them was scratching at his powdered hair, and although they had the height of the real footmen, neither of them stood straight, as they would if they'd been trained from boys.

The children listened to them trudging away down

the passage, making rude comments about each other's outfits. Then they focused their attention again on the figure they had come to see. She was sitting tensely on the edge of the low bed, her hair still pretty with its bronze-colored streaks, and trailing down past her shoulders. Perhaps they wouldn't let her have hairpins, Rose thought. In case she did something awful with them.

As they watched, Rose's mother pushed down hard against the bed with her fists and stood up unsteadily, stretching out a foot to take a step into the center of the room. She turned her head from side to side, her eyes wide and gray in the dim light. "Who is there?" she asked, her voice dangerous.

Rose flinched from it. It was the voice of someone who had spent the last several years unable to rest. How could she have slept with a gang of thieves around her? She had been on guard all the time, and now she was fighting. One hand went up into the air and started to pull, like someone bundling washing off a line, reeling it in.

Rose and the others felt the spell tugging away from them, pulling at their clothes and hair like a fitful wind. Bella, the youngest and least practiced in her spells, twirled around, her skirt spinning, and fell straight into Rose's mother's hands, gasping in fright.

Miranda gripped her by the shoulders, a strange, half-there child, still disguised by the rags of the spell, but already starting to fight back like a little wildcat.

"Stop that!" Miranda shook her, just a little, and Bella seethed, her fingernails reaching out to scratch and tear. But she couldn't free herself from that tight grip. "What are you? A magician's child? What are you doing here?" Suddenly she caught Bella·even tighter and pulled her forward to look closely at her face, scanning her with eyes that were doubtful and confused. As she stared at Bella, the little hint of hope in her eyes died away, and she shook her head. "No. No, you're not. And too young, anyway... What are you doing here, child? Is this some new trick of Pike's?"

"Please let her go." Rose pulled the spell off herself with the same gesture her mother had used and stepped forward. "She isn't the one you're looking for. We came to find you. She doesn't mean you any harm. She's only frightened. Bella, *stop* it!"

"More of you!" Miranda muttered, looking around wildly as Freddie revealed himself and Bill. But then her eyes fixed on Rose, and she seemed to turn even paler, although Rose would not have thought it possible.

"*Hope...*" she whispered.

Rose nodded. It didn't feel like her name, but somehow it seemed to catch her and tug at her insides, so that she took another step forward, her feet faltering. "Yes..." she murmured huskily.

Her mother let go of Bella and reached out her arms, but before Rose could take another step toward her, her mother suddenly shrank back, her mouth twisting

151

in pain. Her arms slammed straight to her sides, and she writhed as though she were in agony, and screamed out loud.

"What is it? What's happening to her?" Rose cried.

"It must be the spell," Gus said swiftly. "She was too happy. There was an alarm set into the magic. Get away, quick. Run!" He leaped down from Rose's shoulders and tried to herd them all out of the door, but Rose could not be torn from the sight of her mother, quivering and ashen faced in the middle of the room, and Bella had collapsed against the bed. Bill and Freddie were trying to pull Rose away, but she struggled and wouldn't let them.

A thundering rush of feet sounded from the passageway, and then the doorway was full of angry faces.

Nine

S HE IS MY DAUGHTER. She is my daughter."

She said it again and again and again in a dull, mechanical voice, and it was clear from the twitching and bulging of her eyes, and the way her lips were drawn back over her teeth, that she did not want to say it all.

A tall, pale, red-haired man, whose mustache was a glorious fiery explosion, came into the room, smiling brightly. "Is she? Is she now? This is our little stolen baby?" He stopped in front of Rose, held tightly by one of the footmen, who had been the first to come racing back when Miranda began to scream. He lifted her chin in his hand. "I hardly need to ask. You look very like your mother, girl. So. What happened to you? Where did you go? Hey?"

His voice was not unpleasant, and he did not swear, but Rose had the most terrifying sensation of a banked-up fire. It was as though old turf had been laid across the embers to keep the fire going till morning.

Then, when someone poked it, it would spring up into a blaze again and consume anything that came near it.

She stared back at him, too frightened to speak, and had the sense to realize that this was a good thing, and that being dumb with fright might be useful.

"She hasn't her mother's wits, then?" He turned to Miranda and waved a hand sharply across her mouth.

She broke off midsentence, gasping, as though someone had poured a jug of cold water over her. Her eyes stayed desperate. "I—don't—know." The words seemed dragged out of her.

"And the rest of them. Four." He looked from Bella to Freddie to Bill. "Three little rich brats and a servant."

Rose realized with a start that the servant was Bill, and not her. She supposed she shouldn't have been surprised, since she had her good clothes on. There was no mention of Gus or Eliza. Rose searched the room as carefully as she could, imprisoned against the brass buttons of a scarlet footman's coat. No, Gus was gone. And presumably Eliza could melt through walls or something like that. She couldn't be shut away. But then, neither could she manipulate locks or carry keys with her wispy fingers. It was better to pin their hopes on Gus.

They needed someone. The more Rose saw of Pike, the stranger and more powerful he seemed, not like any other magician she had met. The magic seemed to be spilling out of him, so that his hair glittered like red-golden wire and his eyes burned. Even his voice, soft though it was, wrapped around her and pulled, holding her like silken ropes. Was it the same spell he had used to entrap her mother? Her eyes as wide as a startled rabbit, Rose stared at him. She didn't think he was even trying.

"Ransom," Pike muttered, fingering the braid on Bella's favorite velvet cape. "Or are we better off keeping you?"

Bella was standing petrified, her face pale with fear. The color even seemed to have leached out of her blond curls, so that she looked like carved marble, something that should have been on a grave. Freddie had fought so much against the huge man who had seized him that they had tied him up and shoved him onto the bed. Now his eyes blazed furiously over the dirty cloth they'd bound his mouth with.

Creeping from child to child, Pike sniffed fiercely, like some sort of hunting dog. It was horrible having him so close. He smelled of metal, and his eyes were a pale shade of blue, so pale it was almost white, like china. His hair looked red, but Rose could see many colors in it, like flames in a fire, as he sniffed and prowled around her. "This one we'll definitely keep," he muttered. "I can smell it on her. Everywhere. Buckets of it. You should be proud of your daughter, Mrs. Garnet," he called with a malicious little grin.

Then he tweaked one of Bella's curls and stroked one

finger down her stony cheek. Watching, Rose waited for Bella to bite him, but she seemed to have disappeared inside herself and did nothing. "A great well of it, but too far down, and at the same time oozing out of her skin. She doesn't know what she's doing with it yet. Dangerous."

He was enjoying himself, Rose could see, sniffing out their magic, and perhaps because Freddie was bound, Pike wasn't as cautious as he should have been. He bent over close to Freddie and then reeled back with a cry of shock, his blazing red hair truly blazing now. Freddie had always been good at fires.

It went out, of course, in seconds, but it left an ugly scorched patch all down one side of Pike's head, and Freddie was laughing. You could see it behind the gag—and even worse, some of the gang, those huge men pressed into the tiny room, were smirking a little too.

Pike hissed with fury and hurled Freddie against the wall with a dreadful, soft crunching sound. Rose cried out in horror, and even Bella came to and gasped. Bill struggled in his captor's arms, but the man hit him carelessly, like he'd push away an overexcited dog, and Bill reeled and sagged.

Stop it! Rose shouted, but silently, inside all their heads, even somehow Bill's, who she had never known she could reach before. *Just don't. We can't fight them now. We have to wait, and—and sneak. Pike is better at fighting magic than we are, and they don't care very much if they kill us.*

She had to strain her mind to hear Freddie's reply, the faintest thread of a whisper, but at least it meant he was alive and conscious. *Actually, they do care. I think they'd rather enjoy it.*

* * *

"That Pike is over the moon," Bill muttered. "Three of you! He thinks all his Christmases have come at once. He hesitated. "They ain't never letting us go. You know that, don't you?"

Rose didn't say what they were all feeling. That they might be shut up for ten years, just like her mother. They had been so close. It had been stupid, she supposed. They should have been more careful, watched and waited longer. But she couldn't wait. It wasn't fair to expect her to wait, was it? Not when her mother was only the width of a room away?

"Gus will have gone to fetch Papa." Bella nodded as she said this, as though she was trying to convince herself. There was no getting around the fact that Gus was a cat, and his feelings and attitudes and, above all, his sense of time could be very different from everybody else's. Despite his criticism of other cats, Gus on a life-or-death mission could still be easily distracted by a passing sardine (even if canned).

"And there's Eliza," Rose added. "I think she'll come back. I think so. But she must have been terrified, seeing Pike again. And it might take her a while to find us, if she ran far. She'll have to try and find the mirror again."

The men had bundled them down into a tiny, cramped little room, which seemed not just to have been made from a boat's timbers, but to be the tiny cabin at the bow end of a smallish fishing boat, transported in one huge piece. Surely it had been done with Pike's magic, for Rose could not see how it could have been carried. The hatch they had been shoved in was locked with a sort of magical seal that had burned Rose's fingers when she'd tried to push it delicately away.

Would the magical locks stop Eliza from getting in to find them? Rose wasn't sure. If she came back, perhaps they could send her to fetch Miss Fell, if Gus hadn't thought of that already.

Freddie had the marble light he had made in Miss Sparrow's cellar all those months ago, and they had all put extra strength into it, but the light was still dim and grayish inside the boat. The room still smelled of fish too.

"How long do you think we've been here?" Bella asked irritably.

Freddie frowned. "Only a few hours. I wonder if they're going to feed us. It ought to be teatime. Or maybe past teatime by now." He looked wistful, and

Rose could tell he was thinking of buttered crumpets. They were his favorite. She stared at him in the dusky light. She was hungry too, but she didn't want to eat. She thought she might be sick if she did. Her stomach kept twisting and jolting every time she thought about Pike and what he might make them do. He had imprisoned her mother for more than ten years. How long would he keep them?

"For always," Bill said dully beside her, and Rose jumped.

"How did you know what I was thinking?"

He blinked at her owlishly. "Didn't you say it out loud?"

"No. I never knew you could hear me speaking in your head."

Bill shrugged. "Didn't do anything. Just listened, and there you were."

"We can't stay here for always, Bill. We'd—I don't know—wilt. We'd die in here."

"Maybe not in here. He'll move you out of here once he's got you properly trained, I reckon." He drew in a shivery breath. "He ain't going to keep me, Rose. Waste of food."

"You don't know that," Freddie argued.

"What would he want me for?" Bill muttered. "I'm no magician, and I ain't going to join their gang, not that I should think they'd trust me to, anyway. He'll do what he did with Eliza."

"No, he won't," Rose snarled, like a vicious little cat. She sprang up, her fists clenched. She had been feeling hopeless, sick with fright. Beset with so much awfulness that she didn't know what to do first, she was doing nothing and simply trying not to howl. But she was not going to let anyone drown her Bill. "Three magicians. We can't be this feeble. We have to be able to get ourselves out. There's only one of him, and frankly, he can't be that clever, or he'd be an awful lot better known."

"What I keep thinking is, why aren't they richer?" Freddie muttered. "I suppose they have to keep hidden, but this place is falling apart."

"Don't you think his magic is odd?" Rose asked. 'I've never seen magic so obviously all over someone before. Usually you have to look so hard." She frowned. "And he hit you, Freddie, really hit you, I mean, not with a spell. Why would he do that? Perhaps he isn't as strong as he looks."

"There's your mother too," Bella said hesitantly.

Rose nodded. "I know. She's forced to work for him, though. If we could break the spell, I know she would come with us. She wanted to, didn't she? I know she raised the alarm, but I don't think he could actually make her do anything to hurt us. He's on his own. And his gang are idiots."

"Rather large idiots," Freddie muttered.

"But not the slightest bit powerful, if we could use our magic," Rose reminded him.

"We're stuck in here though, ain't we?" Bill was looking at her with just the slightest hint of hope in his eyes now. "Can't fight from behind these walls."

Rose frowned. There had to be a way—the things she had seen Freddie do in their lessons with Mr. Fountain—and she was supposed to be as powerful as he was, just not as practiced. Let alone how strong Bella was. She had believed they were stuck when Miss Sparrow had imprisoned them in a stone cellar underground, but there was no stone here, no solid walls, only a battered old boat. Surely it couldn't hold them.

But they hadn't gotten any further toward an escape plan by the time Bella gave up and fell asleep against Rose's shoulder.

"They're leaving us to stew for the night," Bill reckoned. "They'll roust us early in the morning when we're really scared. We should all try and sleep. No point lying awake and worrying."

It was easy to say. But Rose leaned against the wooden wall, her arms prickly with the slumped weight of Bella, and thought about her mother.

* * *

By the next morning, Freddie's longing for crumpets had spread to everyone, and they still couldn't think of a way to get out. Bella was getting more fractious and difficult by the minute, and Rose was beginning to wonder if perhaps they should encourage her. If they could stand the agony and bleeding ears, perhaps Bella could scream their way out. She would surely be able to break down the boat timbers.

Freddie lifted the marble up, looking around their prison. "You know, we've only tried getting out of the trapdoor. I wonder if his spell goes all the way around." He climbed up onto the old box he'd been sitting on and peered at the timbers. "It feels very old, this boat. Maybe it's not too solid."

Rose knocked against the nearest wall and sighed with frustration. "It feels solid. Heavy." She remembered the mast, back in Dover harbor, and sighed. Her magic hadn't worked then either. But she knocked at the wall again, more thoughtfully, and then pressed her hands against it, flat palmed, feeling the wood, and remembering the water, crumpling against the harbor wall.

"What's the matter? Have you found a weak point?" Freddie asked eagerly, and Bill stood up to see what she was doing.

"No...but I can feel the sea."

"Rose, it's a river we're next to. The Thames."

Rose rolled her eyes at Freddie and stroked the timbers again. "It remembers the sea, Freddie. I don't think it likes being run aground."

"Someone's coming!" Bella said sharply, and Rose jumped down. Freddie blew on the marble and stuffed it into his pocket, and they tried to look cowed and sad and not as though as they were considering escape at all.

The hatch creaked and whined as it was wrenched open, and Rose tried to see the spell as it died away, but she couldn't get a grip on it. Pike hung over the doorway, looking foxlike and pleased with himself, and Rose thought again that his magic didn't seem to fit. Could he have stolen it somehow? Most of the magicians she had met inhabited their magic like a well-made suit of clothes. It moved with them. They belonged in it. Pike seemed to use his instead, picking it up and throwing it at people. She was almost sure he was not a natural magician. It would explain why he had had to steal Miranda.

However, even if the magic wasn't his, he used it very well. She tried pushing against it with the merest feather-light touch of her own magic as he dropped gracefully into the room, and he swung around and smiled at her at once. "Be careful, girl. I'm still watching, and two of my men are up there, ready to nab slippery little children." His smile grew wider. "I only came to see if you would like to visit your mother." His voice was a purr, and Rose flinched away from it. She looked helplessly back and forth between Bill and Bella and Freddie. What should she do? Of course she wanted to see her mother, but was this some sort of trap?

Bill shook his head slightly, and Rose could see that he thought they should stay together.

"May we all go?" she asked, trying to sound polite, while her fingers curled into furious little claws.

Pike stared at her blankly. "No."

"Then I won't."

He blinked, as though he simply couldn't believe that she had just denied him. Rose supposed not that many people did.

"Be careful," Bill breathed behind her. "I think he's crazed."

Rose was quite sure Bill was right. It was something about Pike's pale, pale eyes. They were unstable. He clambered back out the trapdoor, and it slammed shut, shaking the whole boat room and making Bella squeal.

Freddie began to mutter worriedly about whether it had been wise to upset Pike, but Rose was standing in the center of the tiny room, her arms outstretched, smiling to herself.

"What is it?" Freddie demanded, pulling out the glowing marble. "What have you done?"

"He let it go. His magic. And now it's high tide," Rose told him dreamily. "Can't you feel it pulling? When Pike slammed the trapdoor, he hit the boat with all that furious magic, all loose. He likes to bind things together, like he bound my mother, and that magic wanted to cling on to something. I'd spoken to the wood already, and it was waiting."

Freddie grabbed her shoulders. "Rose, *what have you done?*"

"It isn't me; it's the boat."

Bill frowned. "There ain't a boat, Rose. Just the beaten-up old parts of one. It ain't going anywhere."

Rose smiled. "It thinks it is." She could feel the boat now, straining at a mooring rope, its old, dull-red, gaff-rigged sail starting to swell and fill and flap. "It can feel the water, and it wants to be gone. A little of my spells, from when I wanted to get out, and a lot of Pike's loose magic. Now the boat wants to escape too…"

The little room shook suddenly, and Bill sat down, his eyes panicky. "Rose, this ain't a boat. You can't sail off in nothing and old wood!"

Bella patted his knee. "She likes sea journeys. She invented one inside my head a few days ago. If she says there's a boat, there probably is."

"There's boats and boats. I bet it's got holes in it," Bill muttered.

Freddie snickered, sharp and hysterical. "It's all hole!"

Then there was a splintering, crashing explosion of sound, and they shot forward, grabbing on to each other and yelling in fear and joy and excitement.

The half-boat flung itself against the stones of the outer wall, and as they broke out of the warehouse, Rose felt Pike's magic tearing away, like an ugly coat of slime. There was a sickening lurch as they slipped over the little causeway, and then smoothness as the water sucked at the strange memory of a boat. The boat's timbers quivered with their newfound freedom, and Bill reached up to the hatch. "Can't get to it. Climb on my shoulders?"

Freddie nodded and scrambled up, shoving hard with his hands flattened against the boards. "It's still bolted, but his spell's half-torn off. Can you hold me up here a minute?"

"Mmpf," Bill muttered. "Hurry up."

Freddie drew a series of interlocking patterns on the underside of the hatch and then swept his hand across them. Then he shoved again and cried out gleefully as the hatch sprang open. His head and shoulders disappeared out of the hole, and then he called down to Bill. "Push me out; then I can pull you all up."

Bill boosted him out, then stood on one of the boxes to make it easier for Freddie to haul him up, and then they dragged the girls out of the hatch, Bella kicking and yelping indignantly. They huddled together up on the bow, staring back into the well of the boat.

"Oh…" Rose gazed around them, wide-eyed.

"Mmm. Imaginary boat," Freddie agreed. "I'd never have believed it."

"Not completely imaginary," Bella disagreed. "I can see it. Can't you? Just very faintly?"

The bow of the fishing vessel, the part they had been imprisoned in, looked like any old boat, although very worn and battered. But the rest of the boat was—not there. Or almost there. As Bella said, one could see it very faintly, a honey-golden haze of new timber—there was even a sweetish whiff of cut wood. And the boat was sailing, wallowing through the wide, pewter-gray river.

"Do you think we can touch the rest of it?" Freddie asked. "I mean, would it hold us? I don't feel very safe clinging on up here."

Bill snorted. "It don't look very safe down there. I'm staying where I can see the wood. No offense, Rose. But I can only see water down there, and it looks cold."

"They've seen us." Rose had been staring back toward the old Beloved's warehouse, watching for Pike. He was easy enough to spot, even from this distance, his hair a flaming spot of red against the tumbled gray stones. The rest of the gang were gathered around him, pointing. A small rowing boat was tied to a metal ring on the wall, but no one seemed to be about to give chase.

Rose sighed and looked away, out to the other side of the river. The warehouses were shrouded in early-morning mist, but the odd boat was busy plowing up the river already, and its occupants were staring at the strange little craft.

"We should make for the bank again. Try and moor somewhere further down, away from Beloved's, and then we can get back," she suggested.

"Back?" Bella squeaked. "We aren't going back! We've just got away."

Rose nodded. "That's all right. You can go home. I'm going back."

Freddie rubbed a hand across his face. "Sorry, Rose. I'd almost forgotten why we went there in the first place. Your mother's still there."

"And I should think Pike will take it out on her that he's lost us," Rose said quietly. "We've only made things worse for her."

"No." Another voice joined in, and the children wriggled around to face the well of the boat, where a silvery figure was watching them, as insubstantial as the timbers she stood on.

"Eliza! We didn't know if you'd come back!" Rose frowned. "Be careful, won't you? We don't know what that part of the boat actually is."

Eliza smiled. "I'm not afraid of getting wet, Rose. Besides, it feels solid to me. I've seen your mother. I went back. She saw me too, or she almost did. Pike tried to cripple her with the spell, but it didn't take this time. She's growing away from him—you broke his hold on her, Rose. She's happy."

"Can she get away?" Rose demanded.

Eliza shook her head. "No. He still has her bound, but I think her real magic is waking up inside her again. I don't know how much longer his spell will hold."

Rose laughed. "But then we did it! We've freed her. If Pike's spell is wearing off, she'll be able to get away!"

Eliza was silent for a moment, staring down at the strange deck of the boat, her wet hair trailing over her face.

"What is it?" Rose asked uncertainly. "What's wrong?"

"Pike knows too. He can tell he's losing her." Eliza looked up, shaking her hair back. "He'll kill her first. He could do that now, while he still has her just enough under his control. He can't let her escape. She'd have the law after him, and if they knew what they were fighting, if she told them how to fight him, he knows he wouldn't have a chance. He doesn't want to be hanged, Rose."

Rose laughed bitterly. "So she's going to die happy, that's what you meant by us not making things worse? We have to go back and get her." She smacked the roof of the cabin angrily. "How do we make this thing move? We need to turn around."

"It's partly made of your magic. I should think you just tell it." Freddie reached out to touch the side of the boat, his fingers stroking wood that was hardly there. "It feels like you, Rose. You and the memories in the wood, that's all."

"Look!" Bill nudged them both. "That cat running along the slipway there. Is that Himself?"

Freddie peered across the water. "I think so. Gus! Gus, we're here!"

"I can see you, you idiot," came a mewing cry across the water. "Why else would I be down by the river on a freezing February morning?"

"Is the master with you?" Freddie called back, ignoring the insults, which was second nature by now.

Gus shook his head. "Stuck at the palace." His

whiskers were bristling with tiny, silvery sparks, Rose noticed, frowning. The white cat often glittered when he was working a spell, but this looked different. Gus was worried and trying not to show it. She had a dreadful feeling that she knew why. Her mouth was suddenly full of a strange, bitter taste of dismay.

"The Talish invasion is about to begin, according to some intelligence the king had smuggled out. They're preparing to embark, and Aloysius is desperately trying to gather everyone together to fight." Gus's tail swished anxiously. "I decided I'd better save you myself, since we ought to get back and help. Although you seem to have saved yourselves without me, which is most ungracious."

Their odd craft had turned, with a great creaking of phantom sails, and was now cutting through the water toward Gus's slipway.

"Did you tell it to do that?" Bill asked, impressed.

"Not really. It just did. I suppose I hadn't told it anywhere I wanted it to go before, so it was just going. Now it knows we want to be over there."

There was a certain smugness about the sails as the boat drew up alongside the wooden slipway where Gus was sitting, staring down at them disapprovingly.

"Really. An imaginary boat? Could you not manage something better?"

"It's getting more real, I think," Rose noted, as they scrambled off onto the slipway. She held out her hand to Eliza, who was hesitating over the band of dark water between the boat and the wooden boards. "I won't let you fall in it," she whispered. She knew that Eliza couldn't drown again, and so did the ghost, but the water was as dark and thick and sucking as treacle. Eliza gripped Rose's hand with her own chilled fingers and jumped, her eyes closed in fear. Then she scurried along the slipway toward the solid stone walls of another tumbledown warehouse.

"Look, you can see proper wood, almost." Rose kneeled down and stroked the honey-yellow wood gently. "Where will you go now?" she whispered, and felt the boat rock excitedly under her fingers. She smiled. "Good luck, wherever you are."

"Do you think a strange boat is just going to turn up in someone's mooring?" Bill asked, watching it shear off into the wind.

Rose smiled. "One that always seems to weather the storms better than anyone else's. It's a good boat. They'd better look after it." She stared fiercely across the water as the boat seemed to melt into the dancing February sun. Then she shook herself and turned to Gus.

"Listen, my mother is still in the warehouse. We escaped by accident. We didn't really plan, and so…"

"Oh good." Gus's whiskers perked up a little. "I was beginning to think you had managed that without me, which would have been disappointing. So we have to go back and rescue her."

Rose nodded. "How did you get away before? Did you find a different way out? We didn't see."

Gus snorted delicately. "Of course you didn't. When Miranda began to raise the alarm, I shot out into the passageway and back the way we'd come. It was fairly obvious you idiots weren't going to get out in time—no point in all of us being caught."

Freddie rolled his eyes. "Always heroic."

Gus simply yawned, showing all his sparkling teeth. "I'm here, aren't I? For the actually dangerous and difficult part. All you managed to do was get out. You need me to do anything useful."

Rose put a hand in front of Freddie, who was starting to seethe. "Don't, Freddie. We haven't time to fight. Gus, Eliza thinks Pike is going to kill my mother so she can't escape."

Gus nodded brightly. "A challenge, then. What do we know about this Pike?"

"Well, he's mad." Freddie shrugged. "That's about it."

"I don't think he understands how to use the magic properly," Rose said slowly. "He seems to just—fling it about… Gus, could he have stolen it? Could he have a thing, a talisman, like the mask that Gossamer stole? And that gives him the magic? He seems very, very strong, but not quite right, somehow."

Freddie frowned. "Oh. I thought that was just because he was mad."

"It's how the boat happened, I think. When he was

angry that I wouldn't do as he said, the magic got loose, and because my magic was already in the boat timbers, Pike's magic followed it there…"

Bill frowned. "If half his magic's just sailed off down the river, does that mean he isn't a magician anymore? Did you steal his power, Rosie?"

Rose longed to say yes, but she looked doubtfully at Gus and Freddie and Bella, and shook her head. "It'll grow again, won't it? Do you think?"

Gus nodded. "But the boy is right. That could take time. We should hurry, while we might still have an advantage."

Freddie folded his arms. "It's all very well saying 'hurry.' What are we hurrying to? We don't have a plan—we can't just walk in and ask for her back."

Gus smiled a cat smile, his eyes narrowing in pleasure. "Actually, I thought that's exactly what I might do. Walk, boy, and listen."

They set off, hurrying down the slipway to solid ground and following Gus through a series of dark, winding alleys.

"Pike may be a magician, but the rest of the gang are not, hmmm?" Gus explained as they scurried after him. "And he is weakened at the moment, or so we hope. So if we stay out of his way, we should be able to do this with a relatively simple series of spells."

"Don't we need to go this way?" Bill asked, pointing down a dark passage, the roofs of the warehouses almost touching overhead. "We want to get back to the water, don't we? So we can find the hole the boat made."

"Too obvious," Freddie disagreed. "They'll be expecting that. It'd be guarded."

"And the front won't?" Bill folded his arms disgustedly and stared down at Freddie.

"Shut up!" Gus hissed. "We don't have time for this. Where's that ghost girl gone?"

Eliza, who had been lurking behind Rose, shuffled forward a little. Rose frowned. Was Gus hoping to use her to get them inside? She wasn't sure it would work. Eliza seemed so fragile, and it was obviously hard for her to control how she moved outside the mirror.

"What sort of things was Pike involved in when you lived there? Extortion? Gambling? Robbery?" Gus demanded.

Eliza nodded. "All of that. But he got a lot of his money off the protection racket. He only had to look at a grate, and the fire would start burning—it persuaded people pretty well."

"What does she mean?" Bella whispered to Rose.

"I think people paid him not to burn down their shops," Rose told her, shuddering.

Bella looked intrigued. "How clever."

"Bella!"

"Well, it is. To have people paying you not to do things. It sounds ideal."

Gus prowled on, the tip of his tail twitching

174

thoughtfully. "So if a boy came to them, looking for a reward… Perhaps he wanted to tell them about a new grocer's opening, not too far away—just far enough to be into the respectable streets. They'd let him in—right through their front entrance. And really, once one of us is in, it should be no trouble at all to open a door to the rest, especially as Pike might be indisposed."

Rose frowned. "I suppose we know where my mother is now. She knows we might come back too. She'd be ready, perhaps. She could help us to set her free."

"You've forgotten something," Freddie pointed out gloomily.

Gus pricked his ears up curiously.

"This boy who's got to get us in. They know what I look like, Gus. They aren't going to let me anywhere. Unless we do a glamour, and that takes ages to get right. We aren't all as good at it as Rose's mother."

Gus sighed. "I wasn't talking about you, dear boy. I meant me."

Eliza hissed loudly in Rose's ear. "But he's a cat!"

"That's what you think," Gus spat out irritably before disappearing behind a rickety iron staircase. When he came back, he was a boy about the same age as Freddie, with similar whitish-blond hair—but unlike Freddie's, it looked grubby and uncombed, and he was wearing scruffy trousers and a jacket with patches. Only his eyes were the same as before—one amber, one blue, and both sparkling evilly.

175

Rose stared at him. She had seen Gus as a boy once before, in Venice, but only behind a mask. This was the first time she had seen his human face. He had a very pointed chin, and his eyes were rather round and set far apart like a cat's, but that was the sort of thing you only noticed if you knew.

"Hello, Rose," he purred, and she jumped, realizing how rude it was to stare so. Bill was scowling, which Gus seemed to think was very funny. He kept chuckling to himself. But at last they rounded a corner, and he held up one finger to shush everyone. "Look, there's the warehouse. Stay here. I'll call you once I'm past the guards, if the story works."

"What if it doesn't?" Rose murmured anxiously. Gus as a boy didn't have the same air of unshakeable confidence as he did when he was a cat.

He sighed at her. "Well, then I won't." And he sauntered off up the alleyway with his paws—hands—in his pockets.

* * *

They sat hidden behind a pile of old packing cases, watching the door of the warehouse anxiously.

"He's been a very long time," Freddie muttered. "We should have made him take Eliza. Then at least he'd have more idea where he was going."

Bella scowled. "This coat is ruined."

Rose!

Rose sat up sharply. "Freddie, that wasn't you, was it?"

"No! Did he call you?"

"I think so…"

Of course I did, idiot! Come on, there's not a lot of time. I've sent the two men by the door to sleep so you can sneak in, but I can feel Pike's magic, and he's getting stronger again.

"I hope he's right about this," Bill growled, as they peered around the shabby door to the warehouse. "I don't like just walking in the front door."

"Stop complaining." Rose took hold of Bella's hand and dragged her into the shadowy building. The front part was simply a cavernous warehouse, piled with boxes and barrels. The two sleeping guards were collapsed on a pile of oriental carpets, which looked quite valuable.

Gus was beckoning to them from the other side of the space, by a small door. "It's this way," he whispered, as soon as they reached him. "I got to her room, but I think we'll need all of us to break Pike's spell—you especially, Rose. And once we start to try, he'll know what we're doing, and he'll come running."

"Leave me here, outside her door," Eliza whispered. "I'll warn you if he's coming."

This time, Miranda wasn't hopelessly facing the wall. She was still sitting on the bed, but she was staring intently at the door, as though she had been waiting for them to arrive. Her eyes were bright with hope and excitement, and as soon as she saw Rose, she tried to leap to her feet.

"Ah! I can't." She held her hands at her sides, squeezing her fingers into painful fists. "I'm holding back the alarm spell, but I can't do it for long. He'll be here. Please, help me break the binding."

"Do you know how he set it?" Freddie asked, kneeling beside her.

She shook her head. "No. Except that he's been adding to it for years—like layers and layers of silken ropes tying me down. There must be a way for someone to slice through them."

Gus sat down on the bed beside her and stretched out one finger. His nails were slightly hooked, like claws. He pulled at the air around Miranda, and made a spitting sound. "Tight," he muttered. "Nothing to get a grip on."

Rose's mother gave him an odd look, and Rose explained hastily. "He's a cat."

"Oh! What a remarkable transformation."

Gus grinned at her, showing off all his teeth, which were still very sharp.

Rose stroked her mother's arm. "I can hardly feel the spell," she confessed. Her fingers were tingling, but it was with excitement, not magic.

Miranda smiled. "Keep doing that. I'm sure it's weakening, even if you're doing it by accident. And if it doesn't work, at least I'll remember you doing it. But promise me, if he comes, you'll run, all of you. You have to leave me here."

Rose frowned. She wasn't sure she could promise. But Bella nodded. "We'll make her go. We promise."

"You need to cut the spell away." Eliza had appeared beside her, and now she whispered in Rose's ear.

"I'll go and take over watching," Bill muttered.

Rose turned to see the silver ghost hovering shyly next to her. "How? Do you know how we do it, Eliza?"

"She is here, then!" Rose's mother exclaimed. "I thought I'd seen her."

"Yes, Miss Miranda. Sorry, miss," Eliza whispered.

"She's sorry—about taking the mirror," Rose explained.

Her mother shook her head. "After everything she did, she has no need to say sorry. She saved you, Hope. She was the one who got you away from this awful place. How did you find her?"

"She's in your mirror," Rose explained, pulling it out of the inside of her coat. "Because she took it, she's haunted it ever since."

"The mirror will break the spell," Eliza breathed in her ear, her breath frosty cold. "If you break the mirror. Then use the largest shard of the mirror glass to cut away the spell bindings."

Rose stared at her. "Really? And then she'll be free?" Eliza nodded. "Powerful spell, that mirror, miss." Rose drew in one delighted breath to tell the others, but then she frowned, turning back to the ghost child.

"Eliza, what happens to you if I break the mirror?"

179

Eliza smiled faintly. "Nothing."

Rose stared at her. "You're sure?"

"Oh yes."

Rose held the mirror by the handle and stared around. There was nothing to break it with.

"Stomp on it," Eliza hissed. "Put it on the floor and stomp on it."

Rose nodded and raised the heel of her boot to crush the glass. She was looking at Eliza as she did it, and she saw the strangest expression cross Eliza's silver-mist face—a mixture of pain and relief and a sort of pleased surprise. And then she was gone.

Rose looked around, expecting her to reappear somewhere else in the room, but she didn't. Her mother twisted painfully inside her spell bindings, and Rose heard her whisper, "Oh, Liza…" Her voice quivered and cracked.

"She's not coming back," Gus said with a certain satisfaction.

Rose turned on him. "You knew, didn't you?"

"Knew what?" Gus asked innocently.

"That she'd go! I shouldn't have believed her when she said nothing would happen."

"Rose, she was telling the truth," Gus told her, gripping her hand. She was sure she could feel fur between her fingers. "That's what she meant. Nothing happened to her. That's what she is now."

"I didn't know she meant it like that," Rose whispered, stricken.

"Don't waste what she did for you," Gus reminded her. "It only worked because she gave herself up. She knew what she was doing, Rose. She'd sacrificed herself to save you once before, remember. And now we haven't much time."

Rose nodded and wiped her hand across her eyes to brush the tears away. She looked down at the mirror glass, broken into lethal shards.

"Hit it on the floor! Quickly!" Bella muttered. "Look, I don't think she can keep the alarm spell under control for much longer."

Rose glanced up at her mother anxiously. She was biting into her lip, and her eyes were squeezed tightly shut. Sharply, Rose hit the boarded floor with the mirror and lifted the frame away, leaving the shattered glass on the floor. She picked up the largest, sharpest piece, and turned to her mother. "Where do I cut?" she asked helplessly.

"I doubt it matters," Gus told her. "Be quick!"

"Oh, Eliza, please make this work," Rose begged, and she sliced quickly across her mother's golden-bronze hair—it seemed the only safe place, although a great pity to cut off such pretty hair.

But the hair didn't come off. Instead a sticky, translucent mass like snail slime seemed to appear for a second, then melt away. Her mother sprang up and hugged her, and then whispered, "Run!"

Ten

THEY ALL PILED OUT into the passageway, and Rose looked from side to side in dismay. She had no idea which way to go, and now they didn't have Eliza to guide them. Gus slipped past her and stood scenting the air. Rose was sure she could see his whiskers, despite his human shape.

"Gus sent the guards at the front to sleep—is that the best way out?" she asked her mother quickly.

Miranda shook her head. "I have no idea. I've never been out of that room. But—no. Pike is coming that way. I can feel him, like some great wounded slug drenched in poison. This way, toward the water. Come on."

There was shouting now at the end of the passageway, and Gus hissed. "I missed those." His fingernails had grown even longer, and his front teeth were cat-like and sharp.

"You'll get your chance," Miranda said, not looking back at him. "Is this where you broke out this morning? Good gracious, Hope, what did you do?"

"Rose," Bill snapped. "She isn't Hope, she's Rose. I know it weren't your fault she got left, but she did, and she's Rose now."

Miranda looked stricken, but she nodded. "I'm sorry. Later, we can talk about these things."

Rose smiled. "Not now." She gazed rather proudly at the enormous hole in the wall. "We enlivened half a boat," she explained, "and sailed it away. Through there." It was the *largest* thing she had ever seen her magic do, and she was quite pleased with it.

"They'll not have left this unguarded," Bill muttered, looking around suspiciously. "Where are they... Oh, blast..."

A tall, chronically thin man had materialized from the shadows, wielding a knife, and he was holding it at Bella's throat. Her eyes were bulging, and she was holding her breath, trying to make herself as thin as possible to escape the blade.

"Where was he?" Freddie muttered. "How did we miss him?"

"The others are coming..." Bill was staring behind them. "Or at least, someone is. I think it's Pike, but he looks—different."

"We stole a lot of his magic for the boat." Rose was still staring at Bella. Why didn't she scream? When they got home, Miss Fell was going to have to stop teaching them etiquette and work out how Bella could control her screaming trick so it only hit the right people.

Rose smiled grimly to herself. *When. Not if.*

The thin man was shaking, and they could all see the blade wavering against Bella's skin.

"He's drugged," Bill muttered.

Miranda nodded. "They trade in opium. They tried to give it to me once."

There was the faintest squeak, and a thin red line appeared across Bella's neck. The thin man laughed. "Master's coming…"

Pike had dragged himself up the passageway. His skin was grayish, and his mouth looked wet, as though he'd been drooling. He moved as if he had to think about every lurching step, but the madness was still there in his pale eyes, and somehow he seemed even more dangerous than before. His eyes were paler now, the pupils shrunk to the merest pinpricks, leaving that flat expanse of blue.

Rose and her mother and Bill and Freddie were pressed up against the edges of the hole in the wall, close enough to jump through and run, but they couldn't leave Bella.

"Go!" Rose hissed to her mother.

"I can't leave you all!"

"You tried to make me promise I would. It's you he wants back. Run!"

Miranda laughed. "I think he'd rather have all three of you. Young and strong, you're exactly what he needs. I'm not going, not without the little one. Hold hands with me, Rose. We're going to get her back."

184

The china whiteness of her face was flushing slowly pinker, and she seemed to be growing more alive every minute. Her hair was crackling with energy, and even her dingy grayish dress was a taking on a silvery luster of heavy silk.

Pike was watching her, grinding his teeth. "There's your escape." He nodded at the gaping hole in the wall. "But you can't go," he snarled. "You won't leave the child…" He sounded doubtful.

"You're right. You would, but then you are a thief and a child murderer. I'll never forget what you did to Eliza, and what you made me do to my baby." Rose's mother seemed to be growing taller as she hurled the words at him, and Pike was cowering backward. "Your magic isn't even your own to use," Miranda snarled, and then she laughed as Pike cried out in horror. "Did you think I didn't know? I saw it in you years ago. All stolen. The very first thing you stole, and from your own brother. You stole his magic, Jonathan Fisher, and all it was ever good for was stealing more things."

Pike sat down suddenly, as though someone had sliced across the backs of his knees. "You know my name."

"And Jacob's. The brother you killed." Miranda nodded, but behind her back she was pulling Bill's sleeve, pointing him toward the thin man and Bella.

"I didn't! I didn't kill him!" Pike screamed. "I didn't. He's over there. Look at him!"

Startled, they looked across at the thin, shaking man

and saw that he had red hair too, under the layers of dirt. He was staring back, looking frightened, and his hands were shaking even more. He wasn't looking at Bella.

Miranda glanced between the two of them. "You drugged him, then. So you could take his power. You really are a slug. Was that why you tried to get me to take the stuff? So that you could steal my magic forever too?" She shuddered. "Was it what you were planning for these three?"

"No one's stealing anything from me!" Bella suddenly screamed as she stomped her pretty high-heeled boot down on Jacob Fisher's foot. Gus leaped from behind Jacob to rake his claws across the man's face, and Bill snatched Bella as she ducked out of Jacob's grip and bundled her through the hole in the wall, grabbing Freddie's arm and dragging him after them. "Come on, Rose!"

Rose pulled her mother's hand, and they scrambled over the rubble, leaving Jacob moaning behind them and Pike dragging himself in their wake, as they raced along the narrow stone pathway that ran around the crumbling warehouse, a ribbon of safety between the walls and the water.

When they were back at the mouth of the alley, Rose threw her arms around Bella, the scarlet line across Bella's pretty throat filling her with fury. She had never thought she would want to kill anyone. She had hated and suppressed and fought against her magic, but now she would never give it up. Pike had stolen it once before by taking her mother and her history away from her, and now he was planning to steal it again.

"Bella, could you scream that building down?"

Bella nodded, her teeth showing in an angry little smile. She had wiped her nice glove across the cut and was staring at the stain. "But won't it hurt you all?"

Rose shook her head. "Not if we're in the hiding spell first, I hope. We never tried to ward it off before."

"Take hands," Gus snapped. His bloodstained claws had retracted into normal fingernails again as he stretched his hands out to the others. "The strongest you've ever done the spell."

The shimmering bubble wrapped them all, leaving Bella standing alone in front of them.

"I can't do it," she muttered. "I've never done it on purpose!" She looked around at Rose, her face panicky.

"He's coming!" Freddie yelped, pointing at the gap in the stone wall, and Bella wheeled around and screamed out of pure terror, a wave of sound that the others felt even inside their protection spell, battering and swinging against the stone walls and their own fragile wall of magic.

"He wasn't coming," Gus muttered to Freddie, and Freddie shook his head. "But he would have been in a minute. She needed scaring into it."

Bella jumped back suddenly, the scream dying away

into a yelp of fright, as the building seemed to shimmer. "It's pulling me in," she gasped, her lace-edged skirts suddenly sucking toward the warehouse. As the others broke out of the disguise spell and seized her, they felt as though a strong wind was sweeping them back toward the crumbling stones of Beloved's.

Rose's mother stood there, her feet planted on the stones, her long, bronze-gold hair streaming out past her face toward the old warehouse. She had grabbed Bella's coat, hauling her back like a sailor rescuing a man overboard. "Hold on to her," she hissed through her clenched teeth to Rose, Bill, and Freddie, and she stood like a rock, her face growing impossibly whiter, until the warehouse seemed all at once to sink into itself, leaving a cloud of choking dust.

The last shreds of the disguise spell faded away, and they stared gaping at the devastation.

"He's gone," someone whispered, and Rose found that she was holding her mother's hand.

* * *

They straggled back through the dirty alleys, gradually reaching the cleaner, more well-to-do streets, but there was still a curious air of desolation. Hardly anyone was about, although it was midmorning now, and those people who were out were hurrying, heads down with anxious faces.

"Something's happened," Freddie muttered, walking faster.

"It has to be the invasion. There must have been news." Gus was a cat again, dancing ahead of their feet and sniffing the air luxuriously. No one cared enough to be surprised by him right now.

"But Papa was going to stop it!" Bella murmured anxiously. "It can't be."

"Who are we invading?" Rose's mother asked, and they stared at her.

She sighed. "Eleven years—no one talked to me."

"Talis is invading us," Rose explained. "Or they were going to. Bella's father went to the palace—yesterday? The day before? I can't think."

"The day before." Bella's hands were clenched inside her bloodstained gloves. "What if he's hurt?"

Gus suddenly stopped and turned back to them, his tail swishing in agitation. "We've been gone overnight."

Rose and the others nodded, unsure what he meant.

"Don't you see?" Gus snarled. "The one thing guaranteed to draw Aloysius away from the war committee. Bella and you two gone. He'll be back at the house, searching. We have to run!"

"Oh no," Rose muttered, starting to dash after him and pulling her mother with her. All six of them raced through the streets, back to the tall house in the square.

Freddie hammered on the front door, and it opened

189

so suddenly that Rose was sure Mr. Fountain had been pacing the hallway, waiting for them.

"You're safe!" He caught Bella up in his arms. "I heard you screaming."

"She collapsed a warehouse, sir!" Freddie told him. "On purpose," he added quickly. "We needed her to."

But Mr. Fountain had seen Rose's mother, standing nervously in the doorway with Rose still clinging to her hand.

"Rose?" He looked at them both, frowning. "Who…"

"Miranda!" Miss Fell was hurrying down the stairs, her stick forgotten and new life in her face. "Oh, Rose, you found her!"

Mr. Fountain swallowed. "Miranda Fell?"

"Miranda Garnet." Rose's mother's voice was proud, and her shoulders were unyieldingly stiff, as her aunt embraced her.

"Miranda, where have you been? I shall never, ever forgive you for going off without telling me!" Miss Fell stared at her niece. "Did you think I would disown you?" She stood holding Miranda, staring at every line of her face. "Oh, my dearest. So changed. But then, eleven years, and it's seemed so much longer."

Miss Bridges, the housekeeper, had appeared discreetly through the green baize door. "Tea, ma'am?" she murmured, and Miss Fell nodded, towing Miranda after her into the drawing room, pushing her into one of the button-back velvet chairs, and simply staring at her.

Mr. Fountain had followed them in, still holding Bella, who looked exhausted. Rose and Freddie and Bill were lurking in the doorway.

"Come here, child!" Miss Fell commanded, beckoning to Rose and delicately kicking a footstool toward Miranda's chair. "Sit there. I want to see you together."

Her cheeks burning, Rose did as she was told. She felt as though she were sitting for a portrait, like the handsome oil painting of Bella as a baby with her mother that hung over the fireplace. The thin white hand that brushed her cheek and then settled cautiously on her shoulder was only part of the pose. Except that it was shaking.

Rose reached back, suddenly ashamed of her dry, stained hands. She held that hand and felt it still and heard her mother sigh.

Miss Fell stared at them, her eyes glittering and hungry. "I was right. Ever since I saw you in Venice that day, Rose, running along the dock. I should never have doubted it—look at the pair of you! I told you, Rose, didn't I, that I thought I would have known if Miranda had died? You found her for me, after all this time… I should have trusted my instincts better."

"Aunt, what is happening?" Miranda's voice was husky, as though she had hardly used it over the years.

"The streets were dead. Fear seems to be seeping into the air."

"It's definite," Mr. Fountain said flatly. "The Talish are bringing the invasion force to Cormanse. They've been constructing barges—dreadful, flimsy things, but then, they only have to make one journey. Now they're waiting for a clear day to make the crossing. February—stupid time to do it, of course. But the Talish emperor has his spies everywhere, and I think the agreement I made for the king in Venice wasn't as secret as it was meant to be. Clearly the emperor didn't want us having any extra help."

Rose gasped. "Sir, did we stop you from fighting it? We had to go. I'm so sorry."

Mr. Fountain sighed and sat on one of the brocade sofas with Bella in his arms. "I don't think it made much difference that I had to leave, Rose. I'd gathered as many magicians as I could—old friends—and we've managed to keep the channel too rough to cross. But we can't do that forever. The Talish magicians are so strong, so many of them, and we're worn out."

"You can't give up." Freddie stared at him, horrified. Mr. Fountain smiled sadly. "I'm not giving up, Freddie. I collapsed. Since Gossamer stabbed me, I don't have the same strength. They brought me home. Then when I got back here, I discovered that you were all missing. Since then I've been trying to scry for you. I found you in some dank warehouse, but then you were on a boat—it was all muddled, and the wound kept making me lose the vision." He hid his face in Bella's hair for a moment. "I don't know if we can disturb the sea again."

Miss Fell glared at him. "Aloysius Fountain, get up and stop mooning about. Don't you realize what you have here?" She swept a hand around the drawing room. "Three generations of the strongest magical talent in Europe. Plus Isabella, who may be objectionable but is capable of screaming down buildings. And Frederick, who probably could too, if only he would make the effort."

Freddie shrugged crossly, but Rose thought he was secretly rather pleased.

"Tell His Majesty that magicians cannot work in that dead stone monstrosity of a palace," Miss Fell commanded. "The sea spells are still working, are they not? The invasion cannot be for a few more days, surely?"

Mr. Fountain shook his head dumbly.

"Then we must move somewhere more suitable. Your gathering of magicians from the palace too." She searched Miranda's face anxiously. "Dearest, I must tell you… Your parents…they died, a few years back."

Miranda swallowed. "I wondered," she admitted. "I don't know if I could have gone back and seen them, not even now."

"The house will be yours," her aunt pointed out gently. "And Rose's."

Gus mewed irritably. "It won't be soon! A bunch of Talish officers will be using it for housing if we don't do something!"

"Quite," Miss Fell told him frostily. "We need every advantage we can get, so the Fells will gather at Fell Hall. Miranda, you will have to be strong. Once this is all dealt with"—she waved a hand dismissively, and Rose had to stifle a little snort of laughter, for Miss Fell looked as though she was having problems with a mouthy second footman, not an invasion— "then you and Rose will be able to go wherever you like. But for now, we need the house on our side, my dear."

Miranda nodded—and Rose noticed that her mother's hand was shaking again.

Miss Fell stood up in a grand sweep of stiff silk. "William, send for the carriage, and tell the admirable Mrs. Jones that we need provisions for a journey to Derbyshire."

* * *

"So many of them…" Rose murmured, peering out the carriage window. She and her mother were sharing a carriage with Miss Fell and Gus, who had apparently abandoned his master for the sake of better gossip in Rose's party. "They look exhausted already. They must have been marching for days."

The column of soldiers stumbled past, their weapons jingling. But the polished swords were dusty, and the men themselves were no better. They hardly glanced up as the carriage sped past. "Are they going to the coast?" Rose asked. "In case—in case the plan doesn't work?"

Miss Fell nodded grimly. "Or perhaps to the manufacturing towns. There are metalworks around here. It would be disastrous if the invading force should seize those."

Rose watched the tail end of the dusty column disappearing behind them. The soldiers didn't look capable of defending a great deal. Miss Fell's plan had to work—or Rose could imagine the Talish forces simply sweeping their way across the country.

Miss Fell's determination that morning had seemed to fire up Mr. Fountain. He'd slid Bella—who was now fast asleep, worn out by her destruction of the warehouse—off his shoulder and laid her on the sofa, while he paced up and down the drawing room.

"You've never worked together, of course," he'd muttered, suddenly glaring at Rose and her mother. "And no time to test it. But three Fells, as you say… immensely powerful." He stared at his perfectly shiny shoes for a few seconds and glanced up. "If we were to gather the whole invasion fleet close together—all those hundred barges that our agents have been gabbling in a panic about—could you destroy them? With my help and that of the other magicians I've recruited?"

Rose had simply stared at him, and then glanced up at her mother and then her great-aunt with her mouth half-open. But Miranda had wrinkled her nose and nodded, and Miss Fell had sniffed. "Undoubtedly. Rose, well-bred young ladies do not sit around like frogs after flies. Close your mouth, dear."

Mr. Fountain had hurried off to the palace without even putting on an overcoat and demanded an immediate Council of War, at which he outlined the plan. It was a neat little trap, sending the major part of the British navy off to rendezvous with the Venetians and leaving the Channel hardly guarded. The Talish emperor and his generals would be forced to make a rather hasty decision. The whole invasion force, hopefully, would embark at once, straight into the hands of the waiting magicians.

It was all very well setting a trap, but now Rose and the others had to spring it—and if they didn't, it wouldn't be a trap at all. It would simply be the most disastrous defeat—one that had been predicted by the Admiralty and the Horse Guards. Every senior military commander present at the king's council had threatened to leave the service, but as the king had declared himself willing to entrust the fate of the nation to a handful of unreliable magic workers holed up in a crumbling old house in the wilds of Derbyshire—as the First Lord of the Admiralty put it before he actually did resign—there was very little they could do, short of forcing the king to abdicate.

As the last jingling noises of the troops died away behind them, Rose shivered a little. The Talish soldiers probably wouldn't look very different. They would be tired too, after marching to Cormanse to embark on the barges. And they might well be seasick, some of them, perhaps even as bad as Bella.

It was the only thing that disturbed her about the plan. She was almost sure that Miss Fell was right, and they would be able to destroy the invasion force, even though she didn't feel like the blood of centuries of seers and magicians was flowing through her veins, as Miss Fell had assured her it was. The plan would work. Hopefully.

But if it did, she would be as much a murderess as her mother.

* * *

"Rose, wake up."

Someone was shaking her. Rose sat up and winced. They had driven through the night, stopping only to change horses. She had been sleeping slumped against the someone's shoulder, she realized, and now she ached.

Her mother looked down at her, smiling a little. "We're almost there, and it's getting light. So I thought you'd like to see…" She closed her eyes for a second. "I wanted you to see it with me," she added in a whisper.

Rose nodded and crept one gloved hand around

her mother's sleeve. Her mother was wearing one of Miss Fell's traveling cloaks, a gloriously old-fashioned one with masses of capes around the collar and a hat that trailed feathers. She looked very small and slight underneath it, and terribly frightened.

Miss Fell was glaring out the carriage window—she was sitting facing the horses, of course. She had pulled an eyeglass out of her bag and was examining the trees on either side of the drive.

"Bad pruning. Quite obvious. Really, I shall have to speak to Moffatt... And just look at those weeds in the drive!"

Rose thought it all looked immaculate, and she couldn't suppress a gasp as they finally drew up in the carriage circle in front of the house. She had seen it before, of course, but only in a painting, and that had been the terrace view. The front was even more impressive. The house was built of honey-colored stone, not the gleaming white of the building she'd seen in the painting. Only the peacocks were familiar.

"This is the older part of the house," Miss Fell explained, and even her voice had a slight crack to it, as though she too found it hard to be back. "Built in the seventeenth century by our ancestor Richard Fell."

Rose nodded. She wondered if he was the one Freddie had mentioned and where he'd kept his dragon. The house looked as though it could house a whole colony of dragons—they could quite easily sleep in that little arched part over there. Rose blinked as she, her mother, and Miss Fell descended stiffly from the carriage, and the blinding winter sun seemed to catch a glinting scale and perhaps a twitch of scaly claw. She really hadn't had a proper night's sleep, it was clear.

* * *

"I didn't believe I would ever come back." Rose's mother was sitting on the marble terrace with Rose beside her, both wrapped in layers of shawls. Rose kept looking around, frowning. It felt so very odd, as if she were inside that painting she had tried to copy. Or perhaps an illustration from a fairy tale, with the peacocks sweeping haughtily past.

"Are you happy—to be here?" she asked hesitantly.

Her mother stared out across the velvet green expanse of lawn. "It's full of old ghosts. I'm not sure I could live here again."

Rose nodded, a little relieved. They were still feeling their way around each other, but she supposed she belonged to her mother now. She knew she didn't want to live here either. She liked towns. The countryside was strangely empty and still felt like something that ought to stay in pictures. The house itself was amazing, though—as steeped in spells as Mr. Fountain's house, but about a hundred times larger and older. And she was almost sure the story about the dragons had been true.

She could feel them, something old and sly and wise that seemed to dart around the corners just ahead of her.

Freddie was finding it impossible to concentrate on the spells they were supposed to be planning. He kept disappearing on the way from one room to another, to be routed out an hour or so later by a polite servant, his eyes saucerlike, sure that he had only missed seeing a dragon by inches.

Gus strolled up to Rose and her mother, leering at a nervous peacock, and leaped onto the arm of the bench. "You should go back inside." He yawned.

"Oh! Is it time?" Rose's heart thudded.

"Soon."

In the drawing room behind them, there was a whispering of silk dresses and a smoothing of coattails, as forty people set down their afternoon teacups and exchanged last nervous, encouraging glances.

Miss Fell's skeleton staff had risen to the challenge of their mistress and the cream of magical society descending on them for an unexpected house party. As Rose had suspected, the house was immaculate, and all the housekeeper had done when the news was broken to her was to purse her lips very slightly.

Miss Fell was sitting in a straight-backed wing chair, upholstered in purple damask, which had been placed just to the right of the fire. Mr. Fountain was close by, and Miranda and the children were seated on stools around her. The other magicians were in chairs scattered throughout the room, but all facing Miss Fell and close enough that everyone could clasp hands.

Rose could feel the ancient magic that filled every stone of the house. It whispered and called to her, stroking tiny fingers over her skin.

"Where are they now?" Mr. Fountain asked a young man in a plum-colored velvet jacket, with what Rose thought was a ridiculous mauve-spotted cravat. He was seated at a small wooden table with a map spread out in front of him. One hand was laid flat on the map, and the young man's eyes were half-closed.

"Here. Approaching Dover."

"Are there balloons?" Bella asked, her high voice clearly audible in the nervous hush.

"Ssshhh, Bella," Rose and Freddie hissed, but the man in the velvet jacket laughed.

"No, that was only a rumor in the newspapers. It's the flotilla of barges only. The sea is very rough, and the waves are almost swamping them already."

"This is so risky," a young woman seated close to Rose whispered. "They should not have let the Talish get this far. What if it goes wrong?"

Rose turned and glared at her, but she stared back hard-eyed, and Rose shivered. If it went wrong, they would have exposed England to a Talish invasion.

"Are they close enough together?" Rose's mother asked.

The velvet-jacket man nodded. "Very close. It should work."

It had been Rose and Freddie's idea to adapt Mr. Fountain's protection spell into a trap for the invasion fleet, veiling them in a sudden, soundless bubble. Then working together, the magicians would drag the fleet under the waves, sinking it and drowning the entire invading army. That part had made Rose run into the gardens to be sick in the shrubbery. Freddie had pointed out that it was only what the invasion force were intending to do to *them*, after all.

Rose could see his point, but it seemed so brutal. She had wanted to break the barges apart somehow to at least give the soldiers a chance of being washed up onshore and imprisoned.

No one else had agreed, and the half-retired admiral who was their liaison with the military forces had looked as though he wanted to slap her.

"Now." The velvet-jacket man nodded, and everyone drew the symbols for the spell in the air and then caught hands to link the spell into a giant net.

Rose had never felt so much magic in one place before. She had never realized, but everyone's spells smelled different. Miss Fell's smelled of lavender and Bella's of milk bonbons. Mr. Fountain's reminded her of the pomade he applied to his mustache, and the man in the velvet jacket emitted a strong aroma of tobacco.

Her mother's smelled of dark sugar, from being imprisoned for so long in a cell made of black timbers from the hold of a ship. Rose closed her eyes, wrapped in lavender sugar, thinking of lavender icing and Mrs. Jones's kitchen, and how her own unlikely story tied her to these two determined, impossible women.

The strength of the three of them was pulling the others out over the odd calm of the sea.

It was as though she were being carried along on the waves of the spell, as they all streamed toward the invading ships. She could feel Bella beside her, clasping her hand tightly. She knew that they were sitting on stools in the drawing room, but at the same time they were swooping and rushing through the air. Her hair was streaming behind her, and she laughed for joy at the feel of the wind in her face, a hundred times better than leaning over the side of a ship.

Then they drew close to the Talish barges, and the wonderful wind-rushing feeling died away, as she watched the men, ant-sized in their dark-blue uniforms. How could she do this to them? She was quite sure that if King Albert had had half a chance, he would have invaded Talis. These men were only doing what they were told. It simply wasn't fair. How could she have let them persuade her into this?

"We haven't a choice, Rose," she felt her mother whisper in her ear.

"But it isn't fair. It's cruel. A hundred thousand men, they think!"

"It will end the possibility of the Talish invading."

"We could do that just by destroying the ships,"

Rose argued again. "Those men would never let their commanders make them do it another time, would they?" She swallowed. "If we do this, everyone will hate us. And they will be right."

Her mother stared at her for a moment, and then Rose jumped as something patted her shoulder. Miss Fell had let go of Bella's other hand long enough to tap Rose with the black lace fan looped around her wrist. "Miranda, she's right. This is too much." The old lady smiled, hawk-like. "I have a solution. Remember all those times I made you unravel your crochet?"

Miranda wrinkled her nose. "Can we unravel an invasion fleet?"

"My dear, you could unravel anything. You've had quite enough practice. If the three of us change the spell, the others will have to follow. Then those poor soldiers will at least have a fighting chance. Ah!"

The spell bubble began to envelop the Talish barges, and Rose could hear the cries of surprise and horror as the soldiers saw the sky change color to an eerie cast of silvery gray. Perhaps they thought it was some strange, uncanny storm.

Once the spell surrounded the ships, they should have swept them under the water, but there was a moment of stillness, as no one could bear to start such devastation. And in that moment, Miranda, Miss Fell, and Rose swept in like a whirlwind, splitting the boards of the ships apart, ripping the ropes, and scattering the infantry into the freezing sea. Rose couldn't help murmuring, "Sorry," as her magic swirled past, but of course, she didn't know the word in Talish. A sparkling white flurry of fur shot past her as Gus gleefully joined in.

It took a horribly short time.

Rose blinked and shivered and opened her eyes. The fire was burning brightly, and somewhere in the depths of the house she could smell muffins toasting. Two hundred miles away, men were fighting and scrambling to get aboard the scraps of wood that were all that was left of their ships, but at Fell Hall, it was time for tea.

She shivered again and felt her mother's rose-pink silk frock brush past her. It was ten years out of date, but still beautiful after all its years in a cedar-lined dressing room. Miranda kneeled in front of her and caught her hands. "Don't. Think instead what might have happened if they had landed on the beaches, Rose. The Talish emperor is not merciful, and we have been at war, secretly or not, for the last fifty years. It would have been a massacre."

"Can we go back to London now? Can we go back home?" Rose asked stiffly. She wasn't sure if it was her home anymore.

Her mother smiled. "Mr. Fountain was most put out when he realized that my return might disrupt your apprenticeship. He forced me to promise that I would not take you away from his house. So much so that he invited me to live there too and assist in teaching you all."

205

Rose smiled back, and then laughed out loud as she caught Freddie's face displaying an expression of complete horror.

Gus leaped into Rose's lap and stared up at her mother, his eyes jewellike slits. "Shall we bring the peacocks with us back to London?"

Rose stroked him and rubbed behind his ears. "Would you rather have a peacock or a whole fricasséed lobster?" she whispered.

Her mother nodded. "You're a war hero, now, you know. You could probably claim a lifetime of lobster from the king."

"There's not the same enjoyment in stalking a lobster," Gus muttered regretfully. "They're terribly slow. But delicious."

Rose smiled at him, rubbing the back of her hand over the soft, silk fur beneath his ears. It felt quite normal to be using magic to discuss expensive seafood with a cat. Far more normal than it did to be discussing *anything* with her mother. Rose still couldn't quite believe she had one. But she was starting to feel that she might rather like it. Every so often she looked up to find her mother's eyes fixed on her and filled with a strange sort of delighted amazement. No one had ever looked at Rose that way before.

The drawing-room door eased slowly open, and several maids entered with trays of tea. Bill followed them with a large platter of sandwiches, which he brought straight to Rose. He bowed briefly to Miranda and Miss Fell. "You did it then?" he murmured to Rose, offering her a sandwich and pretending not to see as a white paw reached over the side of the platter. "The potted shrimp sandwiches are on the other side, miss, should you wish for one," he added. The paw disappeared, and then a sandwich disappeared from the other side.

Rose nodded. "It worked." She smiled at him, her eyes creasing at the corners and a delicious feeling of excitement glowing inside her. "And now we're going home."

About the Author

Holly Webb was born and grew up in southeast London, but spent a lot of time on the Suffolk coast. As a child, she had two dogs, a cat, and at one point, nine gerbils (an accident). At about ten, Holly fell in love with stories from ancient Greek myths, which led to studying Latin and Greek, and eventually to reading Classics in college. She worked for five years as a children's fiction editor before deciding that writing was more fun and easier to do from a sofa. Now living in Reading with her husband, three sons, and three cats, Holly runs a Girl Scout unit. The Rose books stem from a childhood love of historical novels and the wish that animals really could talk.

ROSE

How would you know if you were special?

Mr. Fountain's grand mansion is a world away from the dark orphanage Rose has left behind. The gleaming, golden house is practically overflowing with sparkling magic—she can feel it. And though Rose has always wanted to be an ordinary girl with an ordinary life, she realizes she may possess a little bit of magic herself.

But when orphans begin mysteriously disappearing, Rose is put to the test. Can she find the missing children before it's too late?

ROSE AND THE LOST PRINCESS

Not all magic is used for good...

Rose's whole life has changed in a matter of weeks. She's gone from being a lonely orphan to a magician's apprentice, though she's learned that power comes at a price. Even Rose's friends don't seem to trust her anymore, especially when rumors of dark magic begin to swirl through the city.

Then the country's beloved princess vanishes, and the king asks Rose for her help. She must find the missing princess and put a stop to the evil magician behind the kidnapping...before all is lost.

ROSE AND THE MAGICIAN'S MASK

Will Rose's magic be enough?

A dangerously powerful mask has been stolen from the royal palace, and Rose suspects dark magicians are responsible. If used correctly, the mask can give the wearer unimaginable power. But in the wrong hands it can cause chaos around the world. It's up to Rose to stop the evil thieves and return the mask to its rightful place.

Rose's quest takes her to the mysterious city of Venice where nothing is what it seems, and she's put to the test to find out if her new magic will be enough to save the magician's mask—and save herself…